THE CHERRY PIT

BOOKS BY DONALD HARINGTON

Some Other Place. The Right Place.
The Cherry Pit
Lightning Bug
The Architecture of the Arkansas Ozarks: A Novel
Let Us Build Us a City

THE CHERRY PIT

Donald Harington

A HARVEST/HBJ BOOK
Harcourt Brace Jovanovich, Publishers
SAN DIEGO   NEW YORK   LONDON

Copyright © 1965 by Donald Harington

All rights reserved. No part of this publication
may be reproduced or transmitted in any form
or by any means, electronic or mechanical,
including photocopy, recording, or any
information storage and retrieval system, without
permission in writing from the publisher.

Requests for permission to make copies of
any part of the work should be mailed to:
Permissions, Harcourt Brace Jovanovich, Publishers,
Orlando, Florida 32887.

Library of Congress Cataloging-in-Publication Data
Harington, Donald.
   The cherry pit.
   "A Harvest/HBJ book."
   I. Title.
PS3558.A6242C48   1988   813'.54   88-16373
ISBN 0-15-616820-0 (pbk.)

Printed in the United States of America

First Harvest/HBJ edition

A B C D E

1

WHY HAVE WE COME HERE TO THIS WATER?

> *Little Rock is, without any flattery, one of the dullest towns in the United States; and I would not have remained two hours in the place, if I had not met with some good friends, who made me forget its dreariness.*
>
> —FRIEDRICH GERSTAEKER, *Wild Sports*, 1842

ONE

Olyphant is the name of the tiny jerkwater town in Jackson County, northeast Arkansas, where the Missouri Pacific train I was riding to Little Rock stalled for thirty minutes in the late hours of a Sunday in late April, leaving me with nothing to do but read the paper and wait impatiently for the (as near as I could make out by expressing my anxiety to the conductor) triple-thierce camming pin on the glaring-rod of the fifth car's starboard glomhefter to be replaced. Olyphant, which has a population of less than three dozen and was named after a much larger town now a suburb of Scranton, Pennsylvania, of all places, has no significance for this story except that it happened to be the place where I was when I began to wonder, perhaps for the first time, why I was on that train, why I had left Boston, and why I was heading for a place which, home town or not, seems in the retrospection of these past weeks embarrassingly pregnant with fortuitous happenings leading to gloom of one sort or another—to shame, to frustration, to disillusionment, to, yes, even tragedy.

But on second thought, I think that I should say that Olyphant does have more than such limited significance, because in a way it became for me a symbol, whether I was aware of it or not and whether the symbol was actually metaphorical or instead only catachrestical, of the whole of the Arkansas which I would find during my brief, transient return; that is to say, Olyphant was small, vastly empty, flat, alluvial, dark in the early morning, quite lonely, and I did not stay there very long.

It took me not more than fifteen minutes to get down off the train, walk back up the gravel roadbed to the highway, find an all-night café where I could get a cup of coffee to go and a Sunday paper, insult the waitress, and return to the train, all without being missed by the five other passengers in the car. Physically I'm a small person, and have no conspicuous characteristics other than a pair of gibbous ears, and I'm usually unnoticed, ignored, until, for example, the aroma of the coffee I began drinking drifted to the others, one of whom came up the aisle to ask me where I got it, the dining car being closed. I told him, and then I unfolded the thick Sunday issue of the Arkansas *Gazette* and let my eyes fall, for the first time in almost four years, on its familiar, neat, unique typography.

In Boston, which I had slipped away from two days previously, I always read the *Christian Science Monitor* because it is the least hideous of all Boston's degenerate dailies and I am less put out by its slant than by that (not slant: tilt, list, lurch) of the *Globe, Herald,* or *Record-American,* and because we live in a section of town where for some reason it is impossible to have the *New York Times* delivered to the breakfast table. My wife comes from Rutland, Vermont, where a very good daily paper, the Rutland *Herald,* has been published continuously since 1794, and I always read it thoroughly during our too-frequent visits to that city. So there are three newspapers in my life: the Arkansas *Gazette,* Boston's *Christian Science Monitor,* and the Rutland *Herald.* Each of these papers has its own distinctive format and outlook, and its own personal appeal. If I had to choose among them, as sometimes I visualized myself reaching the point of having to, I would without hesitation have selected the Arkansas *Gazette,* I can't help it, and that too, I reflected, must have been part of the reason why I happened to be on that stalled train that night in Olyphant on the way to Little Rock, and why I was greatly pleased to find a copy of that paper at that all-night highway café. I had not, let me repeat, been to Little Rock in almost four years, which, for reasons which may later become clear, was entirely too long, and I did not know, when I left Boston, why I was going back there, or who, or what, if anything, I expected to find.

Clifford Willow Stone is my name. Although of Ozarkian extraction, I was born in Little Rock twenty-eight years ago (which also, sometimes, seems entirely too long), educated in the public schools there, at the University of Arkansas (B.A., History, 1957), and at Yale University (M.A., American Studies, 1959). My hair and eyes are a quite ordinary brownish color, I weigh 132 pounds, am five feet and seven inches tall, and, since this is a confession story of sorts, I wear elevator shoes. At the moment I'm living, if it may be called that, with my wife, the former Pamela Calvert (Mt. Holyoke, 1959) on Hammond Street in Chestnut Hill, Massachusetts. We both work in downtown Boston, she as a secretary for an advertising agency, I as assistant curator for the Cabot Antiquities Foundation, an organization devoted to the preservation of certain important relics, both tangible and intangible, of the Vanished American Past, or VAP as we abbreviate it around the office. For quite a long time I was irrationally devoted to my work, often putting in more hours than were good for me, endangering my health, my sanity, ignoring the chance for profitable leisure, not making any new friends and losing many old ones, forgetting nature's call and calls of nature, and becoming, in an age of machines, an apparatus, an efficient but mentally corrupt tool for prying into the miasmic crevices of obscure history. No longer. In a few weeks I'm getting out. I think I'm going to build myself a log castle out in the deep woods somewhere, anywhere, and I'm going to hole up in it. But that's *future*, and I don't know—I just don't know about it. What I'm thinking of right now is *past*, and I know nearly everything about that.

TWO

Say that I went home to Little Rock for any reason: my chronic and hopeless wanderlust, my nostalgia for a motherland, my lonesomeness for old friends, my search for lost elements of the Vanished American Past. But I think the most obvious immediate reason, the *primum mobile*, may be traced back to an embarrassing occurrence at the office shortly before my abrupt departure from Boston.

All through the winter I had been working harder than I realized, trying by sheer industry to extract from my body and brain all of whatever energy and talent they contained, for the service of that branch of scholarship which I had chosen as most suitable for my temperament. I had not had a vacation in two years. Twice a month my wife badgered me into taking her out to dinner and to Symphony; otherwise I had no obligations interfering with my consuming mission, and I was doing two jobs at once, moonlighting, as it were, except that I was doing them together, simultaneously. Although my work at the office consisted primarily of such routine tasks as cataloging items, old furniture and art works and such, for the Cabot Foundation's *Index of American Culture*, and helping locate unusual craft objects and other articles indigenous to the Vanished American Past, I was steadily accumulating materials for a long and conclusive study of the Decay of American Civilization, the deterioration of our institutions, the decline of our standards, etc., etc., which, when finished, would promote me into the vanguard of American cultural critics as swiftly as Athena emerged fully armored from the brow of Zeus. Yale had planted the seed of this noble work in my soul, and Boston had fertilized it. Sometimes, while suddenly hitting upon some momentous insight into the sickness of our society after a hard day of painstaking study of various documents and photographs, I wanted to rise and shout for joy that it was *I* who had made the discovery, *I*, a young little guy from the same sticks of Arkansas that had produced Lorelei Lee and Nellie Forbush, *I*, whose parentage and environment were submarginal, *I*, whose only boyhood ambition had been to capture eventually the Featherweight Boxing Crown of the World. Arriving at Yale in 1957, still wet behind the ears and passionately convinced that American civilization was the greatest in the history of mankind, I had at first affected a style of scholarship which synthesized the mentality of Vance Packard with the prose of Hemingway, spiced occasionally with a dash of Ozarks objectivity, but the result, which I felt was particularly appropriate for verbal exposition of various aspects of American history and culture, offended my professors no end, and pressure was put upon me both subtly (one gentleman suggested that I read through the Adams papers) and harshly (another refused to read my work) until at last I conformed, got in line, *hurle avec les loups,* and acquired a style of thought, speech, and writing which would leave me indistinguishable from my peers but would replace the unrestrained passion of my mind with coolness, detachment, circumspection. Verily, I had been innocent, modest, and overly naïve, and it was not without great difficulty that I eventually persuaded myself that Clifford Willow Stone the learned antiquary, despite his fustian, would be infinitely more valuable to the world than ole Nub Stone (as I was known in my youth), the buddy-buddy cornpone.

But sometimes I missed myself. Of course I wasn't aware of it, but I did, and maybe this is why what happened happened. Arriving for work at the customary time one Friday in late April, I noticed that my superior, Miss Ovett, a brilliant scholar only a few years older than I, was strangely remote, avoiding me as much as is possible in a small office which we share alone. Normally we are quite amiable in our relations, breaking the tedium of the work with an occasional joke or jest. So after wondering for several hours what her reason might be for ignoring me that particular day, I ventured to inquire if she had discovered anything amiss in my work. "Amiss!" she yelled indignantly, and resumed her attitude of insouciant disdain. Later I tried again to worm some word out of her, but again she was evasive. At five o'clock Miss Ovett, who, I will have to say, equaled me in my dedication to the work and often worked late hours overtime at my side, put on her hat and started to leave the office.

"Leaving early today, Clara?" I asked, being one of the few people permitted to address her familiarly.

Miss Ovett fixed me with a look which surely contained bits and pieces of all the great variety of hostile looks she had been giving me all day, and said, "Early? Perhaps my watch is fast, Mr. Stone, but as I recall, I set it by the Trinity Church clock during the lunch hour, and the Trinity Church clock has never been known to be inaccurate, therefore I must assume that if it is not precisely five o'clock, it is either going to be in a matter of a few seconds or else it already was, a moment ago."

Greatly relieved to hear her break her long silence so effusively, I was emboldened to stand up and move toward her and say, "Aw come on, Clara, why don't you tell me what I've done wrong. I'll never know unless you tell me." And to add suasion to my plea, I let my hand fall gently on her arm.

"Don't you touch me again!" she shrilled.

"??" my eyebrows, fluttering upward, said to her, and then I said, "Again?" and began wondering if I had ever touched her before. Miss Ovett, although she was not without certain felicities of appearance despite what eight years in the Radcliffe Graduate School had done to her, possessed the sort of corporal demeanor which automatically discourages physical contact, and I was unable to recall having done more than shake her hand at our first meeting, two years previously. But then I suddenly remembered that once, when we were exchanging confidences over a couple of beers at Jake Wirth's, she had mentioned being troubled by frequent recurrent nightmares of various types. Aha! "Miss Ovett," I intoned solemnly, dropping the familiarity because it was no longer effective and fixing her with a look of rapt penetration such as she might receive from her analyst, "have you been having bad dreams again?"

She started to reply, but her breath caught, snagged on some bewildered, hesitant turning of her mind for several moments before she could shake herself lose from it and say, "No." But timidly now, not indignantly. She gave the front of her sweater a tug, as if to correct a lax swelling of her abdomen. Her sweater, seen and sniffed at close range, was a thoroughly pilled cashmere cardigan the color of mud, sorely in need of a Woolite treatment; her semifeminine body scent was overlaid thickly by a musk redolent of books and papers and old wood. "No, I have not," she said. "It was too clear. How strange that you dare to suggest that, as if it were all only a dream to you."

"What was? What was only a dream?"

"Last night. Surely it wasn't of such little consequence that you've already put it out of your mind."

It was my turn to be bewildered. But my confusion rapidly gave way to annoyance. "For God's sake, Clara, I don't have the foggiest notion what you're talking about. *What* happened last night?"

She studied me for a moment and then said, "One of us is unhinged, and I think it must be you, because Dr. Rosepine assures me that my analysis has reached the point where I am definitely capable of distinguishing between reality and fantasy. Unless, of course, it is possible that last night's experience put me right back where I started from."

"Please, Clara, *please*. I swear on a stack of Nutting's *Furniture Treasuries* that I can't possibly imagine what you're talking about. Look, why don't we step around the corner and get a couple of drinks and talk this over like a couple of mature, rational people?"

"After last night I don't think I'd want to risk consuming alcohol in your company."

"All right. Would it make you feel better if I just gave you my resignation right now, and then you wouldn't have to look at my horrible face ever again?"

She thought about this, and apparently decided that she

didn't want me to quit. Giving in, she let me take her to a cocktail lounge around the corner on Charles Street, and I was very careful, during the first pair of drinks (I had a whiskey sour and she had a gin Alexander and you should always be chary of ladies who drink Alexanders), to discuss nothing but trivia totally unrelated to the matter at hand. For the second round, after I had persuaded her to switch to a sidecar and she had gone through half of it, I delicately reminded her of what we had to debate.

"Come to think of it," she said, coming to think of it gently, politely, like a mature, rational person, "you weren't quite yourself last night. I mean, there was more than the usual bemused detachment in your speech and manner. How much can you remember of what happened?"

I didn't remember very much, because nothing out of the ordinary had happened. It was my custom, three or four evenings a week, to phone a local delicatessen and have a light supper sent up so that I could stay in the office without interruption until, sometimes, nine or ten o'clock. Miss Ovett frequently remained there with me, but both of us were so absorbed with our individual tasks that only rarely did we speak to each other.

"Well," I offered, "all I can think of is that about eight o'clock you asked me if I had seen the 1670 Hadley desk-box which had just arrived yesterday afternoon, and we went down to the storeroom for a look at it, and we talked about it for a while, and then I went home."

"Do you recall anything in particular you said about that piece?" Miss Ovett asked, with her eyes looking down at her hands in her lap.

"No, I only recall that I was quite impressed with it, its excellent condition and rarity and all, you know. Didn't I make some remark to the effect that I wished I could have it for my own?"

"Yes, you did," she said, her eyes still on her lap. Then she looked up. "Clifford, order me another drink, please. Something pure this time, undiluted, unadulterated by extra ingredients."

So I got her a double Scotch-on-the-rocks and one for myself, and we drank them, and she touched one of her palms down lightly on my arm and left it there, moist and nervous. Then she said, "I think you've been working too hard." Then she told me, in a quavering voice, using the third-person narrative form for modesty's sake, what had happened the evening before. I was incredulous, naturally, but when belief at last got to me, I agreed that, indeed, I had been working too hard.

* * *

The woman looks up from her work and says to the man, "Say, have you looked at the Hadley desk?"

The man very slowly raises his head, looks through her, and addresses a cigar-store Indian (school of J. B. Woodhue, circa 1836, Willimantic, Conn.) behind her, "Hadley desk? Hadley desk? Hadley? Desk?"

"Yes," *the woman says.* "We just got it this afternoon. Didn't I tell you? Merrow found it in a junk shop in Delaware."

"Merrow? Delaware?"

"Yes. Near Dover, I think he said it was. Cost him fifteen dollars."

"Dover? Fifteen?"

"That's right. Would you like to run down and take a look at it?"

"Down?"

"Yes, it's downstairs in the storeroom. I thought you'd be dying to see it. Come on."

Rather reluctantly the man follows the woman downstairs. She decides that, as is frequently the case, he has left his mind behind him at his desk, where it is still wrestling with a problem of authenticity regarding a Portsmouth, New Hampshire, firehouse sign of about 1828. But perhaps the sight of the magnificent Hadley desk will snap him out of it.

"There!" *she says, snapping on the lights of the storeroom.* "Isn't it a beauty?"

The man gives it only a cursory glance, as if it doesn't interest him at all. Then he begins to stare at the woman. Often he is abstracted, she realizes. Even more often he is brash, pert, and flippant in his manner. But now she detects in his gaze something trancelike, even evil. Mr. Stone is a strange man, but a profound scholar; like all brilliant people, he has his peculiarities.

"Clifford?" *the woman says.* "Do you like it?"

"Very much," *he says, still staring fixedly at her.*

"Clifford? Are you feeling well?"

"Certainly."

"Don't you want to examine it? Pick it up, see how solid it is."

The man, although he is a small man an inch or so shorter than she, lifts her bodily and places her upon one of the worktables in the room, holding her down with arms whose strength amazes her.

"Clifford! What are you doing?"

"Very solid," he says, and then he begins to stroke her body with his hand.

"Mister Stone!" she gasps, and struggles to free herself, but the little man is very powerful. "What is the meaning of this?" she demands.

"Virgin oak," he says. "Perfect craftsmanship. So nicely put together."

"Let me go, Mr. Stone! I'll scream!"

He climbs onto the table beside her, and gazes soulfully into her eyes. "So rare," he murmurs. "I wish I had it for my own. It's so exquisite, I'm tempted to steal it." And his soft words, mingled with the gentle fondling of his hand, have a curious effect on her, more overpowering than his physical strength.

"The lid," he says, grasping her skirt and raising it. "How perfectly it is hinged!"

"Clifford," she sighs weakly, "don't."

"The drawers," he says, grasping her panties and pulling them down her legs. "How smoothly they slide!"

Then he gets on top of her.

"Would you like another drink, Clara?" I gently inquired.

"I guess not, thank you," she said. "I have those Rensselaer papers to collate, so I'd better get back to the office."

"Shall I help you?"

Noisily she Kleenexed her nose, then looked at me for a moment before replying, and began to smile, the first smile I had seen on her face all day. "No, Cliff," she said and patted my arm. "I think you should stay away from the office for a few weeks. You haven't taken a day's leave in over two years, and I think you've been driving yourself too hard. Perhaps you could let Dr. Rosepine have a few talks with you. He's an awfully good man."

"Oh, I couldn't do that," I protested sincerely. "I mean I couldn't leave the office. I've got too much to do.'

"But you're verging on a breakdown, I can sense it. Last night . . . well, last night was simply the culmination of a series of developments in your anxiety syndrome, and if you don't get away for a while, I fear for your health."

I mulled this over while I finished my drink, and I also thought of something which had been in the back of my mind for quite some time—a trip to Little Rock, a chance to see various good people I hadn't seen for years, including my own relatives, a chance to encounter once again the self of my youth, Nub Stone, a nice, well-adjusted boy who never, never would have done what the adult Clifford Stone did to poor Clara Ovett. "Perhaps you're right," I said to her, "but I could combine some business with the pleasure of a vacation." Then I told her how I might take advantage of a trip to Arkansas to look into some of the aspects of that section of Southern culture and possibly obtain a few items for the Foundation's collection.

"Why, that's an excellent idea!" she said. "But don't spend too much time for us. Get some rest, and do a little fishing or swimming or something. Stay as long as you like."

"Thank you," I said and gave her my most grateful smile. "And, Clara . . . I want to say how sorry I am about last night. I must have been out of my head. Anybody else but you would have fired me for a stunt like that."

Objective Ovett, she said, "I am convinced now that you were the victim, temporarily, of nervous pressure over which you had no control."

We got up and left the bar and I walked her to the corner, where she would turn up the hill to the office and I would cross the Common to catch the M.T.A. home. I shook her hand. "Thank you again," I said. "I'll see you in a few weeks and drop you a card or two while I'm away. And Clara—"

"Yes?"

"Before I go, I'd like to know . . . well . . . last night . . . you didn't finish telling me everything about it . . . did I . . . well, uh, I mean . . . did I—?"

"Did you insert your organ?"

I nodded, my eyes averted.

"No, you didn't. I managed to throw you off in time." Miss Ovett set her jaw and turned to go, saying rapidly yet almost inaudibly over her shoulder, "But I wish I hadn't."

I thought about that all the way home on the M.T.A. Trying like a hungover reveler on the day after to remember the improprieties of the night before, I sought in vain to recall what I had done and at last gave it up, deciding that maybe it wouldn't be such a bad idea for me to see that Dr. Rosepine after all. I knew I was oversexed, I was aware that I often suffered a mild form of chronic unmitigated satyriasis, which in my personal punning manner I think of as "Stone-ache," but there had only been two times in my life when I had not been aware of what I was doing: once in a boxing match in high school when I had become so punch drunk that I felled my opponent with one thunderously uninhibited blow and then knocked down the referee and my seconds before finally being stopped by the coach; and another time at Yale when I had killed a fifth of bourbon in two hours on a dare and recited all of Lincoln's first inaugural address from a memory which I was not even aware I had had. But both of those occasions had been stimulated by an actual change in the chemistry of my body. The *affaire Clara,* however . . . I just didn't know. It was all a dream I wanted to forget.

Not until I stepped down from the trolley and began the three-block walk to my house was I able to begin thinking about my vacation. Arkansas, as I have already indicated, was repeatedly in my thoughts, although time and again I had told myself that like others who have left it forever I was never very happy there and would not enjoy living there again for long, and had remained away from it primarily in rebellion against its jejune simplicity, its insignificance. Again like most who have left it, however, I often fancied going back to stay, but knew that I couldn't, although I had tried. Now again as I walked up Hammond Street in Chestnut Hill (between rows of houses which were utterly strange to me—regardless of my having passed them many times before—simply because it was Chestnut Hill and I by circumstance had been born and brought up in Little Rock) my mind started already to tease the possibility of the pending vacation as an opportunity for reappraising my old, comfortably familiar birthplace with a view toward resettling there, recapturing whatever stimulus the climate and physical environment had once given me, despite my failure to take advantage of it. I realized it was absurd even to wonder if Little Rock might have any need for a scholarly specialist in certain moribund aspects of American civilization. The University or the public schools could use me as a teacher of history, but I would not apply, firstly because I am shy of speaking to more than one person at a time, secondly because the kind of history which interested me would impart a warped view of our nation to the student. But, I wondered as I approached my house on Hammond Street in Chestnut Hill, would I necessarily have to be employed in something so closely related to my training? Couldn't I perhaps forsake my absorbing interest during eight hours of the day in order to earn a living so that the other eight hours might serve that interest? Costs of living in Arkansas were, I realized, astonishingly lower than in New England; perhaps a simple clerk's job in some Little Rock insurance office would provide a better sustenance than that which I eked out in Boston. And of course my wife might be thought of as independently wealthy. By golly, yes! She . . .

THREE

It was not until I had turned into our walk and placed my foot upon the first step to the door that I realized my wife might be thought of, no, *should* be thought of. By then it was too late to do much more thinking.

She was sitting in the living room athwart the sofa, her feet tucked under one of the cushions, reading her quarterly copy of PMLA, which at one time I had thought was some sort of vowel-less abbreviation of her name, Pamela, but later learned stood for *Publication of the Modern Language Association*. As she often does not, she did not look up when I entered. This may or may not reflect scorn on her part. On the other hand it may or may not indicate oblivious absorption in what she is reading. Probably, that particular evening, it simply meant that because she had looked up on so many occasions when I had entered, she was tired of the monotony of having to look up on this occasion, and so did not. I hung up my overcoat in the closet, looked through the day's mail, mostly junk and bills, poured myself two fingers of tepid bourbon in a tumbler that had clowns and blue elephants decalcomaniated on its sides along with the words EETSUM FLUFFY PEANUT BUTTER, sat down across the room from my wife and said, "Anything for supper?"

Without looking up, she said, "Twocoldleftoverporkchopsintherefrigerator. Andcoldpotatoes. Helpyourself."

I decided that warming up and serving supper for myself would provide some time for further study of the problem of how best to broach the topic of the Little Rock vacation to my wife, who, I was aware, held my home town and hell in about equal esteem. So I withdrew to the kitchen, scraped a blanket of congealed grease from the pork chops and from one side of each sliver of sliced potato, slid them all onto a shelf of the oven, drank off the rest of my drink and refilled it with three fingers, then sat down at the kitchen table to devote my thoughts to

Pamela Calvert Stone, an unusual wife, an uncommonly pretty blonde, intelligent and charming in a patrician sort of way, but, for the nonce, a woman who did not enjoy the responsibilities of wedlock, namely, cooking, housework, and particularly sex; a woman who, furthermore, was no longer able, or obliged, or simply disposed, to communicate with me.

Possibly it is her own fault that she is so pretty and that she hates domestic responsibilities, but it is my fault that she won't talk to me. It is mine because in the fragile months of our courtship and in the first fresh days of our marriage I fell victim to that heedless mistake, that *étourderie,* which dooms so many contemporary marriages through the indiscretion of verbal intimacy. In the early days of the Vanished American Past young couples maintained a proper timidity and taciturnity toward each other. But not any more. Today the intelligent young couple, recognizing in each other potential life partners, rushes headlong into the mutual exchange of their most secret thoughts and feelings, as if to say, *My love, I honor you with these gifts of my private soul.* Indeed, such exhibitionism of the interior landscape is a prerequisite to exposure of the exterior flesh. The admission fee to bed is long and honest confession, wherein the route to the mattress is lubricated with fluent words. Next morning's (or next year's) hangover is a nervous recognition of the extent to which the limits of tact have been violated. But too late. Darling Pamela sees through me as through fragile, transparent glass, satisfying herself that my slightest thought or deed can be interpreted by something I told her during one of those lingering, languorous hours of tender talk. A dominant man needs a certain mystery, a mantle of enigma, which he can wrap like a dark burnoose around his body, concealing the pusillanimous frame beneath, but I have none. At least not for my wife. If for example I am a day late in paying the Boston Edison bill, she understands it as a symptom of my rebellion against the rich little Miss Kilmansegg she is, because I unburdened myself of such a feeling during one of those unguarded moments of conversation which I thought at the time were purely objective and even intellectual, little realizing that one day they might subjectively be turned against me. If I procrastinate the disposal of the daily bag of garbage, her mind automatically returns to an occasion when I confided to her one of my pet Theories of the Leisure Class, whereby honest and dedicated scholars should ideally enjoy an existence unhampered by picayune chores. If I swear vociferously, profanely and menacingly at some taxi driver who without compunction blocks the path of our car, Pamela knows that my bark is worse than my bite because in one of our intimate moments I discoursed at length on the Roots, Nature and Effect of Base Funk in the Human Spirit, confessing bravely several of my own weaknesses (such as a lack of Charles Atlasian "dynamic tension") as examples anent the subject. In fact, my imprecations to the taxi driver have a certain ludicrous aspect, bereft of authority, because it is always my wife who sits behind the wheel of our Buick Skylark, a circumstance which is itself the outcome of gracious confession (once, clinched together in the deep pile of a cabin's rug, our hands stuck in each other's crotches, we spoke of that subject most relevant to the business at hand, and I, rambling onward expertly in my thorough analysis of matters which I considered myself an authority on, let fall some innocent, well-meant affirmation of my belief in the Automobile as Sex Symbol—which amused and edified her thoroughly at the time, but ultimately deprived me of the use of the family car). No matter that I was Featherweight Champion in the Mid-South Golden Gloves tournament of 1953, and have scattered around the bedroom of our Chestnut Hill house several trophies attesting to the pugilistic prowess of my youth. Pamela dusts these trophies periodically, perfunctorily when she is cleaning up, but she does not see them. All she knows is what I revealed of myself one chill autumn night in the first year of our marriage, when we sat side by side on the sofa before the season's first snug fire, in sweet rapport, congenially swirling brandy in the bottoms of our snifters, while I ruminated, aloud but softly, articulately, on the kaleidoscope of fears which dwell in the boxer's breast during those brief but endless moments when he comports himself against his adversary.

Lord, Lord! I cried after another heavy drag on the bourbon. Let us forget that poisonous aphorism of Ovid's: *Si qua voles apte nubere nube pari:* If you wish to marry well, marry an equal. He lied! Or else he thought of Julia, the poor little licentious daughter of old Emperor Augustus, as his equal, which was socially pretentious of him, or else, because we may assume that her small, warped intellect was no match for his genius, he was being maliciously sarcastic. Marriage of equals means conflict of equals and, like our perpetual struggle with the Soviets, nobody wins. A marriage of equals is like a demoniac chess game in which the king may be checked and checked again but never checkmated. Ovid, you old bastard, say what you really meant: If you wish to marry well, marry disparately.

Once I wrote at great length of my marital troubles to an old and valued friend in Little Rock, Dall Hawkins, now a benevolent young policeman, and Dall returned simply a nine-word postcard: *You don't have to put up with that crap.* I suppose he was right, but it was kind of late. I'll say this: Had I been warned, had I but divined the doorless labyrinth which marriage to someone of Pamela's intelligence would become, I would have pulled up short, turned my back on Mt. Holyoke and all its sister institutions, and chosen some unspoiled even if witless heifer from the most remote wilds of the Ozarks.

But never mind. The pork chops burned. Gazing into my fingers of whiskey while negative thoughts of Pamela and positive thoughts of Little Rock waged war in my mind, I was unaware that in shoving the chops and chips into the oven I had turned the dial beyond BAKE to BROIL, until there was considerable smoke in the kitchen and Pamela came stomping into the room, her magazine parted around one finger, and an expression on her face as of Ino rushing to the rescue of Ulysses' wrecked raft.

"Merciful heavens, Cliff! Can't you do *anything* right?" Whereupon she snatched my sad scorched supper out of its crematorium, deftly flipped the helpless potatoes into the garbage pail, scraped the black bark from the surface of the two pork chops and placed them before me on the table without ceremony, returning at once to the living room. The air in the kitchen, as of the air anywhere when she has passed through it on one of her reluctant errands, was abruptly cooler, as of a winter door suddenly swung open and held too long, despite the layers of smoke which still drifted through it.

Ah, I thought as I hacked away at the inelastic meat, *she treats me like this miserable meal: leaves me entirely alone, to my own devices, until I am spoiled or damaged, and then scrapes my surfaces until I am usable again.* For it is true that Pamela took little interest in my work; her own field in college had been French literature of the late nineteenth century, and American culture was of no concern to her, but still I was disappointed that my occupation was to her no more noble than that of any other white-collar Bostonian, and that the only time she had acknowledged my career at all was when, for example, she sought a detailed description of the appearance and personality of Clara Ovett.

What did she want? What *does* she want, of me, of herself, of life? God knows. But *I* knew, that night I swallowed the humble chops and the humble pie of her treatment of me and the meal both, that what she most needed was to get out of Boston *pro tempore*, and I was prepared, as a well-practiced swallower, to swallow my bile for a while, long enough to attempt communication with her once more. Boston, for all its early charm, its evocation of the VAP, can be a depressing place at any time of the year, because of its decadence, its disuse and misuse, the feeling of a gray old lady slightly demented, living on the thin thread of memories, forced to wear last year's tattered dress, taken advantage of by corrupt Machiavellian politicians, suffering a climate which is never exactly right, and fatally jealous of her cousin cities, all of whom somehow are her betters. But that time in April was the worst time of all. Then the place was well-nigh unhabitable: the welcome pink blossoms of the saucer magnolia had not yet appeared, the workmen of the Public Garden sharpened their tools and cast anxious glances at the sky but did not commence their mass implantation of jonquils and tulips and pansies, the streets were still gray; the M.T.A. was prone to breakdowns, and the tempers of Boston's Finest shrank to a new shortness; impatient spring-seekers, egged on by the overoptimism of the *Globe* and *Herald*, trekked out to the Arnold Arboretum but found there only skunk cabbage; the fish did not bite in the Charles; ferns did not fungate in the Fens; the sailors of Scollay Square, bored and disenchanted, went back to sea.

"Pam," I said, standing above her, holding my glass of bourbon casually in one hand, "let's get out of this place." But try as I might to make my voice relaxed and natural, to give my seven-word sentence an easy, ordinary prosaism, I sounded to myself like one total stranger making some absurd suggestion to another total stranger. Lord, how effortless it used to be to say whatever happened to pop into my mind!

She looked up, marking her interrupted place with a polished fingernail, honored my eyes with her glance for two seconds, the glass in my hand for one, and then returned to her magazine. "You're drunk," she said. "Why don't you go to bed?"

"No, I mean it," I protested. "Let's take a vacation. Go South. Sunshine. Fresh air, flowers and all. Recreation. Re-creation."

She chose to look up at me again. "Where South?" she asked.

"Uh, Ah was thinkin of maybe, well, *Little Rock*."

She returned to her magazine again. I waited.

After a while I said, "Well?" but she didn't respond.

I wanted to sit down, beside her perhaps, so her eyes would be on a level with mine, so I could see into them, but I knew she wouldn't want that. "Pam?" I said. She did not look up. "Say something," I said.

"I did: go to bed," she said.

"No, *really*," I said. "I'm not going to work tomorrow. Clara knows, I told her. She says that's okay, for me to take a vacation, stay away as long as I like."

Pamela looked up at last. "Really?" she asked.

"Yes," I said.

"Good," she said. "We'll go to Rutland."

"I don't want to go to Rutland. It's frigid." *Like you*, I started to add, but dared not. But I had a point. Going from the chill of Boston to the cold of Rutland would not help me. In summer and fall the place is wonderful, and we usually go up several weekends a month during those seasons, but I could not abide living under the noses of her parents for more than two days at a time. The Calverts are pleasant people, sound Congregationalist gentility, *arbitri elegantiae*, and they know enough about early New England history and culture to make conversation with them educational, but they had never quite forgiven me for not being a Saltonstall or a Lowell. In late April their beautiful old Lavius Fillmore house on Highland Avenue would be a musty ossuary wherein, imprisoned by the bars of fluted pilasters, I would strive for sleep against the sounds of ancestral bones stirring in the long corridors.

"Suit yourself," she said. "*I* am going home."

Home! she called it, as if there were no other, as if our house in Chestnut Hill were a hole to which I had shanghaied her for the duration of our marriage. Would she if she saw Little Rock in the full flowering of its spring like it better than she had that one week in hot July she had been there after our wedding? "I don't suppose you'd consider going to Arkansas with me, then?"

"Of course not," she said. It was beyond discussion.

"I suppose you'll be taking the car with you to Rutland?"

"Of course," she said. That, too, was beyond discussion. I hated to go to Little Rock and, worse, *be* in Little Rock without that beautiful Skylark. Perhaps the automobile *is* a sex symbol.

Her smug righteousness emboldened me. Upon my mettle I said, putting my glass down with a bang on the coffee table, "Goddammit, Pam! Don't be so obstinate!"

"I?" she said. Again: "I?" She laughed, a false crepitant *ha*.

"All right," I said. "I think I *will* go to bed."

But the last word, as I marched away, was hers: "Good."

Undressing in the bathroom, removing my trousers and hanging them carefully in the closet, I extracted from the right rear pocket my notebook and sat down with it on the john. My notebook is a very small, three-inch by five-inch spiral-bound pad with brown covers, called a Ring-Master. Unlike most such memo books, it opens from the side rather than from the end. I bought mine in a drugstore across the Common on Boylston Street. I would not have been without it, and during my three years in Boston I filled thirty-four of these books with notes written in a small, cramped, page-filling hand; these will form the core of my opus on American civilization, should I ever get around to writing it. They slip easily into my hip pocket, and I am fast on the draw, having once timed myself, with the aid of one of those fast-draw clocks in an Arkansas sportsmen's club, at .09 seconds. On the john I opened book number 34, which was crumpled and sweat-stained, to page 67, the first clean page, and at the top wrote in heavy capitals:

FAMILIARITY BREEDS CONTEMPT

and beneath that, extending onward for several pages:

The source of marital estrangement in our society is nearly always that very condition of the mind and emotions which promoted the original attachment, viz., *intimacy,* or, specif., a verbal intercourse so acute it penetrates the mind as deeply as sexual intercourse penetrates the body. The hapless male ejaculates into the brain of his partner a seed of knowledge, of recognition, which creates in her mind a slow-growing concept of what he is, what he is like, or rather what she takes him to be. He can no more control that image than he could superintend what happens to his sperm once her ovum gets hold of it. Consequently the fully developed image of him which she bears in her mind, like the infant she bears in her womb, may not resemble him at all. The trouble with mankind today is that husbands are no longer content simply to fuck their wives; they must fuck their wives' minds as well. The latter act is just as easy to botch as the former.

But the simile has its limits: a man can, by cajolery, soft words, periodic gifts, and perhaps the assistance of liquor or other aphrodisiac, persuade the woman to open her legs to the incoming seed; but nothing will open her mind to the image of him which he would like to implant there. Also: whereas a woman's womb may be impregnated as often as she and nature will allow, her mind can only be knocked up once. Short of thorough psychoanalysis or some dramatic transmogrification whereby the man suddenly becomes an entirely different person, nothing (repeat: *nothing*—confession magazines and Abigail Van Buren to the contrary) will ever change her concept of him.

This lamentable condition, virtually pandemic today, did not always exist. American women of the past, the VAP, did not receive higher education, and were so reserved and withdrawn that few men would ever give them the affinity of serious talk. As early as the first quarter of the eighteenth century, old William Wollaston was remarking that the good wife was obliged to defer, to submit to her husband simply because his reason was stronger than hers, his knowledge and experience greater. And although Franklin himself argued that the young suitor should make his intended bride accustomed to serious, sensible conversation, he warned that this could too easily inflate her conceit and vanity. At about this same time Talleyrand made his excellent remark: "A clever wife often compromises her husband; a stupid one only compromises herself."

We are hard-pressed to strike a balance in the modern era of marital adjustments. Our efforts are frustrated. We get—

"All right, you awful onanist, come on out of there," her voice seeped through the solid oak bathroom door. Hastily I closed the notebook and popped it into my pajama pocket before opening the door. A twinge of guilt for what I had written flushed my face slightly pink; as I passed her she saw my blush and could interpret it in whatever way she liked.

Let her. I went on to bed.

But later, after she had come into the bed and lay scant inches away from me, I began to think I owed her one more chance. Perhaps the case might well have been that my understanding of her was no less frangible than hers of me. Women are, after all, strange, perplexing, well-nigh inscrutable creatures. Pamela was, at all events, my lawful wedded wife. This is my charity, my softness.

Across the cold bed I reached out and touched her hand, to hold it, but she withdrew it, turning over, away from me.

In the dark I looked where her back would be. Pamela honey, if I go to Arkansas I just might be unfaithful to you, once or twice, or maybe a dozen times or more if I take a notion to. Won't you put out for me this one last time? Won't you, seeing as how I might not be seeing you again for a month or more, put your middle up against mine, just this once? For old times' sake? Huh?

Her backside I embraced, and pressed my mouth against her ear: "Guess this is our last night together for a while."

There were words in her exaggerated sigh, two words I think, and although I could not catch them clearly I think they were: "Thank God."

Further efforts, additional motions, continuance of my meager maneuvering, would not have availed. But I tried anyway. Just, I suppose, for the hell of it. For the unpromised promise, the hopeless hope, the inominous omen of some mumbled utterance or revelative gesture heard or felt in the dark as testament to the restoration of contact, of the frail felicity from which we had absented ourselves for more than a while. *Felix qui potuit rerum cognoscere causas:* Happy is he who has penetrated into the causes of things. She stirred not, nor spake. By and by I burped the last bubble of the humble pie, and thinking of custards and karo nuts and deep-dish blackberries which awaited me homeward, and then at last beginning to feel glad, even overjoyed, that I was going alone, without Pamela, that for the first time in four years of marriage I could escape her, and that that would be, *could* be, a delight worth anticipating, I fell at last to sleep, my Stone-ache drifting away.

FOUR

I took leave of my wife before dawn the next day, before she awakened, sacrificing a leaf from my Ring-Master for a terse parting message, reminding her of my father's address and phone number in case she should ever want to reach me. With my one suitcase I rode a Greyhound bus across the Massachusetts Turnpike to Albany, where I caught the next westbound New York Central, a reasonably decent train called the Dewitt Clinton, which took me all the way to St. Louis, where, after a quick shave and defecation in the men's room of Union Station (I have never been able to attend properly to such business in the cramped, jostling confines of a moving train's lavatory), I transferred at last to a fine blue Missouri Pacific coach which provided excellent transportation through the Sunday afternoon hills of Missouri and on into the Arkansas night, until that triple-thierce camming pin or whatever it was gave way outside of Olyphant.

The sound of the rails I love. There is nothing else like it, and probably no other reason why I travel by train whenever possible. Back cushions which prickle the neck, the omnipresent smell of disinfectant, surly conductors, tepid drinking water, and, above all, those impossible lavatories—all of this can be borne, even suffered, in order to listen to that unique sound. This may strike the habitual commuter as absurd, but just as he has immunized himself against the charms of his wife through long and intimate association, possibly he has also immunized himself against that sound which clicks in his unhearing ears from 7:35 until 8:40 five mornings a week. The way to listen to America, as you move across her, is to focus your ears on that steady *clackety-clack* of hard steel beneath you. Ah, the habitual commuter protests: but the sound of the rails is the same in Arkansas as in New York or anywhere else? Exactly. And the America of Arkansas, these days, is the same as the America of New York. Or anywhere else.

The America of Olyphant, I would have sworn as I prepared to step down from that stalled train, was no different from that of, say, Drury, Massachusetts, a dreary wide-place on the road to Vermont. But I was unprepared. Respiring in the bland, soulless air of Boston as I had all winter, and then knowing only the olfactory interlude of disinfected train coaches and train stations, I was totally unready for the fumes of spring which blasted my nostrils as I placed the first foot on Arkansas soil. A green and yellow smell, fragrant of night air after day blooming, effluvial of rich earth and burgeoning field weeds and flowers: a saturation of ripe, luxuriant vegetation. Having seen Olyphant by day in the days of my youth, I knew that physically it was no work of art: a scattered handful of unpainted boxlike houses, an old store, the flatness of the soybean land, not at all a worthy namesake of the eminent Lord Olyphant. Its sole claim to note was that here on the chill night of November 3, 1893, the desperate bandit Jesse Roper held up the northbound Missouri Pacific (perhaps near the very spot my own train was stalled), robbed all the passengers and killed the conductor, thereby perpetrating the most daring train robbery in the annals of otherwise dull Arkansas history. But in this night, clinging tightly to the handrails of the train's steps as I thrust my nose out into that incredible air, I fancied a sylvan park, a Pandean pleasance such as loom darkly and invitingly in the backgrounds of rococo paintings. O Fructuous Firmament! I was home. My own country, my motherland. Even the drab reality of the truck-stop café on the highway where I got my coffee and newspaper, and of the ugly waitress of overcurled hair who shocked me with her flat Southland drawl, could not spoil the enchantment of that first brave illusion.

The copy of the Sunday Arkansas *Gazette* was the last one for sale in that café, and I carried it proudly and carefully back to the train, along with my cup of coffee. Even the smell of the *Gazette*, the mingling of a particular kind of newsprint with a particular kind of printer's ink, evoked old memories of mornings at the family table. I usually read the funnies first, because the paper comes wrapped in them, but this time the funnies were alien, they came from New York, and neither Li'l Abner nor Snuffy Smith had any relevance to my home state. So I ignored them and drew out the Sports section. The sportswriters of the *Gazette* are the most literate, witty, perspicuous writers of their breed in the entire country; Arthur Daley and his crew at the *Times* could learn things from them. Their only fault is a hearty optimism, a conviction that Arkansas teams, whether football, baseball, bowling, hunting, or whatever, are the best in the country, a judgment which however is often correct. Reading their avid columns is an experience as entertaining as the games themselves, and I absorbed every word of the section, from the fate of the Travelers, now somehow in the Pacific Coast League, blanking Spokane 3-0, to the prospects for bass fishing in Lake Maumelle, Greers Ferry, and Bull Shoals. Here and there a familiar name: my old classmate Billy Compton was top city bowler with a 281 average; Tom Hoffman, who lived around the corner from me for some twelve years, had taken the lead in the Country Club four-ball tournament, 2 up; and old YMCA buddy Ken Vernon had reeled an eight and a half pound largemouth out of Lake Conway with a blue plastic worm and had his picture, same bashful grin and all but getting loose around the jowls, holding up the husky lunker in one meaty fist.

Finishing Sports, I skimmed through the Society section. The sixteen young brides and brides-to-be on the first page, every one of them lovely, were a new generation and I recognized none of them, although several of the family names were familiar, and thus I gave them each only a quick glance, pausing long enough to admire their good blooming Arkansas-type beauty: the fluffed coifs, the doe eyes, the cherry cheeks, the full beaming consummate mouths—hadn't an Arkansas girl been reigning as this year's Miss America? On page 2, the regular column, "Among Ourselves," informed me that, among other things, Marilyn and Steve McComb had returned home from two weeks in St. Croix, Virgin Islands, with their three children; Susan and Guy Hammond had entertained thirty friends Friday night at a special housewarming for their new home at Sixteen The Riverway, Hickory Wood; Cinny and Dick Anderson would leave tomorrow for a week at the harborside chalet of Chuchu and Lonny Heffington on Lake Catherine. All of these people I had known in school.

The Home and Garden section showed three photographs of the new contemporary house built in Pondmeadow for the Ernest L. Jacksons. The Business section had photographs of Steve McComb, now elevated to a partnership in a law firm; of Henderson (Henk) Wainwright, newly appointed account executive for Nash Advertising; and of Byron Drenker, promoted to vice-president of Apex Insurance. I knew these guys too. Long ago, it seemed.

The Entertainment section mentioned a special news broadcast on Channel 8 to be conducted by the regular announcer, Hy Norden, who, if I was not mistaken, had been one of my best friends in high school; we had worked together for a time on the school paper and yearbook, belonged to the same service and social clubs, taken three years of Latin together, and frequently lunched at the same table in the cafeteria. I had not expected that Little Rock would hold him, but if he had to be held it was appropriate that he would be a semi-celebrity in a position of such public exposure.

Two other items, in the News section, which I saved for last, are worth mentioning here. A photograph showed the current contingent of stalwart policemen being honored for various acts of meritorious service and bravery, and in the forefront of the group stood Sergeant Doyle C. Hawkins, who, as plain old Dall, a tall, gangling but sinewy hayseed produced by the same section of the Ozark backwoods that had fostered my father, had been my closest friend through the Little Rock public schools.

We had corresponded irregularly over the years, but I had not seen him the last two or three times I was home, and although I knew he was on the police force, I had not known he was now a sergeant, nor that he was capable of being decorated for an act of foolhardy bravery (persuading, the paper said, a drink-crazed wife-killer to turn his shotgun on himself instead of on the cops who were unable to flush him out of his hideaway.) Possibly I ought to look up Dall this time, for old times' sake.

The other item, *sans* photograph, said simply that the premiere of the new play, *How Many Times Have You Seen* THE RED SHOES? by Arkansas' own Bollington Prize-winning dramatist, James Royal Slater, scheduled to open at the Arkansas Arts Center Theater next Saturday evening, was sold out, but that tickets for the Monday and Tuesday performances of the production, starring Hugh Berrey and Margaret Austin, were still available. Margaret Austin? My old girl friend Margaret? No, it couldn't be. Not old Margaret Austin the pale and wan, Margaret the shy and hopeless, not Margaret the untouchable brunette. Strange, I had not thought of her for quite some time. Or had I? That name . . .

No, I decided, no, there must be another Margaret Austin. It was a common name. *My* Margaret would never—*could* never—have gone on the stage, even a little stage.

But still, somehow, I felt strangely nervous—no, *apprehensive* —as I saw all of these old familiar names in the newspaper, and I began to ponder a question which had troubled me only slightly since I left Boston but would begin to crop up at frequent intervals in the days ahead: *What, or who, am I really looking for?* I could not fool myself into thinking that this was a purely social visit or a mere vacation. Something, or someone, was waiting to snare me or entangle me in some fateful course of events which might well determine the direction of my future. Call this hunch a portentous presumption. Color it a gaudy shade of mauve. But although I am as much an antipredestinarian as the next man, I felt this presentiment in my bones, and I knew that I was looking for something, or, even now as I read this newspaper, someone, and that it might be Guy Hammond or Dick Anderson or Hy Norden or any one of these old friends who would herald some chance adventure of great consequence.

Well, all of these people—perhaps even Dall Hawkins—were ones I would have to see again. They would want to see me. Clifford Stone, the home-town boy who went East and made good, now returning in triumph. Ah, that was a pretty image. They would all want to know why I had come back, and they would like my answer: to see if this was where I belonged. To find out why I had ever left in the first place. Now, reading the intimate old *Gazette* again, seeing familiar names and faces, which never appeared in the pages of those other two newspapers, Boston's and Rutland's, I was tempted to ask: Why, indeed? Had I been so presumptuous as to think that I was better than most Arkansans and thus should seek my fortunes elsewhere? Folks belong where they was reared, my oracular Newton County grandmother had once said to me; and truly it had hurt my father to pull up stakes in the little mountain-locked village of Parthenon and move even the relatively short distance of a hundred and sixty miles down to Little Rock. If there was only one thing held against me by my widowered father and my motherless and now brotherless sister and any of my other relatives, it was that I had betrayed my birthplace, I had cast my lot with the Yankees. But now I was coming home, wasn't I? From Boston, where I had the anonymity of a very small cygnet in a very large lake, I was returning to Little Rock, where I could have the prominence of a grand and handsome swan in a very small pond. It gave me a happy feeling, it beatified me. Abruptly I was aware of two things: first, the train had begun to move again, the camming pin re-cammed or re-triple-thierced; and, second, I was not chewing my hangnails. In Boston, reading the paper or reading magazines or simply working at my desk, I continually gnaw the little slivers of tough skin that fringe the sides of my fingernails. A talented and sophistic therapist might easily interpret this as a semiconscious manifestation of my wish to revenge myself on my wife (or Clara) by biting her. Myself, I figured it was just nervousness. Now I *wasn't*, suddenly, any more.

Now, from a Boston which seemed to me thoroughly feminine —and rather dowagerish at that—because of the quality of the city itself which I have already mentioned and because my days there had been lived in the company of such as Pamela and Clara, I was setting a course toward a Little Rock which was, by positive contrast, thoroughly masculine, a warm river-town, rough, broad-shouldered, a little wild, the feeling of a forceful fellow who had seen enough of the West to be fierce but enough of the South to be gentlemanly, a scrappy chap who, like me, was small but sharp, little but rocky. And the people I would see there would be mostly men: my wiry old dad (my mother died in an automobile accident when I was a teen-ager), shrewd Steve McComb, waggish Hy Norden, rough Dall Hawkins. Lord, what a refreshing change from my emasculated Boston life!

Come on, train, let's *move!*

And it did, gathering speed and rushing on smoothly out of Olyphant, across the broad and flat land between the White and Arkansas rivers. I would be home by dawn. After a glad and near-tearful reunion with the old man, I would begin, one by one, to notify everybody of my return. Steve and I would play tennis and golf; Dall and I would don old khakis and drift across the waters of Lake Maumelle, filling the boat with all manner of bass and bream and crappie, and we would shoot snooker and watch the Travelers and sit on front porches in our undershirts sipping beer the warm night long. Hy might ask me to do a guest appearance or two on his television program: "Little Rock Revisited," or "The Superiority of Arkansas over Nearly Any Place Else." And if all this activity became a little too taxing at times, why, I could simply relieve it with a night of fun in the company of a warm-blooded lass. There was sweet old Sarah Farnley and Sissy Portis and undoubtedly countless others I would meet at Steve's parties. Hell, what was a woman *for,* anyway? Certainly not for dry, juiceless scholarship, as Clara, nor for frigid, sadistic scorn, as Pamela. By God, in a *man's* world like Little Rock, a woman was good for, *damn* good for, a lay, and she knew it, and by God a man could have himself a little pleasure.

Life is, after all, a search for adventure, and I had had precious little of that in Boston. Life is a search for adventure, yes, and you sure don't get adventure *alone,* by yourself. You get it with other people, but first you've got to get to *know* those people. The last time I had seen any of them, I was still a schoolboy, still practically a kid with no real understanding or insight or compassion or simple *savoir faire.* Now I had grown up a little, emotionally if not physically, and I could pry into them, I could find out who all these people really were, I could take the whole town apart piece by piece and examine it meticulously and put it back together again. A creeping quidnunc, an inquisitive gadfly, I would worm my way through every street of that town, and through every heart, and learn everything anew.

The quadrennial homecomer, the sporadic wayfarer, discovered in reaching his native shore that he had come a long way in both space and mind, turning, changing, returning into somebody Pamela would not know, somebody who, even better, would not know her. But only his own, of which she was not one. The *voyageur,* making port, became the *voyeur.*

❧ FIVE

The soul of the air of Little Rock is often the big brown smell of baking bread: the tang of roasting wheat, of dough well done, toasty whiffs of the sharp biscuity savor of many loaves, the tawny nips of the staff of life so sharp they assault the senses: the gentle pain of *pain.* On Sunday night especially, and on into Monday morning, the bakeries—Colonial, Meyer's, Wonder Bread, Mrs. Wright's and others—are stuffing their ovens to freshen the shelves of a thousand groceries, and the breath of that work escapes those buildings, seeping out through their windows and doors, drenching the air of all the streets. I have noticed that essence in no other town, but it has always been that way in Little Rock. Walking off into that fragrant air, I became hungry.

Dawn had not yet broken. The air was still cool, but growing warmer. I would walk home; although it was more than a mile, my one suitcase wasn't heavy, and I wanted to see the town, to watch the simple houses of my street as the morning light crept onto them. My house—I mean my father's house—is on Ringo, which, if not one of the oldest streets in town, has the little-known distinction of being, except for University Avenue, the longest north-south passage in the city, beginning in the mud of the riverbank and running over two miles to end in the scalloped-oak jungles beside the Rock Island tracks. It is a thoroughly pedestrian street, and by that I mean both meanings: firstly it is fit more for walking than for driving; secondly it is commonplace. It is not fit for driving because it has too many stop signs, one at every corner in some stretches; it takes forever to traverse it by car, stopping and starting and stopping again. It is commonplace because, like Cross Street on one side and Chester on the other, it has nothing really conspicuous or special anywhere on its two miles, amalgamate of many different types and sizes of structures, none of them distinguished or circumstantial. Ringo in several ways is like the city itself, and I like to think of it as a typical street, although I realize it is rather seedy, shabby, and haggard in contrast to the newer streets farther west. It is a mellow and manly street, soft, easy, and casual. It may be sullen and rather splendidly splenetic but it is not melancholy like those streets east of Main, which seem to groan, "How weary we are! How jaded and sunk in sorrow, enduring days which are too long!" And it is self-respecting, but it has none of the reproachful hauteur of those proud but bored avenues and boulevards and circles and terraces of Pulaski Heights and the lavish additions, the opulent streets which laugh a laugh that sounds like "Ho-hum" and say, if you ask them, "We are not, after all, of Little Rock, but rather so far west of it that we manage very well, thank you, to establish our own independent coteries." No, Ringo is neither sad nor snotty; if it says anything at all, should you ask, it says, "Buddy, I don't give a shit, what's it to you?"

It begins, as I say, in the mud of the riverbank, beneath the Baring Cross bridge, but leaps up the bank quickly and becomes macadamed and curb-lined, getting a good running start where the old Capitol City Coach Company bus and trolley yards used to be and where the sprawling red-brick edifice of the car barn still reposes in a kind of obsolete, preterit splendor, and then it dashes on for another block before the limited-access La Harpe Boulevard cuts rudely across its path and closes it; but it opens again on the other side and continues on to Markham, where I stood on the corner several blocks up from the MoPac station and looked down Ringo toward the river for a moment before turning south, past Tanner's Café with its White Entrance on Markham and its Colored Entrance on Ringo, on up to West Second and West Third, past Mrs. Wright's big bakery, where all of tomorrow's bread for the Safeway Stores was amaking in its ovens, to West Fourth and Capitol Avenue and beyond, walking slowly and easily on my slow and easy street, letting the dawn come up on my left, the night fade away on my right, the street lights blink out. Ringo Daytime: on to West Ninth, the Little Rock Harlem, where for several blocks Ringo would be the exclusive property of the Negroes and would contain, at intervals, three Negro Baptist churches, the small shack of Ballard's Bar-BQ (where the best sandwiches in town are made, I am told, having never been allowed to buy any, because I am white, ofay) and the Dunbar Community Center and Dunbar Junior High School for Negroes, and several small grocery stores now abandoned because one of the few places in town where Negroes can rub shoulders with the whites is the supermarket. In a newly cleared lot, high with pungent weeds, there was a sign I passed: a new sign stuck into the earth, saying, in large blue and white letters, mysteriously: "Who's Happy?" I paused to ponder this strange sign, decided I was happy, and walked on.

On the other side of the Dunbar neighborhood, but in a block shared almost half and half by white and black, is my father's house. Beyond it Ringo becomes increasingly white again and stays white until it goes past Roosevelt Road, which is Twenty-fifth Street, and gradually shades again from white to black, and ends, entirely black, no longer paved, almost like a country road lined with modest sharecropper-type houses, at West Thirty-sixth. My father's house is extremely commonplace, so familiarly plain and usual that it is beyond description. It has six rooms, a front porch and screened back porch, is perfectly symmetrical, and is painted white. I feel strangely proud and exonerated, like a reconstructed liberal who thinks of himself as a staunch, enlightened integrationist, that there is a dwelling occupied by a Negro family just a few doors down the street which is exactly like my father's house, detail for detail except the pigmentation of the occupants' flesh. My father knows this and does not care; if somebody were callous enough to point this likeness out to him he would undoubtedly respond, "Buddy, I don't give a shit, what's it to you?" For my own part I will never understand that gross hypocrisy whereby all the black folks of Manhattan are consigned to Harlem and all the coloreds of Boston are stuck in Roxbury, whereas in Little Rock, apart from the pseudo-ghettos of West Ninth, the South End and East Side, black and white live side by side in many places.

I entered the house by way of the back door, because the front door is used only at Christmas or when my grandmother is visiting, and because the key to the back door is kept under a flower pot on the back porch while the front door has no key and can be opened only from the inside. I was very quiet because it was too early to wake my father; he is a technician for the Southwestern Bell Telephone Company and would have to put in a hard day's work that day, as on any Monday, and needed all the sleep he could get. He used to beat hell out of me if I ever made any noise before breakfast. The back door led directly into the kitchen; I let my suitcase down gently inside the door, and, closing the door softly behind me, tiptoed across the room and closed the other door which opened onto the hall and his bedroom beyond. Then, as though it were an act I had been performing at that same hour in all the recent days, I opened the refrigerator and took out a bottle of milk, then opened a cabinet door and removed a glass bowl, and then, my hand reaching automatically for the correct door in flagrant forgetfulness of the fact that four years had passed since last I had done it, I opened still another cabinet and breathed a thrilled sigh of relief to discover there the box of Rice Chex in its proper place. But I slipped in getting a spoon: by mistake I pulled out the drawer which contained the heavy utensils, knives and spatulas and tea strainers, but forgave myself that error because those drawers look so alike and there are so many of them. I got the right drawer on the next try, extracted a spoon, and sat down at the table to mix myself a bowl of cereal. This simple performance, and especially my ingestion of the result, gave me a warm feeling of audacious pleasure, of defiance, because Pamela will not tolerate cereal either hot or cold, will not allow it in her pantry, will even prevent me from ordering it in restaurants, by reason of her firm conviction that the manufacture of breakfast foods is America's most dishonorable racket, a clear swindle which returns insipid pap for precious dollars. Fortunately neither my father nor I subscribe to that estimate, and consequently I could philander that bowl of Rice Chex, secure in the knowledge that Pamela was two thousand miles away. While I ate I watched the neighbor's cat, a spayed marmalade whose name as I recalled was Dundee, preening itself in the new morning sunlight in the back yard next door. The back yards of our neighborhood are not ample but neither are they cramped; there is enough room for a garage, an incinerator, a badminton court, two garbage cans, a small vegetable garden, a miniature thruway built by the toy road-graders of junior engineers, a mumble-de-peg arena, three sleeping dogs, six children playing hide-and-go-seek, a dozen preening cats, and a partridge in a pear tree. I grew up in one of them; in fact, in that very yard behind this house.

I was born in this house. Thus it was to some extent disconcerting, not to say utterly confounding, to look up from my bowl of cereal and see entering the kitchen a strange woman, a woman whom I had never seen in this house before. Without the security of that familiar bowl of Rice Chex, I would have panicked into supposing that I had entered the wrong house. But of course it was the right house. Only the wrong woman. She did not see me immediately, but took a teakettle off the stove, filled it with water at the sink, then returned it to the stove, turned on the burner under it, and then, still standing there, half facing me, she began an elaborate yawn-and-scratch: with her mouth stretched agape all the while, she raised a thin hand to her head and scratched her hair, then lowered it to her abdomen and scratched the neighborhood of her navel through the thin rayon of her chemise, then, lowering her hand once more, began a prolonged friction of her pudendum, deciding apparently that that was the best of the three scratching-places. I could hardly breathe, I was so embarrassed. I had no courage for voice, as any sound from me would have parted her from her senses. I waited, witless. The ecstasy of her act had closed her eyes, but now finally she opened them. When they came open the first thing they saw was my flabbergasted face. But for several seconds after she had seen me, brain messages being as slow as they are at that time of day, her hand kept on scratching. Then it, too, stopped.

"Christ all Jesus," she said, not too loudly, but then she flung both arms ceilingward and screamed, a banshee's furious wail, and ran off into the hall toward the bedroom, ululating, "Man sakes alive! WES! There's a prowler out there! Get up, Wes! Quick! A prowler! Quick, Wes! Help!"

Because she called him Wes, I knew I was in the right house, that she was yelling at my father, Wesley K. Stone, and that possibly the old bastard had gone and gotten himself married without telling me about it. Or else she was another one of his concubines, his keptive floozies.

I was standing when he came rushing in to confront me. He was stark naked, and I didn't think he looked much like my father because I had rarely seen him looking that way. In his left hand he held a .38 pistol of such ancient make that probably it was too rusty to fire, but I was frightened because he had neglected to put on his glasses. To a man with extreme myopia, a son is no better than a burglar.

"Daddy," I said quickly before he could pull the trigger, "it's *me*, Cliff!"

"What?" he mumbled and squinted fiercely at me. "Who?"

"It's Cliff, Daddy. Put on your glasses."

It is a wise father that knows his own child. "Clifford?" he said and lowered the pistol, and, suddenly aware of his nakedness, placed his other hand over his parts. He turned his head to his woman: "Sybil, damn your tough tits, don't just stand there! Fetch me my specs and my bathrobe!"

SIX

We waited, my father and I, for the small eternity of time which, like the beginning of a curtainless in-the-round drama, leaves the spectator and the performer facing each other in an imagined timelessness and placelessness until the play can properly begin, until my father's shady lady returned, and he put on, first the robe, then the glasses. Then saw me clearly.

"Hot diggety!" he said. "It *is*, aint it? When did you turn up?" He pumped my hand mightily and clapped me on the back. "Sybil, I want you to meet my boy. This here's Clifford, my own boy."

"Well, I swan," said Sybil. "You sure give me a turn, sittin there at the table like that."

"Beats the devil. Where's your wife?" he asked.

"She wouldn't come," I said.

"Never mind. Glad to see you. Boy, you look good."

"I'm sorry I woke you up," I said.

"Hell, don't mention it. Weren't your fault. Sit down. Go on there, sit down, make yourself at home. Sybil, close your mouth and stir us up some grub. This is my boy Clifford."

"Law me," Sybil said and began banging some pots and pans around in the sink.

My father and I sat down across from each other at the table, and he jerked his thumb at his woman and said, "That's Miss Sadie Thompson, my own horny hussy. Aint she a fine-lookin piece?"

"Aw . . ." Miss Sadie, overhearing, protested.

"Actually her name's Sybil Samuels. Can you beat it? Lookit what big dinners she's got!"

"Shush it, you," Sybil put in. "How do you guys want your eggs fixed?" She held an open carton in her hands.

"Clifford?" my father said.

"Oh, sunny side up, I guess," I said.

"Bacon?" she said.

"Yes, thank you."

Turning, she said to herself, "Grunt and two cackles lookin at you."

"Used to work in a hash-house," my father explained. "That's where she learned that kind of talk. Thinks she's smart."

"Listen to him!" she said to me. Then to him, "How you want yours, hon?"

"Same way, on toast," he said.

"Bride and groom on a raft," she said to the stove.

Boston is a long way off, I thought, I have come a fur piece. But oddly enough, I did not feel dislocated, out of place, but instead a warm gladness, an almost joyful satisfaction, at being able so easily to slip back into the bosom of my people, sloughing off the fusty nimbus of my sophisticated Boston self as though it were the anomalous nature, so that, a moment later when Sybil poured the coffee and dangled the cream pitcher over my cup and asked "Mud *with*?" it was easy for me to retort "Without" and to wink at her.

"My, my," Sybil said, appraising me with a roving eye, "I do believe this boy is littler even than you, Wes, and you're a dinky runt."

"Don't let that fool you," he said to her. "This here kid used to be one of the finest bruisers for his size in the country. Why, I've seen times when Clifford would take on three or four of the neighborhood punks all at once and send ever goddamned one of em home to their mommas in short order. And he won the Golden Gloves, didn't you, son?"

Grateful to the old guy for spieling me, I murmured modestly, "Yeah," and gave Sybil a wry smile.

"But now he's just one of them no-account Boston perfessors," my father went on, ill-concealing his disappointment that his only son, who with disciplined training might well have become Featherweight (or, now, Lightweight) Champion of the World, had developed into a mere broad-browed scholar, a most unmanly calling.

"Not exactly," I said, and then explained to Sybil, "I work in a sort of museum. I'm not a teacher, just a researcher."

"How'd they let you off?" my father wanted to know.

"Well, I haven't had a real vacation since I got married, so I figured it was high time I took one."

"Glad to see you anyway," he said, leaving me to wonder what his "anyway" implied. My father and I, despite our perseveringly friendly connection, implemented all these years by his loose jocular charm, have never been able to talk to each other on equal and equable terms, probably because the purview of his small, complacent world, satisfying though it may be to him, has recurrently estranged me with its strangeness, that mystery of a life so obviously squandered yet in its own way so unsquanderable that I will never understand it. Physically, as Sybil had already noted and insinuated, my father and I are quite alike, and I fully expect some day to acquire that same beady squint of his, that slightly curled upper lip so delicately suggestive of an approaching sneer, that smooth baldness of the forecrown, and that thoroughly bibulous profile of the abdomen. But my parlous mind, my intrepid intellect which at times in Boston seemed to me should have been stamped like a sweatshirt "Property of Yale University," had long since been so emendated by cultural enlightenment that I feared I would never ever be able any more to probe the meaning of his simple pleasures, to learn what joy his trifling strife engendered. And that would be the sorriest failure of my faculties.

"Well, how are things with you these days?" I asked him, as Sybil poured the second round of coffee.

Stirring his spoon in his cup slowly, he answered, "I got no kick. It's a long ways yet to bedrock, and I can still get my pecker up, huh, Sybil?"

"That aint no way to talk in front of your own boy," she said.

"Why Lord, Syb, you oughta of seen the poetry this here boy used to write on the bathroom wall when he was a kid. Tell her one of em, Clifford."

"Never mind," she said.

"Go on, Clifford, tell this holy whore one of them poems of yours."

"Never mind," I said, gingerly avoiding the subject. I could never maintain the nonchalance with which my father profaned his speech in the presence of females. Besides, I had forgotten the gist of those brashly pubescent verses. "How've you been doing at work, and all?" I asked him.

"Just hunkydory. They give me a good raise ever so often, and I got it made." My father's job in the phone company home guard was all day to wire and rewire the intricate innards of switchboards and other equipment, his hand semipermanently soldered to a soldering gun. "How about you? They payin you well in that line of work?"

"I get by," I said.

"You never write much. I never know," he complained, remembering his umbrages.

It was true. I love my father, I think I am very close to him, but I was no longer able to sit down and write him a decent letter. Voice to voice we could always somehow reach each other, through the tangled briers of our private solecisms; but letter to letter we were Babelites exchanging gibberish the other could not fathom: his brief newsy postcards packed with innuendoes, my long gushing shrifts which, confessing ultimately their own senile worthlessness as the hermit talking to the wind finally senses he has no audience, at last stopped coming. Avoiding the subject, I asked, "What's new around this old town?"

"Nothing much. She gets bigger all the time. Nobody goes downtown any more because they got all of them new shoppin plazas out on the west end." He shoved his empty coffee cup aside. "Now I'm a hunerd percent for progress, but I don't much care for the way the whole damn town keeps slippin and slidin westwards, like it was tryin to get as far away from itself as it could. Course it's no skin off my ass where they want to put them plazas—God, aint that a word? *Plaza!* like as if we was in Mexico or somewheres—but afore long Main Street'll be a goddamn ghost town."

"You think Faubus has got anything to do with it?" I asked, trying to draw him out on his favorite subject, the ifs and ands and buts of our beloved ruler.

"Well now, I just couldn't say. Old Orv seems to like it over there in the Governor's Mansion on Center Street, and I guess as long as he stays in the middle of town there'll always be somebody who won't move to the west end, but I just couldn't say."

"You haven't lost your admiration for Faubus, have you?"

"Me?" He made a face. "I'm still straddlin the fence, son. Always have. Just straddlin the fence."

"All right," I said, giving it up for the time being. "Say, I saw a copy of yesterday's *Gazette* with Dall's picture in it. When did he get himself promoted to sergeant on the force?"

"Oh, four or five years back, I reckon. You know ole Dall, keen as a whip. His daddy had more gumption than any other sheriff we ever had up there in Newton County. Matter of fact he was just a little *too* foxy, else he'd still be alive and kickin today. But I imagine your old buddy Dall tended to take after his daddy. You fixin to hunt im up this time?"

"I thought I might."

"Good. He's called over here two or three times the last couple of years to see if I knew when you'd be comin home again, so I reckon he'd be awfully pleased to see you."

I allowed as how I would be pleased to see him too. Then I mentioned another old friend. "Saw that Hy Norden's a television announcer now. Has he—"

"Crud." My father mocked a spit. "Thinks he's Mr. Little Rock hisself or something, the one and only. Got his own ten o'clock news show, Channel Eight, ever night. 'Hi out there, folks, here's Hy!' he says, fruity-tooty. Big splash."

"I think he's cute," Sybil offered. "Reminds me of Van Johnson."

He scowled at her. "I think you oughta go brush your teeth maybe."

"Well I never . . . !" she huffed, got up from the table and disappeared.

We talked for a while about other old friends of mine. I would mention a name and he would bring me up to date. "You remember old Sarah Farnley?" I asked him. "Whatever happened to her, I wonder?"

"Her folks moved away two, three years ago, but far as I know she never got married. Last I heard she was a clerk at Woolworth's." He gave me that notorious Stoney squint, and his upper lip, always imminently about to smirk, curled upward fiercely. "You gonna tomcat around while you're here?"

"Oh, I don't know. Maybe."

My father never laughs, but he made a sound as close to it as he ever gets. Then he said, "How come your missus wouldn't come with you, did you say?"

"I didn't say, but you know how she hates this place."

"Yeah, I remember. You and her doin all right? I mean, you're not bustin up or anything?"

"Oh no. It's just that . . . well . . . Daddy, she doesn't treat me right, sometimes." I grinned, sheepishly I guess, at this blurted confession.

He popped the almost-laugh again, and said, "Well, a man needs to get away from his woman ever so often, aint that right?"

"That's right," I agreed.

"How long you thinkin of stayin?"

"Oh, I don't know. Three or four weeks, maybe longer."

"Fine and dandy. I'll have Sybil fix up your old room for yuh." He turned his head over his shoulder and yelled, "Hey, woman!" Sybil returned to us, smelling faintly of Gleem. My father put his arm around her waist and pressed his jowl against her breasts. She smiled. He looked up at her and said, "Honeybunch, rig up that side room for Clifford, will you? He's gonna be around a while." She nodded her head and patted his shoulder and asked us if we wanted any more coffee. He asked her if she could see the clock. She craned her neck and said it was half past seven. "By Godfrey!" he said and rose from his chair. "I'd better be gettin a move on."

He went to the bathroom to shave and dress, and I had one last cup of coffee. Sybil sat across the table, watching nothing through the window. The wakefulness of last night's dreaming caught up with me: I was suddenly somnolent. I yearned to yawn and sleep. "Ho-hum," sighed Sybil, my glassy-eyed clairvoyant, tapping her fingernails idly on the table top. I yawned emphatically, sucking in an obbligato of noisy air. Her eyes shifted from the window to me, became unglazed. "Didn't sleep much on the train," I explained. "Gnhph," she responded absently, looked off again across the neighbor's yard, and scraped between her teeth with the nail of her little finger.

"How's my dad really getting along these days?" I asked, not just for small talk.

"Just fine, just fine," she said. "Not a worry in the world, far as I can see. He feels right pert and full of beans."

"Does he give you much trouble?"

"Aw, not much," she said and stood up. She started to scratch again but thought better of it. Shuffling out of the kitchen, she added, "He's a pretty good old boy, your paw. We get along fine. It's all a bowl of cherries." She threw me a backward glance, for emphasis, and said again, "Just all a big old bowl of cherries."

I was in my room, unpacking my suitcase, when my father emerged from the bathroom. His jowls smooth, his sparse hair neatly parted, a freshly ironed gabardine shirt on his back, he looked much better. "Well, I reckon I'd better go punch the clock and earn me a few more nickels and dimes," he said. "What you plan on doin today?"

"At the moment I'm thinking of crawling in for a couple of hours. I didn't get any sleep on the train. Afterwards I guess I'll make a few phone calls."

"Give Cindy a buzz, why don'tcha?"

"Sure," I said. Lucinda was my older, married sister, whose husband worked for the Little Rock post office. I rarely wrote to her either.

"Will you be here for supper?" he asked.

"I guess so."

"Be seein you then, Clifford. Glad you're home." He went away.

I finished unpacking, hanging my one suit, a tropical seersucker, carefully in the closet and arranging my socks, handkerchiefs, and underclothes neatly in the top drawer of my old bureau. The last item out of my bag was a new Ring-Master notebook. From some other part of the house Sybil was singing something about "I want to hold your hand," her voice pitched high and piercing, and yet turned in on itself. I closed the door of my room, dimming her song. Then I fell down with my Ring-Master on the bed, and there, the glad scene of so many old evenings when like young Lincoln before his fire I had lain me down to the feast of knowledge, I opened it to the first page and wrote "LITTLE ROCK" in the center and then flipped to the second page and prepared to begin, pausing first to absorb the nostalgic effulgence of that setting, that very room where in the late evenings of pubescent loneliness I had first looked with tingling senses into Gibbon's *Decline*, snatched in a pellucid abridgement from an obscure shelf in West Side Junior High School's library, and into Ridpath's *Popular History of the United States*, and even into Headley's *Life and Travels of General Grant*, and others, more than I could remember, whose substances long ago became rootlets far below the surface of the ground from which the tree of my mind thrives upward. It was there that I first discovered, in Gibbon, those words which would be my private motto, subconsciously for years, quite consciously of late—he quoted the Italian Gothic historian Nicola Rienzi, that *Ultimus Romanorum*, who, looking backward on the glory of antiquity, had been provoked to exclaim, "Where are now these Romans? their virtue, their justice, their power? why was I not born in those happy times?" To a fourteen-year-old boy shut away on his bed with a book, trying to forget the serial round of little aches and larger agonies which are the lot of that age, those homeless words quoted by Gibbon were a rallying cry spoken thunderously from some craggy summit, palliating his pain with the knowledge that others too had been dissatisfied with their own warped worlds. The difference between the idealistic fourteen-year-old and the cynical twenty-eight-year-old is that the boy believed that somehow he could return, bodily, *toto caelo*, into a bygone era, whereas the man, while pragmatically denying the possibility of such a miraculous transmigration, hoped that somehow some elements of the past, *les neiges d'antan*, might be recaptured. I stretched out full length, my feet no nearer the footboard than they had ever been, my jaw cradled in my left hand, the elbow of that arm sunk deep into the mattress, and my ballpoint poised hoveringly in my right hand, while I reminisced. Then I lowered the pen and bestowed a title for that page:

THE SINS OF THE FATHER ARE TO BE LAID UPON THE CHILDREN

I paused again and studied a calendar on the wall, left over from 1954 but kept, I suppose, because my father wanted to preserve my room in its original appearance. The calendar was worthless, but its picture was not: a large full-color print of George Caleb Bingham's "Raftsmen on the Upper Mississippi," the four of them posed calmly and simply, but with a feeling of lost majesty about them, in the hushed and sun-drenched splendor of the watery wilderness. Outside my door the perpetual, transient voice of Sybil was singing "Shimmy shimmy to and fro . . ." Then I tried to write for a while.

But I was too tired. I got up from the bed, closed the notebook and put it beside my wallet on the bureau, undressed to my shorts (the morning was quite warm, almost summery, by then), lowered the shades, and crawled in under the top sheet of the bed, having pulled the spread away.

On my back, I clasped my hands behind my head, stared up at the acoustical tiles of the ceiling (an old innovation installed —futilely as it turned out—in hopes of muffling my constant jabbing of my wall-hung punching bag), and thought for a few moments more of where I was, why I was there, and what I was going to do. I was still not completely home, it would take me a few more hours to become so. Such a drastic change, leaving Boston and everything connected with it entirely behind and returning to a place where I had lived more than eighteen years of my life, could not be made too easily. Perhaps it could not be made at all, because there are always limits to how much of the lost past one can consciously recover. I felt a slight anxiety, not dread but just my usual nervousness again, over the question which was foremost in my mind: *What, or who, am I really looking for?* Who, or what, has lured me to this trivial city? Perhaps I would find nothing, because I had changed too much or, what might be worse, the town had changed too much and I too little. Possibly the Vanished American Past was as vanished here as anywhere else, if not more so. But I gave some credit to the chance that my advanced wisdom could discover something in the town, some delightful places or persons, which the schoolboy had never been aware of. It was this latter possibility, trolling a melodious *amabile* descant in my head, to the exclusion of Sybil's loud but tuneless "She loves you, yeah yeah yeah; she loves you, yeah yeah yeah," which put me finally to sleep, determined to burst in full bloom upon the town as soon as I awakened.

SEVEN

Those few hours of midday slumber were characterized only by a singular, moon-splattered dream I had, which any amateur psychoanalyst might interpret in whatever way he liked. As is true of all dreams, it probably required only a few minutes of actual time, but, again like all dreams, it was longer than a double feature at the drive-in. I hesitate to call it a nightmare.

I am a lawyer in a little frontier settlement called Lewisburgh, no more than a clump of mud-chinked log houses, twenty miles upstream from the flourishing territorial capital which is called, variously, Arkopolis, La Petite Roche, or Little Rock. My cronies in the adjoining shanties call me John Linton. I am passionately fond of raw corn whiskey, which helps me dissolve the specter of my sad background—a shattered love affair in Maryland, no, Virginia I think it was, a short but debasing term in the penitentiary, and a law practice which was spectacularly unsuccessful despite an intelligence which, at least when thoroughly greased, can spout Latin phrases like the most practiced priest, and claims the mythological heroes and heroines of classic Greece as constant silent companions. In territorial Arkansas, although I have no clients to defend nor courts to defend them in, there is an abundance of that potent beverage around which my happy life revolves.

It is night and I am sitting on the doorstep of my cabin, halfway through the first jug, when a rider appears out of the dark road, followed by his servant. He dismounts, shakes my hand, asks me if I am John Linton. "I believe that is correct, sir. *Ave!*" I answer. "*Ave*, yourself," he says. "I'm Gen'l Sam Houston, fresh up from Tennessee by way of Little Rock back yonder." He jerks his thumb over his shoulder in the direction from which he had come. I am taken by surprise, all the more so because the eminent General Houston is rumored to be six and a half feet high, while this stranger is no taller than I. But he seems to be a gentleman, and in these parts one takes a gentleman at his word. "I'm honored, sir," I say. "What can this worthless barrister do for you?" "Wal," quoth he, "I'm tired and weary and a mite put out by that farewell party they gave me in Nashville, and it's rumored hereabouts that you've got some of the finest drinkin whiskey in these parts, so I was just wonderin . . ." "Of course! Come right in. *Post equitem sedet atra cura.*" I usher him into my humble home and pour him a generous amount of my finest sour mash. In the dark I cannot see his face clearly, but he sounds the way Houston ought to sound. "How's that?" he asks. "I'm a bit dull on my Latin." "Oh, just a remark of Horace's, meaning that even the rich man on horseback cannot escape his cares," I explain. He says, "That's me all right, but I aint so rich any more."

We thereupon proceed to get ourselves merrily potted. Houston's servant stands darkly in the doorway, watching, without comment. It is not civil, these days, to offer a drink to a servant, especially if the servant is, as I suspect this one is, either Indian or Negro.

"*Prosit!*" he says, downing his third glass.

"*Prosit tibi!*" I respond, and up goes mine. "*Venia necessitati datur.* That's a nice way of saying we can drink all we want to, so long as we got a good reason."

"I don't know about *your* reason, Mr. Linton, but I sure as hell have got a couple of damn good ones," Houston says.

"*Benedicite!*" I say. "Down the hatch."

We pour another round, and another. "Sure is mighty fine white mule you got here," Houston proclaims.

"Glad you like it," I say, and then, stirred by our good fellowship, our rich conviviality, I am provoked to utter, shaping my lips carefully: "οἶνος Ἀφροδίτης γάλα!"

"Great Caesar's ghost!" Houston exclaims admiringly. "I missed that one altogether. What's it mean?"

"A maxim of Aristophanes: Wine is the milk of love. In this case, whiskey."

"Godalmighty, I sure do admire a scholar," Houston applauds. "Maybe if I'd of been one, I'd still be governor of Tennessee."

His encomiums prod me onward to greater heights of grandiloquence, and make of me even more a *laudator temporis acti*. "Tell you what, Sam," I say, pouring our sixth round. "I think we're going about this all ass-backwards. What we oughta do is make a libation to the good old god Bacchus."

"Sure nuff!" Houston agrees heartily. "What's a ly-bayshun?"

"Sort of a sacrifice," I explain.

"That's the spirit!" good old Sam bellows. "Got to make us a sacrifice to Bacchus afore we can have another snort." Whereupon he stands up, removes his wide-brimmed hat, and throws it into the fire. "There ye go, Bacchus!" The flames catch it and it blazes up immediately, smelling rankly of burning sweat. "Yore turn," he says to me.

"*Tu quoque,* eh?" I say and, entering into the spirit of things, toss my sombrero into the fire.

Houston takes a drink, removes his jacket, cries, "All hail, Bacchus!" and adds that fine buckskin to the flames.

I drink and donate my coat, a linsey-woolsey.

He drinks and contributes his shirt. I mine. He his undershirt. I mine. Drink. Trousers. Drink. Drawers. Drink. Shoes. Drink. Socks. A beautiful conflagration rages in the fireplace, never mind the hideous stench.

"*Hoc erat in more maiorum!*" I cheer, striking a grand posture with my naked body.

"You tell em, boy!" he shouts, standing at my side.

The blazing flames illuminate him clearly. His hairy body I see for the first time; his grizzled face is distinctly visible.

He is not old Samuel Houston at all. He is old Wesley K. Stone, my father.

"Daddy!" I gasp.

His laughter is like thunder. Then he stops roaring and points a finger at me. "Now let me tell you something, son, in that fancy language of yourn: *Vulgus amicitias utilitate probat!*"

Then he rushes out the door and, still magnificently naked, leaps on his horse and rushes off into the night.

"*Siste, viator!*" I scream after him. Stop! But he is gone, I am alone, *eheu!* all alone, *vox clamantis in deserto,* thinking of the meaning of his parting message: The common herd values friendships only for their usefulness. *Ave atque vale,* old daddy.

But am I entirely alone? No, he has left his servant behind him. Emerging from the shadows of the cabin's room, the servant approaches me and in the firelight I see that it, *she,* is not a servant but instead Tiana, little Tahlihina, his Cherokee mistress, left behind as if to prove perhaps he *was,* after all, the bold adventurous vagabond who would one day revenge the Alamo. Tiana gracefully approaches me, her palm raised calmly in the Indian manner of greeting, but to me the gesture is an entreaty to silence. There is a word on her lips. She stands as close to me as her dignity will permit, and I sink helplessly into the dark pools of her eyes until . . . until she puts a hand on my shoulder and I discover with ineffable chagrin that I have been beguiled again, twice-cozened. She is not Tiana, no, not the lovely dark-haired, doeful half-breed who had so agilely charmed the General. She is a sallow-skinned doxy, name of Sybil Samuels.

Hic finis somnium.

EIGHT

"I declare, you're the spiffiest little whang-dilly I ever did see. Cute as a speckled pup. Didja have a nice beddie-bye-bye?" Her face was alarmingly close to mine, as if she had been counting my freckles, and her hand was on my shoulder. As she leaned over my near-nude supine body, her hair, released from its bun, fell over the sides of her face, and there was a dimpled softness, a pasty flaccidity, of her mouth and chin. She still wore the fragile chemise; if I lowered my eyes I could penetrate its décolletage. I groaned, either in dismay at her unabashed advance or in some kind of weird pleasure at her brazen proximity. Her concupiscent scent, rife with cheap cologne and an overpowering bodyness, suggested new developments in her oestrus cycle. She gave my shoulder a shake and said, "Scoot over, honeybunch, and we'll fool around some."

Hoo boy now, I told myself: Go ahead. Here's your chance. She can't be more than thirty-five. Ignore the face, concentrate on the body, the *body!* Wild, hot, rarin' to go. Telling me to scoot over. By jingo! Scoot over, honeybunch, make room for momma.

But that was just it: motherless as I was, she was the only excuse for a dam, a progenitress by proxy, I had in all the world, even if there were scant chance she might ever become my legal stepmother. I would not risk the chance of becoming that most disgraceful of all obscene twelve-letter words.

Oh, I dissembled, of course, I rationalized to myself, I varnished the truth, which was simply that I suddenly remembered a bunch of important phone calls I had to make. I was the Messianic conqueror of Little Rock, the foretokened cynosure returned from the East; my minions awaited me, I could not put them off any longer. Sex-starved as I was (cripes! I had not had, discounting the aborted ride of Clara, a decent lay for weeks), I had a higher duty to perform, a compulsive function to discharge. Later there would be abundant leisure for frisky folly, perhaps, and I was pleased to know the opportunity was there in Sybil's eager utility. Some other time maybe, baby.

Sybil inevitably took offense at my chivalry, and anointed me with florid maledictions all the way to the bathroom, where I locked the door and remained until her wrath had moderated. The bathroom clock said half past one. Then I quietly opened the door, saw that she was nowhere about, and sat down beside the telephone in the hall. Find it in the Yellow Pages! something said subliminally to me, so I leafed through that part of the directory, a book considerably thicker than when last I had used it and bleeding on the cover with a dramatic color photograph of the new Arkansas Arts Center. Flipping idly from page to page, from familiar name to familiar name, I finally came to the law firm of Wheeler, Bristol, Little, Saunders and McComb.

I dialed their number. A secretary answered.

"May I speak to Steve, please?" I asked, making my voice important.

"Who's calling, please?" she responded, honey-toned.

"Cliff." A sharp, brisk, handsome monosyllable.

"Mr. McComb is on another line. Could you hang on?"

I hung on. Sybil, nearer than I thought, was hoarsely screeching a tune, "What's the nitty gritty, baby?" "Break it off!" I implored. ". . . Ev'-rybody's askin, what's the nitty gritty?" "Come on, cut it out, I'm making a call!" ". . . Boop bop boob-a-da bobbp-boop da niddy griddy . . ." "GODDAMMIT, *ENOUGH!*"

"Beg pardon?" the phone said.

"Oh! I was talking to someone else. Steve?"

"Cliff *who?*" the phone said.

"Clifford Stone," I said, and the secretary repeated it to him. Then his own voice came on, deep, staunch, political: "What *say*, Cliff? You in town?"

"Yep," I said, old cornpone Stone. "Just got in. Thought maybe we could polish off a couple beers or something tonight, you know?"

"Can't make it tonight, old buddy. Wife's having some people over. Sorry. But listen, we oughta get together one of these days, hey? Gonna be around long?"

"Yeah," I said.

"Well say, lemme give you a ring sometime, okay, boy?"

"Okay, boy," I echoed, and he was gone, back to his business, working himself up toward the Supreme Court.

Sorry.

Sybil was laughing beside me. "Got the brush-off, huh?" she put in, and laughed even louder, her pink hands on her huge hips.

"Get off my back, will you?" I invoked.

"Your funeral, hot-shot," she said and headed for the kitchen.

To spite her, I called next directly to Woolworth's, to fix myself up with sweet old Sarah Farnley. After an interminable wait, during which I supposed she was required to fill out in triplicate a form requesting permission to leave her candy counter and use the telephone, she came on, and I said, "Hiya, Sallysimple! (an old pet name of hers) Guess who?" "I couldn't," she said. "It's *me*, Nubbin! (an old pet name of mine)" "No kidding?" she said, but not with much warmth. "Yeah, you doin anything tonight, sweetheart?" I breathed. "Somebody told me you was married," she said. "Yeah, well, I was, I mean, I *am*, but, see, well, I thought—" "Not tonight, Nubbin. Sorry. Call me bout the middle of next week maybe. But not here. They don't like it."

Sorry.

I called Guy Hammond. Out of town. Ernest Jackson. In the hospital, kidneys. Byron Drenker. "Well, whaddaya know! Nub Stone! But gee, Nub, the little lady and me are flyin up to Chicago tomorrow for a convention. Maybe when I get back, huh?" Sissy Portis. "How *good* to hear that *nice* old voice of yours, honey! But didn't you *know*? I'm not *Portis* any *more!* Last summer I married *Biff* Simon, you remember *him,* he was *all*-state *quarter*back with the Tigers . . ." Dick Anderson. Didn't remember my name at first, said if it was urgent he might be able to see me in another week or two. Ken Vernon. Gone off on a White River float-fishing trip.

Sorry. Sorry. Who, after all, am *I*?

As a last resort I called the police station and asked for Dall Hawkins. *Sergeant* Hawkins, I added, as an afterthought. But sorry, he didn't come on duty until three-thirty. Could I be helped by anyone else? No, thank you. It didn't matter.

Then I called my sister Lucinda, to discharge that part of my duties. Cindy is a pretty girl, or rather she *was*, before ten years of housewifery had taken it out of her, but an attractive older sister is never very easy for a boy to enamor or become enamored of. We had never occupied each other's good graces; my general memory of her was of petty squabbles, senseless bickering, jealousy, rancor, malice. Our later years, away from home, would *in absentia* soften some of that ill will, but not enough to keep us from feeling like strangers or, more graphically, like a divorced couple. She wasn't exactly tickled pink to get my call, but she did sincerely want to see me, as she and her husband had been on vacation to Biloxi the last time I was in Little Rock, and thus she hadn't seen me for almost six years.

"Why don't you come over after supper, Cliff? Can you play bridge? Monday is our bridge night, but Mary Ann's husband got called out of town so maybe you could take his place."

I wouldn't mind taking his place in bed, but otherwise, No. I hate bridge. Poker yes, pinochle maybe, but not a frumpy trumpy game like bridge. I begged off that night, saying I already had plans, but would stop by tomorrow afternoon for a chat. Before her husband, Victor, got home from the P.O. Victor and I never hit it off very well.

My stomach growled, I wanted something to eat, but I made one more, one last, phone call. To the Channel 8 studios, to catch Hy Norden. But the secretary who answered said that he didn't come to work until after supper. Pressed, she confided that if it was a matter of urgent importance, I might find him at a place called the Deadline Club on East Third, where he often spent most of the afternoon. I decided to go confront him in person right after lunch. This phone-calling was getting me nowhere.

Sybil, bless her heart, had made me a couple of corned-beef-on-rye sandwiches, which she deferentially presented to me at the kitchen table, along with a cold bottle of Busch Bavarian, once my favorite brew but unobtainable in beer-glutted Boston. "No luck, huh?" she said sympathetically. "I know how it is, kid. Things change. Why, just last week I bumped into an old pal of mine and she didn't hardly know me."

I could do without her commiseration, but not her sandwiches. They were excellent, and the old, familiar, Saturday-night bite of the beer returned me yoreward with swifter thaumaturgy than any other sensory aspect of that place or time. I glowed. The contrast between that elegant little lunch and Pamela's tough pork chops was incredible.

Swelling with happy conviviality and gratification, I was moved, first carefully wiping my mouth with a napkin, to approach that woman from the rear as she was bent over the sink, and to osculate the back of her neck resoundingly, wrapping my arms around her middle.

"Unt-uh," she said, turning around to turn me down. "You had your chance."

I groped for her, maundering, "Aw, c'mon, baby—"

"Nope. I aint nobody's second fiddle." She glowered, but then her face softened and she began to laugh. "You been stood up, joker. They hung you on a nail!"

Her laughter, chiming scornfully behind me, followed me to the bathroom, where I showered and shaved and put on my seersucker suit, followed me thereafter, stridently derisive, followed me out of the house and on toward Fifteenth Street, where I could catch a bus. I could not shake it loose. That blatant guffaw, now whinnying, now caterwauling, pursued me relentlessly, as if the city itself were in stitches, as if all those hostile old friends, those tittering forgetters, those snobbish bastards laughing behind my back, shadowed me all through the town.

NINE

Turning into Main on the bus, I snickered back at the town. Roosting low and scyphose in the seat with my knees up against the next one, I peered over the metal window rim and caught sight of the downtown structures of that city: the older little towers—Donaghey, Lafayette, Boyle, Rector—and the one new larger tower, called The Tower itself, surmounting the somber chastity of the others not so much with its height as with its color: a garish yellow suggestive of a week-old egg yolk; and in the midst of all those foursquare shafts the lonely acuminated spire of St. Andrew's church, whose tip seems to poke itself higher than any of the other buildings and is, despite the gaudiness of The Tower, the dominant form of the skyline. Why did I snicker? I will confess that I snickered first and conceived a valid reason later, just as the scathed child will strike back at his tormentors with a fabricated laughter mocking their own, a bootless sound born more of hurt than of reason. My reason, which I had managed to invent before the bus had reached as far as Ninth and Main, was that all that mass, that congeries of brick, stone, and the new steel, for all its manifest show of enterprise in the midst of this languid desert of Arkansas, was yet a superficial, hackneyed, and sterile place, like a lone, vast, intricate, and curious piece of fungus on the empty bark of a tree, but a fungus all the same: fatuous and inane, the uncompleted soul of a town which could have been either another Memphis or only a Clodville, but through its desolate striving became something stale and teamless in between. Suddenly I remembered, in this frame of mind, why I had left Arkansas in the first place, years ago: to get away from this sterility, this deficiency, this cheap and hollow aspiration. Even if Boston had made me less human, more mechanical, it had given me a chance to be productive, creative, as if part of that patch of fungus had been cut away and taken to a laboratory, where, under ideal conditions, it was transformed into an orchid. Now I began to suspect that by returning that orchid to the fungus patch, even experimentally, it might perish.

But the sidewalks of Lower Main at that hour showed no indication of becoming, as my father had forecast, a ghost town. Main was as busy that afternoon as I could remember. My nervous mind, shuttling violently back and forth between extremes of love and hate for the old town, reminded me that if I had still been in Boston at that hour I would have been cooped into my dark cubicle at the Cabot Foundation, still suffering some petty dread over the authenticity of some old firehouse sign and sweating out my life in trivial VAPic research. Here at least I was free, I could stand in the sun. I could relax and breathe. So I stood on the corner for a while, with my back up against the terrazzo façade of a shoe shop, and watched the people pass. Here and there I saw a familiar face, one dimly remembered from the corridors of the high school, but I could recall no names to match the faces. Several people cast blank stares at me, or at my seersucker suit, which, I began to feel, was out of place that early in the season (although that April afternoon was hotter than Boston ever gets in deepest summer), but nobody from out that crowd stepped forward to pound me on the back and say, "Why, Nub Stone! you old punkin-headed rascal you! Where you *been* all these years?" I stood too long, and was slammed back once more to the other side of my vacillating mood: Old Clifford Willow Stone, that pumpkin-headed rascal, might just as well have been still in his cubicle in Boston.

After a while I gave it up and went on to the Deadline Club, where, after climbing a long flight of stairs and passing through the big red door as nonchalantly as any fourth estater, I found Hy Norden. He was sitting across the room with a girl—or woman, I should say. There were four other people in the lounge, a couple of editors getting drunk together at the bar before facing the pace of the evening shift, a leg man sitting alone on his last legs, dregs of foam in the bottom of his empty schooner, and a photographer swearing at his Graflex. The seediness of the clientele (except Norden, whose dapper trappings alone would have made me recognize him) dishonored the splendor of the surroundings, which were just about the best that could be had in Little Rock (where, as in the rest of Arkansas— save the oasis of Hot Springs—liquor cannot be dispensed in doses over the bar to the general non-club public). There was a deep maroon carpet on the floor; the dim, dramatic lighting suggested the staging of a Greek tragedy by an avant-garde theater group, and the bar itself was a lavish affair, all glass and chrome and burnished mahogany. I always felt ill at ease whenever I entered one of those few Little Rock hangouts where the bottles of bourbon and Scotch are stacked tier on tier behind the bar; although this is a common sight in Boston and other cities, I always expected to be imminently raided in the presence of such potency in my home town.

Norden had not seen me for ten years; nor I him, except his picture in the paper now and then. As I stood at his table looking down at him (he was engrossed in some sort of frivolous banter with the girl and did not look up immediately), I saw that those ten years had given him another twenty pounds, but had not changed the shade or texture of that wild blond hair, a sandy shock the envy of countless girls frustrating themselves with peroxide, nor of that puckered peachy mallow mouth always, when not guffawing, about to kiss something, nor of that leonine nose so discreetly suggestive of Semitic ancestry. (His father had descended—as rapidly as he could—from a family of Swedish Israelites named Nordencrantz, and had become a triumphantly successful lawyer, later circuit judge, later federal judge for the Eastern Arkansas district—but he is dead now, having hanged himself from a rafter in his four-car garage during the height of the Sunk Bayou Ferry scandal, so I will not impugn the motive for his name change.) Hy of course was born with the silver spoon in his mouth, which may have given it that peachy puckered aspect that would stamp his mien forever. At one time I thought his appellation was the result of surgery performed on "Hyman" or even "Hiram," but as I later learned it was simply "Harsey," his mother's family name, with the arse removed. He was the head cheese, the Grand Panjandrum, *primus inter pares*, of the affluent Pulaski Heights set at the high school; anyone better would have been sent away to Exeter or Andover. He nudged me out in the election for Eleventh Grade Representative to the Student Council, and later, after I had eaten my boiled crow and put my loyal West Siders on his bandwagon in return for the campaign managership, he was elected Student Body President. His adversaries, intolerant of his success and popularity (and intelligence too; in three years of Latin he was the only student to make higher grades than I), extracted retribution in gym class, where Hy was dismally inept at physical combat, and I had often to defend him.

"Hi!" I said when he at last looked up. That was the nice thing about his name, it spared words in greeting. There had always been those who, trying to circumvent the redundancy, had said, "Hello, Hy!" which was needlessly formal, or "Hi, Norden!" which had a coarsely imperative sound.

The process of recognition proceeds through four stages on the human face: first, an utterly blank stare; then, second, a sudden twitch of interest, often accompanied by a slight tilting of the head to one side and a lifting of the eyebrows; third, a look of intense concentration, during which the eyes are withdrawn and the lip often bit, while the person is trying to place the subject; and, fourth and finally, an ebullient expression of success and pleasure accompanying the loud utterance of the subject's name. Hy Norden, it saddens me to relate, went through only the first three stages; he did not achieve the last. "Charles?" he said feebly.

I smiled, waiting.

"Clarence?" he said. "No . . . Clyde? Clinton? Clifton?"

"Close," I said, smiling, waiting.

He was snapping his fingers in rapid succession, and mumbling to himself, ". . . rock, boulder, pebble, cobble . . . stone—" Then, "Stone!" he said, and, unsnapping his fingers and pointing one at me, "Clifton Stone. How are you?"

"Clifford," I said. "Just fine. How're you?" And, resting my hand tentatively on the back of a vacant chair, tried telepathy: *And now why don't you ask me to sit down?*

"Never can remember names," he said and, gesturing to his companion, added, "You know my wife Marcia?"

I saw her clearly for the first time, but I would not have recognized her otherwise, so great was the change. Marcia Paden, of course! who had been head cheerleader, president of Beta Club and the Gold Jackets, most likely among females to succeed, queen bee of the Pulaski Heights clique; how appropriate that she was matched up at last with Norden. But her tastes, and consequently her appearance, had improved: where once she had been simply a conservatively plaid-clad girl of unkempt mode, of studied neglect, now she was thoroughly kempt: her stunning raiment must have been ordered specially for her by Kempner's: a two-part shirt dress of heavy white linen, the shirt of near-tunic length, slashed deep at the neck; her red hair, plumped Marienbadly from beneath a black Panama straw hat of sewer-lid size, was carefully Clairoled; her lips Cotyed, her scent Cordayed. Stunning. My own wife Pamela had often been capable of making herself look like that when I took her out, and for a moment I wished I had her with me; it would put me on a level with Hy. Pamela was certainly prettier, I had to reflect.

"Paden, wasn't it?" I said to her, giving Hy notice that somebody at least could remember names.

"That's right," she said, doling out a parsimonious smile.

"Glad to see you," I said and returned my gaze to Hy. Ask me to pull up a chair, you bounder.

"Where you live now, Cliff?" he asked, unconcerned, really.

"Boston," I said.

"Married?"

"Yes."

"Children?"

"No."

I am in a goddamned employment office, I thought, and now he is going to ask, Religious affiliation?

Instead he said, "What are you doing?"

I did not immediately perceive the meaning of his question. My first reply, which I deigned not utter, was, "I am standing here in the Deadline Club in Little Rock wondering how long I will have to keep standing here before you ask me to sit down." Maybe I should have been nonchalant about it and pulled out the chair and plumped down uninvited, but I had my principles. He was asking me, I realized, what my occupation was. "I'm a VAP collector," I said.

"Pardon?" Perhaps he thought it was a euphemism for garbage collector or bill collector.

"Research for a foundation," I said, preserving the mystery.

"Oh."

"I see you're on television now," I said.

"That's right."

Come on, Hy, you old jackleg politician, it's *me*, Clifford, one of the boys, give me a seat, I'll buy my own goddamn drink. The conversation, such as it was, began to run out of gas. He sat there entirely at ease, one arm draped casually over the back of his wife's chair, his eyes blank and tired and vague, while I stood uncomfortably at attention, the knuckles of my hand which gripped the back of the chair growing white from the pressure of the squeeze. It was my most humiliating moment in years; not even Pamela's degrading devices could have put me so far out of countenance. My crest fell with a sickening thud.

"Well," I said, but stopped, my voice too dry for speech. A long moment passed.

You wouldn't ask me to sit down?

Sorry. But you see, Clifford, it's like this: I'm the cock of the roost around this place, see? And you? Who are you, fellow, but a back issue, a dud, an also-ran? So pack it off, boy, I got no use for you.

I removed my hand from the back of the chair. I would have enjoyed swinging it into his face. "Nice day," I said and glanced around the room, whose air-conditioned darkness suggested night.

"Yes it is," he said and inspected his fingernails.

"Well, see you around, Hy," I said.

"Yeah," he said.

"Glad to've seen you, Marcia," I said.

She smiled.

I departed.

Crud.

TEN

There is nothing here for me, I decided, scuffing aimlessly and glumly along Main Street. I am a stranger in my own home town, I am a stranger to whatever it might have in the way of redeeming value. There is not anything here. Nor anybody. That answers my question—What, or who, am I really looking for?

Absent-mindedly I window-shopped for a while, then I wandered into the Rib on West Second and had a couple of schooners of Michelob. While I was drinking my beer, I debated with myself whether or not to go see Dall Hawkins at the police station. I had done this before: I had debated with myself. Always I had decided not to. I had nothing against Dall—he was a fine, goodhearted, quick-minded fellow, albeit occasionally ill-humored and bullysome. But my friendship with him had always been more corporal than capital—we had practically nothing in common except our appreciation for rough physical combat, a wish for creative expression by means of a slam-bang application of our bodies, a passion for innocent violence acquired from our Ozarks rough-and-tumble ancestry, through which Dall became a football player and I a boxer: lanky though he was, he had been one of the best fullbacks in the history of the Little Rock High School Tigers; runty though I was, I had been one of their best boxers. It is only my distaste for stereotypes which keeps me from thinking of Dall and myself as a perfect Mutt-and-Jeff combination.

In my memory of him are images of an occasional afternoon's sport when, peeved or bitter over some grievance brought about by the injustices of some teacher or fellow student, we would stand together restlessly on the south steps of the school building after the final bell and complain loudly to each other of our gripes, and then use each other as an escape valve for our rancor. "We gotta police up on somebody," he declared typically on one such occasion, therein unconsciously foretokening his future career. "We gotta beat sap outta some bastards." His anger, cooped up and unfocused, softened my own; I cheered up and told him to do likewise. "Naw," he said, "I gotta lay into somebody." "All right," I said. I would deliver his tension. Plunking a teaser against his chops, I squared off and said, "Come on, mix it up, you big prick!" He laughed and waded in on me, flicked a light left against my shoulder, then swung his steamhammer right toward my head. I blocked it and delivered a thudding wallop to the pit of his stomach. He grunted and swung that royal right again. It nicked my ear and I gave it back to him, a nailer right on the button, which spun him off balance. He staggered back a few steps, but I didn't pursue him. Dall was almost a foot taller than I, and about fifty pounds heavier, therefore I couldn't afford to get him really angry at me. So I waited, and when he came back at me I peppered an assortment of one-two jabs into his pan, then caught one of his potluck shots on my chest, which knocked me down. He let loose several body slugs while I was getting up, but I ripped his guard open and hooked him on the nose with a cracking right. He countered with a straight stab which I rode out of harm's way, then I hung a heavy clout on his ear. He tagged me with a left cross. I unpacked a solid *whump* to his stomach again. We danced around for a while and I could see he was cooling off a little. We pitched a few feints at each other, then I connected with a stinger to his chin, and saw his mighty roundhouse coming for me. I slipped under it and we exchanged a couple of left wipes. His mouth was bleeding and my nose was. "Okay, buster," I warned him, "here comes your corker," and I clipped him with an easy right to open his guard and then threw my blockbuster at him. He got it full in the mush and went down, but it didn't lay him out. "God*dammi*t," he said, sitting there on the grass and wiggling his jaw in his hand, "I think you busted one of my teeth." But always afterward we would feel just fine, and forget our grudges against the world. And I never met a better sparring partner.

Give the guy a chance, I persuaded myself, so I left the tavern and ambled on over to the City Hall, which housed the police headquarters. Walking through the hot sunshine with a belly full of beer is not wise; I became woozy. Yet I arrived at the City Hall and went on inside to have a reunion with this old physical friend whom I had not seen for eight years. But the police station was gone. I mean, it wasn't in the rooms where it used to be. I wandered around the corridors of the City Hall's first floor, looking for somebody to tell me what had happened to the police station, feeling a strange suspicion that perhaps the police force had been abolished entirely in an economy move and thus the town was as lawless as during the steamboat days. I couldn't find anybody. In my wooziness and dejection and continual suspicion that there would not really be anything that I could talk to Dall about, I gave it up, left City Hall, staggered through town again to the public library, its waffled modern façade gone up like a masonry carapace around the homely old Carnegie edifice which, along with the YMCA a few blocks west, had been my favorite refuge in a youth of applied cultivation of my mind and body. The rest of the afternoon I spent in the library, shut away from the hostile town.

In the Periodicals Room my glance fell on the current issue of *Connoisseur*, and I eagerly picked it up and found my name on the contents page, turned to page 136 and there was my short illustrated paper on "Identifying Saw Marks and Plane Marks on Drawer-bottoms of Connecticut Chests of ca. 1750." I sat down and read it through; although I had worked it over so extensively that I knew it by heart, there was a special satisfaction at reading it in print, and I became so suffused with pride and a sense of accomplishment that I abandoned all thought of Little Rock and, reflecting philosophically that every man has a purpose in life and that perhaps my purpose was to explore the harmless properties of American antiquities, the moribund yet picturesque fossils of the VAP, I managed to convince myself that I had come to Arkansas only to research certain relevant aspects of the VAP, and that I had no time for any old friends anyway.

I found two splendid volumes on the archaic indigenous arts and crafts of the Southland, one of them emphasizing Arkansas and Louisiana productions of the mid-nineteenth century, and, using a still-valid library card that I had carried around in my wallet for ten years, I checked them out and took them home with me and began an earnest, concentrated study of them, interrupted only by supper, during which Daddy asked me what I was doing and I told him I was working. I told him I had frittered away too much time already, and now I had to get back to work. After all, I wasn't entirely on vacation. Finishing Sybil's beef stew in fifteen minutes, I excused myself and returned to my room and resumed my swift, alert perusal of the books. A fascinating subject, really. The native art of the Southern homesteaders was unpolished and makeshift in comparison with the more ornate culture of New England, but it had a raw force, a directness, a kind of masculine expedience which perhaps typified the lost American spirit more fittingly than that of any other time or area. I began to transcribe long passages from these books to my Ring-Master. But eventually I had to give it up. The hidden laughter of all those unfaithful old friends, who valued friendships only for their usefulness, was still ringing in my ears. I could not escape where I was.

Why, *why* have I come home?

ELEVEN

"The trouble with you, boy, is, you gotta *unwind*," my hortative old dad instructed me, jabbing at me a free finger of a hand which held a can of Busch. We shared the morose purple sofa of the living room; Sybil had the armchair, but she wasn't listening to us. The television set was on, a limpid silvery rectangle in the gloom of the far side of the room. After abandoning my abortive attempts at scholarship, I had joined them there, and my father, questioning me about my adventures of the day, had decided to play again his old role of fatherly adviser and admonisher. "Yeah, you got to get down off that cloud, get the starch out of your collar. This aint Boston."

"I know it isn't Boston," I retorted, rather loudly.

"Shhhh!" complained Sybil, a punctured tire leaking slowly. She was watching the Andy Griffith Show.

"Turn it up!" her grizzly lover roared at her, and then he turned back to me. "And another thing. You have been around them high-tone Boston folks too much, you forgot how to behave yourself when you're back here amidst us plain old unwashed clucks. No wonder nobody would talk to you."

"I didn't say that," I protested. "All I said was that they—"

"Yeah, but another thing—"

"You guys pipe down, okay?" Sybil beseeched.

"Still and all, you—"

"But, Daddy—"

"If you guys are gonna make all that noise, why don't you go—"

"Aaa," he nasally bleated, "damn pigheaded women."

"Let's go sit on the porch, Daddy."

"Let her go out to the damn kitchen if she don't like it in here."

"I'm watchin this damn show, that's why!"

"Let's take off our shirts, Daddy, and go sit in the breeze on the porch and drink our beer, all right?"

"I like it in here. It's comfortable. Hellfire, caint a man sit in his own goddamn livin room if he has a mind to?" He paused and waited to see if either of us would challenge his rights, and then he continued. "Now another thing. The trouble with you, son, is you've got just a mite too highfalutin and toplofty for your own good. You use to didn't be that way. You use to—"

"Oh, Jesus sake," Sybil moaned, rose, and turned up the set's volume.

"—use to could go up and be chummy with just about any old feller who came along. The trouble with readin all them books is, you get so's you can't look at people, you're so used to lookin at words. And another thing—"

Without a word I shrugged my shoulders in a gesture of helplessness, got up, and returned to my room.

A glass-fronted Victorian bookcase held the remnants of my

adolescent book collection, and I browsed indolently through it, trying to find something to read. But the collection, mostly old paperbacks and textbooks, was stale and immature and there was nothing in it I had not read before or cared to read again. Wedged behind a row of Reader's Digest Condensed Books was a sheaf of photographs of nude women, lolling and stretching and squatting in all manner of ample-assed pose, which I had often used to feed the fires of wish-fulfillment in the dreams of my pimple period, but now, flipping through them again, I was entirely blasé and unstimulated. Constantly restless, I rummaged through more of the papery debris of my irretrievable prime: a yellowed page from the Sports section of a 1953 *Gazette* with a photograph of me, stunning in silk Everlast trunks (purple, as I recall), getting my hand held high by the referee at the conclusion of the Featherweight bout in the Golden Gloves at Memphis; a letter from the Admissions Office of the University, notifying me that I had won a four-year scholarship; two ticket stubs to the Arkansas-Mississippi football game of 1954 (I could still see Preston Carpenter catching that fabulous pass—but who was the girl I had taken with me? Not Margaret Austin); a ribbon-bound stack of all issues of *Ring* magazine between 1948 and 1953; a tenth-grade theme written for a city-wide essay contest, "Why Little Rock Needs Natural Gas" (won honorable mention, no money); an envelope containing a lock of Margaret Austin's black hair and an eight-by-ten photograph of her at the age of seventeen, pretty but doleful-looking; a typescript of my speech in the American Legion oratorical contest of 1951, "What's Wrong with the U.S. Constitution" (a presumptuous subject, missed honorable mention by a half-dozen votes); the cover of a travel brochure for Hot Springs which serves as the false front for a thin, poorly drawn, black-and-white comic book showing an imitation Dagwood and an imitation Blondie engaging in every conceivable form of natural and unnatural sex activity—a classic example of a venerable kind of hard-core pornography known simply as "fuck book"; and a few other less mentionable items of juvenile erotica, including a prophylactic (*rubber* in the argot) which when blown up to the size of a football displayed a Grecian line drawing of Priapus forcing his attentions upon a recumbent maiden under the legend "Courtesy of Nick's Cigar Store, Coldest Beer in Town." This last item, I reflected, belonged rightfully in the Cabot Foundation's collections, VAPish as it was.

Beneath all this mess I came at last to what I had probably

been looking for all along: the yearbook of my high school graduating class, called, with considerable want of imagination, *The Pix*, and bound in black and old gold. I extracted this heavy book from out of its poor company and took it to the bed, where I curled up with it and prepared to be tortured again with the sight of familiar and forgotten old faces. The one familiar and forgotten face which I wanted to contemplate first was, naturally, my own; and I did, finding it fast, my portrait wedged between those of Patsy Stevens on one side and Gladys Stump on the other. The proximity was damaging. There I sat, looking every bit of nine years old, and every bit of What-Me-Worry Alf Newman of *Mad*, idiotic grin and prominent ears and all, between two girls who looked every bit of nineteen or twenty, and every bit of forty pounds heavier, as if they were the two ends of a barbell of which I was the bar. Beneath the photograph was a thick column of print: "Clifford Willow Stone. 'Nub.' *'He thinks, therefore he is.'* Home Room President, Beta Club, Key Club Vice-President, National Honor Society President, Nightcappers, Masque and Gavel, Varsity Boxing, Varsity Track, Intramural Baseball, Football Manager, Chambers Latin Prize, Boys' State, Pix Staff." I appeared again several pages later, more informally, in the "Distinctions" section, as "Best-All-Around" (gee!) on the same page with Hy Norden ("Wittiest"), Steve McComb ("Most Likely to Succeed"), Dall Hawkins ("Best Athlete"), and others. I appeared once more, a whole lace-edged page to myself, as "King of Hearts" at the Valentine Ball. I appeared also in a dozen or so club pictures, in the sports section, in a snapshot with Dall Hawkins above the trite caption "The Long and Short of It," and finally on a special page at the end of the book above the caption, "Appeared Most Often." By God, why didn't Hy and some of those other bastards get out their *Pixes* every once in a while? Then they might remember who I was. Every inch of marginal and end-paper space was covered with their fervent and undying tributes: "To Nub, my best friend forever, Keith." (Who was *Keith*?) "To the only guy I ever envied, yours always, Hy." "To the classiest guy in our class, always remember me, your best buddy, Steve." "For the sweetest boy I ever knew, all my love forever, Yvonne." (Who was *Yvonne*?) And loads of other such unctuous drivel.

Picking up the phone book in the hall, I attempted to find the present addresses and phone numbers of a dozen or so other old friends whose faces smiled up at me from the pages of *The Pix*. But most of them no longer lived in Little Rock. Two of them did, and I called these on the phone. The first call was to a fellow boxer in my own featherweight class. But there was no answer. Bridge night? The second call was to a thin, homely boy named Herbert Stodbecker who had been in my Home Room class, and whom I had befriended because, although he was a scholastic failure and a social flop as well, he had shown some talent for writing imagistic poems. Herbert was delighted to have my call, and we chatted pleasantly for a while. I told him what I was doing now. What was he doing now? Well, he was working for his father in a broomworks over on the East End. Making brooms? Well no, not exactly, it was more of a front-office-type position, you know. Writing any more poems these days? I asked. Any more what? he said. Poems, I said. He laughed self-consciously, burst out, "Aw, naw!" and went on laughing. I gave him up.

My father approached, squinted his beady eyes at me with his jaw set, wagged a finger at me, and began, "And another thing—"

"Oh, the hell with it!" I said, brushed past him, and stomped off through the living room toward the front door.

Sybil eyed me with surprise as I passed her. "You'll miss Johnny Carson!" she warned.

"The hell with him too," I said and walked on out of the house.

I wandered for a long time around the dark streets of the city. Even the incredible spring-night fragrances of myriad blossoming shrubs could not perfume away my growing distaste for the town. I could neither stand nor understand the place. In the glow from a street lamp I saw another one of those strange blue-and-white signs: "Who's Happy?" Not me, I said aloud, and walked on. I was in a frame of mind for nothing so much as walking on out of Little Rock entirely, walking until I came to the deepest, most virginal forest of Newton County, and there I would cut down some trees and build a log castle. I would live on berries and mushrooms and grasshoppers, making my own dandelion wine and growing an acre of corn for sour mash whiskey. If I became lonely, I would hire a local broad-hipped farm girl for housekeeping and humping. I would read, meditate, write, drink, hump: five noble activities for the easy rustic life. Ah, the hopeless fantasies of the idle mind!

For a while I toyed with the notion of going down to one of the whorehouses on Markham Street and getting myself fixed up. I had never been to one of Little Rock's before, but I knew where they were, and I thought this would make an appropriate memory of a disappointed homecoming. But it was too far to walk, and I was not yet *that* hard up . . . or hard on, so I turned homeward. On my way home, in the quiet and dark streets of that mellow residential area, dogs barked at me. Everybody was asleep. For all it mattered to me at that moment, they might as well have slept the sleep of death.

TWELVE

When I woke up the next morning, after a fitful and too warm sleep, the postman had come and left an air-mail letter for me, which said: "Dear Clifford, It was sneaky of you to run off like that. It was uncharacteristic of you, and inconsiderate, and furthermore it was impractical. I called Moms this afternoon to tell her I was coming home, but Iris answered and said they have gone to Bermuda for a month and are renting a house there. Why don't you come and meet me in New York, and after a day or two of plays, dinner, etc., we can fly to Bermuda and join them there. Please reply by wire if this idea strikes your fancy. We could have fun in the sun in that charming old place. Otherwise I would just have to sit here in Boston and twiddle my thumbs, and pine for old you. Please say Yes. Love, Pam." I had not eaten breakfast when I read this, and I had a head, possibly from all the beer I had had the day before, so my first reaction to this curious scrap of foolscap was one of muddled awe, all the more so because of the unusual juxtaposition of those last two words. My wife?

"Your wife?" Sybil asked, hovering.

"Yeah," I said and began rereading it.

"A love letter?" she coyly questioned.

"Yeah," I said. Then, "Could I have some breakfast, please?" and she got off my shoulder. Alone, I studied the letter. I looked at the reverse side, which was empty. I turned it upside down, I held it against the light. Her small, cursive script, laid down in brown ink on tan Eaton's, summoned me. Her proposal had much to recommend it, and I was tempted. In fact, I was more than tempted: I accepted. I would do it. Bugger this miscarried homecoming, bugger this home! But I would not wire Pamela. I would simply take a train to New York, have a few days of fun there by myself, and then phone her to come join me. I would take no gaff from her, then or later, or forever, and if she didn't like it she could shove it. Uncharacteristic of me, had she written? Well, I would show her what was characteristic of me.

"Come and eat," Sybil said, and I went and ate, and then afterward I tried a little sport with her, but she put me off again, saying that she was sorely offended that I had told her, and my father, and nice Johnny Carson, all to go to hell.

"Very well," I said, and I packed my bag and took it to the front door, and when she asked me what I was doing, I told her. Then I made it clear that this was her last chance to play with me, and if she didn't play with me now, I was never ever going to play with her any more, or anybody else in this funereal town. She was put on the spot by that, and almost gave in. But at last instead she laughed.

"You better come and have another cup of coffee, boy," she said. "You're still half asleep." But I declined, and told her I must be on my way. I opened the front door, lifted my suitcase, pecked her a wet one on the cheek, instructed her to explain to my father why I was leaving so soon, closed the door and walked away, leaving her in one heck of a quandry behind me.

First I took a bus to the public library to return the books I had borrowed. This time I noticed in the library's lobby a special display case decked out, in honor of the forthcoming premiere of James Royal Slater's new play, with photographs and books and manuscripts tracing his career as a dramatist. I regretted, briefly, that my sudden departure from Little Rock would prevent me from seeing his new play, but I decided that if the play were any good I would undoubtedly see it soon in Boston or New York, where I had seen productions of two previous Slater plays, *Christmas in Jail,* at the Charles Street Playhouse in Boston, and *The Pedagogic Demagogue,* at the Circle-in-the-Square, New York. I had never met Slater, in fact I had never even seen a picture of him, but he had a certain reputation outside Arkansas because both of these earlier plays had been forerunners of the present Theater of the Absurd, or, as it is more appropriately called, Metatheatre. I had never been able to make much sense out of his plays, but the very fact that he was Arkansas-born-and-reared, and even today still lived not far outside of Little Rock (where, advancing into middle age, he considered himself a horse rancher more than a playwright), gave me an almost proprietary interest in the plays. Thinking back over the intricate structure of his art, I found myself wondering how any intellectual could have survived in the cultural wasteland of this city. Pausing only a few minutes at the display case in his honor, I hefted my suitcase and left the library and took a taxi to the Missouri Pacific station.

There I discovered with considerable distress that the next train for St. Louis, and thence New York, did not leave until after midnight that night. Well, I was not going back to my father's house again. I checked in my suitcase, bought a cup of coffee and a paperback of Dostoyevsky's *The Idiot,* and sat down to while away the hours. Forty-five minutes of this, however, wearied me to distraction. I got up, stuffed the difficult book into my pocket, and went for a stroll around the platforms of the station. These same tracks, I reflected, had by night in the wandering nights of my boyhood tempted me constantly outward and away from this town, and had finally taken me away at last. What now was I doing here again? I had sold newspapers on this platform to servicemen going away or coming in, and had envied them their goings and their comings, until at last I had gone myself. And had come. And now was going again. Is this the consummation of existence, to yearn for departure and arrival, and then to spend all one's born days departing and arriving, until there is no longer any distinction between the two? Until I do not know now whether in leaving this town, I am going home or leaving home? Bitter questions. Do I, leaving, leave, or come; or, rather, by coming, go? Is my returning really removal, or is my evacuation actually approach? Or either neither, or both both? Or should I have accepted that second cup of coffee Sybil offered?

The day now was not just warm; it was hot, and beastly so, the air thick with sticky moisture. Motion and sound both had ceased and I seemed to have the railroad station all to myself. A pall hung heavy as the air all over the place, and if any train ever did come in, I was certain it would be a hearse train, car after car packed with wooden caskets crossing the bar through the valley of the shadow toward the journey's end, the downward path of the way of all flesh toward the Stygian shore where a great neon sign flashes in big red six-foot bloody letters, MEMENTO MORI, and that grim ferryman punches tickets and that reaper rents pillows for a quarter, and that pale priest of the mute people sells paper buckets filled with ice cubes.

The place gave me the creeps, and I got out of there, but not before I had already been somnambulized, like that poor fellow in Dr. Caligari's cabinet, to such an extent that the rest of that day became entirely vague, listless, insensate, almost comatose, and I moved (walked? floated? crawled? seeped?) through a great many places of that city, a zombie at last among his own. I lunched with several fat and thin zombies in Miller's Coffee Shop on Lower Main, and I browsed with several more zombies through Pfeifer's book department, and I wound up, sometime in the afternoon, sitting on a sofa beside one of the zombiest zombies of them all, my sister Lucinda, but for the life of me I cannot remember what I said to her, or she to me. Perhaps we did not speak at all, but only exchanged a series of deathlike stares. Or perhaps I insulted her. Or she me. Or perhaps her husband Victor came home and threw me out. Or I him. At any rate, I found myself again in Miller's Coffee Shop, having supper. I drank a couple of cans of Miller's Hi-Life and read a copy of the *Gazette* which someone had left behind on the counter, and discovered on the Amusements page that a block down the street, at the old Main Theater, there was a rerun movie I had missed the first time but still wanted to see, *Two for the Seesaw,* with Robert Mitchum as a Midwesterner who, as I was about to do, goes to New York and has a good time there. The cooler air of the late afternoon cleared me up a little, and I drifted out of it, and maneuvered my way, arms loose and feet sore and soul all but entirely expatriated at last forevermore, a block down the street to the picture show.

🐢 THIRTEEN

In the titles, he is wandering lonely all day all over Manhattan, he is on a bench feeding pigeons in front of St. Mark's-in-the-Bouwerie, he is searching for the Omaha *World Herald* in that OUT OF TOWN newsstand which shoes the feet of the old Times Building in Times Square, he is shuffling through the Egyptian room of the Metropolitan, staring emptily at a seated pharaoh while behind him the eyes of Anobis, the jackal god of the necropolis, the same conductor of the dead who had escorted me loping all day through Little Rock, follow his progress in and out of that hushed sanctum. Then the movie proper begins, and the hollow gray breadth of his isolation is underlined: he wishes he were back home in Omaha. Will I, if I go to New York, wish I were back here? But soon he meets the beatnik Jewess, Gittel, and is taken with her, and so am I. She is a brunette, and although Shirley MacLaine's wig seems possibly a *bunkin-taka-shimada*—cut short by Mr. Kenneth—left over from *My Geisha*, her brunetteness is of a type that I have always somehow been drawn to, strangely enough in view of my marriage to a blonde. It is a shade of lightless, sooty burnt umber; a kit and boodle of girl friends, one-night dates as well as longer drags, had come into my life wearing that same cast of black, and although this Gittel is, if not actually beat, rather obviously hip, I am drawn to her because she reminds me of them all. Therefore I am with Mitchum tooth and nail as he begins his courtship of her, and I share in his pleasure when his lonesomeness evokes her rich pity, and I sit back and muse, wryly, worldy wise: How rare is the compassion of a woman: How stupid of me to marry a blonde: How inevitable that I would bring such a thing on myself through some unconscious sort of masochism. Ah, Gittel, how charitable of you to put out so easily, so voluptuously, for a poor friendless stranger. But Mitchum—*O tempora! O mores!*—does not want charity, and he skips out on her. From here on, I am forced to think too deeply about the *tempora*, to reflect too painfully upon the *mores*, and I didn't come here for that.

I lost interest. The movie was falling apart anyway, lapsing into a series of involved and impassioned conversations which struck me belatedly as the meaning of the title: the seesaw, up and down, down and up, marjorie daw. Not enough action. I wanted Two for the Roller Coaster, I had come to the wrong show. Taking out my pack of Milk Duds, my favorite cinema candy, I began a restless chomping and chawing. From time to time I glanced furtively around at my neighbors, hunting for an old face, but recognized no one, although the theater was nearly packed: an elderly man on my left, a young lady on my right, a couple of high school kids in front, an assortment of blank stroboscopically flickered faces, young adults, behind me. The sinistral old man was fortunately downwind, so the scent of his age and talc and sweat was only as gamy as what might cling to the walls of a long-abandoned boarding-house room, but the upwind starboard lady smelled of an innocent spangled essence which was disturbingly familiar and which I might have found a name for if I had thought hard enough: Ma Griffe,

Bellodgia, Poivre, or some such namable *eau*, which had clung to my cheek and collar several warm evenings sometime, some long time, ago. I stole a quick glance at her profile, trimly marmoreal and ageless in the flickering light, but as strange to me as a hermit thrush encountered in a tree full of sparrows. Then I glanced beyond her to evaluate her escort, to marvel at what manner of man had brought this fair damsel hither, but he wasn't there, I mean the seat was empty, he was either out for some more popcorn or he had never been there in the first place and would never be there; and it was this latter case which, after I had waited a while for him to return, proved correct. Well now, I thought, well now. From that point on, Gittel had a rival for my attention, and it was odd how, although Gittel's locks were banged and hacked while this lady's were tressed and crested, they were both of the same darkness, it seemed in the pale available light at least, which set me thinking once more about how it is that I have always been moved to take notice of that certain type of brunette, as though it were some inborn compulsion periodically returning to bedevil me. Gittel was in a hot fix, while this lady, watching, was still cool and seemingly uninvolved, but the two of them became as one for me, and I watched Gittel with my left eye and *her* with my right like the two separate but identical halves of an old stereoscope picture. It was impossible for me to treat either of them as cavalierly as Mitchum was treating Gittel, so that, some time later after he had been giving her pure hell and had thrown the chemistry of her poor ulcer all out of whack and it, her ulcer, began to hemorrhage when and because he was running out on her, and she almost fell down the long stairs after him, yelling, "Jerry, *help* me!" and I was helpless to harm that cad for her, but the least I could do was hold her hand in comfort and sympathy, I did, I couldn't help it: I held her hand.

Too late I realized that this was an irrational and altogether immature thing for me to do, something too embarrassingly akin to the old fantasies which possessed me in the crowded catchpenny Rex, Crescent and Roxy theaters during a certain nervous and wistful period of my boyhood, and if I were soon to be summoned before a prim municipal-court judge and required to account for my rash behavior, I could only plead a temporary insanity resulting from the general besotted condition my emotions had been in all day long. Had Clara chosen to have me indicted in Boston for that other offense, I could only have offered the same plea. Some such defense, I suddenly realized, had better be forthcoming very soon, for the lady turned and, with her free right hand, slapped me. Quite hard.

A stir ensued among our neighbors, and it was this which embarrassed me more than either the smart slap itself or the words which accompanied it, which were: "What do you think you're doing?" The kids in front of us had turned around to gawk, the young marrieds behind us were all achatter, and as I gazed forlornly into the full face of my hostile lady, I could feel the eyes of the old gentleman on my left, possibly the municipal-court judge himself, burning into the back of my red neck.

"Oh, pardon me," I hastily mumbled to this outraged maiden. "I thought you were somebody else." I realized I was still desperately clutching her hand, and I looked down at it as I would look at someone's lost wallet picked up from the sidewalk, and then I dropped it.

Then, because, I suppose, of something about the lift of her eyebrows or the thrust of her small chin, I saw that she *was* somebody else, somebody who, astonishingly, I knew. And in that same instant, perhaps because my own features had not changed as much as hers, she recognized me as well.

But instead of gasping my name, as I thought she might have done under the circumstances, she simply made a short, deep chuckle in her throat, and breathed back at me, "I *am* somebody else."

"Hi, Margaret," I said feebly, hangdoggedly, "long time no see."

An usher, or possibly the manager himself, was snapping a flashlight at us from the end of the aisle and rumbling, "What's going on here?"

The white-maned, gamy colonel on my left leaned across me and asked, "You want me to throw this person out, ma'am?"

The high school boy in front of me turned his head and urged, "Hit im again, lady."

Our colleagues in the rear continued their babble of startled surmises, ignoring, as everyone else but me seemed to be doing, the fact that Gittel was prostrated in the rear of an ambulance, being whisked away for an emergency gastrectomy.

All of this seemed as embarrassing to her as it was to me; she slunk down in her seat and commenced shaking her head in reply to all questions, including my own: "You want me to leave?"

"It's all right," I explained to the senior citizen on my left. "I'm her brother and was just playing a joke on her."

He grunted, the usher and his flashlight went away, and all

of us resumed our absorption in the peptic disorders of Gittel Mosca.

A few moments later she whispered, "Why did you do that?"

"I didn't know it was *you*. Honest," was my sincere reply, and I realized, too late, that this was not the most diplomatic way to phrase it. "An accident, I mean." She was silent. "I just happened to be here, was all."

Later she asked, in that same clear and regionless voice which would identify her even in the dark, even in a whisper, "When did you come home?"

"Yesterday morning," I answered.

"Why?" she asked.

How reply? How discuss it properly without annoying our neighbors? They had been kind enough to leave us alone, let us leave them alone. She was holding the violated left hand with the avenging right hand in the center of her lap. Unnecessary, because I was of no mind to try again anyway. "Homesick, I guess," I muttered distractedly out of the side of my mouth, pretending I was wrapped up in the movie.

She said nothing more, and I actually did endeavor to concentrate on the picture, but it was no use, partly because Gittel and Jerry were still bickering in the seesaw of their endless colloquy, partly because I could not unwind the coils of my mind from the tense state that this chance encounter had left them in. After all, there once had been a time when I had suspected that she was not sound of mind, which was one reason I had given her up, and perhaps I was contributing to her obsessive dementia by my presence beside her and by that thoughtless little slip of my hand. Although she seemed to remain as outwardly cool as before, still marmoreal, more whitely so than the glow of the screen could have been held responsible for, perhaps she was inwardly seething with a stark, frantic sort of aberration and thus she might at any moment suddenly begin pummeling me, and then nothing I could say to that municipal judge would do me any good.

I had to get away. If only Gittel would do something really dramatic, if she would only stab herself or stab Jerry or jump out a window or simply expire, then maybe in the excitement that followed I could slip past the grizzled codger sitting to the left of me, and gain the aisle, and made a clean getaway. But no, all Gittel could do was talk, talk, talk.

Later, much later, her left arm came up and lay again on the arm rest between us and I studied it with a fascination usually reserved for the gracefully turned limbs of Chippendale highboys, but I was as helpless to do anything about it as I would have been to tamper with a Chippendale design. My tampering days, my bold and meddling moments, were now over and done with: I had gone into the water too far and was so happy to be safe back on shore that I would never ever, God help me, be tempted to do such a thing again. So I left her hand alone, and eventually she sensed that I was either leaving it alone or did not know it was there, or else she had not put it there on purpose anyway, for she took it away once more, and left it away.

Several long and dull weeks later old Jerry finally got sufficiently homesick for his old wife back home in old Omaha, and, after a few parting pumps of the seesaw, ran off and left old Gittel holding the bag, waiting for the next sad old boy to come bumbling through Manhattan in need of her limitless love and the vacant end of the stilled seesaw. The two sides of the plush brocaded curtain ran out to meet each other and did a little dance together, then the house lights went on.

"Well," I said and turned slowly, casually toward her.

I half expected (or hoped, in some desperate final attempt at wishfulness) that she would be gone, that my eyes would encounter only the empty seat. But she was there, and she was crying.

"Aw," I frowned, never one to feel poised around weeping women, "I'm sorry. Really."

She gouged her eyes with the back of her bent wrist, twisting it in, and managed to blot up most of the lacrimal flow. She sniffled and said, "It was the movie. The movie was so sad."

Yes it was, I allowed, and she had always been overly susceptible to the little sadnesses of this world. I had never known her to cry over her own sorrows, but she was always fluently sobbing about somebody else's, like the time the whole school was made to assemble in the auditorium for an hour to listen to General MacArthur's farewell address on the radio after Truman kicked him out of Korea, and when he came to that part about "old soldiers never die," etc., she began such a flood of tears that both my hip-pocket hankie and my jacket-pocket hankie, not to mention most of my sleeve, were thoroughly soggy before the old soldier finally faded away and left her alone to contemplate in damp silence the mean treatment of Little Rock's favorite son at the hand of old Give-em-Hell Harry. It had disconcerted me at the time, and it did now.

I stood up. "Well—" I began, marshaling my talents for a graceful leave-taking, but that was as far as I got. I couldn't just say "Nice to've seen you," and be done with it.

She rose too, and lifted her tweedy gray handbag from the vacant seat on the other side of her. We looked each other in the eye, levelly; just as I had suspected, she had grown a bit since last I had seen her, and now was almost a quarter of an inch taller than I in my elevators, whereas once there had not been a hair's-breadth of difference between our heights, and we had made a well-matched pair. I used to love this girl, I mused with no little nostalgia, I used to be just wild about every inky hair on her lovely little head.

I waited for her to say something, but she wouldn't. She was not looking at me. After a moment I said "Well" again. Then inanely I asked, "How's tricks?"

"All right," she said, still not looking at me, then, after another long and painful silence, she looked up, studied my eyes nervously for a moment, and finally spoke: "How long are you going to be here?"

"Oh, I'm leaving right now," I said. "Just wanted to stretch a bit before going."

"I didn't mean *here*," she said very quietly, almost inaudibly, pointing at the floor. "I mean here in Little Rock."

"Oh, I'm leaving right now," I said, as if I knew what she had meant the first time. I looked at my watch. "My train leaves in a couple of hours."

"Well," she said. She was not looking at me again. She heaved her shoulders a little, not a sigh but rather a kind of resigned shrug. "I could give you a ride to the station—"

"Why, thank you—"

"—but I don't have a car."

"Oh," I said.

"I suppose we could walk," she said. She wasn't looking at me.

Was she married now? I wondered. I looked down at her hand, searching for a gold band, but her fingers were clinched tightly around the straps of her handbag and I couldn't see them. If she walked me to the train station, might not her husband be out looking for her, and gun me down? The item in the *Gazette* about the play had given her name as always, Margaret Austin, but I knew that actresses usually kept their maiden names on the stage. "Oh, I'll just get a cab," I said.

She frowned, wrinkling her smooth fair brow as though its

marble had abruptly been creased by three savage blows from a sculptor's chisel. "What will you do for the two hours until your train comes in?"

I drew *The Idiot*, bent and broken, out of my pocket and flapped it at her. "I'll read," I said.

"Well," she said.

Damn you, Clifford Stone! my naïve, seraphic, lily-white conscience hissed at me. *Don't be so pococurante! After all—* But I interrupted: I'm fed up with this town, I'm sick of it; the sooner I get away the better. *After all,* my indomitable conscience continued, *what are two hours of your precious time? What if this had really been that strange girl you imagined, then what would you have done for these two hours between the end of the show and train time? Are two hours of friendliness too high a price for what she did for you?* What did she do? *She colored your adolescence.* Lord, it really needed coloring, didn't it? *Yes indeedy.* But she's changed, I'd hardly know her, were it not for those eyes. *Changed for the better, can't you see? Slimmer, smoother, straighter, whiter, plain prettier. . . .* And crazier too, no? That's why I finally broke off with her, ten—or was it nine?—years ago, she bothered me. Those eyes, for pity sakes! they blistered carbuncles on the inside of the back of my skull, they nettled the last shred of my *sang-froid*; alternately green as grass or gray as graphite, they decorated her face while they desecrated my blood, and look, *look!* they are still at it.

Avoiding them, I ushered her to the aisle, and there, lacking any words of my own, borrowed Goethe's: " 'Fair Lady, may I thus make free to offer you my arm and company?' "

Knowing it, she laughed and answered shyly in kind: " 'I am no lady, am not fair, can without escort home repair.' "

But departing from the script, she repaired not home but instead with me, after a ten-block walk in diffident silence, to the environs of the Missouri Pacific terminal, where we located a beer café, one of those drab bored trainmen's oases, and sat down to a couple of bottles of cold Busch and a conversation of sorts. She had removed her khaki trench coat and draped it over the back of the bentwood chair; she sat straight with her arms laid out on the table surrounding her glass and bottle. She was wearing a fetching red paisley dress, silk, and a choker of lumpy turquoise stones. The bright red of her dress, the deep black of her hair, the pale white of her skin, reminded me of those sharp red-black-white color cadences of the Netherlandish primitives. Roger van der Weyden would have loved her.

For a long time before either of us spoke, I feasted my eyes on her, my giddy brain flooded suddenly with a host of old memories, not all of them unpleasant, and then I asked her the question that came first to my mind: "Margaret, are you married now?"

Slowly, almost imperceptibly and still without looking at me, she shook her head.

FOURTEEN

Why not? I almost asked, but I didn't need to. (I had earned my lunches as a busboy for the teachers' dining room in high school, and once I had eavesdropped as an English teacher was explaining Margaret to the guidance counselor: *That girl is just a straw in the wind. She won't ever marry.*) It wasn't that she wasn't nubile; personally I had never met a girl, or a woman, whose muliebrity was so much an almost visible aura as Margaret's. But neither had I ever encountered such an overwhelming inferiority complex in a person, and I suppose it was her bashful withdrawal, her helpless isolation, which had kept her out of wedlock. I think I must have been the only fellow in high school who had ever had a date with her.

I had known her, or known of her, since the seventh grade. My first image of her was still sharply engraved into my memory. It was Martinmas of 1949—somehow I even remembered the day, as well as the year—and she was in her first year at West Side Junior High. She was crossing the playground that bright November morning on the sunny side of the school building, when she arrived at an opened door, an unmarked door leading directly from the playground into the bowels of the basement, a door which she had perhaps never used before simply because nobody had ever told her to use it, and she paused there, peering into the interior, which at first must have been as dark as a cave but became rapidly clearer as her eyes readjusted and a shifting cloud permitted the sunshine to illuminate fully that obscure chamber. Almost immediately she was struck with a great rolling roar of heinously hyenaen laughter, such as would attend a hysteric Saturnalia, but she continued gazing at the scene without any immediate constraint or comprehension. Knowing as I did the curious but green and uncertain mind which Margaret had in those days of early adolescence, I suppose she remained standing there for quite a long moment before finally realizing that she was facing the entire third-period boys' gym class in various states of nakedness, *tout ensemble*, in their locker room, the door to which someone had so carelessly left open. Knowing also the character of her domestic environment, which was as seraphic and righteous as any obsessively religious mother could provide without transferring her allegiance to the Holy Rollers, I could understand her reluctance to depart abruptly despite her awful bashfulness: she had never seen so wondrous an apparatus of nature as a boy's genitalia, let alone a whole room full of them, and was simply fascinated, moral codes be damned. Delight of discovery admits of no guilt. Or perhaps she did not know that we could see her. Ultimately, unfortunately, she had to withdraw from that doorway, for soon the shrill laughter, the shrieks of glee had become so raucous that the whole school threatened to be disturbed, and several of the unclad bacchantes were becoming uninhibited exhibitionists; their inelegant dancing was too much for her. I happened to know about this incident because I was one of those bacchants . . . in fact, the one closest to the door. Margaret never admitted to me, years later, that this had been the first time she became aware of the fundamental physical difference between the sexes, but I suspect it was, for she was an only child until, at the age of fifteen, she acquired a stepfather and stepsisters . . . and a stepbrother who finally took pity on her ignorance and, taking her aside (or, I will assume, up to the attic), explained to her the basic facts of life.

Now also I remembered another reason I had given her up: all around me in the junior and senior years of high school my cronies were boasting of their sexual adventures with their girls, while I, time after time, failed to get anywhere with Margaret; she was still a virgin when I left her.

Pouring more beer into our glasses, I groped for a *mot juste*, or a *mot pour rire*, to get the conversation going. Are you still a virgin? No, not that yet. I thought it best, for the sake of my honor, to attempt to explain why I had accidentally held her hand at the movie. I tried "About the movie—" I began. "When I held your hand, I mean. You see, I—"

Musing, she said: "Your hand was cold."

I said: "It was not."

She: "Yes it was. Like ice."
I: "No it wasn't. Yours was hot."
She: "It wasn't either."
I: "Was."
She: "Wasn't."

"Was." I touched it again, like testing an iron, but without spitting on my finger first. "Ha! It still is. Feel it."

She did. "It's not. Your finger is cold."

"No it isn't."

"It is too."

"Then feel it."

"I did."

"No you didn't," I said.

"The trouble," she said, again in that quiet, practically soundless voice, "is that we both are prejudiced in the sense of having a personal bias in favor of our individual temperatures. It's the same thing that makes the Orientals think we stink, and vice versa."

"All right. Let's talk about something else, hey?"

She nodded. Timidly she asked, "Light my cigarette first."

"I don't have any matches."

She handed me her tiny Ronson. "Use mine," she said.

"Thank you," I said.

"You're welcome," she said.

I lit her cigarette for her. She took a long puff, and exhaled, thank God, through her mouth. I could never abide ladies who exhale through their noses. She extended her pack of Kents to me and raised her eyebrows, but I shook my head. I quit smoking at about the same time I quit dating her.

The conversation collapsed again, and I labored mightily to think of something other than the usual banalities about what-all-have-you-been-up-to-since-I-saw-you-last? Finally—wonder of wonders—she broke the silence herself: "What are you doing in Little Rock—or, I should say, what *were* you doing in Little Rock?"

"I am just a bird of passage," I said.

She grinned. "So now that you've left your droppings all over this poor nest, you have to fly off and find a clean one?"

"In a manner of speaking," I owned. Was she trying to insult me? She never talked so saucy before.

"Why are you leaving, really?"

"This town," I said, as if those two words, inflected ominously, explained it all, and they did.

"Oh," she said, nodding her head. But after a moment of thought she asked, "What's wrong with this town?"

"My dear," I patiently replied, "it would take me all night to tell you, and anyway you should know, you've lived here longer than I have."

"Please don't my-dear me," she said, slightly peevish. "My question was rhetorical, I suppose. I know more about what's wrong with this town than you do."

"I'm sure you do," I granted.

She was not listening any longer. She was studying my face. I could feel her eyes gamboling about on the landscape of my countenance like a pair of ants exploring a dunghill. "You know, you haven't changed at all," she offered, unsolicitedly.

"Not much, I guess. But you've changed quite a bit. Except for my good memory of little details, I wouldn't have recognized you."

"Changed how?" she wondered.

"Prettier. Of course, you were always pretty, but now you're stunning." Her beauty was not the sweet, blooming, cherry-cheeked kind of prettiness that decorates the front page of the *Gazette*'s Society section; rather, a fragile beauty such as one might encounter in late Gothic German art—the jet-black hair and the whitest skin I ever saw. Arkansas prettiness is baroque, but Margaret's was medieval. And I knew there was something fastidious, nearly compulsive about it: I visualized the long hours she spent ironing her clothes and creaming her face and shaping her hair and plucking her eyebrows.

"Thank you," she responded to my compliment.

"You're welcome," I said and then the conversation died again for a while. We ordered another round of beer. Eventually I discovered that we were making idle small-talk about the movie we had seen. Yes, she admitted, Shirley MacLaine was her favorite actress. Yes, I admitted, Robert Mitchum was my favorite actor. We analyzed the plot: as she saw it, the fellow Jerry (Mitchum) had to go to New York and to Gittel in order to discover that Omaha was his real home. I asked her if she would like to go to New York. Not especially, she said, after a long, meditative pause. Why not? I asked. Because it would only make her realize how much she belonged to Little Rock. I was surprised and I said so: Do you mean you really like it here? She answered: I didn't say that. Then what do you mean? I asked. Maybe, she said, I only mean that I would like to like it. Oh, I said, and the conversation died yet once more.

At a loss for a better gambit, I resorted finally to the old cliché: "What all have you been doing lately?"

She shrugged. "Just boondoggling," she said. "Just dillydallying and fiddlefaddling. Nothing exciting or worthwhile or even interesting."

I eyed her with suspicion. "You don't call being the leading lady of a new Slater play very interesting?"

"Oh, you've been reading the papers," she said.

"With surprise," I said. "I never knew you were interested in the theater. How did you happen to get the top role in the play?" You of all people, who cannot even emote to me successfully, much less to an auditorium full of people.

She smiled. "There are only two parts in the whole play," she explained. "And I'm only doing it as a favor for an old friend of yours."

"An old friend of *mine*?" I said. "Who?"

She grinned. "Doyle Hawkins."

I was sorely perplexed. "*Dall*? Sergeant Hawkins of the Police? Explain, please."

She glanced at the clock. "It's a long, long story and I wouldn't have time to finish it before your train leaves." But I pressed her for a synopsis at least and she gave me a few details: she had run across Dall by accident not so long ago, and she had not been in a very pretty mood, and he had tried, in his awkward way, to cheer her up, and eventually the idea occurred to him that she ought to be *involved* in something, as a diversion, because she had lost her job, which was selling shoes, so he suggested that she join the Little Rock Playmakers group as a stagehand or wardrobe mistress or something, just to have something to do. Because of his insistence, she had told him that she would join the group just as a favor to him, and when she did, almost by accident she was given the part in the play.

I recalled that there had been only one class in high school which Dall and Margaret had both taken, an art class, and his only awareness of her seemed to be that he was, if anything, a little jealous of her at one time because she was taking up so much of my companionship, which he probably thought belonged rightfully to him. Now here I was in the strange situation of learning that my ex-girl friend and ex-pal had been consorting with one another, and I wondered why.

"Was that in the line of duty for him?" I asked her.

"In a way," she said.

"How?"

Her gestures indicated that it was something she would rather not discuss. "Oh, I don't know," she said. "He's a very conscientious policeman, and I guess he thought he could . . . could, well, *save* me, or something, I don't know."

"You were despondent?"

"Sort of."

"Not suicidal or anything, I hope?"

She didn't answer. In the silence that followed, I pondered an assortment of conjectures: somebody had jilted her, her life was a mess, stalwart Dall to the rescue. A mysterious girl. I regretted that I could not remain long enough to learn what the facts were. There was only about half an hour until train time.

The little café we were sitting in was quiet; two brakemen from the MoPac yards were having coffee at the counter; the other tables were vacant. It was a dreary, stuffy place existing in that tasteless manner which was thought modern in the war years but now was as outmoded as a second-hand top-heavy Hudson. On the wall above my lady's beautiful dark hair was a sign in faded day-glow: No CREDIT. Again she was not looking at me; her jaws were working as if she were trying to crush a stubborn piece of hard candy or to force a raspberry seed out from between two teeth. These motions transformed the lower half of her face, and although they were performed with a ladylike grace they disturbed me, as a certain nervous tic of a lunatic might do. I asked her what the blue blazes she was doing. She said she was writing a letter on the roof of her mouth with the tip of her tongue. I asked her if she often wrote such letters. Now and then, she said. Whom was this one addressed to? I discreetly inquired. To me, she said. Why was she writing me a letter on the roof of her mouth? I asked. Wouldn't it be awfully hard to read under such circumstances? Didn't I ever have odd little compulsions? she wanted to know. Didn't I ever knock wood, or go out of my way to avoid cracks in the sidewalk, or trace designs on the carpet with my toe, or stick out my tongue at old ladies? Not that I could remember, I said. Oh well, she said, and stopped writing her letter.

"Margaret—" I began, and she looked up at me again, but there was a great frog in my throat.

We had never done much talking in our courting days, probably because she was so inordinately shy, so difficult to talk to. Perhaps the reason I talked too much to Pamela, confessed too much of myself, exhibited my soul to her, was in reaction against the few years I had dated Margaret in near-silence. It was not that we didn't have anything to talk about. We just didn't know how. There were times when she would get all moody about something (sex? me? her own shortcomings? what?) and I would ask her what was the matter, but she couldn't—or wouldn't—tell me. I would plead, "Come on, Margaret, tell me what's wrong. Is it something I did? Something I said? Just tell me, and I'll do something about it. I'll never know if you won't tell me. Please tell me." But she would clam up tighter than ever, and I never knew what the deuce was bothering her. That, too, was why I had relinquished her.

Yet I felt the minutes slipping away from me, I could picture the train already approaching the town at eighty miles an hour from the southwest, I felt this last fragment of the past seeping through my fingers, and perhaps that was why there was a sudden, untypical desperation in my voice. "Talk to me, Margaret," I suddenly pled, leaning forward over the table and clutching her arm. "Talk to me!"—my voice almost wheedling now—"I've been home two days now and nobody has talked to to me, and now I'm leaving, and nobody has said a word to me."

Her mouth did something—not exactly a smirk, but close to it. Then after a moment she tonelessly replied, "I've been here twenty-seven years now and nobody has talked to me."

I leaned back in my chair and regarded her from more distance. "Except Dall?" I said.

"Except him," she said. Then her face softened, was almost benign. "What shall I talk to you about?" she asked.

"*You*," I said. "I never understood you. I never knew what you were all about. It hurts me when I can't figure people out."

Her gaze turned in on itself—or back upon all the times, ten or eleven years ago, when I had failed to fathom her. "I guess you thought I was crazy sometimes, didn't you?" she asked.

"Frankly, yes . . . sometimes."

"I am," she said.

"Why do you think so?"

"There's no one reason, nothing encompassing. On the whole I guess I give most people the impression of being simply an aloof snob, but there are just a lot of little things—fragments from my childhood and so forth—which pop up to bother me ever so often and remind me what a sorry wreck of a mind I accumulated over the years."

"Like what?" I asked, pleased beyond words to hear her talking at last. I don't think she ever spoke more than twenty consecutive words to me before.

"Like this," she said, holding up a few salted peanuts for my inspection. I had bought her a bag of the things because she had said she liked something salty with her beer. "Watch," she said. She popped the peanuts into her mouth and swallowed them whole.

"What did you do that for?" I asked.

"When I was a little girl," she explained, "I had the weird notion—I don't know why—that I had a set of beautiful teeth, perfectly formed molars and incisors and bicuspids and all, right down inside of my fat tummy, and that therefore it was not necessary for me to chew my food before swallowing it, because the other set of choppers down below would take care of it. So I gulped all of my food down with nary a nick from my mouth-teeth."

"Gee," I said.

"Every night at bedtime I would swallow a great big gooey gob of toothpaste so that my tummy-teeth could stay all white and shiny."

"Horrors," I said

"You'd think I might at least have realized that it wasn't necessary for them to be white and shiny so long as they weren't visible. But that simple piece of cogitation never got through to me. It required about three years of cramps, colic, gas, and plain old constipation to make me realize that either my extra teeth weren't functioning properly, or else I never had any in the first place."

"My goodness," I said.

"Wouldn't you hate yourself if you had been guilty of that kind of stupidity?" she asked.

"I certainly would!" I agreed.

"But that isn't all," she said and paused, and I had the happy feeling that she was winding herself up for a good confession. "That's only a random example, picked out of the air like a peanut picked from a bag. The list of my mistakes—my errors and faults and crimes—would read like a Concise Encyclopedia of Human Numskullery in one heavy, thumb-indexed volume. When I was six years old, I realized how poor we were—that was when Mother had to go back to work as a waitress again—and I set myself up on the front sidewalk to solicit nickels and dimes from all passers-by, and I had collected almost two dollars before my mother discovered what I was doing, just in time to prevent me from accepting the invitation of a generous old gentleman who was offering me a whole dollar if I would get in his car and go for a bye-bye with him. When I was seven, I developed an incorrigible grudge against the cranky old widow who lived alone in the nasty house next door—I can't even remember what I had against her—and began a campaign to part her from her frail senses: I would sneak into her stale old rooms when she wasn't looking and set all of her clocks two hours ahead or behind, I would remove pages from her calendars, I would steal her morning paper off her porch before she could get to it, and replace it with a six- or seven-year-old paper retrieved from our attic, I would do the same with her copies of *Life* magazine, spiriting them out of her mailbox as soon as the postman had turned his back and substituting issues from a year or two earlier, and I was never caught, never discovered. One day she moved away. So I never had the satisfaction of knowing what lasting effect my campaign had on her, but one afternoon not long before she moved she called to me as I was passing her house and asked me how old I was, and when I told her she said, 'Now that's odd. Here I've been thinking you were only three,' so I asked her how old she was and she said she wasn't sure. Well. When I was eight, I entered a period of hostility toward the colored race, particularly toward the ugly, slimy Negro men who came twice a week in the Sanitation truck to collect our garbage, and I would sit in the window of my upstairs room and look down at them passing beneath me up our driveway, and they were so ugly I had to do something to them, so I would pee into a tin can and pour it down on them as they passed below, and that went on for about three weeks before one of them got up enough nerve to tell my mother, but of course she didn't believe him and she threatened to report him to his superiors, but I quit anyway because I felt sorry for him the way my mother was cursing him and intimidating him."

She paused for breath, and, seeing the way my face must have looked—quizzical, surprised, yet smiling with delight withal—she blushed, her superwhite skin pinkening. Then, apologetically, she said, "You asked me to talk. You asked me to."

"Yes," I said. "Please go on."

She gave me a skeptical look, shrugged, and went on. "When I was nine, I almost caused the death of little Karl Schnitzer, a boy at school whose great-grandfather had been Austrian and therefore made it seem likely to me that Karl was a Nazi, and that was '44, the hottest part of the war, and I knew Karl's father had a plaster statue of the German eagle down in the basement of his grocery store, which proved they were Nazis and convinced me that Karl should die, just in time to keep him from growing up and becoming another Goebbels. I thought it should be a school project in which everybody participated, but I wasn't very popular myself and didn't have enough leadership qualities to talk anybody else into it, although I tried, so I had to do it all by myself: I caught him after school one day and dragged him off into a vacant lot and tied him up and set fire to him with a bunch of newspapers, but when he started burning he started crying, so I put him out, flagellating him with my coat, and he was all right, only a few slight burns, red places on his face and hands, but all I can remember of Karl to this day is the way his clothes—his corduroy knickers and his wool mackinaw—stank as they singed. When I was ten, my mother determined that my 'spiritual growth,' as she put it, was not all it might have been, and she forced me into a strict regimen of church participation, so that I had to attend everything that happened at the church—twice on Sunday, once on Tuesday, once on Wednesday night, once on Saturday afternoon, everything except the Monday night Men's Bible Class—for six solid months, until I was so fed up with the subject that I told my mother I was never going again, and if she made me go I would sit in the front row reading comic books, and if she came and took away the comic books I would stand on my head and if she spanked me I would scream and tear the hymnals and if she took me home I would run away and if she found me and brought me back I would lock myself up in my room, but I would never, no never, open the Bible ever again, and I never did, except once at junior college when I wrote an essay on "St. Paul as a Pink Poputchik" or fellow traveler. When I was eleven, my mother sent me away to live for a year with my aunt and uncle—her brother Hollis—in Bowling Green, Kentucky, and I liked it better than Little Rock and even made a couple of friends, which was bad in a way, because one night my father showed up and said he was going to take me off to New York and Uncle Hollis got in a fight with him, so Father said, okay, let's ask her what *she* wants to do, so he said to me, 'Margie, do you want to stay here with your Uncle Hollis or would you rather go to New York with me?' and because I had made some friends in Bowling Green and didn't want to give them up I said I would stay with Uncle Hollis, so my father went away without even kissing me good-bye and I never saw him again, he died in New York less than a year after that. So when I was twelve, my mother brought me back to Little Rock and I told her I was never going to speak to her again because of whatever she had done to my father, and I managed for at least three months not to say a word to her, and it broke her heart, and she was never quite the same afterward, and she has been taking it out on me ever since."

Margaret stopped again, hung her head, and lapsed into a silence which lasted until I put my hand on her arm and she looked up and, seeing the smile on my face, smiled herself, but weakly, and asked me if I wanted her to quit now or if I wanted her to keep babbling on like that. I told her she was at the age of twelve and had fifteen more years to go and I honestly wanted to hear about them.

"Clifford," she protested, "I'm being silly, talking like this."

"You haven't even started," I said, thinking: If experience on the stage can open one up like that, I ought to urge Pamela to join some theater group.

"Well," Margaret said, sighing. "When I was thirteen, I was lying face down on my bed reading a book one day—I remember it was *Tom Sawyer*, although the particular book didn't have anything to do with it—when all of a sudden for no reason at all I got a very tight feeling as if the hands of a giant were squeezing me, and then those same hands picked me up and held me in a kind of seismic seizure about a mile above the earth and then let me go, dropped me, and I was falling, falling, plunging down fast and free from that dizzy height, with nothing whatever below me to stop me, and although it scared the everlasting heck out of me I reflected that it had been a wonderful, a really thrilling sensation, and I discovered not long afterward that I could voluntarily make it happen . . . and it was all so grand that I began to worry if maybe there was something wrong with me, if maybe it was some kind of epilepsy even, or if maybe this was the way God had chosen to punish me, and I knew this thing, this phenomenon, never happened to anybody else, because you could tell it from their faces if it ever did, because once I watched my face in the mirror while it was happening and it looked like this, *look:* all warped and crooked, with the eyes all pinched and the nose cockled sideways and the mouth agog, astonished, so I began to be frightened, almost terrified, and I quit, I was even religious again for a while, but I quit that thing, I gave it up entirely, and when it happened by itself a couple of times later, I cried, I was so scared I prayed and cried, and eventually it never happened any more.

When I was fourteen, this girl friend of mine, Amanda Hadfield, maybe you remember her, the blowzy redhead who was always in trouble with Miss Dorland in the tenth grade, told me that she had experienced similar sensations herself, and she was even about to instruct me in the methods when I warned her that it was a form of punishment from God and that you would die after you had done it a dozen times, and Amanda quit too, she became even more alarmed about it than I had been, it drove her batty. When I was fifteen, my mother married again and I had a stepbrother and two stepsisters and not a one of them had the least bit of decency or modesty or chastity, and although all three of them were younger than I they were continually talking about things I couldn't understand, all I knew was that it was wicked and I should stay away from them, so I did. When I was sixteen, I never spoke a word to anybody, and I discovered how much I was being excluded from all the activities at high school, *all* of those things, remember them? the talent assemblies, the awards assemblies, the social clubs and all? When I was seventeen, I started having dates with one of the big shots at high school, a glib, fast, sharp little boxer called Nub Stone, and I liked him and he almost cracked me out of my shell and we had good times together and I probably felt closer to him than to anybody else except my lost father, because he was intelligent, but as it turned out he was wicked too, just as bad as all the rest. When I was eighteen, he gave me up. When I was nineteen, I decided that I didn't care about anything or anybody, that nothing mattered, that there was nothing I was good for, that since my striving would only turn out an embarrassing failure I would not bother to strive at all, adopting as my motto the first two lines of one of Landor's cornball quatrains: 'I strove with none, for none was worth my strife. Nature I loved, and next to nature Art,' but ignoring the last two less cornball lines of that same quatrain until, after those next eight years of the most unstriving sort of existence you could imagine, I was ready at last to add them: 'I warmed both hands before the fire of life; it sinks, and I am ready to depart.' Of course I kept on making errors and mistakes and committing little crimes and stupidities, and I cared too little, and wanted nothing. It was the last, the most recent, of my errors which was my undoing. When I was twenty-seven, which I am, that is: once upon a time, two months ago, I was doing my things at that self-service laundromat on West Seventh Street, and when I took everything out of the dryer and went home I discovered that I had six pairs of white cotton panties with a name label sewed into each: Sister Mary Dolores. I might have folded them neatly and taken them to the diocesan office or even mailed them in, or even given them to the priest who lived two doors down the street, but I didn't. They were my size, so I wore them. I still wear them, and as a matter of fact I've got on a pair right now and I'd show them to you if you didn't believe me, but I guess you believe me because it really isn't very incredible at all, but anyway I'm ashamed of myself. Wouldn't you be? I mean, *after all*, anybody who would walk around all over God's earth wearing a pair of nun's panties . . . it's just the kind of thing that is a good reason for wanting to jump off a bridge or something . . . because, well, because I—"

"Margaret," I said. I said Margaret because it had two syllables and she had run out of breath two syllables too short of finishing the poem, two notes too soon before the end of this aria, this elegiac, dirgeful tune.

Then she unwound herself from that frenetic pitch, she tamed her eyes and her tongue, she sighed. It had been her best performance. For all I knew, it had been her *only* performance. Whatever it had been, it was what I wanted, what I had asked for. She had talked to me. Now she looked at the clock and said it was late.

She walked with me across the street and down the cobblestoned drive to the train station. Where is your suitcase? she asked. I told her I had already checked it in.

We walked out onto the elevated platform above the track level. I discovered that we were holding hands. Men were loading baggage onto the train, but it would not leave for a while yet; I wanted to hang on to Margaret until the last minute. We leaned against the railing and looked out across the tracks, and the lights along Cantrell Road, and the sky above the river. Dark and still was the view; darker and stiller were my feelings. We said nothing to each other. I thought again, for a long while, of why I had come home, and why I was leaving. Then abruptly I realized how much the town and this girl had always been bound up together in my mind, even if subconsciously, but consciously too sometimes: how when I thought of Little Rock, I thought of her; when I thought of her, I thought of Little Rock. Is that, really, why I came home? Is she really, though I have not known it, precisely what I was looking for?

Down below us an aged Negro in a conductor's uniform was baying *Board!* at the empty station, his hoarse voice the only sound in all that silence.

"They're calling you," Margaret mused.

"Ma'am," I said to her, smiling, "I ain't gettin on no train."

🌿 FIFTEEN

For hours we walked, talking, excited, making a fuss over each other. Down dark sidewalks, through tunnels of crepe myrtle and flowery abelia and the ubiquitous honeysuckle, tripping over our tongues, we rushed to get it all said. I wondered when, and if, she was going to ask me if I were married yet, because I wasn't going to tell her if she didn't ask me. We talked mostly about her.

Why was this strange girl, so bright and fair, unwed? Hadn't *any*body proposed? I couldn't ask these questions of her, but gradually I gathered a general notion of the direction her life had taken in the years since I had known her: all the few fellows who had known her (or known *of* her, because she never had a really close friend) in high school or junior college had long since either married or gone away (I had done both); she would not attend church socials to meet the few prim bachelors still available, dried-up pious finks who crooked their little fingers when holding teacups and got cookie crumbs on their chins; and her succession of petty jobs exposed her to hardly any eligible males except occasional loud swaggering louts, salesmen and minor executives and such, all of them self-appointed Lotharios who wanted to see if that detached, reserved loveliness of hers masked a passionate rutty fire, but who were unwilling to be patient or gentlemanly or even nice about it; or else the already-married and frustrated bucks who saw in her a chance for quick illicit congress and made no attempt to conceal the ugly baseness of their motives; or else the shy and withdrawn idealists in whom she sensed kindred spirits but was not ever able to find out, for the simple reason that apparently these timid souls took it for granted that a pretty girl like her was already spoken for, was already taken, was already out of their league and thus it would be presumptuous of them to approach her even if they had the nerve for approaching anybody. This was her prime failing: that no one knew her or could know her, because if the face, the bearing, the visage was all they had to go on they would learn nothing and make all kinds of misconceptions or distortions, and if they went beyond the surface it was because their interest had nothing to do with anything outside a half-foot radius of her crotch anyway, and their inguinal obsessions got them nowhere, and got her even lesswhere, if that were possible.

She had, up until recently, sold shoes at Alexander's, a cut-price footwear emporium on Lower Main, but she had become progressively disenchanted with the work of dragging out box after box for the rejection of capricious and indecisive ladies who didn't really want to buy anything anyway but just wanted a place to sit down and somebody to stroke their sweaty feet until the next bus came. The foot is a phallus, Margaret knew; she had read all about it: the foot, an appendage, is dependent, it slips into the shoe, it is a frank substitute for the missing penis that women never had but always wanted. This is why almost all shoe salesmen are men. Margaret got all the lesbians. They oohed and they ahhed and they groaned when she slipped a shoe on their foot. They loved it. It made her sick. One day a fat customer rubbed her the wrong way, and she got angry and said to the customer, "Kiss my foot!" and Mr. Turner, the manager, who liked her, did not fire her but kicked her upstairs into the stock department, where she languished for the duration of her employ, which terminated not long afterward when she told Mr. Turner she couldn't stand the sight of another shoe, thereby putting her foot in her mouth, as far as he was concerned. But her ultimate unemployment came not because of her incompetence or even the discouragement which had created that incompetence but because of the defeat, the frustration which had created that discouragement: she was thoroughly convinced that she was good for nothing, and it was at this point that her depression took a turn for the worse.

But she didn't feel like talking about it, that period of dark depression. She tried to shift the conversation to me, she said she wanted to know about me, what I was doing now, and so forth. She was all right now, she said; she was happy again, and if I would stay in Little Rock, she would be even happier yet. We could go places together, do things, see things that she had never been able to see alone.

We had stopped now, resting, sitting together on an old carriage stoop beside the sidewalk in a seedy residential area. I couldn't see her face; some light from the street lamp filtered through the boughs of a giant catalpa overhanging us, but not enough. Her voice sufficed, I guess, it availed my need to remember all the times I had thought of her in the years between, all the times I had not been able to bury the image of what once she had been to me.

I could not talk to her about myself—not yet, at least. But as a substitute I could let her know why I had not caught that train, and I did. "I guess," I said, taking one of her hands again suddenly, "I guess I've really never forgotten you—I haven't been able to. All these years I guess I've still been meeting you in dreams and idle moments—you've been my own private succubus."

She laughed, and, my perfect counterpart, replied, "Then you've been my own private incubus."

Two of a kind, we kissed.

Disengaging, she somewhat breathlessly asked me, "Would you like to go up to my room?"

"Your room?" I said. "Sure. Where is it?"

She turned and gestured behind her. "Here," she said. I looked up and saw the large and dark old house behind the trees.

"Hey!" I said, surprised. "That's your same old house, isn't it?" She nodded. I asked, "Do you mean you *still* live here?" She nodded again. "Well, I'll be damned," I said, thinking again of her mother, a bloated old scatterbrained ex-waitress who had domineered the poor girl and made my rare visits to this house miserable and embarrassing. "Your mother—?" I wondered aloud, my chest pounding.

"My room is all by itself, way up in the attic, and we could tiptoe up the back stairs. I think I've got half a pint of brandy hidden up there, if you like brandy."

"Great," I said, standing up and appraising again the big old house. This house, on Victory Street not five blocks away from the train station, was the same house I had always associated with her in my mind because except for a year in Bowling Green she had lived there all her life. Its present impoverishment was exaggerated by its size: twelve or more wide, high-ceilinged rooms put together in the Reconstruction era into an Arkansas version of Romantic Gothic architecture: balustraded porches and verandas, bracketed and gingerbreaded, crocketed and finialed, fretted and beetled, with a small mansard roof drooping above a desultory nest of gables capping a maze of L-shaped masses of room. Once it had all been bright yellow, I suppose, but had not been repainted during Margaret's liftetime, so that, lurking behind these two outsize catalpas, surrounded by a chaotic privet hedge, and ensnared forever by a profuse web of wisteria and ivy, it might have served as a model of Southern decadence were it not totally lacking in sobriety; a ludicrous, gauche, tawdry old monster which made me smile just to look at it. But now the neighborhood was all seedy and run-down, like this house. Low, squat brindle-bricked business buildings were cropping up all over, and many of the other old houses had been torn down. Nearby were several newly cleared lots with those ubiquitous "Who's Happy?" signs planted in them.

Creeping up the driveway toward the rear of the house with Margaret, I quietly asked her, "Why do you still live here?"

But she wouldn't answer. I had to ask her again, insistently. "Can't you ever get away from your mother? Why do you want to stay here at home?" Still she would not answer. I continued to pester her about it, and she hushed me.

"Oh, Clifford," she paused to say, tiredly, before opening the back door. "I just take what I can get, that's all. I tried to move into a place of my own once, but it didn't work. I live here because it's a place to live." She touched my lips with her fingers. "Now be very quiet," she said. Then she opened the door.

I am an expert at soundless stealth, and so, I discovered, was she. The only sound, as we pussyfooted up the steep rear stairway, was our gentle breathing. It is difficult for me to understand how anybody could have heard us. But somebody did.

As we were rounding the turning of the stairs at the second floor, a hall light flashed suddenly on, and there, emerging from a bedroom, was an enormous ogress, spectral in a floor-length nightie and her hair all up in curlers, swiftly approaching. Unable to sink through the floor, I could only stand and hold my breath and tremble.

"Margaret, *what* on *earth!*" she boomed in a shrill flighty voice that I well remembered. She outweighed me by a good fifty pounds. One of her large forefingers shot out and touched the tip of my nose. "And *who* is *this?*" she demanded.

"This is Clifford, Mother. Don't you remember Clifford Stone?" Margaret's voice was calm, but her face—good Lord, her face wore an expression unlike any I had ever been before: a mingling of fear and loathing such as one might see on the face of a convict confronting the jailer.

The woman glanced down at me with a thoroughly contemptuous expression, removed her finger from my nose, and returned to her daughter. "Do *you* know what *time* it is? *Do* you? A *quarter* past *three!* Who *gave* you *permission* to go *out?* And *where* have you *been?*"

"I went to the movies," Margaret said in a small, cowed voice.

"*Alone?* Did *you* go *out* all by yourself a*gain?*"

"No. Clifford took me."

The woman glanced at me, and I nodded my head. Then she said to Margaret, "We've been looking *all! over! town!* for you. *Dall* and the *police* and *every*body! I just *don't* know *what* to *think* of you. And *now! Now* what do you *think* you're *doing*, child? Bringing this . . . *this* . . . this *man* into the *house.* Do you *think* you're going to make a *doll* out of *him* and take him to *bed* with your *other* dolls?"

"Mother—" Margaret said.

"*Enough!*" She pointed her finger down the stairs from whence we came. "*Out!*" she said to me.

I glanced at Margaret for confirmation of this command, and she nodded her head resignedly, then she suddenly put her arms around me and, there in front of her mother, gave me a long kiss. Then she whispered in my ear, "Call me tomorrow, please."

I nodded. She released me. Her mother took her by the arm and led her away. I went on back down the stairs.

Half an hour later, sneaking into my father's house, I suddenly realized that my suitcase was probably halfway to St. Louis or beyond. When is the next train? I wondered.

🐾 SIXTEEN

Wednesday morning, after a fitful and dreamful sleep wherein a tangled skein of old images played one upon another as though a cedar box of family snapshots were upset and jumbled into an omnium-gatherum of queer but familiar arms and ears and noses, I woke up shortly before noon and discovered that I was, oddly enough, filled with cheer and zeal. I had a mission now, I realized, I had a duty, a function: to help this girl. The Fates had destined me, had lured me to Little Rock, had appointed me this poor girl's rescuer. Jumping out of bed, I faced the day with a smile. Sybil gave me a big fine brunch, and then announced that she had changed her mind: she was so glad that I hadn't really left town after all, she said, that I could have her now if I wanted her. I thought about it. At length, impressed with the loyal celibacy Margaret had left imbedded in my usually fiery groin, I turned her down. Then I called Margaret immediately. Her mother answered. I did not identify myself but asked for Margaret. Her mother said that Margaret had gone to rehearsals. I asked her when Margaret would be back She couldn't—or wouldn't—say. I asked her to tell me where Margaret was rehearsing, but she claimed she didn't know. I asked her why she had kept Margaret at home all these years, and she hung up on me.

Then I called the Missouri Pacific baggage agent, to inquire if my suitcase might be retrieved. It might, he said.

Then for a couple of hours I moped, pondered, and plotted. Finally I decided to go find Dall and have a talk with him. Perhaps he could help me help her. Or, if he was already trying to help her, perhaps I could help him help her. At any rate, I wanted to see him again. Whatever my reasons had been for avoiding him during my previous visits to Little Rock, I had a good reason now for cultivating him again. My watch said a quarter past three; I would get right on down there; from the phone book I learned that the police headquarters had been moved a block westward on Markham Street.

But first I had a short letter to post. Borrowing a begrudged sheet of lined paper from Sybil's Cary Grant letter pad, I sat down to write. The day was becoming sweltering; seemingly the temperature, like an oven preheated for a frozen pot pie, had risen steadily from the moment I first stepped off the train and now it was insufferably close to that of the human body's natural degree. Globules of sweat congregated in the fringes of all my hairy places and, congregating, became heavy and fell, trickled, lathered me. In parody of that ubiquitous john-wall ditty which admonishes "No matter how much you shake your peg the last few drops go down your leg" I conceived an apt analogue for this occasion: "No matter how much you stir the breeze the last few drops get to your knees." Blotting them up somewhat by tapping the baggy knees of my seersucker trousers, I recomposed my mind for the work at hand, and worked fast: "Darling Pamela, Your letter received and dully noted. Bermuda sounds nice, but the fact of the matter is I'm frightfully indisposed. Things are a bit hot here, and getting hotter. Get me? Anyway, my schedule is packed for the next two weeks, at the inside, and beyond then I cannot honestly foresee. If you should become too bored or restless in the meantime, let me suggest that you join some local little theater group. Experience on the stage, I have learned, can have several rewarding effects—particularly for taciturn females. Ta ta, Clifford."

I didn't even use an air-mail stamp.

SEVENTEEN

After posting the letter at the corner mailbox, I took a bus down to the new police headquarters, a low, long, austerely modern edifice, where I learned that Dall was out on a call and would be back shortly. I sat down on a bench to wait. Sitting there I tried to pre-formulate what I would say to him, what I would ask him. I could not recall a single occasion when we had discussed anything more serious or intellectual than the relative merits of spinners and flies in the capturing of sunperch and bream. Our long and abiding friendship had been based almost entirely on a nearly maniacal love of physical sport and contact, through which our habitual greeting to each other was not a weak "Hiya!" nor a formal handshake, but instead a playful pummeling, with fists and elbows and the butting of heads and shoulders, until one or the other of us cried uncle.

Now he was coming down the hallway, followed by a couple of his patrolmen, and he was beautiful. His light-gray epauleted short-sleeved shirt bore its gold badge and purple chevrons like magic heraldry ensigning his new power among men. From a heavy bullet-studded belt hung low around the hips of his dark-blue trousers he harnessed a formidable black-sheathed service revolver, whose demeanor suggested he knew how to use it, and had. Love of beer and spaghetti had made him a little less lean and lanky, but the face beneath the crushed-crown white cap was the same old Dall: the green lynx eyes below two heavy brown hedgerow brows growing toward each other in the center above the steep cliff of a craggy nose, the wide, colorless mouth which even immobile seems to mutter "crud," the cudgel jaw cleft neatly by a dimple in the center of the chin. A gorgeously ugly old boy.

I always wanted to slug a cop. All men, resentful of authority, have this yen; but few ever discharge it. I did.

Rising from my bench to meet him, I caused him to halt and to study my face for the rapid moment necessary for recognition. Then, in the instant that his hard features softened at the sight of me, I let him have it, a swift short-arm smash to the pit of his muscle-bound gut. Then I stepped back, ready to parry his counter-blows.

The ceiling descended. The floor ascended. Factory whistles celebrated New Year's, and wedding bells tolled; for a while asteroids, meteors, and other luminaries flashed and flickered in the dark sky, but then even those were extinguished, and all was completely black and still.

Much later, dawn came up out of the east accompanied by a waterfall, a roaring Niagara over which I had plunged, under which I was left spluttering. The light of that dawn revealed, hanging in the sky, a giant arm, the hand of which held an enormous Dixie cup upended, dripping the last drops of the cascade. So terrible was the spectacle that night returned for a while more, and then, when the timid dawn tried again, that same Brobdingnagian hand was slapping both of my cheeks in rapid, jolting succession.

It was the old familiar voice, calling to me out of the lost past, which restored me, brought me back to life. "Nub? Hey, Nub? You all right?" I tried to come out of it, but every time I neared the surface, that flat palm would smash against the side of my face a couple of times and sink me under again. "Nub?" Bang, smack. "Say something, boy." Smack, bang. "Come on, snap out of it." Bang smack, smack bang.

I gasped enough breath to say, "Goddammit, you dumb prick, quit slapping me and maybe I can get up."

He laughed. I raised my head, gyrating it achingly on my neck, and saw that I was sitting in a chair against the wall of a little room. The floor was rocking, and I thought we were on board ship, but through the window I could see the Health Center across the street, which was rocking too. "Please remain seated while the room is in motion," I said drunkenly, then groaned loudly several times and asked, "What happened?"

He pulled a chair up in front of me, and sat down backward on it. "Jack hit you with his billy," he said, "then Curly got a double-nelson on you and threw you to the floor. They didn't know you from Adam, and I had one hell of a time trying to tell em who you was." He doubled his fists and made a few swinging motions at me and said, "But we're alone now. You want to mix it up?"

"No, thanks," I moaned, and mopped my brow. "Could I have a glass of water?"

"You just did," he grinned, and pointed to the front of my shirt, which was soaked. "But I'll get you one to drink, if that's what you want." And he left the room.

I always do the wrong thing. Leave it to me to botch up something so simple as a pleasant greeting. My good intentions always, *always* backfire.

He returned with another Dixie cup and a handful of paper towels. While I drank the water he wiped my wet hair and face and tried to mop up some of the water on my coat and shirt. Then he rubbed the back of my neck vigorously and pointed to the empty opposite corner of the room and said, "Okay, kid. Round two. Get in there and murder that sonofabitch!" So conditioned had I been to the sound of those words that I immediately rose groggily to my feet. He laughed, and the absurdity of my Pavlovian behavior dawned on me at the same instant that my head reeled in the sickening aftereffect of its ordeal. My legs gave way and I spun around as I fell, but he caught me and hugged me to him. We remained there thus, clenched in each other's arms, for a long moment.

"You old half-assed bastard," he said.

"You old rattleboned beanstalk," I said.

"You dinky little stinking turd," he said.

My eyes moistened in solemn rapture. "You worthless old egg-sucking polecat."

His voice choked with emotion, he replied, "You runty shit-eating dog." Then he held me off at arm's length and looked at me. "Where you been for the last goddamn two hundred years, anyway?"

Then we sat down and I brought him up to date. He had difficulty understanding why I remained married to Pamela, after all the complaints I had once written to him about her. He also wanted to know why I had stopped writing him, and why I hadn't been by to see him the last couple of times I had visited Little Rock. I said the pressure of my work was the reason behind both shortcomings, but I hoped to make it up to him now. He said I seemed to have grown a bit since he saw me last. I told him I was rich enough now to buy elevator shoes. Then I expressed surprise that he had got himself promoted to sergeant, and I said I wondered how a dumb yokel like him could have accomplished it.

His eyes narrowed at me and he said, "Listen, buster, I like to of got myself killed more times than you ever jacked off."

"Yeah, I read the papers," I said, hinting at the appearance of his picture in Sunday's *Gazette*. "No kidding, how long've you been wearing those stripes?"

"Nigh on to five years, buddy," he said. "If you read the papers, do you ever recall seeing something about a little trouble we had a few years back when they started stickin the niggers into the schools?"

"Certainly," I said, but flinching at the sound of his use of that word. For years I was properly careful to say nigro, until Pamela pointed out to me that it is nee-gro and should always be capitalized.

"Okay, then," he said. "Maybe you read about the second battle, not that first one in '57 when the whole mess started, but the next one, in '59, when a bunch of rednecks took a notion to see if they couldn't put something over on us cops."

"I think I read about that one, too," I said. "Wasn't that the one where the police got sued afterward by a bunch of innocent bystanders?"

"Yeah, only they wasn't *all* so innocent as you say. There was a bunch of real mean bastards in that mob. We call it the Battle of Fourteenth and Schiller because that's the intersection where we stopped em. There was about three hundred of em comin up Fourteenth Street, headin for the high school, looked like a goddamn parade with flags and all, and there wasn't but about two dozen of us out there with the Chief. The Chief stopped em and looked em right in the eye and he said, 'We're not going to stand for any foolishness.' But they yelled 'Nigger lover!' and 'Get the Chief!' and then three of the biggest guys rushed toward him, with the whole damn mob backin em up. I got the first one and smeared him, and the Chief got the second one; and then the third guy, a mother-fuckin elephant must of weighed over three hundred pounds, he come rushin at us, and I tried that trick you showed me once where you slam your knee into his balls to double him and then clip him on the back of the neck, and that old boy went down so hard there's still a dent in the asphalt out there, and by that time the other men had turned the rest of the tough ones back and we had the fire hoses goin on em. Next day the Chief give me these stripes."

"Did that experience improve your attitude toward the Negroes?" I asked, careful to give it a long *e*.

"Hell," he said and glowered at me. "One thing you Boston carpetbaggers aint never got straight yet is that we was just doin what we was told to do and not cause we wanted to. The only thing kept me from being on the other side was this here uniform on my back."

"All right," I said, palms outward. "You would've made as good a redneck as any of those other racists or rabble-rousers."

"You damn right," he said.

"All right," I said, wondering why a level-headed and usually compassionate fellow like Dall could have fallen victim to racist feelings. Then I asked, "Dall, you old flat-headed flatfoot, what you aim to do with yourself by and by?"

"Boy, I'm gonna make chief one of these days, you wait and see. Come September I'm eligible for lieutenant, and then, by God, you watch my dust."

"That's your ambition, is it, to be Lord of the Fuzz?"

"You just wait."

"Then if I get a ticket for jaywalking, you'll fix it for me, huh?"

"Any old time." He winked.

"That's good, because I've been thinking about moving back to this town."

"*No shit?*" His bushy eyebrows arched capward.

"I've been thinking about it," I said noncommittally. Then I told him of the yearning I'd had, that same paralysis of the intellect which chronically corrupts all the wandered sons of that town and makes them keep coming home, sometimes to stay, long after they have no further use for it. I did not tell him of my memory of oak-leafed tunnels down summer night streets, or of the fragrance of shortleaf pine and sweetgum on winter mornings, or of the baking of bread, or of the October winds and June clouds and the grass now of April. Instead I mentioned such things as going fishing or sitting on the front porch in one's undershirt with a beer after supper in summer, or watching the Razorback football games. These are the things that may be mentioned between us, man to man. The others, the magnetic baits hidden deep in that dull city which draw us recurrently to it, are unutterably vague and unfathomable; it is useless to talk about them. Dall, having never left home, would have no conception of their poignant, piquant sway anyway.

"It's a right nice old town," he agreed, his eyes glued vacuously to some blank block of stone in the building across the street, and there followed a long silence, a lull, without any specific meaning, in the course of our talk. Somebody once told me that when a conversation lags, the time magically always is either twenty minutes past the hour, or twenty till it. I looked at my watch. It said four-forty.

A minute passed, and then I asked, "How's your wife, Dall?"

"Yeah," he said.

"Well?" I said. "How's the wife and kids?"

He was still gazing out the window. "Aint got no wife," he said. Then he swung his head to face me; his eyes refocused fiercely on me and suggested the scrutiny of a vicious cop about to administer the third degree to a hapless suspect. "Yeah, Nub, I aint got no wife nor kids no more."

"Well?" I waited politely. Had they been in a car wreck or something?

"I've a mind not to tell you about it, but you'd worm it out of me sometime, wouldn't you?"

"I just might," I said, returning his fierce glare.

"That's what I mean, you snoopin little creep." His tone was not entirely hostile. "Okay, it was like this. You know she was a skittish gal, one of them Newton County jobs come from up toward Jasper, flighty as a humminbird, anyway she told me once she'd leave me if I ever hit her, and I sure had never hit her before nor even acted like I would, but I did then, just to see if she was givin me a bunch of junk, you know, just a light little smack, you wouldn't never of felt it, and sure enough, she up and lit out for home with the two kids and I aint seen her since, last I heard tell she'd taken up with some bricklayer up around Jasper, you got any more questions?"

I shook my head. We looked each other over for a while, both of us obviously trying to think of a better subject to talk about. It was still too soon, I felt, to mention Margaret. One of the other cops, the one he called Curly, stuck his head in the door and said, "Sergeant, there's a call for you out here," and Dall left me for a while.

When he returned, I asked politely, "Am I keeping you from anything important?"

"Naw, it's pretty slow this time of day, unless there's a bad wreck somewheres or somethin. Make yourself at home."

I shifted my weight in the chair. "Well, Dall—" I said.

"What about *your* wife?" he asked. "Did she come with you?" I shook my head. "Good," he said. "Me and you are both bachelors again, huh? We can have us a few good old times." I said that would suit me fine.

He was stuffing a pipe with tobacco. I suppose I had expected he would chew Day's Work or roll himself a cigarette with Bull Durham or chomp on a fat King Edward, but then he stuck the pipe into his mouth and began lighting it, and I saw how well it seemed to fit his scraggy mountaineer's face. I waited until he had his furnace puffing, and then without further ado I bluntly said to him, "Tell me about Margaret Austin."

"Who?" he said and made several rapid puffs—too rapid—on his pipe. "Oh," he said. "That old girl you used to run around with back in the old days. Yeah. Sort of a black-haired girl with a nice figure, but kind of a wallflower. Yeah, I remember old Marge. What about her?"

"*You* tell *me*," I said, giving him my old Stoney squint which, he damn well knew, meant: Come on, let's not beat around the bush.

"Me?" he said. "Why, son—"

"Let's start with the Slater play," I suggested. "You advised her, for some reason, that she ought to—"

The chair he was leaning back in snapped abruptly forward. "God*damn*," he said, peering at me up close. "I should of knowed. You aint been home two days yet and already you got them big ears tuned in on everything in town. Most likely you know so much already, maybe you should tell *me*."

"I don't know anything but what she told me, and that wasn't much."

"You *seen* her?"

"Yes."

"When?"

"Last night. I met her at a movie."

His mouth fell open. Then he closed it and spoke: "Oh. It was *you*, then. I'll be." I gave him a puzzled expression, and he explained. "I had two or three of the boys out lookin for her most of the night. That crazy, screwed-up old—" he became red in the face, his neck muscles bulging; it took him a moment to get himself under control "—mother of hers, that . . . that *bat*, she wore herself plum near to death worrying about Margaret, and then she just called me a minute ago—matter of fact, that was her talkin to me on the phone just then—and she told me what happened. She said some man picked up Marge and brought her home and was fixin to take her upstairs to rape her or somethin, when she—the mother—come along just in time and run him off. So it was you, huh?" He paused, grinning and eying me narrowly. "Now of course I long since learned not to put no stock by what her mother says, so I figgered whoever it was didn't really aim to rape her or nothing noways. But you might just tell me what you did happen to have in mind."

I told him that I had had nothing particular in mind, but that I was escorting Margaret up to her room. Then I began at the beginning and told him exactly what had happened. He listened attentively—I had the feeling that his mind was taking down meticulous notes. When I finished he began nodding his head.

"Now," I said, "perhaps you can explain to me why it was necessary for you to delegate two or three of your patrolmen to hunt for her. Is she on parole or something?"

"Well, Nub," Dall said, smacking ruminatively on the stem of his pipe, "I'll tell you how it come about that I got mixed up in this thing, and then maybe me and you can string along together on this business." He leaned back in his chair again, closed his eyes for a brief moment, and passed his hands a few times up over his brow and hair.

"It was back in March," he began. "Early March. I was settin out on my front porch—I got a little place out on West Fourth—and I was settin out on the porch late one Friday night, after midnight, just settin there because Friday is my night off, and it was the first real good night of spring, with the weather purt near warm and all. Well, anyway, I'm just settin there in the dark, see, and I'm kind of down in the dumps, frettin about them little boys of mine that their feisty no-good momma took off with her, and I happen to look up, when here comes this girl walkin down the street, all by herself pretty as you please, like it was broad daylight and she was aimin to grocery-shop or somethin. Well sir, she stops at the corner and looks up the street and down the street, and then she heads on across, but halfway to the other curb she stops and turns around and goes back to the corner and turns down the other street but she don't go very far that way neither before she turns around once more and comes back to the corner and then she just stands there like she's bad lost. She aint even totin a purse or a pocketbook, so right off I figger she left it behind at a party, or she's drunk maybe, or she run off from some itchy-fingered boy friend that was tryin to mess around with her or somethin. Anyway, she looks like she could use some help or leastways some advice on street directions, so I get up out of my chair and walk down to the sidewalk and I says, 'Pardon me, lady, but could I do anything for you?'

"And she turns around all wild-eyed and lookin like she was fixin to holler, and right off I recognize her, but she's so skeered she don't know me, or maybe cause she aint seen me for ten years she's forgot who I am, and she tells me not to touch her or she will scream for the police, and I caint say as how I blame her, me bein so ugly and skeery-lookin, you know, but I tell her not to worry about that none, cause I'm the police myself, but I don't have on no uniform so I reckon she don't believe me, but I says to her, 'Margaret, I'm old Dall Hawkins, don'tcha member me?' but that don't cut no ice with her neither, cause she never knew me very well back in high school and maybe figgered that I was just as likely to molest her as the next feller. 'Honest to God,' I says to her, 'I'm a sure-enough policeman, only this is my night off so I aint wearin my uniform.' She calms down a little, and I says, 'Honey, it's nigh on to one o'clock. What're you doin out so late all by yourself?' But she don't answer. I says, 'You look like you're kind of lost. If you'd just tell me where you was aimin to head for, maybe I could tell you how to get there.' Still she don't say nuthin. 'Is somebody after you?' I ask her. She shakes her head. 'Where's your pocketbook?' I ask her, and she looks down at her hand like she was lookin for it. 'Did somebody rob you?' I ask her. She shakes her head. 'You been in a fight with your boy friend?' I ask her. She keeps on shakin her head. I don't know what to make of her. I've seen ever damn whore and streetwalker in Little Rock at one time or another, so I know for sure she aint one of them, she's way too pretty for one thing, and I knew old Marge wasn't that type noway. So I don't know what to make of her.

"Then I think she begins to recognize me at last, cause she kind of loosens up and says, 'Weren't you a good friend of Clifford Stone's?' and I smile real big and says 'That's right, Marge. That's me all right. Me and Nub was thick as thieves.' And by God, we just stand there for five or ten minutes talkin about you, like we just met at a party or somewheres and was just makin chit-chat about old friends, just as pleasant and all. I tell her what all I know about you, which aint much, how you live in Boston now and married to some society girl and—"

I interrupted: "You told her I was married?"

"Yeah, but also I mentioned how you'd wrote me a couple of letters once sayin what a raw deal you got with that wife of yours, and how you kept gittin lonesome for Arkansas and all. Remember? Well, anyway, me and Margaret are just standin there beside that light-pole passin the time and I near bout forget what it was I came out to ask her or do for her. After a while she says, 'Well, it was good to see you again, Doyle,' and I says, 'Yeah, take care of yourself, Marge,' and she goes on down the street. But she aint gone thirty feet when it suddenly hits me again what in tarnation she is doin and where in tarnation she thinks she's goin, so I holler after her, 'Hey, wait just a dadburn minute!' and I catch up with her and I says, 'You still aint told me what you're doin out this time of night.'

"Now I reckon if she'd said it wasn't none of my business, I'd of just had to let her go, but she starts to give me some cock-and-bull story about how she has to go out to Allsopp Park to try and catch some goddamn luna moth to add to her bug collection, and I know right off the bat that the only bug collection she's got is up in her head, so I get right suspicious, and I says to her, 'Allsopp Park is a long ways off from here, and looks to me like you're so lost already you aint never gonna get there.' Then she just looks at me and says, 'Show me the way.' I tell her I caint even draw her a map, it's so far off and out of the way, but if she really has to go out there and get her a goddamn luna moth I'll put her in my goddamn car and drive her out there, for godsakes, but for her not to try and set out on foot.

"Then she commences walkin on down the street, like she's afeared I might really put her in my car. Well, I just walk along with her, and we just keep on walkin, and she turns at the corner and I see she aint even headin in the direction of Allsopp Park, but anyway we just keep on walkin, and when she turns at another corner, I turn with her. 'Nice night, aint it?' I says and she says yes it is, and we just keep on keepin on walkin, she don't say I can but she don't say I caint, and I don't mind a little exercise now and then. Well, by and by we come to the state capitol grounds, I guess she's just walkin with no particular place in mind, and we finally wind up out back of the Game and Fish Department building, where there's this big old pond out there, you know the one, where the kids and niggers fish at, and we set down on the grass at the edge of the water and we just stare at the water and talk a little bit. It's a awful dark night, but a few light-poles over on West Third kind of light up the water some, so I can just barely make out her face. I talk to her a little bit about the old high school days, cause I figger she'd like to do a little talkin, it would be good for her and all, you know. So we talk about this, that, and th'other. I even get her to laugh a little bit, but finally she says, 'I don't want to talk about those things. I hated high school and I don't even like to remember it.' So I quit.

"Right along about now we hear a noise and turn to look behind us and here comes one of the squad cars at full blast down the hill to the pond. It screeches to a stop and a cop jumps out and runs up to us and says, 'All right now, no screwin on the capitol grounds. This here's state property and no screwin around here or I'll run you in.' By his voice I know it's old Curly, but he don't recognize me in the dark. Now it just so happens that Curly is one of them hard-shell Baptists and except for a game of poker now and then he don't tolerate no sin of any kind. I can tell Margaret's pretty embarrassed about all this, and old Curly's just standin there like he was waitin for us to try to screw or somethin right in front of him, and then he says to me, 'Buster, what d'you think you're doin out here at three o'clock in the mornin with this here girl anyway?' and I don't say nuthin, so he says, 'Better let me have a look at your i.d. card,' and he holds out his hand, so I fish out my wallet and take out my police card and give it to him and he takes it over to hold it under the headlight of the squad car, and he studies it for a while, and then he near bout drops dead, and he comes back over and says in this squeaky little voice, 'Is that *you*, Sarge?' All I says is: 'Yeah.' He says, 'Well, gee, Sarge, I didn't know it was you, honest. I sure didn't mean to butt in on you or nuthin. God. I wouldn't never of butted in if I knowed it was you.' Pore Curly's so mortified he just keeps on runnin off at the mouth. 'Sarge,' he says, 'you just go and screw if you want to, I don't keer. Aint none of my business.' I caint help it, I bust out laughin, and Margaret she starts laughin too. Then old Curly gives me a salute and jumps back into the squad car and tears off out of there. After he's gone me and Margaret just keep on laughin, and we set back down on the grass again and look at the water again and she just keeps on laughin, like she had it stored up for years and aint had a good chance yet to let some of it out. After a while she quits laughin, and she says, 'You're a sergeant,' and then she laughs some more. By God, for some reason or other I aint felt so good in a long time, and I caint hardly wait to get back to the stationhouse to tell the boys what old Curly said.

"Then it gets real quiet. Me and her both aint laughin no more. We just look at the pond. A long time we just set like that and not say nuthin. I sort of almost forget about her and start in to frettin about my own problems again, and I reckon she's got her hands full frettin about her problems, whatever they are. Anyway, we just set there, and then a good bit later she ups and speaks in this sad little voice: '*Why have we come here to this water?*' And I say it after her, like it was what I was wonderin too: '*Why have we come here to this water?*' and I guess in that moment she figgers she's given herself away, let the cat out of the bag, because in that moment I suddenly get a pretty good notion of what she'd been aimin to do that night, of what she was lookin for: and that maybe what it was was a piece of water somewhere deep enough for her to drown herself in, and that she hadn't come out here to the Game and Fish Department pond completely by accident. So when she realizes that maybe I know what she's been up to, she makes this kind of sound in her throat, and I knew what the sound is: like a cry tryin to get out but caint, like a bawl caught in her throat and barkin to be let out—so I says to her, real quick, 'You led the way, Margaret, I was just afollerin you,' and then real quick I get out my handkerchief and poke it at her and she takes it and looks at it like she was studyin what to do with it, and then she knows, and she breaks down and commences weepin. And after a while I put my arm around her and she puts her face up against my chest and goes on weepin, and gets my shirt all wet, and I hold her. And she cries a long time, longer even than she had laughed, and then she gives it up, I guess she runs out of teardrops, and then she goes to sleep. For a long time we just set like that, with her sound asleep up against my chest. I reckon she aint slept so good for years. Of course my back gets to hurtin some, but I don't mind. No sir, I don't really mind at all.

"By and by it comes up dayspring, the sky lightin up in the east and that old pond turnin almost white. It looks like glass. Ever so often some old fish leaps up breakin the glass to get him a gnat or some other bug. My back don't give out, but I get kind of hungry. She don't show no sign of wakin up. I let her sleep for another hour or so, and then I whisper, 'Marge,' and I give her shoulder a little shake. She don't wake up. I see her now, how pretty and all she is, whereas I couldn't much tell in the dark. Even though I'm hungry and kind of sleepy myself, it makes me feel good settin there like that with a pretty girl sleepin with her head up against my chest, and my arm around her. 'Marge,' I says. 'Marge.'

"Far's I'm concerned she can sleep till three-thirty that afternoon if she wants to, which is when I have to be back on duty.

But soon she wakes up. She just moves away from my chest and stretches a bit and looks out at the pond for a while. Then all of a sudden she turns around and looks at me, like she just now knows where she is at. Then she smiles real big, but in a sleepy sort of way, and pats me on the side of my face. Then she stands up, and I stand up, and I walk her home.

"On the front porch of that old beat-up house of hers she says to me, 'You're a very conscientious policeman,' and I tell her I am glad to be of any assistance. Then I ask her if I could come over sometime and talk to her. The reason I ask her this is that I aim to do somethin for her, I mean, I aim to find out what her trouble is and see if I caint be of some real help. But before she has time to answer, that big fat momma of hers comes stormin out the front door mad as a wet hen and she grabs me and starts in to slappin me and sayin she's gonna call the police and have me electrocuted. And Margaret is standin there tryin to tell her mother that I'm the police myself and I aint done nuthin to her, and me, I'm just tryin to protect myself from gettin the shit slapped out of me by that crazy old woman. And Margaret is shoutin in her ear, 'He's Sergeant Hawkins of the Little Rock Police!' Then her mother stops bangin on me and says, '*Sergeant?*' Then she says, 'Then *where's* your *uniform?*' I tell her I'm off duty, but I don't think she believes me. She takes Margaret into the house and slams the door on me.

"I go on home, and take a nap for a couple of hours, and then I put on my uniform and my gun and all and go on back over there. But Mrs. Austin won't let Margaret come out again. I stand there and ask her a bunch of questions, like what all does she think seems to be botherin Margaret, but she says there's nothing wrong at all, for me *not* to *worry* about it, *thank* you *very* much, *good* day."

Dall stood up and stretched, his hands on the small of his back. "That woman," he said. "I swear . . . she . . . sometimes . . . it just—" He couldn't find the words.

"I know," I said. "I know exactly what you mean."

"Well," he said. "Anyway, I kept on goin back to that house ever day or so, and finally it got to where her mother would let her come out and talk to me, and first thing I asked her was how come she still stayed at home, but she just said somethin about it was 'force of habit' and she'd been doin it for so long, she'd been doin what her mother told her to do for so long that she didn't even think about it any more. Well, I guess you know the rest. One day we was just readin the paper together on her front porch, and she showed me this item about how those Little Rock Playmakers were lookin for people to work with em, and I told her she ought to join up, it would give her somethin to do, workin on costumes or scenery or stuff, and maybe she would make some friends and all, you know. Well, I had to argue with her a long time about it, because she was too bashful to try anything like that, but finally she said she'd do it just as a favor for me, so I even took her over there in the squad car one afternoon, and then about a week later she told me how Mr. Slater had asked her if she would care to read for this part in this play of his, and how when she read for it he was so pleased with her that he gave her the part. Seems there wasn't nobody else that was cut out for it. I was right proud of her and I told her I knew she could do it well."

I inquired if his interest in her was purely professional, that is, if he was only doing his duty as a policeman or whether he might have some personal interest in her.

He scowled, sat down again, and said that as far as romance was concerned he was plum fed up with women.

Then he asked me if my interest in her was pure too, or whether I might have some romantic interest in her.

I shrugged, and reminded him that I was a married man.

He guffawed at that.

Then I asked him if he thought she might be mentally unbalanced.

He said he didn't think so.

I asked him if he thought she was suicidal.

He said that he thought she had been, but that she didn't seem to be any more—although he had been worried last night when her mother reported her missing.

I asked him if he would have any objection if I continued to see Margaret and have dates with her.

None at all, he said. He said that if I could think of any way to get her permanently away from her mother, I would be rendering a great help and service. But, he added, as far as dates were concerned, he didn't know if I would have much luck, because Mr. Slater the playwright was taking up most of her social time.

"Mr. *Slater*?" I said. "You mean he's been *courting* her?"

Dall nodded.

"But he's old enough to be her father, isn't he?"

"Forty-nine, goin on fifty," Dall said, deadpan. "And that aint all. He's a married man too."

I was stricken. "Tell me more," I beseeched him.

But we were interrupted again by Curly, who stuck his head inside the door and said, "Sarge, we finally caught that Howard nigger for you. Caught him doin seventy on Roosevelt Road. We got him out here now."

"Well, well," Dall said, and his face was transformed: he sneered in an evil cat-after-mouse expression of gloating. Then he glanced at me, saw that I was watching his face, and said to Curly, "Just a second." Then he turned to me. "Looks like I got to get back to work. But listen, Nub, Friday's my night off, why don't you come over and have supper with me and we can talk some more about Margaret or take in a ball game or somethin, okay?"

"Sure," I said, but disappointed that I would have to wait that long—two more days—to find out more about Margaret and James Royal Slater.

"You like spaghetti?" he asked.

"Anything," I said.

"I'm a pretty good cook," he said. "Bet you didn't know that."

We stood up and I slammed a hard right into his ribs. "Nothing about you ever surprises me," I said genially.

He clouted me a good one on the shoulder. "Don't be so sure," he said.

Then he gave me his address and phone number and we said "See you Friday evening" to each other, and then I left.

🙚 EIGHTEEN

Passing through the anteroom, I gave Jack and Curly my nicest, most indulgent smile, pardoning the brutal error they had made. Both leered back at me with a couple of savage expressions suggesting they would like to do it all over again, but I suppose that is only what happens when policemen try to smile. I went on.

"Nub?"

Had one of them called? I paused, turned, looked first at Jack and then at Curly, but both were just as my eyes had left them a second before, grinning fiercely.

"Nub?"

Was it Dall, then? I turned further, but the door to his office was still closed, as I had left it.

Completing my full, bewildered circle, I saw that the only other person in the room was the Negro sitting on the bench. I looked at him. He was looking up at me, and all thirty-two of his ivories were gleaming in sharp relief against the exceedingly dark hue of his skin.

The tightly stretched lips snapped back into place, covered the teeth, formed a puckered vowel: "You Nub Stone?" Here was a face, dimly remembered from out of the past, without a name. Negro faces in general, and very dark ones in particular, are difficult for a white person to distinguish one from another. This face belonged to a person who, if he were dressed in silks and had a reins-ring in his hand, could pass for one of those waiting livery boys who lean forward on lawns in perpetual cast-iron, little as he was. My first thought of him was that I had liked him, had at one time enjoyed being with him so much because he was one of the few guys I had ever known in Little Rock who were smaller than I, and I will make no attempt to conceal this feeling, this fact that my spare stature had once been magnified by his sparrowness. But what *was* his name? The first time I had seen that face, that feral moon smudged more black than ash-buds in the front of March and smiling as broadly as it was now, was under a sprawling oak tree beside the caddyhouse of the Riverdale Country Club in the summer of my tenth year. Wanting a few dollars for a pair of boxing gloves, but having a penurious father who insisted that I earn my own money, I had gone to that golf course in hopes that it would be one place in the whole town where a ten-year-old might be employed. I was not overly disappointed when, arriving on my bicycle early one Saturday morning, I saw that all of the other caddies were darkies. Watching them for a while, I observed that their method of being hired was simply to sit under a large oak tree and wait until they were called. So I selected a neighboring, segregated oak and sat down beneath it, laying my bicycle on the ground. I waited a very long time. The other caddies cast a few curious glances at me from time to time, and, I imagined, made a few remarks. I might be sitting jobless under that oak tree yet, if it had not been for this same pitchy Negro, at that time a thread-bare pickaninny who couldn't have been more than eight or nine years old but was old enough to sense what had escaped all the others (even the white caddymaster, I later learned, had no idea what I was doing there), namely, that I wanted to caddy, for he said, poking his face close to mine and exposing all of those pearly grinders in the same grin I would see now, "You not just sittin here cause you likes the sunshine, is you?" I told him no, I wanted to caddy, and he asked me if I had ever toted bags before, and I told him no. "What you called?" he asked, and I told him Nub Stone. He extended his hand, and I clasped those long brown bony fingers, touching Negro flesh for the first time in my life, and he said, "Stick with me, white boy, you git took care of. Call me—" Call him what? *What*, dammit? . . . Something with an N . . . Nick? No. Nate? Nat? *Oh* . . . Nub? No, that's me. Nup? Nep? Nap? Nap . . . *Naps*.

"Naps!" I said and extended my hand.

He shook it vigorously and said, grinning wider than ever, "Thought for a moment you wouldn't remember it."

How could I forget it? He had taken me under his wing that day, introduced me to the caddymaster, a redneck bully who wondered why I wanted to work with them niggers but assured me there was no law against it, and Naps got me a couple of loops of the course as a Grade-C or neophyte caddy attached to a duffer playing a handicap game against a Scotchman for whom Naps caddied, so that we could remain close together and he could show me how to carry the bag and how to tell a mashie niblick from a putter, and how and where to stand when my man was driving or chipping or dinking, and how and when to pull the pin.

"What they got you in for?" he asked solicitously.

"Oh, I'm not in for anything," I replied. "Just been visiting an old friend of mine, the sergeant."

"That *Hawkins*? He your friend?"

Naps was well dressed, in a tasteful tropical suit, whose dark Prussian blue reflected the bluish accents of his complexion, and a yellow oxford shirt with striped tie. But that old day he had been wearing a pair of frequently patched blue jeans and a torn T-shirt and holesome tennis sneakers without socks; and after sunset, when the last golfer had gone, I offered him a ride home on my bike, and discovered to my great surprise and pleasure that he lived on the same street I did, Ringo, and had lived there, not two blocks away from me, all of his life, which was only ten months shorter than mine. And he rode behind me for the first mile home, and then he took over and I rode behind him for the second mile, and thus we reached our neighborhood and our houses in a spirit of teamwork and concert, a consort of equals which establishing our friendship on that day would preserve it for several years thereafter. So really he antedated Dall.

"Yes," I said.

"You got influence on him?"

"A little," I said and smiled, thinking of all the times I had bent Dall's flexible nature to suit my ends.

The one called Curly was standing beside us and said, "Nigger, who tole you you could get up from that bench?" Then to me, "He botherin you?"

"Not at all. He's an old friend," I said.

Curly blinked at this, and his upper lip curled slightly, but he did not comment on it. Instead he said to Naps, "Boy, you git on in there and have a little talk with the sergeant." He put his hand on Naps's shoulder and urged him forward toward the door.

"Wait a minute," I said. "What's he accused of?"

"A whole bunch of stuff," Curly said evasively, "but mainly he was goin seventy miles an hour on Roosevelt Road."

"What's the fine for that?" I asked.

Curly looked irritably at me and said, "It's forty bucks, but the sergeant would like to have a few words with this boy."

"Can you pay it?" I asked Naps.

He was staring down at his shoes, a fine pair of shiny oxblood brogues. Slowly he shook his head.

"I'll be right back," I said, stepped around them, and walked to Dall's door and opened it and went in.

He was standing at the window, with his back to me, and I had to wait a little while until he turned around. His face, when he turned, would have made brave Achilles wet his pants, but it relaxed at the sight of me, and he said, "Oh, it's you. Leave something?"

"No," I said. "Last time I was in here I was here for pleasure. Now I'm here for business."

"What in hell you talkin about, Nub?"

"Allow me to introduce myself. I'm Clifford W. Stone, lawyer for a client of mine who's been arrested. I'm here to argue with Your Honor in an attempt to have him released."

He grinned. "Okay, smart guy, court's in session." He banged the gavel of his fist twice on his desk. "Who you defending?"

"A gentleman name of Naps Howard."

His grin collapsed all of a heap, and he leaned across his desk at me and said, "Look, Nub, why don't you go eat supper or see if you caint take Margaret to another movie or somethin, huh?"

"Naps is an old friend of mine," I said. "An older one even than you."

"I wouldn't admit it," he said, severely reproachful.

I took out my billfold and withdrew four tens and put them down on his desk. "Here's his fine," I said.

He looked at my money with sickened contempt, and then he looked up at me and said in a quite cold and hard voice which I had never heard from him before, "Son, you are gonna get me honestly mad and I am gonna kick your ass out that door and then we aint never gonna be friends no more. You don't know what you're doin. You come round stickin your nose in other people's business, you're liable to get it knocked off. That nigger's your old buddy, you say? How well d'you think you know him? Anybody ever told you that that Howard bastard is the most uppity, biggety, rambumptious coon in the whole state of Arkansas? Anybody ever come up to Boston and set you wise about that, huh? Why, that boy is so all-fired squirty and cocky and stuck-up it makes me plain sick to my guts. He's been tryin to put one over on us for the last goddamn five or six years, and if you think I aim to let you let him, you got a couple more guesses comin to you, buddy boy. Anywhere there is ever nigger trouble in this town, I can bet my last nickel that that buck crow is right square in the middle of it. Any time there's a demonstration, he's always at the head of the parade. Any time there's a sit-in, he's always the first to plump his fat ass down on the stool. He gives us more trouble than all the rest of em put together, and he's slept so many nights in the jail we ought to of charged him rent. But one of these days, by God, he's gonna learn some respect, if I have to ram it up his butt with a crowbar! Now you pick up your fuckin money and get out of here!"

"Dall," I said pacifically, "I've known you from way back. I've also known Naps Howard from way back. Both of you are good old boys, and neither one of you is any better than the other. I'm sure he doesn't hate you. Why should you hate him?"

"Listen, buster—"

"But I'm not going to argue race relations with you," I went on, leaning across his desk to press my attack and remind him that he had never successfully intimidated me and I was of no mind that he begin now. "I'm simply going to tell you, as one old friend to another, and as one responsible citizen to another, that I know enough about law to know that unless you have a clear case against him, unless you can prove that he is guilty of anything other than a traffic violation, you had better take this money and let him go, or I'm going to get a lawyer and have him in here breathing down your neck for false arrest, and I'm not fooling."

Dall sat down. He leaned back in his swivel chair and placed his hand on the butt of his revolver, which was his last contact with authority. *Draw it!* my eyes dared him. But he smiled, and between his smiling teeth in a low voice he said, "You must really love that black boy. Is he gonna fix you up with some nigger pussy?"

I stepped swiftly around the desk and grabbed his collar. "Get up!" I yelled. "Get up and fight like a man."

"No, Nub," he said. "I aint skeered of you, but if you start mixin it up with me, Jack and Curly would be in here before you could say balls, and Jack has a mighty itchy trigger finger. You go on and get out of here. Take your damn money and your damn nigger and to hell with all three of you. But you're gonna think there's somethin awful fishy about a nigger who drives a goddamn limousine convertible but won't even pay his own fine. Now get out."

He stood up, took the money off his desk and stuffed it into my hand, then ushered me to the door, where, before opening it, he looked me in the eye and said, "Never mind about coming over to my place for supper Friday."

Then he opened the door, shoved me through it, and said to Curly, "This gentleman has bought the nigra out of hock. Kindly escort both of them out of the building."

Then he slammed the door on me.

Outside, conveyed to the front steps of police headquarters by Curly's tight hands gripping our arms, we stood alone and looked at each other sheepishly in the late, low sunlight which streamed down Markham from the direction of the train station and was slowly beginning to change white to black. My wristwatch said fifteen after six. The traffic on Markham had all gone home to supper.

"You oughtn't've," Naps said.

"That's okay," I said.

"Here," he said, drawing out his wallet from his coat pocket, "let me pay you back."

I flapped my hand at him. "I didn't really pay him. He wouldn't take it," I said, and Naps put his wallet back in his coat, but not before I had a glimpse of all the greenery. "But I thought you were broke?"

"Naw," he said, and split his face with that Cheshire grin again. "But the law not ever gon get a penny out of me."

"I know how you feel," I said. "I never pay traffic fines myself."

"Much obliged to you anyway. I spect that sergeant sure made it kind of hot for you. Heard lots of hollerin goan on in there. Well, Nub," he asked, "can I give you a lift anywheres?"

"Which way are you going?"

"Just whichever way *you* want to go, my friend."

"Still live on Ringo?"

"Yeah, but not the same place. I'm stayin down on the far end now."

Down where the shacks are, poor Naps. How like a Negro to spend all his money on fine clothes and a car, yet dwell in a shanty. Well, if he was heading that way, I supposed he could drop me off at my father's. But Daddy and Sybil would have finished eating; he always had his supper at five-thirty on the dot. I was feeling morose and outcast and unwanted, and I didn't much care to sit around and watch The Farmer's Daughter and Ben Casey with my old man and his floozy. But what else was there to do, if Margaret was out on a date somewhere with James Royal Slater?

We turned down the sidewalk toward the parking lot. Naps had grown considerably in fifteen years, but still, walking beside me, he was a good inch shorter. This is a great comfort to a small man.

"Funny," I mused. "The first time we met I gave you a ride home on my bike. Now you're giving me a ride home in your car."

"Aint that sump'm?" he said. "You was in trouble that day. I was in trouble *this* day."

"Odd," I said.

"Yeah, Nub, you was what the caddies called a *horror*. I guess you know about that, it's a outside boy who comes in and tries to caddy with the reg-lars. It's kind of like a ice cream caddy, who caddies just for spendin money, only you was a *horror*, and that's worse."

"I'm still a *horror*, Naps," I said sadly.

He cast me an impish sideward glance, and grinned. "Taint much difference between a hornet and a yellow jacket when they both get under folks' clothes," he said cryptically, and I grinned back at him.

We arrived at the parking lot. His car was—Good Lord!—his car was a marvelous, soul-stirring Lincoln Continental convertible of the same shimmery Prussian blue as his suit and the patina of his skin, a mammoth hunk of sleek steel which, parked uncomfortably between two homely police cars, seemed a splendid queen in the company of drab yeomen. If the automobile is a sex symbol, that was one machine I would love to have slammed on the internalexpanding & externalcontracting brakes of Bothatonce, after a wild ride around the corner of Divinity.

Naps, seeing my mouth agape and reading my thoughts, beamed proudly and said, "Aint she a fine-lookin job?" He patted her door fondly. "This wagon goin on a bore and stroke of 4.30 by 3.70, and she got a three-speed torque converter transmission."

"I don't know much about bores and torques," I said, "but I would consider it an honor to ride in this baby." So fresh and clean was she, as though she had just emerged from the dealer's showroom, that I half expected to see a fantastic price tag still stuck to her.

"You get in the back," he said, winked, and held the rear door open (a convertible with *four* doors!).

"Oh, come now," I protested, "let's not be hypocrites. I'll ride up front with you."

"Naw, later maybe, after it's dark. But if we gon enjoy us some fresh air with this here top down, we best sit separate. You know how it is." He winked again and gently guided me into my throne, a supple, yielding couch of finest white leather. Then he closed the door, bowed, and walked around to the other side, getting into the front seat behind the wheel. From the glove compartment he took out a chauffeur's cap and put it on his head.

"Don't I look good?" he asked, turning to show me. He looked splendid.

"Naps, are you making fun of me, boy?" I asked threateningly.

"Oh, nossuh!" he said, all mock-servility, turned, started the powerful engine and placed his hands lightly on the wheel. "Where to, Boss?"

"Don't call me boss," I said, a trifle irritated, but a trifle pleased with this ridiculous scene we were making. In spite of myself I felt rich, regal, powerful, and even debonair, the troubles of my cumbrous day suddenly lightened. It went to my head. "Where would *you* like to go?" I asked.

"You name it, man," he said.

"Well, Naps, I haven't really seen this town for four years. Could we just drive around some?"

"Right," he said, shifted the stick into drive, and we floated away.

That was a magnificent, unspeakably thrilling ride, coasting up and down the streets of my city in such luxurious splendor. First we went all the way down Broadway and crossed over Roosevelt Road to Main and back down Main Street. People stared.

"Naps," I called to him. "What did you say you do for a living? You run a gambling syndicate or something?"

He laughed. "Naw, I'm a book salesman," he called back over his shoulder. "I'm the number one salesman for the Christian Souls Book House. Would you maybe be interested in a nice fine Bible?"

I didn't know whether he meant it or not. "I'm not religious," I said.

"Well, ne'mind. How about a nice unexpurgated *Fanny Hill*?"

"Sure," I laughed. "Put me down for half a dozen."

"You think I'm foolin you, man?"

"Naps, you never fooled me in your life, did you?"

"Not me," he said.

"All right. What do you do for a living?"

"I'm a book salesman," he said, and I would, for a while, let it go at that. "How you doin back there, Nub?" he asked.

"Just fine," I said. "Just fine. I feel like Winthrop Rockefeller himself. All I need is a good fifty-cent cigar."

"Shoot, why didn't you speak up?" he said, leaned over and drew a box out of the glove compartment. He flipped the lid open with one hand and held it back over the seat.

"Aw, I don't smoke," I said.

"Won't kill yuh," he said. "Go on. Hoo now, we gotta show um, boy! We puttin on airs."

"We really are," I agreed, and selected a long stout Havana belvedere maduro.

He giggled. "We tellin um!" he said. Then, "Lighter's on your left back there. Got it?"

"Got it." I lit up. It might make me sick, but by God if I could be king for only one evening, I was going to do it in style.

We were stopped at Third and Main by a red light. While we waited, the car purring soft and expectant beneath us, a couple I once knew came strolling up to the curb and also stopped to wait for the light to change. They turned their heads and gawked at me. The man was a tall, fat blond-haired television announcer named Hy Norden. The woman with him was a chic socialite named Marcia Paden Norden. From somewhere in the dim recesses of my memory of my impoverished past, I recalled having met them briefly. Slowly raising the hand which held the cigar, I condescended to acknowledge their presence with a stiff disdainful wave. Norden's mouth fell open and he stretched his hand toward me and started to speak, but the light changed and my man drove me away from that ghastly rotter left standing all aghast.

"Naps," I called, a block later, "you just did me a great big favor."

"How's that?" he asked.

I explained.

When I finished, he said, "I've seen him on the TV, that boy; he a high-up big-mouth keltch, so brassy, so snotty, he the kind of white makes me glad I'm a nigger."

"Thank you," I said.

"What *for*?" he said.

"You're a good old boy," I said.

"Go on, now," he said, and we broke up into laughter.

We turned up Markham once more. The sun was sinking into the pine hills of Perry County, far away. Dusk was setting in. We drove all the way out to the west end of town, exploring the vastness of the new housing developments: Briarwood, Leawood, Robinwood, Kingwood, Birchwood, Grandwood, Brookwood, Westwood, Coolwood, Point O'Woods, and others; the innumerable ranch-styles and split-levels, faceless in the dusk but not shapeless, swarming in the butchered pine woods like a herd of neoteric mammoths munching and masticating bushels of green trading stamps. "Don't it make you wonder?" Naps said, getting us lost on some twisting, terraced drive dipping through the center of what once had been a pleasant woodland in Boyle Park but now was cancerously crowded with the bedrooms of subexecutive insurance men who had driven home from the Tower Building in Comets and Corvairs. "It makes me wonder," I said, and we found our way out of there, getting on Twelfth Street and heading back toward town, past the less pretentious outpost houses of the early Eisenhower era, then past the outmoded ranch-types of the Truman years, the stuccoed duplexes of the Roosevelt reign, on past the symmetrical white clapboard bungalows of the Hoover bad times, until finally we were back among old and faded parts of the nineteenth century again, where a brilliant idea suddenly occurred to me.

"Naps," I called to my chauffeur, "could you do me just one more favor?"

"Any*thing*, any *time*, any*where*," he sang back at me.

I gave him Margaret's address and explained what I wanted to do.

We pulled up at the curb in front of her house, and Naps honked a melodious tattoo on the Lincoln's horn. The front of the old house was dark, but lights went on in a front room almost immediately. We could see a fat face peering out through the window. Naps honked again, and then Mrs. Austin came out onto the porch and stood there straining her eyes at us. There was enough light from the street lamps to give her an impression of the Lincoln's size and awesome beauty. Then Naps leaped out and raced around the car to hold my door open for me. He bowed as I exited the car and walked up to Mrs. Austin. "Good evening, madam," I said in a genteel voice.

"Oh, it's *you*," she said, a bit frostily, but then she felt obliged to re-examine her opinion of me. "What a *lovely* automobile," she said.

"Thank you," I said. "May I speak with your daughter for a moment, if you please?"

"She isn't *here*," Mrs. Austin said.

"Really?" I said and sprinkled my cigar ashes on her weedy lawn. "May I ask where I might find her?"

"She's *out* at Mr. *Slater's* house."

"Oh. Do you happen to know when she will return?"

"*Not* until in the *morning*, I *suppose*."

"Do you mean to say that she's going to spend the night with him?"

"I *believe* so."

"You mean you don't care whether she sleeps with him or not?"

"I *beg* your *pardon*?"

"Are you telling me that you actually *know* that your daughter is keeping company with that man?"

"*Clifford!*" she said, gasping, offended. Then she said, "Mr. and Mrs. *Slater* are one of the *oldest* and *finest* families, and I see *nothing* improper about my *daughter* being their *house* guest."

"Oh," I said.

"What makes you think—?"

"Nothing," I said. "I just didn't understand you the first time." I turned to go, but turned back again. "Well, just tell her, when you see her, that I'd like to talk with her at her convenience. Thank you."

Driving me home, Naps asked, "Did she say *Slater*?" I told him that was right. "This girl," he said. "She's *your* girl friend?"

In a way, I said. "Lordy," he said. I asked him why he was saying Lordy. He said he had heard that Slater was keeping a mistress. I asked him how he had heard.

"You remember that little colored boy that lived next door to me, when I lived up there in y'all's part of Ringo Street? Feemy Bastrop he was called, and we used to all be such good friends. Well, he workin at the Slater place now, what Mr. Slater call his manservant. He the one tole me Mr. Slater had him a fine-lookin black-haired mistress."

🐗 NINETEEN

Sleep that night was hopeless. I tried counting sheep, but was too weary to count, giving it up when I got the sixties and seventies hopelessly confused. I tried willing my body to sleep, piece by piece beginning with the toes, but got only as far as the privates before succumbing to exhaustion. I tried playing soporific melodies in the silent sounding chambers of my brain, but the thirteenth rendering of "Pop Goes the Weasel" drove me to the point of tears. I quit.

Margaret Austin. Marguerite Margherita Margarete Austin. Meg. Mag Maggie Mamie Margie Marge Margot. Peg. Peggy Meta Maisie Margery Marjory Marge, meaning: A Pearl. Miss Margaret Rose Austin. Backwards: Ssim Teragram Esor Nitsau. Send a telegram to Teragram. Leave a margin for margarine and marjoram. Austin, Texas. Jane Austen. Austin-Healey.

MAWR-GRIT AWS-TIN! My God, how all night that name and its forms, its deviates, they bumped restlessly from node to node, from adyt to adyt in the sweaty and tortuous windings of my intricate brains, until, in proliferating surplus, they surged downward into every passage of my vitals, permeating long-dormant saccules and ventricles, and setting the whole works ablaze with furor, with fidgety twitching that put sleep entirely out of the question.

I might go on back to Boston tomorrow after all, I had told Daddy.

What is Little Rock?
Who is Margaret?

Naps and I had driven past another one of those large blue-

and-white signs which asked only: "Who's Happy?" and I, thinking they had been planted all over town by some fairy spirit trying to remind me that I was not happy, had asked Naps what they meant. He had said they had been erected by the Little Rock Housing Authority, and the answer to the simple two-word question was: "He's *Mr. Happy Fixit! Helping Rebuild Neighborhoods!*" Oh God, I had groaned.

One Saturday afternoon of our teens I had taken Margaret into my room; my mother and father were both away; I had joked with her awhile and then playfully thrown her down on my bed and wrestled with her, but she had been terror-stricken at my innocent but tactless act and had pounded at my chest, crying, "What are you doing?" and continued that theme, like a repetitive motif in a fugue, all the way home, "What were you doing? Why were you doing that?" I remembered it, and I recalled my embarrassment on that occasion; I had done the same thing to Sarah Farnley not two weeks before, and old Sal hadn't seemed to mind at all. I wondered: Could Margaret's shock of outraged astonishment at my sportive, frisky gesture have confounded forevermore her dignity so that at a time ten years later there would not remain enough of it, that self-respecting dignity, to keep her from her own destruction? or out of the viceful vise of a lascivious old playwright?

Is Margaret crazy?

And the town—is it sane at all?

Two Little Rocks: one a slow, easy old Southern town of old bricks and boards and friendly sidewalks where walking unfolds, block after block, new quaintnesses; the other, a sprawling sidewalkless jungle of ticky-tacky suburbs where walking seems prohibited by law or at least impossible.

Sleep. Oh, sleep!

Two Dalls: one sitting beside a pond on the capitol grounds in the early morning darkness, holding a sleeping girl against his breast; the other, stripped to the waist and sweating, brandishing a whip over the prostrate bodies of Negroes.

The common herd values friendships only for their usefulness.

Two Margarets: one very shy and sad-eyed, cool and mute, strolling hand-in-hand with me through night-fragrant tunnels of blossoming shrubs; the other, a bold loquacious actress, wild and open, romping in sin with a nasty old playwright.

I have been meeting her in dreams all these years.

Two Cliffords: one scholarly and staid, aloof in a tower of dispassionate contemplation, impotent, dusty, and nervous; the other, a chummy pint-size ex-boxer stalking through a dull hometown in search of . . . what? Yes: sex, adventure, friends, and the lost, lost past.

Why have we come here to this water?

Naps had talked about this man Slater, had even attempted to describe him to me, and now a spectral image of the aging playwright seemed to hobble to and fro through the eerie illumination of my sleepless consciousness.

He sho aint no looker. No more tall than you or me, but bout twice as big around. Face kind of like a fish. Fish mouth. Big pop eyes. Lumpy cheeks. Not much hair, and what there is of it all glued down with vaseline. Nose looks like he was smellin somethin bad all the time, you know what I mean. No neck atall; his head just sits there on his body like a punkin on a stump. Wears fine clothes, though. Yeah, real fine clothes: silk shirts, Harris tweeds, all that. Country squire type of fellow. See him trottin around on one of them Morgan horses of his, he look like a million dollars, but he aint got a cent to his name. Everything he got, his wife owns it. He never earned a dollar in his life. She in a wheelchair, been in a wheelchair for a long time and caint get out of it, but, man, I'm tellin you, she's runnin the whole show. The whole show.

I had told Naps that if Margaret was involved with Slater, I didn't want to intrude. I had told him I thought I would just go on back to Boston. We had stopped in front of my house and I had thanked him for the ride. There, before I got out of the car, he had asked, "Is you sho you wanter go?" and I settled his doubts on that score. Then he had said, uncertainly, "Me and you couldub been good friends." Me and you *are* good friends, I had assured him, and then I had shaken his hand. "Well," he had concluded as I got out of the car, "good luck to you, Nub." Then he had made me a present of a fine parting aphorism: *"If you obliged to eat dirt, eat clean dirt."* Touched at this gift of what probably had been his personal motto, I had choked up and could only mutter "Thank you" before I had turned and walked to the house.

Now I turned on the bed lamp and lifted my watch from the night table to see what time it was. Fifteen after four. Then I lifted my billfold and took out the card that Naps had given me. "Case you ever come back, or case you don't even go," he had said, "here's my cod." As such cards go, it was rather fancy: raised letters, elegant type, fine heavy white stock.

• • •

N. Leon Howard
Books, Religious and Otherwise
Agitating, Non-Violent and Otherwise
Lunch Counters a Specialty
3700 Ringo Street   Little Rock, Arkansas   FRanklin 8-9635

I put it in my wallet, reflecting upon his name. Obviously "Naps" was only a nickname, but what did it shorten? Naphthalene? Napkin? Napalm, as in the bomb? I was too tired to speculate. I put out the light again.

But I didn't sleep.

She is a witch who haunts, who shamanizes me, preying on my skittish nerves, violating the chastity of my scholarship with the vulgarity of her animate being, who will not ever let me alone.

Dawn came anon. I watched as the back-yard buildings, the toolsheds and garages and doghouses, took on blear cold coronas of early yellow sunlight. Even then she would not let me alone.

Now I suppose it was only what they said of her, and not what I had learned from her myself, which did this to me. Fortunately I have always been one to bank upon my own senses, my own discernment, before swallowing the views of others, and because of this laissez-faireism I stuck adamantly to my original conception of Margaret the provocative and unfallen goddess. I was on her side, come what may, or went what did. Poor kid.

But what the hell is going on?

This question is what kept me awake, kept me aflicker like an all-night candle, afflicted. It gave me a feeling of helplessness, of paralysis, isolated exclusion, of being an interloper unable to do anything but stand in the midst of it and watch, an impotent spectator, or, in the word of those darky caddies, a *horror*.

When I see her again I will have much to discuss with her.

The kitchenward voice of Sybil, cockcrowing the morn with a flat but spirited rendition of "You Are My Sunshine," accompanied by the banging of skillets and pots, roused me out of what had not been even a shadow of slumber. Staggering up out of one of the godawfulest nights I have ever endured, I let Sybil saturate me with black coffee; the eggs wouldn't go down. Even she, thickly simple and ungifted, perceived my haggard fever and asked me what kind of powder keg I was sitting on. I couldn't tell her, beyond explaining that I hadn't been getting enough sleep. After my father had gone away to work, she rubbed the back of my neck for a while, and that helped some.

After breakfast I received a surprise phone call. Hy Norden himself called to say that he had been trying to get in touch with me and that it had just occurred to him to try my father's number, but, well, anyway, he had seen me in my car ("That's truly a swell-looking piece of transportation you've got there, Cliff, man") and, well, anyway, he and Marcia were throwing a little patio party Saturday night out at their place after the opening of Slater's play, and he and Marcia would be damn pleased if I would honor them with my presence. I told him I wasn't positive yet that I would still be in town on Saturday, but that if I was, I would try to make it. He thanked me profusely and I hung up, laughing to myself.

I showered, put on my seersucker suit, girded up my loins, and walked on over to Margaret's house.

TWENTY

At the curb where the walk to her house meets the street is, I noticed again, that stone carriage-stoop which we had sat upon the other night, one of those obsolete hunks of pale granite that disencumbered the high-buttoned lady's exit from the four-in-hand or the cabriolet or even the buckboard in the days when the streets were still dirt and the twin giant catalpas in front of that house were only ornamental shrubs of modest size. On the street side of the carriage-stoop were six letters sepulchrally engraved: AUSTIN. It was oddly incongruous, considering the present poverty of the house and neighborhood.

Mrs. Austin met me at the door. "Where's your *car* and show-*foor* this *morning?*" she asked. I told her I always gave my chauffeur Thursday mornings off so that he could polish the car. Mrs. Austin moved her great bulk out of the way so that I could enter the house, then she led me into the parlor, where we sat down in a couple of threadbare balloon-backed chairs of cherry-red button-tufted velvet, amidst a flock of similar side chairs, marble-topped rosewood tables and taborets with bracketed feet, veneered chiffoniers and étagères, a white marble rococo fireplace beneath a huge oval mirror with a winged gilt frame about to soar off through the air of the room like an overgrown parakeet. Beneath my feet was a luxuriant profusion of huge roses, scarlet and sulphur, burgeoning out of the rank verdure of the well-worn rug. Above my head was an obese cluster of dusty milk-glass bubbles and crystal spangles and pendants in what is without question one of the largest lighting fixtures in town. Somehow I felt very small, yet this parlor furniture was the only thing of value in the whole house, and I also felt embarrassed by this false front. "How *good* to *see* you *again,* Clifford," said big Mrs. Austin affectedly, crossing her hands wrist over wrist on her lap. Margaret, she said, was upstairs dressing and would be down any minute. Make myself at home. "I understand you live in *Boston* now," she said. "What *are* you doing *way* off up *there?*" In short sentences, struggling to keep my voice from imitating the flighty trill of her own, I explained how I worked for the Cabot Foundation in a curatorial capacity. "How *fascinating!*" she falsely remarked, giving her mealy mouth some exaggerated exercise. Then she paused, and, after a moment, asked me, "What's a *curatorial* capacity?" I explained that it had to do with the evaluation and maintenance of valuable old works of art, craft objects, and so forth. She asked if I would care to have a look at some of her figurines; she was making plaster figurines of children in charming postures, all lively colored by hand. Gingerly I suggested that my rather limited province of connoisseurship would not qualify me to pass judgment on items of that particular nature.

"Well," she said, a trifle crestfallen, "they're not en*tirely original,* I suppose, because you *order* the rubber *molds* from Gutta *Percha* Enterprises in *St. Louis,* they send you an *assortment* of *twelve* of your *choice* for a dollar ninety-eight, and *instructions* for *mixing* the plaster of *Paris,* and all, but then *of course* it's up to *you* how you *decorate* them, you *need* a lot of *ingenuity* for mixing the *colors* and deciding *which* color goes *where* and so forth. They're really *cute* if you know how to *do* it."

My face frozen in amity, I allowed as how it must be a truly rewarding diversion.

"Oh *yes,*" she said. "It's very *relaxing,* and it gives you a feeling of satisfaction and *workmanship.* What are you doing in Little Rock?"

Caught napping by her question, I mumbled something about how I was taking stock, so to speak, reconsidering the old home town, retracing my steps and so forth.

"I *see*," she said with irksome and officious cheek. She let a couple of moments drift by, then said, "You *haven't* changed a *bit*."

Unflattering as this observation was, I knew it was well-intended, because it was what everybody else had said; so I smiled bashfully and did not utter my rejoinder, which was: "Well, at least I shave every day now, and I used to be just downy."

Silence, more silence, then she cleared her throat noisily and said, "I guess your *job* must pay *very* well."

Bad manners! Like my father. As a waitress, probably she had never seen more than fifty dollars a week in her life. "I get along," I said.

"*Margaret*," she reflected idly, after another of those interminable, uncomfortable pauses which left me with nothing to do but gaze at the gallery of oval-framed chromolithographs, views and genre subjects, which lined the walls of fleur-de-lis flocked wallpaper, "is *so* much *love*lier than she *used* to be. And you *must*'ve heard, she's going to be the *star!* of a new *play!* which starts *this* Saturday night!"

"*Yes*," I said, with all the aplomb I could muster.

"*Well*, what do you *think?*" she asked.

"Very lovely," I said.

"*Yes*, but I *mean*, what do you think about *Little Rock?*"

"A nice town," I said.

"So you've come *back*," she told me, "to get yourself one of our *good* Southern gals, and *settle down*."

"Oh, I'm already married," I said.

Her heavy eyebrows fluttered upward against her will. "I *see*," she said, but she didn't. After another moment she excused herself. There was, she said, a cake or something in the oven. Margaret should be down any minute.

Alone, I paced the room, inspecting the miscellany of threadbare and horsehairbare furniture, which, the last time I had seen it, had seemed merely an olla-podrida of smothering, inept heirlooms, but now was easily recognizable for what it was: a chaste if somewhat eclectic grouping of Victorian gewgaws, each of which was more or less familiar to me as an authentic piece which probably had been handed down from one of those earlier Austins who had possessed some degree of wealth. This is Louis XVI, I said to myself, running my hand over its smooth walnut. And that is Sheraton, with a touch of Adam. That chiffonier over there is Drawing-Room Gothic, probably about 1874.

And so on, my well-posted mind clicking like a computer. But this was a front, a resistance, an intentionally distracting game covering up my real thoughts, which were lost in Margaret, already grilling her for an explanation of her conduct, past and present.

I sat down again, partly because my knees had begun to quiver, partly because I breathe more efficiently in a sitting position. On the marble top to my left was a stack of magazines. The magazine on top was *Reader's Digest*. I flipped indolently and indifferently through it. "Face Adversity and Smile!" advised the condensed memoirs of a retired Marine sergeant who had been through hell and had not blanched. I read it through, ashamed of myself at first for such profanation of my time, but gradually, as the import of the man's philosophy got through to me, I began to be moved, affected, helped. In my heart of hearts I *know* that such inspirational stuff is trash of the worst sort, but somehow, once I read it, I cannot help but be inspired, elevated. I guess I'm just a hapless sucker for that kind of thing. Anyway, the ex-Marine had a lot of worthy hints for weathering the thousand natural shocks that flesh is heir to, and I even took the liberty of transposing a couple of his sentences to my Ring-Master. Nothing, he summed up, is really worth worrying about, nothing is so terrible that we should live in fear and apprehension of it. I thought this was a rather nice dictum. I smiled, helplessly. After the horrors, both military and domestic, of the ex-Marine's life, the next article, "Let's Forget the Little Mistakes," came as a mild and undramatic chaser, but it was just as pithy, just as aphoristic. Written by a warm and pleasant man who was a reformed fault-finder, a penitent ex-nitpicker, it advised that we should endeavor to make this world a pleasanter place of living by ceasing to make mountains out of molehills. Nothing, he summed up, is really worth getting into a stew about, nothing is bad enough to ruffle the dignity and good sense of a benevolent man. Reading these things, I confess, suffused me with cheer, gave to me an almost defenseless feeling of *bonhomie* and strength and loving-kindness, *deliciae humani generis*, and I resolved to go straightaway and find Mrs. Austin in the kitchen or wherever she was and tell her there was nothing I would like better than to have a look at her plaster figurines of children in charming postures.

But as I was rounding the corner out of the parlor door, Margaret came skipping out of the cobwebs down the winding walnut stair. "Clifford!" she hailed me ardently. Dressed in a

Florentine scroll print shirt of pink-green-blue silk, and olive-green silk slacks, barefoot, she was a vision, a sight, the handsome incarnation of that phantasmagoric succubus I had seen so often in the trance of sleep or sleeplessness.

She drifted down, light as a leaf, seized me with long engulfing arms, kissed me: gave me a robust, liquid, durable, throbbing kiss that I will long remember. Pamela's kisses were as dry as parchment; their relative humidity was always several degrees lower than mine, and her mouth never seemed to fit my mouth, and she never moved her lips once they made contact, and the kiss was over in a few seconds, and she never, never put her arms around me. Margaret's mouth fit mine like a tooth fits its socket. "Wow!" was all I could say when we disengaged, but instantly I began to wonder if this was the other Margaret, the straightforward courtesan whose heart belonged to Slater.

"Let's go sit in the swing on the porch," she sighed, and linked her arm through mine and ushered me thither.

I was glad to get out of that house. On the porch we tranquilly swung ourselves and took in the late morning air, now soaked with the merged perfumes of honeysuckles, hyacinths, and primulas. A beetle lacery of gossamer lavender wisteria, wistful and wispy, tingled the trellises all over one end of the porch.

We sat in silence a long time. I was not going to be the first to speak. If she couldn't talk herself out of her own shyness, or if she couldn't think of anything worth saying to me, I was not going to say a word of my own. Perhaps she sensed this, because finally, in that timid, quiet but precisely articulated voice of hers, she began to talk.

"Sometimes," she said, her hands resting gracefully palms upward in her lap, her knees flexing rhythmically to make the swing move, "sometimes I think I would like to be a cat. Not a Persian or a Siamese or anything fancy, not even a well-striped tabby, but just an ugly tortoise-shell or something, a plain old *felis domesticus,* fat and bodacious, unloved but tolerated, sitting all day in the sun on the porch."

"Now that's curious," I said cordially, although it wasn't, although it seemed a banal, corny remark for her to make, "because what I've always wanted to be was a rat, a small, fierce *rattus rattus* with cute pink ears." But, having said this, I regretted it; it was malign and was not altogether true.

"Ugh," she said. "Rats are disease-carriers."

"So are cats," I said. "Last year in Boston sixteen cases of hydrophobia were traced to cats."

"Rats are lawless," she said.

"Cats are conceited," I said.

"Rats are vile and vicious and ravenous and . . . and *horrible*."

"Cats are destructive and unreliable and lazy and obnoxious."

"All right," she said. "I'll be a rat too, and mate promiscuously all year long."

With whom? I wondered. A rat named Slater? I said nothing.

"Anything is better than being human," she went on. "When you're human, you spend the first third of your life waiting for the future, impatiently waiting to be grown up, and then one day you discover that the future is here, and that you are living it, and that it is not at all what you had hoped it would be, had been led to expect it would be. Animals aren't like that. They live only in the present, from the first moment they are born. When we were growing up, we didn't even know what the present was. It was just a hypothetical and insubstantial point, a flicker of time, where the past and future met each other. It was tiresome and impatient and we let it slip through our fingers like sand. Now we have nothing else. We are buried in the sandpile that fell around our feet."

"Where did you learn that pretty little speech?" I asked, rather severely. "From Slater?" But instantly the humane souls of *Reader's Digest*, the forbearing elves who dwell in its pages, reminded me: Be nice.

She pouted, and retreated into her tight silence again.

"Where shall we go today?" I asked. "Or do you have to go to rehearsals again?" She didn't answer. A minute passed. "Margaret," I said, "could I just ask you a few questions?" No response. "Could I, please?" Oh, all right, she said at last. "One," I said. "Why do you live here in this house?"

She meditated for a moment, then she said, "I told you, when you asked me that question the other night. Where else can I live? It's a place to sleep, is all."

"You didn't sleep here last night," I said, and waited for her to say something about that, but she didn't. Then I said, "Question number two. Why have you always been so shy and reserved with me? You talked so easily and fluently the other night."

"You were desperate then," she said, "and I thought you were leaving, so it didn't matter what I said."

"Are you sorry I didn't leave?"

"Don't be silly. Of course not."

"All right. Question number three. Ready? Are you having an affair with James Royal Slater?"

"No."

Her answer was too immediate. "No?" I challenged her. "Honestly?"

"It depends on what you mean by an 'affair.'"

"I mean, are you sleeping with him?"

"I'm a virgin, mister," she said, almost inaudibly.

"And I'm a celibate but unfrocked priest," I said.

"Very funny," she said.

"Margaret, look, what I want to know is—I don't know how to say this—but just what is going on? I mean, I don't know anything. I feel like a stranger. I'm not trying to pry into your life or anything, but I just wonder where I stand with you."

She did not answer for a while. She was looking down at her hands in her lap. Then, without looking at me, she said, "The other night you told me that if you stayed in Little Rock that you and I could go places together and do things together."

"Yes, but—"

She looked up at me. Her voice was dead serious. "Clifford, would you—could you afford—to get a room in a hotel or a motel or somewhere so that I could stay there?"

My heart leaped up. "You mean you and *me*?"

"You wouldn't have to stay with me if you didn't want to."

"Uh, I, yeah, uh, sure, I—" I stumbled, struggling to get my emotions under control.

"So I could get out of this house," she said.

"Hell yes!" I agreed. "You've got to get out of this house, that's for sure!"

"It would just be until after the play has finished its run, and then maybe I could find some place else to go."

"As long as you want," I said. "I'm loaded with dough." Not really, but I had about three hundred dollars in traveler's checks, and I could always wire my bank for more.

"You know," she said, musing, "I've never been to dinner at the Embers or the Lamplighter or Brier's or Bruno's Little Italy or Mexico Chiquita. Would you take me to those places? And I've never been to the Brown Jug or Shakey's Pizza Parlor. Or gone dancing at the Westwood Club. Or even rode the Ferris wheel at War Memorial Park. Could we do those things?"

"Sure, anything," I said.

"And take long walks at night down all the streets."

"Myself, I'm a great one for walking," I said, nearly bursting with delight and anticipation. I grabbed her hand and held it.

"I don't want to live here any more," she said.

"I don't blame you," I said.

"I don't even want to go back up to that room again," she said. "And I'm not going to. Ever."

"Fine," I said. "To hell with that room."

"To hell with it," she bravely echoed. Then again we lapsed into silence for a time. Eventually she asked, "Does that answer your question?"

"Which question?"

"You said you wanted to know where you stand with me."

"Oh yes," I said, but then I remembered that I had been questioning her and had not finished. So I asked casually, almost flippantly, "But what *was* the extent of your relationship with Slater?"

"He not only wrote the play, but also he's directing it," she said. "In a sense, he's my boss. I have to see him every day in the course of rehearsals and so forth."

"You're not his mistress?" I asked. "I heard he had a mistress."

"Who told you that?"

"A friend."

"Was it Doyle?" she asked. "Have you seen Doyle?"

"Yes, I've seen him, but he wasn't the one who told me."

"What did he say about me?"

"Oh, he just told me that he didn't think I would have much luck if I tried to get a date with you, because you were dating Slater."

Margaret smiled. Then she said, "I wonder where he got that idea."

"Dall seems to know quite a lot about you," I said.

"That's true," she said. "I think I must have talked more to him these past couple of months than to everybody else I've ever known."

"Why?"

"*Why?*" She shrugged. "He keeps asking me questions, that's why. He asks more questions than you do." She giggled.

"What's funny?" I asked.

"Oh, I was just thinking," she said. "You know, I used to think I was very stupid, maybe because I never could open my mouth, or when I did open it something stupid came out. But after talking to Doyle so much, I learned that I have *some* intelligence, anyway."

"Anybody would seem intelligent in contrast to Dall," I said.

"You think so? Well, let me tell you, Professor, Doyle is one of the most intelligent persons I've ever met."

"You've never met many people," I said.

She sighed. "That's true. But even so—"

"Why has he asked you so many questions?" I wanted to know.

"I was very unhappy, I guess. He wanted to know why."

"But you're not unhappy now?"

"Not really."

"Why? Because of Dall? Because of Slater?"

"Because of you," she said.

We held hands and rocked the swing gently. I seemed to hear music playing somewhere, far off, banjos and harmonicas and French horns and violins, soft and tender. I stopped pestering her with prying questions, and we made small talk for a while. She talked about her room, a small attic room. She had tried to fix it up, to decorate it, but it was really a dismal room, stuffy and badly lighted, and she didn't like it, although she had lived in it for fifteen years. There was nowhere else she could go. She hid up there, she shut herself up in that room because nobody could get her there, nobody could find her there to laugh at her or scold her, not even her mother, who was never permitted to come up there. It was her nest, her safe warm snug womb, but now she was going to abandon it forever.

"I've come out of it," she said, "and discovered that nobody really wants to laugh at me, nobody has anything to scold me about, nobody even notices me, or, if like you and Doyle they do, they don't really think ill of me, and this makes me glad." Her voice rose. "Oh, it makes me want to scream with relief and gladness! But if I did, if I screamed with relief and gladness, you'd think I was crazy, wouldn't you? I mean insane. You don't really want to start thinking that. Now do you?"

"No," I said, in truth, "I don't."

Her voice calmed, she said, "Tell me about your wife. Let's talk about you now. Your life and your wife."

What could I say? I put her off with a few vague, bored, critical remarks about Pamela, and then I didn't say anything else about myself. My experience with Pamela had taught me a lesson about revealing too much of myself to others. Carefully I steered the conversation back to Margaret, and then I asked her to tell me more about Slater. Oh, she felt sorry for him, she said. He was a strange person—perhaps a deranged person. It could be that he was damned, a fallen angel, under a curse. He was the first person Margaret had ever met who was more wretched than herself. But she personally didn't think he was awfully talented as a playwright. His early plays, perhaps, but not this one. I asked her to tell me a little about this strangely titled drama, *How Many Times Have You Seen* THE RED SHOES? She said she didn't want to give away the plot before I had a chance to see it—and she hoped I would come and see it—she would give me a free ticket. But anyway, she didn't really like the part. She played a girl named Wanda who is overly idealistic, a dreamer, a petty fool. She felt that Slater hadn't done a very good job of understanding Wanda. I asked Margaret why she wanted to be in the play if she didn't like the role or the play. She gave me a surprised look, then said, "It's the only chance I've ever had to do anything with myself." Then she added, "Jimmy thinks I might be able to make a career out of professional theater if I wanted to."

"Who's Jimmy?" I asked.

"Mr. Slater," she said.

"He's fifty years old and you call him Jimmy?"

"He's forty-eight years old, and he asked me to call him Jimmy."

"I see."

"Are you jealous?" she asked me out of the corner of her eyes.

"Frankly, yes."

"I suppose you would be jealous of Doyle too."

I told her I saw no reason yet for *that*. She said that was good, because Dall (Doyle she persisted in calling him, with her un-Arkansan diction) was like a brother to her, a kind, helpful brother. She had never had a brother or a sister. She wished she had. (Her stepbrother and two stepsisters had all long since married and moved away, and she had never been close to them anyway.) But Dall was such an awful racist, she said, a real white-supremacist, and she couldn't respect him for his views on that problem. She said she didn't see him much lately, anyway, and he had never offered to take her to a movie or to dinner or anything, so she assumed his interest in her didn't go beyond the compass of his police work. For a long while, she said, Dall had appeared faithfully at her house every day, to talk with her, and for a stretch of three or four weeks he became almost a pest, and her mother complained long and loud because she didn't like for the neighbors to see a policeman sitting on the front porch for two or three hours every day. Still and all, she was very grateful to him. She would never forget how he had helped her understand herself.

Now, as for the immediate future, we had to take care of a few plans. Where would we stay? We discussed the possibilities, and she told me about a very nice, modern motor hotel downtown on the east side, called the Coachman's Inn, where businessmen often stayed whether they had cars or not. I preferred something old and quaint, but she said this place was new and quaint. It didn't matter. Anywhere. Anywhere at all.

She would have to rehearse the play out at Slater's hacienda that afternoon ("I don't want to," she said, "but I have to") and she would be free after five o'clock. Her bag was all packed now, waiting to go. (Confident girl!) We could go on over and check in at the Coachman's Inn whenever I was ready to.

"Any time," I said, afire, nearly panting. "Just *any* time."

"I'll have to sneak out," she said. "Why don't you go on around the corner and wait for me at the alley, and we'll catch a cab from there." She stood up, and so did I, although my knees were weak.

The front door, a large Gothic affair with twin panels of frosted glass, swung inward without warning, almost too violently, and there was the hulking matriarch, her eyes sparkling wildly not at me but at her daughter. God help us! Had she been listening? Something about the way she glared fixedly at Margaret without glancing at me gave me hope that she had not, but all the same I felt a tremendous and bitter disappointment, a detumescent frustration, knowing already that our glorious tryst was shot to hell.

"Margaret!" she wailed. "Margaret Margaret *Margaret*." In this re-echoing drumfire was the clang of some sickness, some unutterable disgust and anguish and chagrin.

"Y-y-yes, Mother?" quaked Margaret, dissolved in dread.

"Margaret, what*ever* on *earth* have you *done* to your *room*? Good gracious *sakes!*"

"*Mother*," Margaret said, her panic suddenly eased by righteous indignation, "*what have you been doing up in my room?* You promised you would never, never go into my room."

"May *God* look *down* upon us in the infinite *mercy* of His *heart!* May this cup *pass!*" Mrs. Austin, her eyes rolled heavenward and her hands clutching her bosom, looked like one of those extravagantly pious Magdalenes in late baroque painting.

"Mother, you snoop!" Margaret accused.

"*Margaret,* you *nasty* demon!" her mother rejoined. "The *devil* has *possessed* you. You *knew* I would see it. You *wanted* me to see it. Oh, of *all* the *most*—"

"Pardon—" I began, one hand timidly raised.

But I was ignored. "I was *afraid* it would come to *this*," Mrs. Austin went on. "*Time* and time *again* I *told* you you should *talk* with Dr. *Ashley,* but you wouldn't *listen.* Now *I'm* going to *take* you, young lady. *Right* this *minute.*"

With that, she gripped Margaret's arm and almost pulled her off the porch, down the front steps, across the lawn, and into the car, an old Hudson parked in the driveway. I might have been ignored, forgotten completely except, just in that last moment before she was pushed into the front seat and the door was slammed on her, Margaret raised her eyes and looked at me through the wisteria vines, giving me a sheepish, apologetic, almost idiotically helpless look. Then she blew a kiss at me. And was gone.

TWENTY-ONE

I was still smiling, so help me. That was me all over. Like an outworn circus poster still clinging to a brick wall six months after the show has left town, a senseless grin was still stuck on my face. The fault of the recklessly optimistic *Reader's Digest,* I suppose. Not even my loss, the bitter deprivation of a voluptuous and gratifying rendezvous in a motor hotel, nor my sudden Stone-ache, could quite squelch that unwitting master passion of benignity, toleration. Nothing, I had been advised by *Reader's Digest,* is really worth worrying about, worth getting into a stew about. So I would not. Eventually Margaret would return and then we . . . But would she? Would she return, or would this Dr. Ashley impound her? I had a picture of a black Vandyke, thick lenses, sunlight struggling through Venetian slats into a darkened room, knouts and thumbscrews and Procrustean chaises longues. If the old lady didn't like the way she decorated her room, why hadn't she just politely asked her to change it? Or, better yet, live and let live; Margaret was a full-grown woman, after all, and she ought to be entitled to a little free will, at least in matters of personal taste. Whatever could she have done, I wondered, that would so affront her mother? Put up scenic wallpaper of Sybaritic orgies? Planted marijuana in the window boxes? Made a mobile out of whiskey bottles? The front door was still open; Mrs. Austin had not even paused to close it behind her. I might just run up and have a look. I glanced up and down the street; except for a kid riding his tricycle two doors down, it was empty. I tiptoed in. Closing the door, I addressed the house, "Is anybody home?" Nobody was. Automatically I wiped my feet on the coir doormat, the block letters AUSTIN obscurely visible in the tawny warp of its woof. Then I began to climb the long staircase. Near the top of the first flight I heard the quick patter of footsteps, and stopped, waited, listening, but it was only the quick patter of heartbeats, my own. The staircase ended in a wilderness of khaki corridors, alcoves and doors. "Try me," one passage seemed to suggest, so I groped down it, past more doors, all of them shut, and came at last to a narrow terminal door, which I opened. Behind it was a steep slender stairway hurdling up behind, and parallel to, the wall. Light from the summit lit my way. When I got up there, pausing to catch my breath, I saw that this was sunlight and that it was infiltrating from all over: louvers in the gable tops, a fanlight, thin clerestory windows in the mansard cupola, and a galaxy of pinholes in the roof, planetariaed above me in the murky and musty clouds of crepuscule that hung like cobwebs from the rafters and corners, looming over the rough purlins and the bare lathwork, shrouding a jumble of dust-caked trunks, corrugated boxes, decadent metallic gimcracks and contrivances, a wasteyard of dispossessed belongings. There was a ragged smell of old cedar, wool, mildew, grease and the thin vegetal spoor of nocturnal insects and vermin. The attic is the subconscious, the id, of every house, somebody—Margaret?—once said to me. The attic receives into its snug and secret shadows the unwanted refuse of the rest of the house, and will keep it up here forever or until some of it, any of it, might possibly be needed or wanted again. No matter how lovely the rest of the house is, the attic will always somehow be frightening, haunted by all manner of dreadful things made even more awful by the darkness in which they are kept. To heal the derangement of this id is to convert it, with partitions and asphalt tile and lighting fixtures and curtains, into a sane and normal floor: rumpus rooms or guest rooms or studios, and this had only been done in part to this particular house: I saw at one end of the attic how broad lengths of sheetrock had been erected within a framework of two-by-fours to form a room, one room, a large room made small by the way it was up here alone, fastened into a corner of this vast dim chamber like a nest precariously leeching the limb of a tree. It had a door, and the door was open, and I went in. The change, the contrast between this charming and personal room and the chaotic gloom outside, relieved me, gave me a sense of welcome which assuaged the guilt of my intrusion. Nice furniture, strikingly modern in contrast to the rest of the house, was tastefully arranged, artfully composed: a desk, a dresser, an easy chair, a studio couch, a coffee table. Everything had a pleasant turquoise color scheme, feminine without being effeminate; the only purely girlish objects in the room were a bevy of homemade rag dolls aligned in sitting positions on the couch. . . . But the walls—the *walls,* for crying out loud! Assaulting the chaste immaculate air of the furniture, the walls were cataclysmic explosions of riotous earthy strokes and slashes and smirches; a chimpanzee-painter could not have done these murals in his most rambunctious moment. I gasped aloud. Only a fraction of time would I remain standing in this state of shock, less than a minute before I would get out of there, but in the swift course of those few seconds I tried to take it all in—this overpowering maelstrom of ustulate shades, this umbered and ochered expression of some terrific, unconscionable anguish or panic or hatred. With palpitating, fibrillating heart I focused my eyes momentarily on individual parts of it, and perceived that the whole creation was a fuscous meshwork of letters and cursive swirls, a crisscrossing, overlapping, superimposing signboard of dozens of words, vengeful stigmata block-drawn in a thick vile impasto—a graphic, verbal defilement of the wall. "M is for the muttonhead you are, O is for the offal in your awful heart, T is for the tits you never let me nurse," began a scurrile diatribe obviously addressed to Mrs. Austin, but the rest of it was mercifully obscured beneath a general overlay of lurid epithets. Elsewhere were dithyrambic ditties in which nearly antonymic words, most of them off-color, were forced to rhyme with each other; other less fescennine jingles; double-entendred behests ("Slater, put your money where your mouth is"); unkindly but fecund remarks ("Ethel Slater is a disabled lesbian"); and, strewn helter-skelter all over it all in the same tainted brown tints, vortical streaks suggesting the turmoil of a muddy river, one of which, as I gazed at it in heart-stopped horror, began to slip slitheringly down the wall. It didn't matter. I had had enough. More shocked than sick, I turned to go and, in aiming at the door, dropped my eyes to the place where the artist had signed her work, signed it traditionally in the manner of the old masters, using Latin, albeit flawed Latin imperfectly modified, but still all too clear, adust, feeble but defiant: *M. Austin fecit cum feces.*

2

HOW TO GET DOWN OUT OF TREES

Many mountain damsels carry love charms consisting of some pinkish, soap-like material, the composition of which I have been unable to discover; the thing is usually enclosed in a carved cherry pit, and worn on a string round the neck.
—Vance Randolph, *The Ozarks*

ONE

I got stinking drunk. Shambling southward block after block, lost, I finally came upon a liquor store at Fifteenth and High, went in, asked for a pint of bourbon, was asked what kind, replied anything, was requested to furnish proof of age, produced a stale draft card, was sold something in a paper bag, took it half a block down the street, eased the paper down below the neck, wrapped it around there, removed the cap, tilted it up and, *ah*, took a long swallow. In broad daylight, on the street. Fully aware that this was a weak, craven, despairing surrender, I convinced myself that it was completely in character and therefore not only pardonable but also reasonable, under the circumstances. Like a mordant cathartic the raw whiskey scoured through me, like Lysol, like Drano, it routed and rinsed my stricken soul. *Venia necessitati datur,* I had told Sam Houston in that dream: Indulgence is granted to necessity, we can get tanked up so long as we got a good reason. And he had said: I sure as hell have got a good reason. And now so have I. Pausing every block or so for another liberal gulp, I flounced homeward. Sybil would help me, she would drown my megrims in the deep soft oblivion of her spontaneous yielding; my heavy heart would achieve amnesty through the heart-pounding sweat of a lusty romp.

But she wasn't there. This day of all days she probably chose to go shopping. I checked each room, but the house was indeed deserted. Just me and my bottle, my little old bottle. I flopped down, all asprawl, in an easy chair, pressing the flat bottle to my chest, peering down into its neck alternately with one eye and the other. Half empty. Maybe I could pass out.

So I finished the bottle, but I couldn't. I lay face downward on the living-room rug and closed my eyes, but I couldn't go, I couldn't make it. A noncompos nincompoop, I lay there for ten minutes and then I had to get up, rising like a bloated and ponderous submarine, to go to the bathroom. Afterward I made another attempt to phone the Missouri Pacific baggage agent. Please, I said to him, please get me my suitcase so's I can go home. I can't go home if you won't get me my suitcase. I have to have it. I've been walking around for four days now in the same suit, the same tie, the same goddamn smelly old shirt. Please. And he said: Buddy, I'm doin the best I can, keep your shirt on.

Tottering around the house, in and out of rooms, of closets and cabinets, I looked high and low for the secret cache of Daddy's liquor. I knew he had some, I knew he had a lot of it, but I couldn't find any. After I had already reeled out of the house and was heading southward again down Ringo, I remembered that I had forgotten to check the bottom of the dirty-clothes hamper, where often there had been a bottle or two in the past, but by then my lurching gait was so swift that I couldn't turn around and go back. Naps would have some anyway, a jar of rotgut at least, a little homemade stump with some sissing kick in it, and me and him could go off on a hellbender. My only friend.

The sun was hot, oh Lord the sun was hot, and the heavy white oppressive waves of it boiled my skull and thickened my fuddle. At Roosevelt Road, I had to wait a long time for an opening in the traffic before darting across, and then I tripped on the curb at the other side and sprawled, fell hard to the sidewalk, skinning my hands, one cheek, and tearing a rip in the knee of my trousers. An old woman, trailing an empty grocery cart, paused to help me up, but smelled me and went on. I pushed and arched and hauled myself up and pitched onward, into the last white residential part of Ringo, blessedly deserted unless scared housewives peeked through jalousied windows to watch the staggering progress of this bruised seersuckered lush as he headed inexorably toward Darktown.

Leaving the rows of nice white houses, I set stodgy foot in that final segment of Ringo which is increasingly poor and colored. The street thins and becomes dirt, it elbows sharply to the right at West Twenty-ninth to avoid an open sewer, then straightens out again and, still dirt, for another half-dozen blocks moves on between brown tumbledowns with chicken coops and even a hogsty behind some of them; houses, some of them without electricity, many without plumbing, where janitors and laundresses embrace on iron beds in small rooms and produce caddies.

"Where you goan, white man?" somebody asked of me, and I turned to see a gathering of truant gnomes playing mumble-de-peg in the scarred earth of a front yard, their game interrupted by my unique coming. One of them had straightened up, still on his knees, and was addressing me.

"M'lookin fnapshod's house,"I said. "Zee liveround here?"
"Who?"
"Naps Hod," I said, as clearly as I could manage, then I added, "Misser N. Lon Hod."
"Sho he do," another one said. "But what you want with him fo?"
"Za goofren amine," I explained.

They pointed in unison toward the end of the street. I nodded and moved on. Behind me, one of them advised, "Always drink pure water. Many a man get hisself drunk from breakin dis rule." His colleagues cackled appreciatively. They made other remarks among themselves, their voices a surreal and diminishing drone in back of me.

I plodded on to the end of the street. On opposite corners were two similar frame houses. The one on the right seemed somehow to suggest Naps's character—something about the cocky slant of its porch roof—so I tried it. There was no doorbell; I knocked. I knocked for a long time and then pressed my face against the small pane of glass set in the door. When my eyes readjusted to the darkness of the interior all I could make out was a strange blurred swaying movement, but then when my eyes readjusted once more I was startled to discover that this was a Negro woman's face not five inches away from my own and that it was shaking back and forth while its eyes gazed steadily and coldly at me. I knocked again, but this ulotrichous head only shook more stubbornly. "Naps Hod!" I cried, but she couldn't hear me through the closed door. I mouthed the name with exaggerated lip movements several times but she couldn't read it. At last at least she opened the door a crack and said, "We doan want nuthin today." "Ma'am—" I said. Bam! the door closed again. But unless she was Naps's mother-in-law or something, this wasn't the right house anyway. I tried the other. The woman there didn't want nothing today either, but before she closed the door I managed to convince her that I was only looking for Naps Howard. "Huh-yeah!" she aspirated, and pointed to the woods on the other side of Thirty-sixth Street, where Ringo ceased to exist. A thick little forest of post oaks, their scalloped leaves already deep green and thick. "*Where?*" I said. "In *there*," she said, still pointing a finger straight at the woods. "*Where?*" I said again, squinting in the direction of her point. "Y'mean elivesun one those *trees?*" She laughed. "Naw. You go on now. Get off my porch, Mister Alcohol. This a Christian house. You lookin for Naps Howard, that's where you'll find him, over there."

Sure enough, on the other side of Thirty-sixth Street, in the shade of the thick post oaks, I found a mailbox, a long barrel-domed post-mounted one of the kind used for RFD, with the name on the side: N. Leon Howard. I also found near it the beginning of a driveway, a long, smoothly paved asphalt drive which wound its way among the husky oaks and between two rows of gas lanterns mounted on tall poles. This strange driveway led me on thus through the woods for another fifty yards before I saw the house. The house. House? I wondered, vertiginously summoning up Yale's History of Art 166b: Stylistic Development in American Domestic Architecture, in which Professor Meeks implanted in me the ability to recognize the sources of style in any house in this country, from Colonial times to the present, but had not equipped me to deal with this one: Japanese-inspired, perhaps, in its lines, the angles of its roof and the proportions, on a kind of oriental *Section d'Or*, of its various parts; but in general a preponderance of features characteristic of that free contemporary class called "organic hillside"; yet its materials clearly seemed to be on loan from the more humble rural domestic architecture of the nineteenth-century South: wattle-and-daub, narrow clapboards and fieldstone, all used in elegant disavowal of their low-born origins. In short, it was a unique, thoroughly modern house of great size, one which tastefully echoed certain pleasing elements of the Old South era. What it was doing out here on the edge of Africa, I couldn't understand, but I did at last comprehend an important fact about my friend: he was indeed only a chauffeur, hence the cap he wore, hence the fine automobile he periodically borrowed from his master for jaunts about town, hence this bold and wonderful mansion, behind which I would find the modest servants' quarters where he had his domicile. A glorious but scoundrelly deceit.

Wishing not to attract the attention of the owners, I stealthily stumbled off through the trees and around to the rear of the manse. But the only detached building back there was an open garage. The Lincoln was nowhere in sight. Maybe, I reflected, the servants' quarters are incorporated in the house proper. I went to the back door and pushed the button, what the hell. A bell chimed and the maid appeared, a young Negro woman, bronzely handsome, wearing a stiffly starched apron. "We don't want anything today," she said through the screen door.

"Snaps aroun?" I asked.

She studied me closer. "Who?"

"Naps Hod. Zee work here?"

"Yes he does," she said. "But he's not here at the moment. Could I help you?"

"Whenlee beback?"

"It's hard to say," she said. "What did you wish to see him about?"

"M'un olfrena his," I said. "Olfren."

"I'm Mrs. Howard," she said.

"Zatright? Youn apswife?"

"Yes."

"Well well."

"And what is your name?" she asked.

"Clifferstone," I said.

"I don't recall his mentioning you," she said.

"Ecallsme Nub."

"Nub?" Her face lighted up. "You're *Nub*? Well, my goodness! Of course. Come on in." She held the screen door wide open for me. "He should be back soon." I walked into the kitchen, a chromium and copper and blue-tiled electronic servolab. She motioned me on, through the hall, and followed me. "Just make yourself at home. Could I fix you a cup of coffee?"

"Don wanna benny trouble," I said.

"That's all right. Just make yourself at home. I'll be right with you."

"Don wanna botherin body."

She just smiled and went back to the kitchen, abandoning me in the hall. What was I supposed to do? Why didn't I just sit in the kitchen and drink my coffee and wait for Naps? But maybe this hall led to their quarters, maybe they had their own sitting room or something. I shuffled on through it, conscious of being watched by the eyes of Audubon birds in several prints from the original elephant folio. The hall ended in a vast, multi-level living room, and one look at it told me I had come the wrong way. A huge free-standing fireplace of fieldstone rose up in the center of the room and rammed its end through hand-hewn beams and out through the ceiling. A plush crotcheted rug with a muted parquetry pattern in taupe covered the larger floor area and was anchored by antique ladder-back and arrow-back chairs with seats of woven, twisted cornhusks. Against one wall stood a foursquare milk safe with panels of black tin perforated in eagle designs; I had seen only one like it before, in the tavern room of the Arkansas Territorial Capitol Restoration. Elsewhere in the great room were unique chests and cabinets of cypress wood, flowing flame grain; trestle tables, slatted country Sheraton settees, primitive sculpture and other artifacts. My God, it was incredible, and I wouldn't have known what to make of it had I not, just the other evening, seen all of these things in those books on Southern furniture and crafts. A veritable one-room museum of the best of old-time Dixie artisanry. So fascinated was I by this spectacle that I completely forgot to worry about being an intruder. My intoxication was replaced by a giddiness of a new kind: a breath-taking thrill at having stumbled upon this treasure-trove. Maybe I could get the master's permission to make photographs of his collection for the Cabot Foundation. Wouldn't Clara be entranced! By golly, I could just sit down right here in this room and do enough work to fill a whole filing cabinet at the Cabot.

"Nub?"

Just look at that pine statue over there! Lord, what sheer power of expression and

"Mr. Stone?"

And sense of proportion. Uncanny! And these draperies: primitive but variegated appliqué designs of war-painted Choctaws in combat with white settlers. Must be about 1810, at least, because the linen threads are

"Mr. Stone, here's your coffee."

Obviously unloomed handweave. What? "What? Oh, thank you!" I said, and then, as I took the offered cup, I realized my voice was too loud. Lowering it, I mentioned privately, "Fabyous room. Was jus mirin the furshure."

She smiled. "Won't you sit down?"

"Here?" I looked around me.

"If you like. Or would you rather go out on the terrace? But it's hot out there."

"Well—"

"Let's just sit in here," she said, taking my arm and leading me down into the level of the living room. "I'll turn up the air-conditioning."

Reluctantly I sat down in one of the rare cornhusk-seated pieces and she, after tinkering with the Honeywell, sat down in another one beside me. She had removed the starched apron, revealing a pair of tight blue jeans which did not strike me as properly menial. She had a good figure for a small woman, smaller even than Naps. I'm afraid that I can't properly judge beauty among Negroes, but it seemed to me she was awfully attractive in contrast to her husband. Her wide-set eyes had a mischievous slant to them, and the irises had a greenish cast. Her mouth naturally was quite full, but not as thick as is often the case. Through the thin liquored haze over my eyes she even seemed enravishing, like the furniture.

Apparently she had been alone here, except for a small child whose distant soliloquies I kept hearing off and on. Naps had probably driven the master down to Worthen's Trust or Merrill Lynch, and the lady of the house was most likely off at a club luncheon somewhere. Thus we had the liberty of the living room.

"Where'd they fine all this stuff?" I asked, indicating the furniture with a sweep of my hand.

"Well," she said, "the dealers picked it up at various places, mostly by just snooping around, you know. But a lot of it came from my granddaddy."

"*Your* granfather? How'dee get it?"

"Well, his people had been slaves and, you know, the landowners gave their cast-off furniture to their slaves. You'd be surprised how many fine heirlooms are still in the hands of poor colored people."

"Tha sybird oar there," I said, pointing at a big maple sideboard at one end of the room, "tha dint come from any slave. Thassa Loozanna Cajun sybird, eighteent censhry. Valble. *Priceless.*"

"Yes, I know. I found that at a small antique shop out on the old Hot Springs highway. How that dealer got it I can't imagine, but he wasn't aware of its provenance, so I picked it up cheap. But how did you recognize it as Louisiana Cajun?"

"M'a speshlust," I said, allowing myself a little braggartry. "N'expert. Connasewer ovold furshure 'n all like that."

"Really? Naps told me you live in Boston now, but he didn't say what you do."

"Assissant curetur of th' Cabot Fundayshun."

"You don't say! The Cabot. Why, I've got just dozens and dozens of their pamphlets!"

"I wrote half avem."

"Well, I'll be! And here you are, sitting in the flesh! What a surprise!" She shook her head back and forth at the wonder of it, and then eagerly she asked, "Would you . . . would you care to see some of my other things?"

"Be dlighted," I said. So she took me for a tour of the house, into bedrooms where I inspected gracefully turned four-posters and fine old boudoir chairs and unusual blanket chests, into bathrooms and half-baths where I saw original cabinets constructed of persimmon wood and porcelain fixtures which she claimed were of the first type used in Arkansas bathrooms of the late nineteenth century, into the dining room where a whole new panoply of splendid fittings charmed my eye.

Then she led me downstairs, into an enormous workroom, where countless other pieces of old furniture were stacked in various conditions of disrepair, waiting to be restored or refinished. "And here is my lair," she said, "my hive."

One glance at this pile of raw jewels turned my knees to glutenous pap, and I staggered to the wall for support. "M'ask you apersnal question?" I begged.

"Certainly," she said, all charm.

"Zis *your* house?"

She laughed. "Well, if it isn't, I'll be awfully surprised to find out whose it is."

"But . . . what's your husband . . . Naps, whazzee do fr'lving?" I asked, as I began to wander among the fine plethora of tossed chairs and chests and all.

"He sells books," she said.

"Thas wha he tells me," I said skeptically.

I glanced furtively away from the stock furniture at her long enough to see what her face was doing. She was just smiling, with her hands clasped behind her. Was she smiling because Naps did more than sell books, or was she simply beaming with pride as she watched me examine this hoard? An unreal and a mysterious and a perplexing situation. I roved on, bending to study a chair bottom here, pulling to look at a drawer mortise there. This is a peculiar cherry wood, which will look just great with a rubbed oil finish. That is sassafras wood, by George, but who would've thought you could make a taboret out of it? And this . . . a ball-footed gate-leg table, unlike any I had ever seen before, with a singular stippled grayish-white coloration, a peculiar nacreous surface. I ran my hand lovingly over it. . . . And discovered to my horror that its finish clung turbidly to my fingers.

"Oops," I said.

Nap's wife giggled, then said, "Oh, heavens! That's a table that my granddaddy had out in his chicken coop, and the chickens . . . they . . . it's just covered with— But you can wash your hand at the sink over there . . ."

Christ Almighty, can I not escape? Am I to be haunted, *plagued*, with it? Reeling, I struck myself on my already-ripped trousers with the contaminated hand, wiping it off. Foul! My soul all sullied, soiled! All the world a vile midden!

TWO

When Naps came home he perceived at once that something was wrong with me, and he became solicitous and ministerial, taking away my coffee cup and replacing it with a full glass of iced straight whiskey, and it wasn't rotgut, it wasn't stump, but good Jack Daniels, smooth. His wife and I had still been in the workshop when he arrived, and he had yelled, "Tatrice, what the devil you doin down here in the basement with a white man?" jokingly, kiddingly, jubilant at finding me in his house, but his sudden appearance and his mock outrage, coupled with the distressed frame I was already in, had set me to trembling helplessly, and I consumed considerable of his Jack Daniels before I could stop. To his questions I could only reply that I had been struck all of a heap with misery and sorrow, and that I was going back to Boston as soon as I could retrieve my lost suitcase, or without it if necessary, and I only wanted to drop in and say good-bye to him.

But I didn't leave. I woke up about noon the next day, in one of those four-posters upstairs with a fine view of the granite hills and the Fourche Creek Valley south of town. I stood at the window staring at that view for a long time, jittery, stale, drymouthed, my brains on fire, before I could remember where I was, what had happened. Then my first thought was simply: Goodness, I've not only sat down at the table with niggers, I've slept in their house as well. But I could recall very little of how the evening had passed. Talk, mostly, and drink. We had lounged in Naps's study most of the afternoon, and I remembered being envious of the size of his book collection, which I had got up to examine from time to time; among other things, he seemed to have every book on the Negro that had ever been written, from Gunnar Myrdal to Margaret Just Butcher, and including every written word by Negroes themselves: Frederick Douglass, Saunders Redding, G. W. Carver, Booker T. Washington, Dunbar's poems, W. E. B. DuBois, and the moderns, Langston Hughes, Richard Wright, James Baldwin, John Williams, even LeRoi Jones, as well as, of all things, the complete Frank Yerby, which I thought might have been overdoing it a bit. I had accused him of chauvinism and we had argued, but I could not remember his words. The children had come home from school and I had been introduced to them: Lucy, a tall skinny girl of seven; Mart, a six-year-old spitting image of his father; and the baby too, little Jimmy, whose babble I had heard earlier in the day. Lucy had looked shyly at me and had asked, "You from the school board?" and Naps had winked at me and then explained to his children who I was. A beautiful family he had, a beautiful house, a beautiful car; how did it happen, I had asked him, that he was still the same ugly runt I used to tote bags with at Riverdale Country Club? We had joked a lot and had exchanged many friendly insults, and it seemed to me that he had become almost as tipsy as I was.

The rest of the evening after dinner had been an archipelago of small islands of consciousness, short broken moments which lay suspended and isolated in my mind's drunken eye. There had been a lot of words spoken, but I didn't know whether they were mine or theirs. We had listened to music; a great many Negro spirituals had been played on the elaborate stereo hi-fi, but I remembered only two: "Sometimes I Feel Like a Motherless Chile," and one that Naps himself surprisingly had sung in a deep, repercussive baritone full of cadent surge: "There's No Hiding Place Down Here." Later some jazz had been played, and I recalled learning, with Tatrice, how to twist. They had tried to teach me another dance too, a weird thing called limbo, which consisted of me falling on my back several times while a broomstick was passed over me like a voodoo wand. It had all been great fun, Tatrice the soul of charm, Naps the convivial host, but at some time or another it had died, faded, gone to nothing . . .

Nothing all night except a vague notion that somehow before or maybe after I was put to bed I learned the answer to an old riddle. Perhaps I only imagined it or at last solved it myself through some kind of drink-stimulated cleverness, but it seemed I had learned it from him. It was his name, his real name, and it was Napoleon. Napoleon Desha County Howard. If I dreamed anything that night, my dreams were of Arcole, Rivoli, Eylau, of Waterloo and Saint Helena.

Despite my crapulous chemistry the day after, I felt in good spirits, almost cheerful, having shoved out of my mind whatever it was that had been bothering me. Naps called me down for a brunch which he had spread out for us himself: poached eggs on toast, smoked turkey, Benzedrine, and a beverage he called bullshot—hot beef bouillion laced with bitters and vodka. Tatrice was in her workshop, he said, removing hen droppings from a table. I shuddered and looked askance, and, in looking askance, saw beside my plate a cardboard box.

"What's this?" I asked.

"Your order," he said.

"My *what*?"

"Your order. Open it."

I did. The box contained six identical copies of *Fanny Hill*. "Oh my gosh!" I said.

"I just got it," he said, beaming proudly.

"Well, golly, Naps, I . . . I thought you were just kidding. I didn't really mean to order all of these."

"Well, you *did*, and there they are."

"How much do I owe you?"

"Seven dollars."

"For *all* of them?"

"Apiece."

"Hell, Naps, I don't have that kind of money. Besides, I wouldn't know what to do with *six* copies."

"You said half a dozen. That's six."

"Yes, but I was just joking, and—"

He slapped me on the shoulder and laughed. "Sho," he said. He took five of the copies away. "I can sell these mighty easy. You keep that one. My compliments."

"Well, *say*, thanks a lot." I picked it up and thumbed admiringly through it.

"But don't read it *now*. You doan wanta get goona-goona this time of day."

I chortled self-consciously and put the book aside. We plunged into the brunch. The dog hair in the bullshot did wonders for my disposition. "Naps," I asked, "did you or did you not tell me what your full name is last night? I don't remember."

"Yeah, I tole you. That's about the time you passed all the way out, just as I was beginnin to explain how come I got that name."

"I'm sorry," I said. "I didn't mean to be rude."

"Aw, that's okay. I passed out myself not long after you did."

"How *did* you get that name? Because you're short and brash and saucy? And ambitious?"

"Naw, they didn't name me after *that* Napoleon," he said. "My daddy he was born in Desha County down on the Mississippi, and he named all his chillen after towns in that county. My dad wanted to name me McGeehee cause that's his home town, but my momma wouldn't let him name me that for some reason, so he named me Napoleon, but the town Napoleon aint there no mo, it aint been there for a long, long time. Mark Twain tells in his *Life on the Mississippi* how the river come up a big flood one day and washed that whole town down toward N'Orleans, and they aint nuthin out there on that muddy bank no mo but a piece of lumber here and there and some old bricks. It washed away before my dad was even born, but it was a big place once and they still tell about it to this day." After a sip of coffee, Naps went on. "They's a lot of Little Rock folks come from Desha County, for some reason or other. You know Feemy Bastrop, well, he come from there. . . . And Mr. Slater, too, he was born in McGeehee, same town as my dad. Matter of fact, that's how come Feemy workin for him. Mr. Slater figured that Feemy's granddaddy had most likely been *owned* by Mr. Slater's folks and therefore he had a sentimental attachment for Feemy."

"I suppose the feeling wasn't reciprocal."

"It was for a while. Feemy used to think Mr. Slater was a fine man, but he says he's been going downhill for the last few years, and aint worth a hoot no more."

"From what I've managed to learn about Slater, I've got a pretty low opinion of him myself."

"I know," Naps said, grinning. "That's nearly all you talked about last night."

"Really? I can't remember a thing I said."

"Him and that girl. You were awfully bothered about um."

"What did I say about her?"

"You said a awful lot."

"Like?"

"Like what all she done to her room."

"I told you *that*?"

"Yeah, man, you really did. Tatrice got kinda upset. She don't know her, but I mean, well, she got kinda upset hearin you tell about it."

"Gee, why didn't you shut me up?"

"Me? Not on your life, boy. Wasn't no call for me to interfere, specially as curious as I was. You know me, Nub, I'm just like you, always stickin my nose in other folks's business."

"Was I very obnoxious?"

"Now I wouldn't say that atall. You was just tired and sorrowful, but you didn't cause no offense. Seemed to me you was pretty heartbroken, and the least I could do was hear you out."

"I was, I guess. I feel a lot better today, but just thinking about it again gets me sad all over again."

"Aw, don't let it bug you. Just blame it all on Mr. Slater and forget about it."

"That's just it. I don't know whether he's really to blame or not."

"Sho he is. I spoke with Feemy on the phone this morning, and he said she was out there the other night, and he said they didn't get along none too well, lots of hollerin and cursin at each other."

"Does your friend Feemy know what they were saying?"

"Says she tole um she didn't need him no more, cause she had somebody else now, and he got mad."

"She didn't say who else?"

"Naw, but I do believe she must've been meanin *you*."

I sighed. Lost in thought, I contemplated the bitter poignancy of it. Was this sorrow I felt sorrow for myself, or was I beginning to feel it for her again, all over again?

"Last night," Naps said. "Last night when you were pretty far gone you tole me you liked it here so much, I mean here at my place, that you just wished you was a nigger, wished you was a *Howard*, you said, so you could just stay here and not see no white folks again."

"I did?"

"Yeah, and I tole you you just a white nigger, but I don't believe you could hear me. Well, there's a lot of whites seem to feel that way. They say, Oh, lookee how musical the black man is, lookee at how *creative* and all he is! Oh, what joy and *color* he gets out of life! He don't never get bored, he don't never feel stale, cause everthing he does is just one big jamboree that suits him right down to the ground, just a livelong whoopdeedoo. Shit, I say. You want to know how come the colored folks feel so deep, how come they got such pepper and passion in um, I'll tell you: It's cause they *suffer*. They aint nobody got any heart or soul until they done a little sweatin and bleedin. The more you hurt, the more you weep, and *sing*. The more you die, the more you get a big kick out of livin. That's the way it is. Me and you are past that, it don't matter that you're white and I'm black. Me and you are just a couple of fat cats with satisfied ways, we on Easy Street now. But, Nub, I'm still fightin, some, I aint halfway across that river yet. Are you?"

"I'm not sure I understand what you mean."

"Aw, I doan mean you not welcome to stay here. Naw. You one of the finest peckerwoods I know, and they not many fine ones in this town. I just mean it won't do you no good to be a nigger, even if you could. You aint even learned how to be a white man yet."

"Now that sounds a trifle insulting to me. Not to say contradictory."

"Maybe it is. What I'm tryin to tell you is: What do you know about raisin ruckus nowdays? what *principles* you got that you would stick up for? how many chips you got on your shoulder?"

"I'm no crusader. I don't have any reason to be. If I can just watch out for myself, I'll be doing all right."

"But you aint even watchin out for yourself, that's what I mean! The world stompin all over you, man, and you not doin nuthin about it."

"What am I supposed to do? What the hell *can* I do?"

"You lissen a me, Nub. You been knockin around like a chicken with his head cut off, and you got me worried, man. You gimme all that truck bout runnin back to Boston, and I say to myself: What kinda yellow-gut fraidy-cat is this boy, my old buddy who used to whale tar out of anything or anybody that got in his way? Why don't he get wise to hisself? Wants to scoot back to his Boston mammy with his tail tween his legs. I got to laugh. No, man, that just aint you, that just aint ole Nub. If you got any gism in you, if you got any shine at all, you wouldn't let yourself get so bothered by a little thing like what Miss Margaret done to the walls of her room."

"A *little* thing? My God, Naps, it—"

"Hold on, man. Just pardon me for sayin so, but you the kind of fella jumps to conclusions too much. Lemme just ask you: did you *smell* it?"

"Certainly," I shot back, offended. But then I had to pause and ponder. Come to think of it, I had been so stunned by the sight of it that I hadn't taken the trouble to notice what impression, if any, my olfactory sense had been registering. I could not honestly recall any precise smell.

"How you know it wasn't plain old mud, maybe?" he asked.

"Maybe it was," I allowed.

"Okay. There. Don't go runnin off from your projects just cause they got a kink in um."

I asked him what he recommended that I do. He said that was entirely up to me. I said I wondered if he expected me to return to Margaret's house and say to her mother, "Madam, may I run upstairs for a moment to smell your daughter's room?" Don't get smart, Naps admonished.

Most of the afternoon I spent in meditation. Where was Margaret now? What had her mother done with her? Some of the things written on that wall probably tipped Mrs. Austin off to the fact that there was more than simply a professional relationship between Slater and Margaret, in which case Mrs. Austin might be all the more outraged. And what about this Dr. Ashley whom Mrs. Austin had whisked Margaret off to see? Would he commit her to the state hospital for observation? Would he give her a long series of ink-blot tests or something? Was she really crazy? When, if ever, would I see her again? What, if anything, could I possibly do for her—short of eloping with her? And wasn't there something rather odd—*loose*, even—about her eagerness to shack up with me in a motor hotel? I couldn't cope with all these questions by myself. I needed help, and I knew who that help was.

Later in the afternoon, as Naps was in his study working on his accounts, I interrupted to ask what day it was. He said it was Friday. Good, I thought. Dall had said that Friday was his day off. I told Naps I had to go see a man about a dog. I was reseersuckered again; Tatrice had laundered my suit, my shirt, even my underclothes, and had neatly mended the rip in the knee of my trousers.

"Hey, wait a minute," Naps said. "Lemme give you a ride."

I had Dall's address written down on a scrap of torn Wanted poster in my billfold. I dug it out and told it to Naps, and he drove me over there. When we got there he asked me who it was I was going to see. I knew that he and Dall were violent enemies, but I told him anyway.

He chuckled. "Well, just remember what I told you. If you obliged to eat dirt, eat clean dirt." I got out of the car, and Naps sat there watching me walk away.

THREE

He was in the back yard of what I took to be his house, a simple small white frame hutch tickled by itchy fig trees on a narrow lot in a rather dumpy neighborhood of West Fourth Street. He was out of his uniform, dressed in a white T-shirt stretched taut over his muscular middle, a pair of khaki ex-army pants, and loafers; he looked less commanding. He was playing with a dog, a strapping, sinewy German shepherd of lustery gray coat streaked with black, and of rather menacing mien. The way he was playing with it suggested that either it wasn't his dog or else he wasn't very accustomed to it.

"Hi," I said.

He grunted.

"Your dog?" I asked.

"Yeah," he grunted.

"Splendid-looking beast," I observed. For my compliment the dog snarled at me, baring teeth which seemed to have been filed sharp as a shark's.

"Sit," he grunted.

"Don't mind if I do," I said, surprised and pleased at his hospitality. I sat down on the grass, casual-like, hoping it wouldn't stain the seat of my suit.

"I didn't mean you," he said. "I was speakin at this here dog."

"Oh," I said and got up, stuck my hands in my pockets and stood as inconspicuously as possible to one side, like a sidewalk superintendent observing the progress of an enormous hole.

"Sit, damn ye," he growled at the German shepherd, whacking it on the rump with the back of his hand. Reluctantly, and with considerable snarling, gnashing and frothing, the dog sat. I observed that it had a kind of leather loop attached to its collar and that Dall was clutching this tightly, like a blind man hanging on to a seeing-eye.

"What's his name?" I asked, trying to be sociable.

"Bowzer," he grunted.

"Really? That's interesting," I said affably. "Hi, Bowzer," I said to the dog. He snarled, curling his black upper lip more sneeringly than my father can do. "I don't guess he likes me," I said.

"Who would?" Dall said unpleasantly, but at least it was good to hear him make a substantial remark, ungrunted. "Up," he said to the dog and kicked him in the tail. The dog rose, chomping at imagined butterflies. "Whuddayawant?" Dall gargled, turning to look directly at me for only the second time since I had arrived.

"Dall, let's be friends," I suggested.

"Why?" he said, and scrutinized my face for a moment as if trying to answer the question for himself. Then he turned back to his dog. "I got no use for you," he said. I was hoping he was addressing the dog, but he wasn't. He and Bowzer moved away from me, to the other side of the yard. I remained where I was, watching them from that distance across thirty feet of weedy turf. The two of them resumed their play or work or whatever it was, although the dog was as stubborn as before: Dall would grunt some command at him, and then repeat it, and then reinforce it with a kick or a backhanded whack. This went on for some time; such a battle of wills could not fail to be spectacular and I watched with interest. Silently I was rooting for the dog, and for a moment or two Bowzer's intractable nature seemed to be getting the upper hand. But ultimately Dall succeeded in extracting a measure of obedience from the dog, for he (Bowzer) would now spring and chomp at an imaginary foe, pulling frantically at the leash. Satisfied, Dall hooked his leash to a clothesline pole for a moment, entered the toolshed, and emerged carrying a limp figure which appeared at first glance to be some sort of intricate but threadbare scarecrow. He attached this big floppy mannequin to the clothesline, hooking its shoulders to the line in such a way that it appeared to be standing upright. I gasped in sudden recognition; this huge doll, fashioned with a skill that I would have put completely past Dall's limited talents until I remembered that he had taken art in high school and had some experience with simple sculpture, was, down to the last detail, thick painted lips and broad nose and all, a perfect simulacrum of an insolent Negro man. Although it tended a little too much in the direction of caricature, it was a likeness sufficient to curl my hair and curdle my blood if I had run into it in some narrow alley at night.

Whether or not it could fool Bowzer remained to be seen. Dall unhooked the dog with one hand and with the other gave the clothesline a violent shake, causing the fake Negro to begin a disjointed but audacious dance, like a crude marionette, or like one of those old wooden toys with a string-manipulated darkie automaton. "Sic im!" I heard Dall snort, turning the dog to face the wild dancer, and urging him on. "Sic im!" he said again. "Bad nigger! Bite his pants! Gnaw the bastard!" Bowzer, however, fascinated with this strange creature and its weird convulsive dance, remained rooted to the spot, his haunches planted firmly on the ground and his head tilted sideways in an expression of extreme curiosity and dispassionate observation. Dall's mouth was making a sort of dry flat whistling sound, "Fftt! Fftt! Sic im, boy! Fftt!" but this earnest urging became progressively vehement in the face of Bowzer's disinclination to co-operate. "Goddammit, boy, sic im, I'm tellin yuh! Get im! G'on, kill the black bastard! Eat im up!" He began kicking the dog in the rump, which I immediately sensed was a grievous error. "Stupid mutt!" he yelled. "Sic im, you no-good yap-headed shit-eating fleabag! Sic, SIC, *SIC* IM!"

Bowzer slowly turned his head and gave his master a look of sad, tired, pitying beseechment, then he bit him. He scissored his strong jaws around the calf of Dall's leg and came away with bits of khaki and flesh all commingled. Dall, for all of his great height, managed to rise about four feet skyward, hung there howling for an instant, and came down kicking. His foot connected with the dog's ribs, and the dog howled too, once, then resumed munching Dall's limbs. "Sonofabitch!" Dall yelled. "*Down,* you motherfucker!" Bowzer, stretched on tiptoe with his teeth aiming for Dall's neck, was almost as tall as Dall, and I was a little surprised to discover how equal this match was turning out to be. It would have pleasured me immensely to witness the conclusion of such a contest, but I felt a sense of moral obligation to this old comrade-in-arms, however much he was hostile, and thus because of this ornery onus I determined to furnish a helping hand.

Leaping into the breach, I straddled Bowzer, locking my ankles around his belly and throwing him to the ground. I got a tight, viselike grip on his jaws, keeping them shut, and commanded Dall, "Get his muzzle, quick! Muzzle him!"

"Aint got ary!" Dall replied, bewildered, forlorn.

"A rope, then! Anything!"

Dall scattered in three or four directions at once, and I took advantage of his absence to pacify Bowzer. "Easy, boy," I said.

"Bad man gone away. There now, calm down." I scratched his neck and ears with a free hand and whispered sweet nothings into his ear.

When Dall returned, trotting up with enough hemp to bind all the canines in Christendom, I was sitting relaxed while Bowzer licked my hand. Dall made to fetch him another kick, and Bowzer made to fetch Dall another chomp, but I stayed them both.

"Dammit all to hell, didja see what he *did*?" Dall demanded. "He *bit* me, for godsakes!" Dall rolled up the remains of his trouser leg to show me his wound, which was dribbling a steady trickle of gore. "Twenty bucks I paid for that pooch, and he *bites* me! What kind of a police dog does he think he is?"

It was awfully hard for me to resist the temptation to say, "It served you right." But I resisted. Dall and I had to make up, at all costs. There was a chance, in the excitement of the moment, that he might forget his grudges. So I said, "Let's put Bowzer in the toolshed and then let's see if we can't do something for that nasty leg of yours." Almost absently, distraught and distrait by his ordeal, he yielded to this suggestion. After insuring the dog's comfort in the toolshed, I led Dall into his house, bade him sit, and rounded up some first-aid stuff from his medicine cabinet. While I washed his leg and disinfected it and dressed it with a gauze compress, he kept up a flow of muttered grumbling, speculating about the dog's ancestry, its intelligence, and letting fall enough clear keywords to make it plain that he had bought the dog, out of his own pocket, intending to train it himself for the use of the police in some pending racial crisis. At last he realized who was listening to this incriminating muttering, and he clammed up, staring at me silently and coldly until I finished the bandage. "There," I said. "Maybe you'll live, if Bowzer isn't rabid."

"Thanks, Doc," he said, not smiling.

"Keep in bed for a week, take plenty of aspirin, stay away from dogs and Negroes, and you'll be all right," I said.

"Maybe you oughta drag-ass on out of here anyway," he said. "Ever fool thing you say just makes me mad."

"With your leg like that, you can't throw me out," I said.

"Wanna bet?"

"Yeah."

He sprang to his feet, and for a man with a game leg he was remarkably agile. I backed off, but he didn't come at me. He turned and hobbled off toward his kitchen, saying over his shoulder, "Wanna beer?"

"Yeah," I said, taking a deep breath.

While he was engaged in the icebox I took stock of his living room, a tacky arrangement of second-hand items which could never have had any taste to begin with and now, in the absence of feminine management, had all gone to seed. Two atrocious Sears Roebuck murals, one a Rocky Mountain landscape, the other a trite New England pastorale, covered most of the available wall space. The only other picture in the room was a framed photograph, propped atop a mahogany chifforobe, of a young woman flanked by two small boys, towheads slightly cross-eyed. The ex-Mrs. Dall? All three of them were simple examples of Newton County homeliness, the mother especially, although none of them were quite as much an eyesore as Dall. In one corner of the room stood the inevitable television set, a twenty-one-inch Motorola. In another corner of the room was—wonder of wonders!—a bookcase. It was a small three-shelf affair made of black tin and brass wire, but what surprised me was that it was there at all. I inspected its contents. A number of police manuals; Sykes's *Crime and Society*, Fink's *Causes of Crime*, Blackstone's *Of Public Wrongs*; Bolitho on Murder for Profit, Fisher on Detection, Hill on Sadists, Quentin Reynolds' *Headquarters*, W. T. Brannon's *Crooked Cops*. Sherlock Holmes, complete, and Ian Fleming, complete. *The Fanny Farmer Cook Book*. Manual of Small Arms. Manual of Large Arms. Dittman's *Insanity Laws*. Les Giblin's *How You Can Have Confidence and Power in Dealing with People*. Judo, Jiu-Jitsu and Karate. Vanderbilt's *Etiquette*. Lindgren's *How to Live with Yourself and Like it*. Palmer's *Understanding Other People*. Making the Most of Your Face. How to Spot Card Sharps and Their Methods. How to Make Psychology Work for You. Sewing Made Simple. How to Train Dogs and Win Their Love. And others.

Dall returned and placed two pilseners of beer down on an issue of *Gun* on the coffee table. I indicated his little library and asked, "Have you read all this stuff?"

"Yeah," he said. "You want to sit in here or you want to go out on the porch?"

"The porch," I said. The afternoon was hotter than ever now; the interior of his small house was close and stuffy.

He handed me a pilsener. "Here's yourn," he said.

"Urine?" I said, my eyebrows arched.

"*Yours*, dammit," he said. We went outside and sat down in a couple of old rush-seat straight chairs on the porch. He said, "You're a pain in the butt, Nub boy. You're a real smarty-pants."

"Wasn't I always?"

"Yeah, I guess you was, at that. It's a marvel to me how come you never got took down a peg."

"I'm so little there aren't any more pegs to take me down to."

"Somebody ought to of knocked the everlastin horse-hockey out of you long ago."

"You tried," I reminded him.

"Yeah," he said. We became silent. We drank our beer and watched a few cars pass down the street.

After a while I observed, "Awfully hot for April."

He was squinting at the sky. "Might come a rain fore too long," he said. Then he corrected me. "May," he said. "Today is May Day."

I attempted some ice-breaking reminiscence. "Remember that time we had the Maypole dance in the seventh grade at West Side, and you got all hung up with Sissy Portis, and—"

"I don't rightly recall," he said uncordially, so I shut up. Neither of us spoke for several minutes. Then in the tone of a pawnbroker or a loan shark, he said, "Well, what can I do for you?"

"Dall, let's talk about Margaret," I entreated. *Sure,* he uttered, shrugging his shoulders and spreading his hands in a gesture of compliance. I began: "You said the other day that you don't believe that she is crazy or anything, but I just wonder if she might've done anything . . . well, *peculiar,* you know, when you were around her."

"I don't rightly recall," he said, but then his face assumed a recollective expression, and after a moment's thought he said, "Well, there was this time once when she was screwin her face all up—like this—like she had a bad toothache, and I asked her what in tarnation was the matter, and she just said she was writin a letter on the roof of her mouth with her tongue. But I don't reckon that was so awful crazy. I seen worse."

"Anything else?"

He pondered. "Aw, yeah, there was one other time. She come over here for supper one night—I invited her—and we was eatin spaghetti, cause that's about the only thing I'm any good at fixin, and she took one of these long spaghettas—" he spread his hands two feet apart "—and tilted her head back and swallowed it whole like it was a snake or somethin, thout even chewin it." He paused, reflectively, then went on. "But that don't mean she's crazy. Marge is a real bright old girl, she's got all her marbles far as I'm concerned. Yeah, Nub, she knows all the answers."

After he had refilled our pilseners with beer, he seemed to open up on the subject, and we spent some time discussing the intellect and personality of Margaret Austin. We agreed that considering how crazy the mother was, there was always a possibility that such lunacy could be either hereditary or contagious, or that living in the same house with that woman for twenty-seven years would certainly have *some* damaging effect. Be that as it may, Dall remained convinced that Margaret was of such strong fiber that she had immured herself from the mother, had immunized herself against her.

"Six or seven years back, when she finished out at the junior college," Dall said, "she found out that she couldn't get no scholarship to go on and do the other two years somewhere else —she told me she had wanted to go up to the University cause that's where you was at—but her mother couldn't afford to send her there, or anyway her mother'd *said* she couldn't afford to send her up to Fayetteville, so Margaret had to get herself a job, and she got her one as a file clerk in one of them insurance offices downtown, and she figgered she'd move out of that goddamn house and get her a room of her own somewheres, so she did, but all she could afford out of what little salary she got was this closet-sized little hole in some old boardin house up on Louisiana Street, and she lived there in that place for near bout three months, while all that time her momma kept callin her up on the phone and sayin, 'Why don't you just save your money by living here with us?' and Marge did her level best not to go back, but finally she figgered she wouldn't never have no spare money as long as she had to pay rent and all, so finally she gave it up and went on back home.

"Bout a year after that she took a notion to try and see if she couldn't make out in some big city like New York. So she asked her mother to loan her a little money, just a hundred dollars or so, for the train ticket and to get started on and all, but her mother wouldn't do it. Well, she asked her stepdaddy, Mr. Polk, and he thought it was a good idee and all, but he just didn't have that much spare cash. She told im she'd work hard and pay im back in no time at all, but her momma said New York was 'fraught with dangers'—that's the way she put it, fraught with dangers—and there was just too many risks involved. So there just wasn't a blessed thing that Marge could do. She couldn't even get a bank loan. She'd lost that file clerk job, so she worked for a while in a supermarket, but never did learn how to operate the cash register. Finally she got that job at Alexander's Shoe Shoppe, and somehow managed to keep it for five years. Trouble was, it didn't hardly pay enough to cover her share of the groceries, and her clothes and all.

"The day she told me about this, I offered to loan her a hundred or whatever she needed to get to New York on, and she said that was awful nice of me and she would keep it in mind, but she didn't think much about New York any more, and even if she did go up there, her mother would keep tryin to get her back home, and besides, now that she had this part in Slater's play, she didn't really care to go to New York anyway. What she meant was, I guess, was that Slater was more interestin to her than New York would be."

What hope, I asked Dall, had Margaret held out for Slater? If it were true that she was involved with him, or *had been* involved with him, did she think he would send her to New York to be in the theater? Or what?

Dall was silent. He stared reflectively at the dregs of beer in the bottom of his glass. Then in a subdued tone he mumbled, "I think maybe Slater was fixin to marry her."

"*What?*" I said, astounded. "But what about his wife?"

"Aw, she's kind of pore and sickly, been in a wheelchair for God knows how long, and I reckon Slater was countin on her not lastin much longer." Dall looked at me sideways and smirked mischievously. "Or maybe," he said, "if Mrs. Slater lasted much longer, maybe Mr. Slater would of found some way to kind of *dispose* of her. Who knows?"

FOUR

Apparently there remained a good deal of explaining for Dall to do, and he, sensing this, broke down and invited me to have supper with him. He served spaghetti—properly *al dente*, I was amazed to notice—and a sauce he had made himself, along with a chef's salad and plenty of beer. Between mouthfuls—or during them, all too often—he divulged most of what he knew.

Preambling his disclosures, he said, "You mention *one* word of this to *any*body, and I'll whup the daylights out of you." I gave him my oath.

He had visited the Slater rancho on several occasions, he explained. The first time had been shortly after Margaret won the part in Slater's new play, and she wanted her "best friend," as she referred to Dall, to meet the playwright-director who had given her the role. Dall spent an afternoon with them out there getting acquainted with Slater. When they arrived Slater kissed Margaret. "It was just one of them how-do-you-do kisses," Dall said, "but it kind of took me by surprise, so next time I got a chance I asked Margaret if Slater was on the make, and she said he was just being 'affectionately avuncular,' but that sounded pretty goddamn fishy to me, whatever it meant, and anyway he's the kind of guy has a look on his face all the time like he was about to put his hand up somebody's dress, you know what I mean, so right then and there I got kind of suspicious, and I aint stopped bein suspicious yet."

Slater, Dall opined, was a somewhat cocksure and smart-alecky individual, and had been rather condescending in his manner toward Dall. "Just like you," Dall said. "By God, *yes*, I been tryin to think who he reminds me of. Just as smart-alecky as *you*." He had heard of Slater before, had seen his picture in the paper a couple of times, but wasn't prepared for what he would see in person. "You think *I'm* ugly?" Dall said to me. "Lordalmighty!" And he attempted to describe him, the bright red face, those bulging eyes, the crooked porcine nose, the slick sparse hair, the neckless head: a bestial fright, yet somehow having an emanation of gentility and superiority, enhanced by his clothes, the tweedy coat, the tieless blue silk shirt.

"He's one of them free-thinkers," Dall stated. "Not a communist or anything, but pretty damn radical, and he's always pokin fun at me, just like you. I cant say I blame him, cause I'm a pretty easy feller to poke fun at, but it does kind of rile me, sometimes, when he says things like, 'Well, Sergeant, have you nabbed your quota of shoplifters today?' or 'Well, Sergeant, how's your electric cattle-prod working these days?' or when he calls me 'the long leg of the law' and crap like that. One day he was baitin me about somethin or other when Margaret spoke up—first time I'd ever heard her speak up without bein spoke to first, and it surprised me—she spoke up and said, 'Jimmy, why don't you leave Doyle alone?' Embarrassin.

"Anyway, I begun to get the notion that he was playin around with her, you know, and maybe even gettin into bed with her—long about that time she started going out there to spend the night, and Mrs. Slater tied down to a wheelchair and all, no tellin what kind of mischief they was up to. I'd ast Margaret if Slater was sparkin or spoonin with her, but she'd never say for sure. But one day me and her was talkin, and all of a sudden she says, 'Now, let me ask *you* a question for a change' and I said sure, anything, so she looks at me in this funny way, and says 'What would you think if I were to marry Jimmy?' Well, it took me a minute to get up off the floor, and then I said it wasn't none of my business who she married, but if she wanted my personal opinion, I thought Slater was a pretty good old boy, smart and lively, but I didn't much see how she could be happy with somebody twenty years older. Then it hit me that I ought to ask her how Slater aimed to marry her if he already had a wife, and she just said that Ethel Slater wasn't expected to live much longer. Well, I've seen Mrs. Slater myself a couple of times, and unless she's got a secret disease or somethin, she's still gonna be rollin up and down the halls in that wheelchair when you and me both are long dead and gone."

Dall wasn't so sure about Slater, but he had a hunch, and he had been keeping his eye peeled, waiting to make a move at the first sign of any perfidy on Slater's part. Lately, for the past couple of weeks, there had been no new developments. Margaret no longer spoke of any potential marriage with Slater, and Dall began to suspect that she might have been making the whole story up—or imagining it, or simply saying it to poke fun at Dall. Still he felt a deep sense of personal guilt, because, after all, he had talked Margaret into joining the theater group in the first place, and he was, in a sense, responsible for her involvement with Slater. Now Dall had only one objective: to find some way, short of marrying her off to Slater, of getting her permanently away from her mother and out of that awful old house. He hoped I would help him.

How? He suggested that I "take up" with her. By that I assumed he meant the same thing she had meant: set up cohabitation in some local hotel or motel. He said he didn't care what I did with her, so long as I got her away from her mother. I reminded him that I was a married man. He snorted derisively and reminded me that I was not a very happily married man. I said I didn't know if I could "take up" with her very comfortably, because if it were true that she had been—or perhaps still was—potentially self-destructive, then I would be to blame if anything happened to her during the time we were staying together. He replied that if I were very nice to her, and showed her a lot of attention, she wouldn't even contemplate any self-destructive act.

I asked him why he didn't "take up" with her himself; he seemed so absorbed with her already and involved in her life. He reminded me that he was a policeman and just doing his duty as the law gave him the light to see that duty, etc. Besides, he had already tried. For a period of one week back in March, he explained, shortly after he had met her and shortly before she tried out for the play, she had stayed at his house. He was trying to get her away from her mother. It didn't work. The mother made such a nuisance of herself, by calling the police station every day to ask them what luck they had had in finding her kidnaped daughter, that finally he had had to let her go back. But it had been a nice week. Dall saw the way I was looking at him, and he hastened to explain that he had been a complete gentleman—sleeping on the sofa and letting her have the bedroom. Flirting was out of the question.

"When I think of her," he said, "I remember that old house a little ways up Viney Creek from where your grandmaw lives in Parthenon, you know that old brick house, it's the only brick house in that part of Newton County, and even though it's old it's got a kind of forever-new look to it, but the shutters is always closed and you never can see who lives there. Well, that's Margaret."

The ringing of the telephone followed this metaphorical speculation.

"Yeah?" he grunted into it, annoyed. Then he said, "This is Hawkins." Then he clamped his hand over the mouthpiece and whispered to me, "Slater!" "Yeah," he said, listening to the phone. "No foolin?" he said to the phone. "Well, how about that!" he said. Then he said, "No, I haven't seen her since . . . since last Monday afternoon, it was. But I called her up early yesterday morning, though, so I know she was there then." A pause. "Yeah." Another pause. "Yeah, well, that's for sure." Then: "She's just *bound* to turn up before *then*." And finally: "Well, look, let me hunt around some, and then I'll call you back later, okay?" Then he hung up.

"That was Slater," he said to me. "He says Margaret didn't come to rehearsals yesterday afternoon or *this* afternoon either, and he's been callin her house ever since last night, but there's not any answer. He's awful worried that somethin has happened to her, and the play is supposed to open tomorrow night, and of course she's got to be there for the opening." He scratched his head, looking awful worried himself. "I wonder where the hell she could be. When did you see her last?"

"Yesterday morning," I said.

"Did she say anything about where she was going or anything?"

"No, but as I was leaving, her mother was taking her off to a psychiatrist, and that's the last I saw of her."

"Taking her off to a *what?*"

"A psychiatrist. You know. Fellow named Dr. Ashley."

Dall gave me a queer look. "Ashley aint no psychiatrist," he said quietly in a tone of disgust. "He's a preacher."

Aha. Fancy that. Typical of the mother, that she would put the needs of the soul before the needs of the emotions. "Oh well," I said. "Mrs. Austin took her off to see him, and that's the last I saw of her."

"How come you didn't mention this before?"

"Well, I was going to, but then you started talking about Slater, and about how Margaret is a brick house in Parthenon and all that stuff, so I—"

"Nub, just tell me how come was it her mother took her to see that preacher. Margaret aint religious."

"She was upset. Very upset."

"Who? Margaret?"

"Her mother."

"Yeah? How come?"

"Margaret messed up her room."

He was silent a moment, perplexed, then he said, "No joke? You mean she busted up the furniture and stuff?"

"No, she didn't break anything."

"What'd she do, then?"

I wondered how to tell him. "She messed up the walls," I said.

"How?" he persisted.

"What difference does it make?" I said evasively. "She messed up her room, and it made her mother awfully mad and her mother took her away, and that's the last I saw of her."

"Come on!" he said, grabbing my arm and beginning to haul me out of his house. "We done already wasted too much time. I *wish to hell* you'd told me about it the first minute it happened."

"Where are we going?" I asked.

"Her house, you bodacious fool! Come on."

FIVE

But his car wouldn't start. An ancient, rust-eaten Pontiac, it reposed at the curb of his house like a tired old horse put out to pasture and reluctant to stand again on all fours. After coughing and spluttering in a tentative sort of way, it became completely silent, and Dall got out and opened the hood and disappeared into it all except for his buttocks. I stood aside and watched. From the depths of the vehicle's innards came muffled curses. All I could make out was something about how the goddamn triple-thierce camming pin on the goddamn glomhefter was shot to goddamn hell. Minutes passed, and eventually I heard him suggest that I run into the house and phone for a cab.

I was about to follow his suggestion when a car pulled up alongside and stopped. A long sleek Prussian-blue Lincoln convertible. "Evenin, gemmens," said the driver in an atrocious mock-darkie accent, tipping his chauffeur's cap. "Could dis pore stupid nigger be of some hep to you good gemmens?"

Dall emerged from the bowels of his car and stood to gawk open-mouthed at the black apparition. Then Dall put his hands on his hips and said, "Well, hush my mouf, if it aint the old boogerman hisself!"

"Evenin, Cap'm Hawkins, sir," said Naps politely and bashfully in the same mock-darkie tones. Then he said to me, "Evenin, Mister Nub, sir."

"You sho do turn up at the funniest times, in the funniest places," Dall said, not without a little admiration in his voice.

Naps grinned modestly. "If you gemmens is got car trouble, my car am at yo disposal, Cap'm."

"I don't ride in nigger cars," Dall rejoined.

"Lordy, Cap'm, aint I done gone and rode in yo police car a whole lot of times? Just returnin the favor, Cap'm, just returnin the favor."

A cantankerous retort was on Dall's lips, but he thought better of it. Time was awasting. He snorted in resignation and got into the rear seat. I sat up front with Naps. "Margaret's," was all I said to Naps and he sped the car down the street. Dall sulked in the rear seat and hung on. I asked Naps what coincidence of fate had caused him to come along at that particular moment. He replied that he had been parked down the street from Dall's house for a little while, waiting to see if I would come out again. He said he wanted to help too, if he could.

We arrived at Margaret's house. Naps started to get out of the car too, but Dall said, "*You* stay here, nigger boy."

"Yassuh, Cap'm."

"And another thing, goddammit," Dall said, pointing his finger at Naps's nose, "don't call me captain."

"Yassuh, Lootenant."

"*Sergeant*, dammit."

"Yassuh, Sawjunt," said Naps and made himself comfortable in the car.

Dall and I went up to the front door and rang the bell. There were no lights in the house. We waited and rang it again. Then we tried the door. Surprisingly, it wasn't locked. We opened the door and went in, and Dall groped along the wall until he found a light switch and turned on the hall lights. Then he moved into the parlor and turned on the great chandelier. "What the dickens!" he said.

"What?" I asked, and he pointed. There was a man in there. A thin, bald, somewhat disheveled old man, sound asleep on the Victorian sofa, an empty whiskey bottle held against his chest.

Dall moved quickly to him and began shaking him. "Mr. Polk," he said, and slapped his jowls. "Come on, Mr. Polk, wake up." He continued shaking him and slapping him for a while, but Mr. Polk wouldn't wake up. "Goddamn," Dall said, at a loss. Then he said to me, "Go out there and get that nigger and tell him to come in here and make us some coffee."

I told Dall I would make the coffee myself.

"Get the nigger," he said, so I went outside and asked Naps if he would like to come in and give us a hand. *With pleasure,* he said, and accompanied me back into the house. We located the kitchen, turned on the lights, filled the teakettle and put it on the stove. I explained to Naps that nobody was home exccpt Margaret's stepfather and he was dead drunk up in the parlor and we had to revive him. We made a pot of coffee, diluted it and cooled it with cream, and took it to the parlor, where Dall still was joggling the man. We got him into a sitting position and held the coffee cup to his mouth.

After we had managed to get two cupfuls down his throat, he

began to come out of his fog. "Mr. Polk," Dall said. "Sit up a bit and talk to us."

"Who?" Mr. Polk muttered.

"It's me, Dall."

Mr. Polk looked up and stared at Naps. "You nah Dall," he said to Naps.

"Here, Mr. Polk," Dall said, taking his shoulders and trying to turn him. "Look here at me."

Mr. Polk slowly turned his head and his eyes came to rest on me. "Youn nah Dall nee'er," he said.

"Goddammit, Mr. Polk, *here*, look at me," Dall said and he finally got Mr. Polk to see him. "How come you're so drunk, Mr. Polk? What for did you go and get all tanked up about?" Mr. Polk didn't say anything. "Where's Margaret, Mr. Polk? Where's Margaret and her mother?" Mr. Polk stared blankly at him and mumbled incoherently. "Come on, Mr. Polk, don't you *know*? Tell me where they went." *Who?* muttered Mr. Polk. "Margaret and her mother! Your wife and your stepchile!"

Mr. Polk's head was teetering dizzily from side to side, as if it were perched precariously on a tightrope and might at any moment fall off. Then he opened his mouth. First some saliva trickled out. Then a word trickled out: "H'sprigs."

"What?" Dall said. "Hot Springs? Did you say Hot Springs, Mr. Polk?" Mr. Polk nodded. "What'd they go to Hot Springs for?" Dall asked. Mr. Polk shrugged. We gave him some more coffee. "*Why?*" Dall said. "Why'd they go there?"

"Wan geddouta Li'lrock," Mr. Polk said. He shrugged again, and belched thunderously. "She . . . she . . . don wan Margit t'be in Li'lrock. Gon shtay'n H'sprigs tree, four weeks." *Why?* Dall repeated. *Why?* "Margit bad," Mr. Polk said, "badgul. Messerroomallup." Dall began shaking him again, too violently. "Hurtin me," Mr. Polk said. Dall, beside himself, continued to shake Mr. Polk. Naps and I had to grab Dall's arms and restrain him.

"Talk!" Dall begged him. "How come you're so drunk?"

"She . . . she . . . sh'says t'me, *you* clean th'room. Me? Aint gon cleanit. *Caint* cleanit. All covered'ith potpot."

Dall turned to me. "Where's her room, Nub? You know?"

"Dall—" I began, trying to say something monitory.

"Tell me where's her goddamn room!" he ordered me, so I told him. He dashed out of the parlor and took the stairs three or four at a time. We waited. Naps and I exchanged nervous glances. Mr. Polk hung his head and began mumbling to himself. We gave him another cup of coffee. In little over a minute Dall returned. He held up one of his hands, the fingers outstretched, and rotated it slowly on his wrist. The finger pads and the palm were brownly stained. "Mr. Polk," he said, "you got any turpentine around here?"

Mr. Polk said, "Wha y'want turptine for?"

"Mr. Polk," Dall said, "there's some paint on the walls up in Margaret's room."

Naps turned to me, beaming, and whispered, "I tole you! I *tole* you!"

"Paint?" Mr. Polk said. "Tha'aint paint, y'idiot, it's *doodoo*."

"Boys," Dall said to Naps and me, "let's see if we caint find us some turpentine and old rags and then let's see if we caint get this old feller to stand up and walk, and then let's see if we caint all go upstairs and do us a little housecleanin."

Which we did. It was a tableau, a weird but jolly spectacle: these four workmen busily removing thick brown oil paint and linseed oil mixed with dirt from the walls of a small attic room. A police sergeant. An old, bald, drunken bank clerk. A Negro book salesman. A Boston museum curator. Each of us wielding a spatula or scraper and a rag soaked in turpentine, we took it all off and put it on some sheets of old newspapers. We worked fast—except Mr. Polk—and in twenty minutes we were finished. Now, Dall said, all it needed was a new paint job. I felt a great burden lifted from my shoulders.

We went back downstairs, and Mr. Polk treated us all to a cold can of beer. He was soberer now, and obviously much relieved himself, although rather sheepish at having been fooled by the appearance of the room himself. Poor bastard, I couldn't blame him for having hit the bottle, if his wife had browbeaten him into the responsibility for cleaning up the room. I reminded myself that I, too, had become drunk in reaction against it. Dall asked him where in Hot Springs the mother and Margaret were staying. But Mr. Polk didn't know. Some hotel or motel, he figured. His wife hadn't told him, except to say that she would send him a card later on. Dall asked Mr. Polk if he weren't aware that Margaret was supposed to be in a play which was opening tomorrow night at the Arkansas Arts Center. Mr. Polk said yes, he knew all about the play and even had tickets for it, but that his wife was determined to prevent Margaret from being in the play. Why? Dall wanted to know. Well, Mr. Polk said, partly because of what Margaret did to her room, and partly because the mother had become suspicious, on account of certain things Margaret had written on the wall, that Margaret and Slater were "fooling around together," and she didn't want her daughter to see that man ever again, or be in one of his plays.

Dall thanked Mr. Polk and expressed the hope that Mr. Polk would not again bedrunken himself, and then we left the house, walked out to the curb near the old carriage-stoop, and hunkered down on our heels in the old country fashion of farmers discussing the weather or meditating the problems of a defective hay-baler or manure-spreader. Dall was the first to speak, after a long silence.

"Don't that beat all?" he said. "First chance Margaret ever has in her whole life to do something really important like be in a play, and then along comes that . . . that—" he swelled with rage in search of a sufficiently vehement expletive "—that *mean*, low-down, no-good mother of hers, and robs poor Margaret of that first and only chance."

A great pity, we all agreed. But what was to be done?

Furthermore, Dall said, he was convinced that he knew *why* Margaret had messed up her walls—because she was counting on some way developing for her finally to get away from that house—perhaps the play would be a success, or perhaps she thought that either Slater or I would provide some way for her to escape her mother permanently—and therefore she had defiled the walls of that small prison as a kind of parting gesture. Margaret was not crazy at all, just bitter and vindictive.

Good for her, we all agreed. But what was to be done?

"And another thing, goddammit," Dall continued to reflect aloud. "Most likely Margaret is pretty damn upset and depressed about the whole thing, and no tellin what she might do over there in Hot Springs without nobody to watch out for her except that screwed-up old bat of a maw of hers, who aint even got sense enough to come in out of the rain by herself, let alone keep Margaret from doin somethin drastic like . . . like hurtin herself or maybe worse or maybe God knows what the hell she might do!" Gently I tried to reassure Dall by reminding him that he himself had told me that he didn't think Margaret was actually suicidally inclined. "Hell yes, I did!" he blazed back. "But what I meant was that she was happy and all because of the play, and even because of Slater, dammit, but if her mother won't let her be in the play, she might just get unhappier than she's ever been!"

A dangerous situation, we all agreed. But what was to be done?

"Gemmens—" Naps began.

"Shut up, nigger, I'm tryin to think," Dall said, and we all lapsed into silence and meditation again. Call Slater and let him try to handle it? No. Cancel the play? No, Margaret had an understudy who was ready to take her place at a moment's notice. I suggested that there was a possibility that Margaret might escape from her mother and come on back to Little Rock by herself, but Dall reminded me that Margaret had never yet in her life successfully escaped from her mother.

"Gentlemens, I—" Naps tried again, but Dall hushed him.

Dall was patting his pockets in search of his pipe and tobacco, without luck. He needed a smoke bad. "Nub, you got a ceegret on you, any chance?"

"You know I don't smoke, Dall."

"Hab one ob mine, Cap'm, sir," said Naps, offering his pack.

"You call me *cap'm sir* one more damn time, nigger, I'm gonna kick your goddamn teeth down your craw right where you're sittin."

"Well, I got some fine ceegars in de car, Sawjunt, sir, if you druther hab one ob dem."

"I'll get them," I offered, and stood up to get the box of maduros out of the glove compartment. I opened the lid and thrust them at Dall.

He scowled. "Nigger ceegars," he said.

"Aint nebber touched one ob dem, myself," Naps said. "Dem is *clean* ceegars, Sawjunt, sir." Naps's exaggerated Negro dialect was beginning to annoy even me. Did he have to talk this way in front of the police?

"Well—" Dall said and, as I waved the fine box under his nose, he gave in to the temptation, took one, unwrapped it, smelled it, stuck it in his mouth and lit it.

"Say thank you," I prompted.

He ignored me. "Now," he said, exhaling a cloud of smoke, "where was I?" And we all lapsed into silent meditation again.

After a while Naps hesitantly spoke up. "Sawjunt, sir, could I just open my big fat stupid mouth long enough to say just a word or two?"

"Awright, goddammit, what d'you want?"

"Sawjunt, sir, I just been thinkin. Dey's a whole bunch of folks in Hot Springs is friends of mine, and dey ever one ob um owe me a favor, so dey'd be just *de*lighted to hep us hunt fo Miss Margaret, if you gemmens would care to hop in my car and git right on ober dere."

Dall stared at Naps and then he stared at me and then he

stared at Naps some more. "Nigger—" he said, harshly, but then he softened his tone. "Mr. Howard," he said, "I don't believe you ever told me your first name."

"Hit's Napoleon. Just call me Naps."

"Naps," said Dall, "what're you tryin to do to me, anyway?"

SIX

There is a new road to Hot Springs now, half part of the Interstate 30 out of Little Rock, half a new stretch of U.S. 70 laid alongside the Missouri Pacific tracks in a relatively straight course in contrast to the old twisting and dipping Route 5. With a good car you can take the fifty-four miles in less than an hour. We did it in forty minutes flat, the mighty Lincoln given plenty of rein but still under wraps, held back from getting us a ticket. ("Okay, Naps," Dall yelled to him from the rear seat as we were whizzing past Meadowcliff, "you better slow down now, cause we're out of the city limits and if you get a ticket you're all on your own, I caint help you.") Thoroughly I enjoyed that ride. I have been to Hot Springs a number of times by several means—bus, train, car, even a bicycle once—but never before in a big convertible with the top down. The night air, the cool spring-drenched breeze whipping around my face, the craggy silhouettes of pine-forested hills against the starlit sky, and the lights, the nebula of scintillating house lights speckled and sparkled out there in the darkness of the plain and the glade and the hollow—these particulars refined our mad dash and lifted it out of the realm of necessity and into the realm of delight. Getting away from Little Rock was in itself a deep satisfaction. We talked the whole way. "That Hawkins," Naps whispered to me and winked. He drove relaxed, his left arm crooked free over the door, the fingers of his right hand delicately responding to the power steering, his head tilted slightly sideways as he studied the running domain of the headlights. "That Hawkins," he said again, just loud enough for me to hear. He bore no malice, no resentment; there was even a tinge of admiration in his assessment of the efficient way Dall had handled the situation at Margaret's house. Naps had never been injured by the sergeant, he explained, speaking loud enough now for Dall to eavesdrop if he cared to; one time when Naps had foolishly resisted arrest at the beginning of his career as a sit-in demonstrator, Dall had kicked him in the seat of his pants, but not viciously. "I do believe he must really kinda *like* me," Naps opined, "else why would he cuss at me so hard?" Go to hell, Dall called from the rear seat.

"De bess time fo de black man to hep de white man," Naps concluded idiomatically, "is when de white man caint hep hisself no mo."

Very soon I got an inkling of what he meant. We dropped down into Hot Springs, where the streets and their buildings are scattered every which way like water bursting forth from a spring. I suggested that we ought to try the Arlington, the Majestic and other large hotels, to begin with, but Naps ignored me and did not turn into Central Avenue at all but continued on, until we were lost in a dark residential section. He turned left, and turned right, and I had not the least idea where we were, but he seemed to know what he was doing. At length he pulled up in front of a long old shotgun house, completely dark except for the faint red glow of a single bulb in one window. Beyond explaining that it was "Miss Melba's place," he said nothing but indicated that we were to accompany him inside. "*I* aint gonna go in *there*," Dall protested. "I know what kind of place that is, plain as day, and you aint gonna catch me dead inside of that kind of place." Suit yourself, Naps said to him, and Naps and I left him sitting out in the breeze under the night stars. Naps did not knock but opened the door and walked on in, with me timidly at his heels. After a brief wait in the large, glaringly lighted foyer, which was empty except for a dozen or so chairs lined against the wall, we were greeted fervently by the most immense Negro woman I have ever seen. Over six feet tall, at least four hundred pounds heavy, she caused Naps to vanish from sight entirely by hugging him to her bosom. Loudly she upbraided him for having failed to visit her more often. When Naps introduced me, she did not shake my hand but instead made a sort of curtsy which resembled a circus elephant trying to execute some difficult and uncustomary maneuver. She opened us both a can of beer, then she said to me, "Let's just take our pick," and started to push a button, but Naps stayed her hand, saying, "Naw, honey, we just here on business." She sat down again, sighing, whether in disappointment or simply to rest after the exertion of moving about, I could not tell. She beckoned to Naps, and he went and sat on her lap. "Well, tell me what," she said, and he told her what. "I see, I see," she punctuated his explanation, glancing over at me from time to time. Naps looked like a doll—no, like a ventriloquist's dummy. I hoped she wouldn't require that I sit on her lap too. When he finished his explanation, she said to me, "See can you reach me dat phone," and I picked it up off its table and handed it to her. With Naps still on her lap, she began to dial numbers. "Sherm? Melba. We lookin for a white woman, please. Mawgrit Austin. Twenty-seven, black hair, bout five foot seven. Got dat?" She hung up, dialed again. "Dat you, Lyle? Melba. Naps's here. We lookin for a white woman, friend of a friend of his. Mawgrit Austin. Yeah. A-u-s-t-i-n. She got black hair, bout yo size, twenty-seven years old. Git to it, chile." Another number. "Scooter, what you doin? Well, dis is Melba. Put down dat funny-book and go look see fewken find Miss Mawgrit Austin, snow-white, black hair, twenty-seven, five seven. Right. *Jump,* sweetie-pie." She dialed again, and Naps slipped off her lap to come and explain to me, "She's callin bell captains," then he climbed up on her lap again and snuggled there while she called a dozen more numbers. The bell captains and porters taken care of, she contacted a few maids, a few waitresses, a few taxi drivers, a few peripatetic pimps. Wondrous are the workings of the underground, I mused. At last she was finished, and she said to us, "Well, guess they nuthin to do now but sit tight and stick aroun. Mo beer, boys?"

We twiddled our thumbs and drank our beer and waited. Replies began to trickle in. "Naw, Ozzy, it's *Mawgrit* Austin. M-a-r-r-g-r-e-t," she said to one caller. To another: "Well, thanks just the same. Loosh. Keep lookin, anyway." The front door opened and a squadron of white teen-age boys, pimple-cheeked punks, came shuffling in, their faces cracked with forced grins which were supposed to be worldly but only succeeded in being hangdog. Miss Melba lumbered to her feet and went to welcome them. She asked them to sit down and to produce their wallets for inspection. Satisfied that they had real money on them in sufficient quantities, she pushed the button, and a moment later a slender Negro girl, dressed in nothing but a green camisole and an expression of bored and supercilious distraction, came and got them and escorted them to the rear of the house, whence came the remote thumping and throbbing of a syncopated phonograph. The last of this file of horny bucks, a short towheaded kid in a windbreaker and dungarees, turned and winked at me and rounded his thumb and forefinger in an A-Okay sign, conspiratorially, fraternally, and I admired him, thinking: That's me. There I go. O Hot Springs, the first true bed for our young appetites! With fond nostalgic recognition I raked up the memory of how I in one impetuous evening of my seventeenth year, not knowing what to make of or do with shy Margaret, had accompanied Steve McComb and Guy Hammond and a bunch of others on an expedition to Hot Springs, to kiss good-bye forever my virginity in some white side-street bordello off Grand Avenue. Fierce leaps the first pulse of the urge! hot springs the young spurt from the glands! Rachel she said her name was, and for fifteen minutes she was my first wife. With a *tendresse* that could come only of being twenty years older she had admitted me, hiking her skirt above her hips as she scrootched supine on the grayed sheets with a fresh hotel towel spread to catch the glue. Throughout I was conscious only of the sound of my breathing, and of my regret that she was the wrong size, her aperture seemed too large for me. When my quarter of an hour and my five dollars and my virginity were all gone, Rachel scoffed at my plaintive self-accusation of inferiority, telling me tonelessly that I was the equal of them all, and I told her I would never forget her and she smiled tolerantly and walked with me to the door and said, *Next*. Guy Hammond anointed me with beer, and we all got drunk and drove somewhere, and they held me down and painted my parts with a stolen cherry-red lipstick and we drank and cavorted and we woke up the next morning tangled head-on-foot inside Steve's car, parked beside the patina-green waters of Lake Catherine, and we spent an hour in naked swimming, and I created a lot of spectacular dives, double-gainers and somersaults and belly busters, yelling, "Look at me! I aint a tadpole any more! I'm a goddamn *bull*frog now!" and they all laughed and threw rocks. O yesteryear. Now I am old and inhibited and backward, cold and funless, sitting here in a nigger whorehouse on a chivalrous, eunuchal, harebrained errand. Pamela would be flabbergasted if she knew where I was, what I was doing—or even more flabbergasted if she knew where I was but didn't know what I was doing. *Who, or what, am I really looking for?* And now I realize that I am stupid too, because I've been sitting here all this time without being aware of the essential possibility that if Margaret and her mother were registered in a hotel, they would most probably be registered under the name of Polk, Mrs. Austin's acquired name.

I conveyed this revelation to Naps and he was not pleased. He told Miss Melba, and she was less pleased, but began making her round of phone calls all over again, anyway. "Dat's right, Sherm. It aint Austin. Austin is the young lady's name. Her momma's name is Polk. Miz Theron G. Polk. Thank you, Sherm, you're a sweet old daddy." When she had finished all of the calls, I went to her and personally apologized for inconveniencing her. She made light of it, satisfying me that there was no favor which she would not do for a friend of Naps Howard. She loved him like a mother, she said; there was not a finer colored gentleman on earth. "Aw, Miss Melba," Naps protested.

They bantered with each other and took no further notice of me. I discarded the idea of going out and trying to persuade Dall to come inside; he would be too difficult to persuade and I was in no mood for arguments. I wandered restlessly around the spacious foyer, inspecting various calendars and signs and business cards (the latter of lawyers and physicians) tacked to the walls. "Don't ask for green stamps," said one home-fashioned sign. "Because the only green thing around here is your money." In a lower corner some customer had penciled: "Don't ask for no blue stamps neither, because the only blue thing around here is my balls." No PROFANITY IN THIS HOUSE responded another sign. There was a small and discreet ad for "Knights, the *man*'s prophylactic," and, conveniently nearby, a long wall-mounted dispenser, requiring a quarter; on its white enameled surface someone's ballpoint pen had scrawled an admonition: "You'll get the clap if you don't strap this rubber wrap into your lap," and beneath that a sight-rhyme in pencil by a dissenter: "I'd rather have the dose, Than wear one of those." Officially the dispenser bore the usual printed hypocrisy, "For the Prevention of Disease Only" which someone had amended by scratching out the "Dis." At the deep, nether end of the foyer I came across a card which advised: "After a night on the town, why not sober up at Campbell's Deluxe Grill. Free Alka Seltzer until six A.M." The omission of the question mark after "Grill" irked me; I always chafe at such illiteracies. I took out my pen and was about to emend the oversight when a plump black hand shot out and grasped my arm and almost hauled me off my feet through a door and into a hallway, where I was embraced by the owner of the hand, a Negro girl no taller than myself but twice as thick, who heaved: "You waitin for *me*, chickabiddy mans? Well, come *on!*" and, deaf to my panicked squawks, dragged me on through the hall and into the room where the phonograph was jiggling and churning in a rhythm to which she began to dance with me, exclaiming, "Oh, you the *richest*-lookin man I ever saw! You mus be jus *made* of money!"

Out of step and out of wits, I stammered, "I don't want to do this. I—"

"My, but you in a hurry! Well, let's go, then!" Again I was all but jerked out of my shoes, and spirited off to a side room, hardly more than a closet, containing nothing but one small cot. She let go of me for an instant, long enough to close the door and shuck her scanty garment, then she turned and, seeing that I was doing nothing but trying to get around her and open the door again, besieged, "Here, let's us take off that Sears sucker coat."

She succeeded in manhandling me out of my jacket and was fumbling around with my belt when the door opened and there was liberating Miss Melba, who snapped, "Bernice! How many times do I got to tell you? Doan come out less I pushes the button! Shame on you!" She snatched me from the jaws of that vice and led me back toward the front of the house, leaving poor naked Bernice pouting behind us, on the verge of tears. "We got a bead on yo lady friend," Miss Melba informed me. "One of the boys spotted her and her momma headin into a place over on Hooper Street. Naps's waitin on you out front." She walked me to the front door and said, "Y'all come back and see us soon's you get the chance. Night-night." I thanked her for her help and wiggled into my coat while running down the front walk to the car. Naps had the engine going, and impatiently pulled out before I had the door closed.

"What a time to fool around," Naps reprimanded me. "Yeah," Dall joined in. "What the hell?" I started to explain, but Naps began to fill me in on what was up. Vinny, a cab driver, had seen two women, one young, one old, both brunettes, walking down Grand Avenue, and had followed them until they turned into Hooper Street and entered a place at Number 55. It wasn't a hotel; Vinny wasn't sure what the place was, but he knew it wasn't a hotel, it wasn't a motel, and it wasn't a brothel. Maybe a tourist home, he had suggested. No sign or anything out front. Did he say any more about what they looked like? I asked. "Yeah, sounds like them, all right," Naps said. "He said the young one was slim and pretty, the old one was fat and mean-lookin."

Knowing his way around, Naps got us to Hooper Street quickly and we found Number 55, a squarish and unhomely building which, contrary to what Vinny had said, did indeed have a sign over the door: *Home Hotel*. There was something perfectly familiar about this place to me. And to Naps too, who said, "Shit. This just one of them ofay cathouses. Vinny got bad eyes." I suggested that perhaps Vinny got the number mixed up, or gave the wrong street, or that Miss Melba might have misunderstood him. "He said Fifty-five Hooper," Naps repeated wearily. "This is Fifty-five Hooper. It's all we got to go on. Mi'as well make sure. What I've heard bout that Miz Austin, she such a penny-pincher she'd stay at the cheapest place they could find."

I got out of the car and asked Dall if he wanted to go with me, but he said he wasn't fixin to go into no *white* whorehouse neither, so I told them I would probably be right back and entered the building. A thick-set oaf with a wizened Jewish face was sitting behind the desk, reading a racing form. "Pardon me—" I said, but without looking up at me he jerked his tough thumb brusquely in the direction of the stairs. "Would you happen—?" I tried.

"Just go on up," he snarled impatiently, still not removing his eyes from his tip sheet.

"Would you happen to have a Miss Austin or a Mrs. Polk registered here?"

He looked up at last and regarded me tip to toe before replying, "Ask me something easy. We got Miss Smith and we got Miss Jones and we got em all. I don't know *who all* we got, pal, to tell you the truth. Why don't you just crawl up there and find out?"

"You don't understand. I'm not—"

"I don't understand *nothing*, pal. I just work here. I just sit here and watch the door."

"I take it this is not a legitimate hotel, then?"

"Don't be insulting. If you want a room, we got lots of rooms. With and without."

"Do you have a registry? I just want to see if—"

"Pal. *Look*. You trying to find someone? Okay. So just walk up those stairs already, all right? I can't help you. Sorry." He returned to his tip sheet.

So I gave it up and returned to the car and we went back to Miss Melba's. This time Dall condescended to go inside with us. He said he'd just as soon sit in there as all by himself out in the car. Naps introduced him to Miss Melba, explaining that Dall was a policeman. "Police?" Miss Melba demanded, indignant. "Naps, what you mean, *police*? I done paid all my hush money this week, and I can prove it!" But Naps hastily explained that it was the *Little Rock* police and Dall was simply trying to help me find Margaret. Still Miss Melba eyed Dall suspiciously, and was not very cordial in her attitude toward him. But the big, kindly old lady started the wheels turning again, trying to contact Vinny and check his information. We hung around. In a vague sort of subliminal way I was hoping that we might never find Margaret, and then I could slip away and have a romp with Bernice.

Vinny, we eventually learned with dismay, had bagged a long haul, somebody who wanted to go to Little Rock, and he might not be back for a couple of hours or more. Wasn't that just too dandy? Two o'clock had already passed. Naps and Dall and I hadn't waked up until nearly noon, Naps and I because we had been drunk, Dall because he had been on the night shift, and thus we still had some energy left, but we couldn't last indefinitely. We sat down to a game of gin rummy with Miss Melba for a fourth. All of the customers had gone except for those who had elected to spend the night by spending ten dollars more. I lost eight dollars after a dozen or so rounds and threw in my hand, retreating to a side chair for a doze. Dall was hot, and played on, eager at this chance to rob some niggers legitimately. I drowsed off and on, capturing an occasional short-subject dream in which Margaret was cast as a red-haired Hot Springs prostitute and I was a badged and badgered member of the vice squad, hot on her tail. I mean trail. The last and worst of these cinema chimeras Naps shook me out of. Vinny was back, he said. He said I had been mumbling aloud, "Got you now, you witch!" Vinny was back and had been contacted again, he said, and his information had been untangled: it was not 55 Hooper Street after all. It was 59 Hooper Street.

Off we went again, doggedly. Light was seeping into the sky above the village of Morning Star to the East. We passed through town to Hooper Street and found, two doors down the street and not fifty feet away from the previously visited address, Number 59, which truly, as Vinny had said, seemed a strange dwelling, without any sign or anything out front. It was large enough to be a tourist home: fifteen or twenty rooms in a cuboid chunk of fake English Tudor with stuccoed and half-timbered sides, and a screened porch girdling it all around. In the early morning light it did not look ominous or sinister or even ludicrous like the old Austin house but instead it looked . . . well, perhaps institutional. Institutional? Then it's a private sanitarium, maybe. A shame.

Naps stopped the car at the curb in front of it. "Now what?" I said.

"That's just what I was going to say," Naps said. "But since you asked it first, I'll tell you what. Why don't you just sorta tippytoe up there and see if them doors's locked?"

"Nothing doing," I said. "What if they aren't locked? Are we going to go in and prowl around all over the place, checking every room? Not me."

"I'll go," Dall volunteered, holding up one of his feet for our inspection. He had on crepe-soled shoes. "Got a flashlight?" he asked Naps, and Naps produced one from the glove compartment. Dall took it, got out of the car, and disappeared into the morning twilight.

Watching him go, I remembered that it had been at this same time of early morning that Dall had sat with Margaret beside the pond, when she asked *"Why have we come here to this water?"* and he had comforted her and provided his chest for her to sleep against. Now he was entering a place where again she—supposedly—was sleeping. Naps dozed off at my side, and I ruminated. In the course of his sermons Naps had told me that he thought I was too detached to be involved with other people, but now I was involved, wasn't I? I was trying to help, wasn't I? "The common herd values friendships for their usefulness." . . . And we were all using each other. In these intervals of reflection I came upon something easily recognizable and even expected but which I held up and turned over in my mind as though I were trying to extract some unique significance from a commonplace article: the breadth of my feeling for her was, if not love, at least a kind of fervent compulsive sentiment born partly of bare lust but mainly of lost desperate affinity and kinship. The world was stomping all over me, this wise boy napping at my side had told me; but if there were anybody really getting stomped on, it was her. It takes one to know one, and I saw now why Dall was helping too, and why Naps was helping too: we formed a perfect Quartet of Stompables, a foursome of abused, oppressed, rebuffed, and buffeted nobodies, losers, children outside the gates, eternal wanderers and wanters, tumbleweeds languishing in the anguish of a search for identity. And we had to look out for our own. We had to band together into a mutually protective junto and vanquish our demons, our archtyrants, the grin domineering specters and malfeasors who thwarted our striving. And we had to start winning, somehow, especially Margaret, because she was the lone and defenseless female. We *would* win, by dingies, even if we had to go in there and whisk her right out from under the old hen's wing, which is what I resolved to do if nothing else worked.

Eventually Dall returned. It was full daylight now, after eight o'clock. "They're in there all right," he said. I asked him how he knew. "I saw her," he said. He got back into the car, this time not in the rear seat but up front with us. He sat in silence for a long moment. Then he said, "I talked to her." Naps and I badgered him for a full explanation, and he said that it was just a plain boarding house and that he had prowled noiselessly through it, trying doors, opening unlocked ones, skillfully picking the locks of some of the locked ones, flashing his light for an instant into the sleeping faces of the occupants, without incident, until at last he had found the mother, who was sleeping alone in a bed beside another bed which had been slept in but was now empty, and then Dall had roamed on through the house until he came to a screened sun porch and saw there a glow from the tip of a cigarette and a figure huddled into a deck chair, and it was Margaret, and he sat down and talked with her. She did not want to go back to Little Rock. She did not want to be in the play. She did not want to leave her mother. She did not want to see Slater, or Dall, or me, or anybody again. Dall argued with her, as quietly as he could, but then it was time for her to return to her room, because her mother would be waking up soon. Dall appealed to her to come with him to the car, but she would not.

Naps and I pestered him with more questions, but he held up his hands and said, "Just let me think a bit. I aint had a chance yet to do enough thinkin."

Patiently I waited for him to give his brains a thorough workout, but when after fifteen minutes or so he still had not spoken again, I said, "Dall, I'm going to get her." I began to step out of the car. "I'm going to just go on in there and grab her and bring her out, if I have to carry her." To Naps I said, "You start the motor—"

"Git back in dis car!" Naps hissed. "Here they come! Git in here and hunker down!" I obeyed, and Dall and I remained down below dashboard level, bumping our heads together until I heard Naps switch on the ignition. Then he took his heavy hand off the top of my head and I rose up and peered over the dashboard.

They were getting into a taxi. "Follow that cab!" I implored.

"Easy, Nub," he said, letting the Lincoln drift out after them. "Let's us just keep cool."

We followed them east into Ouachita Street and then north up Central Avenue, past the bathhouses and the hotels and on to the end of the avenue, where they turned to the right, into a road leading up Hot Springs Mountain, and drove on toward the top, slowly, while we followed them, and I sat back to ride and endure. We were steadily mounting the mountain, and there was nothing else for me to do but admire the scenery: the woods full of thick red cedars forming a complimentary background of viridian for the blossoming shrubs and the wild flowers—columbines, sweet williams and ladyslippers—reminding me it was spring and that I was surrounded by a performance of nature that I could never see in Boston, especially not at this time of year. It was a beautiful sunny day with the sky full of white mountain-like cumuli; I suddenly realized it was Saturday.

At the top of the mountain their cab stopped at the base of the high, lanky observation tower, and they got out and went into the building beneath it. We pulled up short and sat for a moment deliberating. Were they going to go up in that thing? If Margaret was really depressed and unhappy, was Mrs. Austin stupid enough to risk being able to control her on a platform a hundred feet or more above the ground, or was Mrs. Austin totally unaware of her daughter's frame of mind? Were we going to just sit here and be witnesses to a spectacular plunge and pulverization?

Fortunately there were several other sightseers on the premises, and I was able to mingle among them, less conspicuous than Dall would be with his height, so he remained in the car with Naps, ready to help if an emergency developed. Once inside the base building, a gift and card shop, I turned my back on Margaret and her mother and pretended to be absorbed with a stack of boxes of pecan pralines. Margaret was looking at some rag dolls. Mrs. Austin was looking at some picture postcards. Eventually I heard Margaret speak to her mother, but I could not catch her soft words. Mrs. Austin's reply, considerably more distinguishable, was: "You *know* I'm frightened of *high* places. But *you* go on up, if you *want* to. I'll just stay *here*." . . . Fool! Idiot! Thoughtless carelessness! What a boneheaded blunder!

Margaret bought her ticket at the counter and then entered the elevator, and I lurched toward the counter to buy myself a ticket, but Mrs. Austin intervened. "I just don't *know*," she said to the clerk. "*All* of these are *so* pretty, I just don't know *which* to get." She held a sheaf of picture postcards in her hand. The elevator door closed and Margaret ascended. I wanted to shove Mrs. Austin out of the way. Or try to buy my ticket with my back to her. Or just go ahead and tell her what a senseless error she had made. But there wasn't time for that. Perhaps there wasn't even time for me to wait for the elevator to come back down and get me.

The stairs! So I took to them. Nine zigzagging flights of metallic, open-aired stairs, and my natural pathological acrophobia killed me nine times, with vertigo and heart attack and dyspnea and angina pectoris, before I could reach the top. *Don't look down,* I kept remembering. And after the seventh or eighth flight I began to have the curious notion that when I finally got up there all I would find would be an attic room with mock-feculent murals smeared on the walls. I climbed on, forever.

Then, somehow, miraculously, I was there, and so, somehow, miraculously, still was she. And about six other people. Past the last step, I kept stepping. Every effort I made to walk, across the smooth metal floor of the observation platform, was a spasmic parody of stair-climbing. One of the sightseers eyed me suspiciously. Margaret was leaning against the rail—one might say *over* the rail. I clung to it desperately and began to work my way along it, my feet still rising and falling upon a phantom set of stairs. Finally I was within inches of her, and I let go of the rail and lunged. And got her. Then there was nothing for me to hang on to but her.

She twisted around in my grasp, gasped "Clifford!" and a shadow passed across her face foretokening some inner evasion, and she withdrew from me, easily slipping out of my hands and leaning with her back against the rail. "Why have *you* come after me?" she asked, her voice hesitant, timid. "I," I managed to say, but that was all. I was really panting, and could not speak. I sucked at the thin high air, desperately gulping at it, but my lungs were only so much paralyzed gangrene, and my heart had gone berserk. I grabbed the rail again for support and hung there wobbling and shivering. I think I may have been frightening her with this display of helplessness, this embarrassing incapacitation, and I tried to smile, but it is virtually impossible to smile with a gasping mouth. *"Clifford—"* she said solicitously now but still timidly. I tried sign language: with a palsied gesticulation I pointed at her and then down at the ground far below, and then made a diving motion with my hands and shook my head vigorously. When I repeated this pantomime, she caught it. "Jump?" she said and laughed a feeble giggle. "You thought I was going to jump?" I nodded enthusiastically and managed to close my mouth for an instant of smiling. "Oh, Clifford!" she sighed and embraced me tightly for a long moment, then she said, "Here, let's sit down," and we both sat down on the floor of the platform, with our backs up against the rail. This more secure position succored me considerably, but still it was a long time before I could get my voice back. People continued to stare at us for a while, but eventually left us alone, having decided apparently that we were just a couple of fun-loving frolickers. "Your face," she said, running her fingers along my cheek. "You're all whiskery. I've never seen you with whiskers before." I eked out my weak smile. A breeze came up and tousled her long black hair. Beyond her shoulder I could see all of western Arkansas spread out in green waves of shallow valleys and billowing hills. "How did you find me?" she asked. I shrugged, spread my hands, and accomplished two whole words: "Just looked." "I mean, how did you know I was up here?" she asked. Three words from me; I had become a loquacious orator: "Just followed you." "Oh, did you come with Doyle?" she asked. I nodded. "How did you and Doyle know I was in Hot Springs?" she asked. "Your stepfather—" I coughed. Her face clouded over again; she bit her lip and withdrew inside herself, throwing brief nervous glances at me. I put my hand on her hand, but could not decide whether the electric vibrations were generated from her or from me. "You saw my *room*?" she asked. I nodded, "Yes, and I thought it was rather f—" She sprang to her feet. "Forget me!" she wailed, and I thought she might have said, Forgive me, I wasn't sure. Then she headed for the stairs. "Marge! no! stop! listen! I!" I stammered out, my rotten voice more helpless than it had ever been, but she went on down the stairs. I struggled to my feet, a painful process. I made it to the stairs and groped down them, but more damn sightseers coming up the narrow passage blocked and slowed my descent, so that when I reached the lower level the elevator had already descended, with her in it.

To the stairs again, and down. Easier, at least, than going up. But still fatiguing. And frightening, having to look down, down at that abyss of crisscrossing steel beams and the ground far below. Twice I closed my eyes, reeled, and almost lost my balance. Twice I closed my eyes and continued downward sightless, by feel.

When I attained the earth again at last I discovered that there was nobody in sight, neither Margaret nor her mother nor Naps nor Dall. On foot I began trotting down the mountain. I heard swift footsteps behind me, and turned to see Dall trotting down after me. Catching up with me, he explained that when Margaret and her mother emerged from the base of the tower, Naps had ordered him to get out of the car and hide around the corner of the building. While he was not given to taking orders from a nigger, he had acceded to the request because it was no time to quibble, and then he had watched as Naps drove the Lincoln up beside the two women and said to them, "Mornin, ladies. Hot Springs Limousine Service at yo service," and the mother said, "*Goodness*, we couldn't afford *that!*" but when Naps told her it was only thirty-five cents, she had taken him up on it.

Dall and I sat down beside the road to wait. Within ten minutes Naps returned. "Cheapskate didn't gimme no tip," he said. He said he had taken them to one of the bathhouses. We got into the car with him and he took us there, one of a number of those prosaic awning-draped edifices constructed on Bathhouse Row in what might be called county-health-center-federal architecture, half hidden behind two magnolia trees. NIRVANA it said over the door of this one. "Let's go see what we can see," Naps said. "I think I got a friend or two works in this place." We got out of the car and I started down the front walk, but Naps came and took my arm. "The back way," he said. "We got to use the back way." So we did.

Inside, Naps abandoned us in a hospital-like corridor beside the valve-control room while he went off in search of his contacts. He was not gone long, and returned bringing in tow a white-uniformed Negro girl. He asked us, "Have one of you gentlemen maybe got ten dollars you would like to spare? Here is Miss Virgie Mae Humboldt, who, in consideration of the aforementioned sum, will escort one of you to Miss Austin's private sudatorium, providing you proceed with caution and play it cool."

"Why can't you talk like that more often?" I asked him, admiring the sudden absence of his darkie patois.

Dall took a half-dollar out of his pocket and flipped it. "Call it," he said to me. "Tails," I said. It came down heads. "You pay," Dall said, so I gave Miss Humboldt ten dollars.

Then Dall flipped the coin again. "Who's gonna go and try to talk to Margaret?" he asked. "Call it," he said. "Heads," I said this time. It came down tails. "You go," Dall said. "I'm a good listener, but I aint much when it comes to talkin."

The Negro girl led me up a chambered stairway, down a

narrow hall, and to a door. We met no one en route. The place seemed deserted. She pointed at the door and whispered, "She in there." She pointed at another door across the hall and added, "Her momma in *there*." Then she smiled and said, "Best not stay too long," and departed.

I opened the door. A not very large room, choked with steam. Through the hot vapors I perceived her sitting on a tiled bench, wrapped in a white Turkish towel, reading a limp copy of *Vogue*. She looked up, and her mouth did something I had never seen it do before: it fell open.

"Muggy day, isn't it?" I said, fanning my face.

She did not scream or anything. She narrowed her eyes, closed her mouth, and said, "I'm losing my mind."

I closed the door and went and sat down beside her on the bench. "Maybe," I said.

"You must be a . . . a sorcerer, or something. How did you find me this time?"

"Actually I'm just an incubus, as you said before. Now if you will kindly remove that towel, I'll proceed to incubate you."

"At least you have your old voice back this time." She touched me, hesitantly, on the sleeve, as if to make sure I was real. "Please," she said. "Tell me how you found me."

"Just followed you," I said.

"You *couldn't* have. I was watching."

"Apparently you didn't see me sneak up and latch on to the rear bumper of that limousine that you rode into town."

"Did you, now? I'm amazed."

"Just fooling," I said, and then I gripped her hand tightly and began to talk very rapidly. "Margaret, I know what you did to your room wasn't really *real* and I know you did it because you hated that room and I don't blame you a bit and I think your mother is horrible and anyway did you know that she is so mean to your poor stepfather too that she forced him to have to be the one to clean the room? but anyway Dall and your stepfather and Naps and I went up there last night and cleaned it all up, so—"

"Who's Naps?" she asked.

"A colored friend of mine. The fellow who brought you and your mother down here from the mountain in his car. Anyway—"

Margaret smiled. "You're clever," she said admiringly. "It's like a special Secret Service or something."

"Anyway," I went on, still talking as fast as I could, "you've just *got* to go back to Little Rock with us because we're all counting on you to be in that play tonight and if you pass up this chance you might not get another chance so this is your golden opportunity so to speak and you know there's going to be a New York producer and a bunch of other New York theater people in the audience tonight because they flew all the way down here to see the play and they want to see you too and maybe you might even get a job offer or a screen test or something out of it, so you just *can't* pass up this swell chance . . ."

She said nothing. She did not look at me.

"Margaret," I said, trying to be gay, "I knew you were being deliberately fecetious in what you did to your room." I waited to let the pun sink in, but she didn't seem to catch it, so I went on. "Anyway, I thought it was funny and so did Dall and we want to do everything we can to help you because you've had such a raw deal from your mother and everybody, and—"

"And Jimmy too," she said.

"Yes, and Jimmy Slater too, and we want—" I stopped. I looked at her.

She flipped idly through the flaccid *Vogue,* not really looking at the pages. She addressed the magazine, quietly: "It's really a very bad play and I don't think I could do the role the way Jimmy wants me to do it, and besides I'd be just as happy if I never saw him again."

"Why?" I asked her. She didn't answer. "Why?" I said again. "Has he hurt you in some way? Has he taken advantage of you? What did he do? Just tell me and I'll kill the bastard."

She glanced up at me. "Leave him alone," she said. "It's all over. Just forget about it."

"But the play—"

"It's a horrible play and I get murdered in the end of it, and the whole thing is just too absurd for words."

"It's supposed to be the Theater of the Absurd," I said, rather pedantically. "Maybe you don't understand it or something. If—"

"*Please,* Clifford," she said, and I hushed. Then she spoke again, quietly: "It's really flattering that you and Doyle are trying so hard to help me, but I'm just a hopeless failure and I've always been one and I'm too old to try to change the situation even if there were anything I could do about it, but there isn't, so why don't you just forget about me?"

"You actually want to stay here in Hot Springs?"

"It isn't too bad. And it's certainly better than that house in Little Rock. You can't make me go back to that place."

"I don't intend to," I said. "We were going to stay at the Coachman's Inn, remember? Or anywhere. And when the play is over

I'll take you to New York, or *send* you there, or just anything you want to do."

"Why?"

"*Why*? Because I like you, that's why. You're very special to me, and I have great hopes for your future and all."

She smiled but said nothing to that. We sat in silence. I was drenched with sweat from all the steam. I searched desperately for something to say, some gambit, some conclusive, decisive word or words which would sway her.

I tried. "Margaret, if you stay over here, we'll all be very much worried about you, because obviously you're unhappy, and you might just try to kill yourself or something." She said nothing. "I mean, *really*," I said. Then I asked, "Isn't it true that you might have drowned yourself back in March if Dall hadn't come your way? Isn't it?" She didn't answer. I said, "Yes, I think it is. So you're badly mistaken if you think Dall and I could stand to go off and leave you here in Hot Springs where you could do just about anything without anybody to stop you or help you. Come on, Margaret, *go with us*." She said nothing. She did not look up at me. There was only one more tack remaining, one last card up my sleeve, and I tried it: "I thought you didn't like your mother."

"I can't stand her," she said.

"Then why—"

"Because," Margaret cut me off, her voice rising, "because she has been telling me what to do for twenty-seven years, and for twenty-seven years I have been doing what she has told me to do, and it is rather late to do otherwise now! *You see*? Because although it is really nice of a couple of friendly, decent boys like you and Doyle to want to help me, it's just too late! So leave me alone! Leave me alone!" Gesturing at the door for me to leave, she cried these words with such vehement motions of her hands and her whole body that the Turkish towel sprang loose and flopped around her hips on the tile of the bench, and she sat there exposed, her marmoreal chest cleaved by two memorably bold breasts hoisted high by the thrust of her arm as she pointed at the door, and the satin skin of her abdomen stretched around the most lovely dent of a navel I have ever seen, and the crisp thatch of her crotch as raven-black as her hair, and the whole creature a delightful feast for famished eyes.

"Nice," I mumbled, agog. "You've got a lovely body." She dropped her arm, hung her head, gave up, began to cry. I lifted the towel, wrapped it around her, tucked it in. "Well," I said and patted her shoulder. "Guess I'll just go on back to Boston." She did not look up. I shifted my weight from one foot to the other. "Me and you could've been good friends," I said sadly. Where had I heard that before? Yes: Naps. "Well, good luck to you," he had said, so I said it too, now. *"If you're obliged to eat dirt,"* he had said, *"eat clean dirt."* So I said this too. Then I turned and opened the door.

A door was opening across the hall and the head of Mrs. Austin was appearing around the edge of it. Quickly I retreated back into the room and whispered to Margaret, "Your mother!" *Think fast or die!* I warned myself. I wriggled out of the seersucker coat and tossed it into the corner, then I forced Margaret to lie prone on the bench and I began to knead the back of her shoulders, keeping my rear to the door and my head down. I heard the door open and Mrs. Austin say, *"Margaret,* I'm going *on* into the *pool.* Will *you* be out *soon?"*

"Yes, Mother," Margaret said. The door closed, and Margaret began to giggle, grinning up at me. "You're cunning," she said, wiping away her tears.

But then the door opened again and I quickly resumed my professional manipulations.

"Margaret," Mrs. Austin said. *"What* is that man *doing* to you?"

"He's giving me a massage," Margaret said and then she could not resist adding, "What does it look like he's doing?"

"Oh," Mrs. Austin said, and I waited with bated breath for the sound of the door closing again, but I couldn't hear it. Instead I heard Mrs. Austin's voice in protest: "Do *you* think that's *proper?* You weren't *supposed* to have a *massage,* and you *lying* there like *that* with hardly *anything* on. That *won't* do. *Now* you *just—"*

"Mother," Margaret said irritably, "will you get out of here and leave me alone? I'll have a massage if I want one."

"Don't you *talk* to *me* like *that!"* the woman said, and approached and put her hand on my arm and said, "That's *enough,* young man. *She* doesn't really *need* a massage. *You* go on, now." And although she craned her neck to address me head-on, I managed to keep my eyes averted, and so intent was she on depriving her daughter of a massage that she did not bother to recognize me, and I mumbled, "Yes, ma'am," and slipped behind her and out through the door. I lurked around the corner of the corridor and waited. I could hear them yelling back and forth at each other for several minutes, incensed and petulant, and then I heard Margaret wail, "I'll come to the pool when I get good and ready to come to the pool!" and Mrs. Austin stormed out through the door and slammed it and went stomping off down the hall.

Then I went back into the room. Margaret was sitting up, trembling, her mouth quivering, her eyes burning into the floor. I sat beside her and put my arm around her. After a moment, when her body stopped shaking beneath my arm, she said, "Was that clean dirt? Did I eat it clean that time?"

"You ate it clean," I said.

On the return ride to Little Rock, after a brief stop at the Hooper Street boarding house where Margaret picked up her suitcase, she sat in the rear seat with Dall and went quickly to sleep, and slept all the way to Little Rock, and we did not wake her until we arrived at the Arkansas Arts Center theater in the early afternoon. There would be time for a couple of run-through dress rehearsals before the opening curtain. Hugh Berrey, the co-star, and Agnes Galloway, Margaret's understudy, were there waiting, but Slater had not arrived. Dall phoned him, and told him that he had found Margaret and brought her back. Then Dall had to go to work at the police station and he asked us to drop him off at his house. We did, and then I went home with Naps to his house and collapsed and slept all afternoon.

SEVEN

"Get up and call it," Naps's voice woke me out of my long afternoon nap. Dressed only in his shorts and undershirt, he held in his left hand two hangers from which were suspended two tuxedos, one with a white dinner jacket, the other with a violent violet hopsacking dinner jacket with satin shawl collar. In his other hand he held a half-dollar which he was about to flip. "Call it," he said. "Heads," I mumbled, waking up. He flipped it, and it came down tails. "You wear the purple one," he said. "Come on, we got to get dressed." My watch said half past six.

While I did not wish to question Naps's taste (a glance at his three-closet wardrobe had convinced me that he possessed a certain sartorial impeccability, and I was happy enough that his sizes were the same as mine), I was still bothered by two slight details: firstly I was not convinced that formal evening attire would be required for the occasion, and secondly my brown elevator shoes would not go well with a purple dinner jacket. To the first objection Naps replied that he was confident that other gentlemen in the audience of this world's premiere of a new Slater play would be similarly attired; and to the second objection he suggested that I call the Missouri Pacific baggage agent once more and attempt to retrieve my suitcase and the pair of black elevator shoes which it contained. So I did, but the baggage agent said my suitcase was still at large. Naps then considered but discarded the idea of padding the heels of a pair of his black shoes for me, and after trying unsuccessfully to persuade me that I could forgo the need for elevators on this one occasion, he got out a bottle of Dyan-Shine and covered my shoes with a thick coat of black polish.

Then we dressed, and I admired myself in the mirror. The tux was a perfect fit, and although its gaudy color made me rather uncomfortable I felt that I looked considerably distinguished, as would befit a native son returning all the way from Boston to see his old girl friend star in a play. Naps said I owed him ten dollars. For rent of his tuxedo? I asked. No, he said, but he had phoned Vestal Florists and ordered four dozen red roses to be delivered to Miss Margaret after the curtain of the play, one dozen each from himself, from me, from Dall, and from Stepdaddy Polk. "You think of everything," I said admiringly, forking over my ten dollars.

We had a quick supper with Tatrice, who was stunningly garbed for the play in a white cocktail dress. Making conversation, she asked me, "How many times have *you* seen *The Red Shoes*?" Oh, dozens, I guess, I replied. Then I asked them if they had any idea why the play was given that odd title, unless the author was simply aiming for a long title like Oh Dad, Poor Dad, Momma's Hung You, etc. Tatrice replied that she had heard something to the effect that the play was a kind of satire on the type of person who goes to see *The Red Shoes* again and again. In that case, I commented, I should probably consider myself one of its targets.

Naps and Tatrice had never seen a Slater play before—this despite the fact that both were college graduates (Arkansas A. M. & N. at Pine Bluff) and Naps, I had learned with some surprise, was a Phi Beta Kappa. So I took it upon myself, during the supper and during the drive afterward to the Arkansas Arts Center theater, to prepare them for the play by recounting my impressions of the two Slater plays I had seen before.

The first, Slater's initial effort written during the last years of the war, was called *Christmas in Jail* and was a long four-act piece about a small group of black and white shoplifters, young and old, who had been arrested on Christmas Eve and spent most of the following day talking to each other in their cell. All of it was rather on the icky side, a little too heavy with symbolic pathos and sentimentality. Cleveland, Ohio, had liked it; it had premiered with the community theater there in 1947 and had run a full three weeks before moving on to Philadelphia for a pre-Broadway tryout which flopped after two performances. It was a dozen years too early for its time, and it rested in limbo for that many years before the Broadway boom of Negro dramas caused it to be revived and added to the repertoire of little theater groups, one of which had presented it successfully in Boston, where I had taken Pamela to see it. Pamela thought it stank.

The one other play of Slater's I had seen, called *The Pedagogic Demagogue*, had premiered at the University of Arkansas theater in February of 1955, had a sensational reception there (although I missed it then), and later opened off-Broadway at New York's Circle-in-the-Square in the autumn of 1958, where I caught it just before it closed, after a one-week run, probably because, in the words of the *Times* reviewer, "It gives the impression of truthful reality and great meaning, but is actually untrue, senseless and perhaps without any meaning at all." It was a kind of stage biography of the career of a state senator in the legislature of a Southern state (not Arkansas, Slater had claimed, although a little research was enough to show that the man was modeled closely on Senator Webbing of Lonoke County, who had terrorized the capitol back before the war and had finally been committed to a private sanitarium) who had such tremendous personal power and magnetism, such uncanny charismatic presence, that he could make anybody believe anything, that up was down, left was right, fire air, black white, rich poor, day night, or whatever he wished, and became eventually so charmed with his own oratorical skill that he set about to see just how far he could go in making people believe nonsense, and before long had brainwashed all the legislature and half the people of the state into accepting as truth all kinds of ridiculous junk, until, in the end, everybody was confused and half cracked and he alone remained sane and rational. It was intricate and involved, richly comic, rife with symbols and double entendres, and was rather bewildering as a whole—one critic was brave enough to admit that he too was left half cracked in the end.

"What I've heard bout Mr. Slater," Naps offered, as he drove the Lincoln into the Arts Center parking lot, "he's kind of half cracked hisself."

I had never seen the Arkansas Arts Center before, except a color photograph of it on the cover of the Little Rock phone directory, and I was rather taken aback by its size and the ultra-modern architecture of its lines, strongly suggestive, I thought, of one of the old Civil War ironclads—*Monitor* or *Merrimac*, I forget which. Erected on and around the shell of the old Fine Arts building with a generous donation from the Winthrop Rockefellers, it seemed almost ostentatious in this humble neighborhood of MacArthur Park.

The lobby of the Arts Center was packed with a crowd that spilled over onto the sculpture courts and out to the parking lot. Immediately I began to spot familiar faces—old high school friends and people I had known at the University—but no one came up to speak to me, perhaps because I was unrecognizable in the purple dinner jacket. But I was relieved to notice that a number of the other men were wearing tuxedos, particularly one group which, to judge by the bored and condescending expressions on their faces, was probably the New York producer and his entourage. I caught a glimpse of a distinguished-looking gentleman, also in a tuxedo, who, Naps thought, was Winthrop Rockefeller himself. Naps and Tatrice kept to themselves at one end of the lobby—although the Little Rock theaters have all been integrated now there were no other Negroes present, and I observed a couple of weasel-faced businessmen, probably denizens of the Capitol City White Citizens' Council, casting angry and resentful looks at my two colored friends. I spotted Mr. Polk, Margaret's stepfather, standing alone at one side, and I waved to him, but he did not seem to know me. Hy Norden rushed up and glad-handed me, and gushed a babble of pleasantries, then said he hoped to see me out at his place for the party after the show, then he rushed on to glad-hand somebody else.

Wandering outside for a brief breath of air, I passed one tall, magisterial personage, dressed in a conservative business suit and a porkpie straw hat and looking like nothing so much as a chief of police or county sheriff, and there was something so familiar about him that I moved up for a closer look. He saw me and grinned. "Got here on time, didje?" he said and his voice gave him away.

"Dall!" I said. "Good Lord, I wouldn't have recognized you." I fingered the lapels of his coat, and told myself how perfectly he would seem to fit the role of police chief if he ever attained it. "Are you going to the play too?"

"Wouldn't miss it for the world," he said. "Been waitin for this a long time."

I asked him how he had got off duty, and he said that he was still on duty in a sense, and drew aside his coat to give me a glimpse of the lethal hardware strapped to his chest. But officially he was off duty and would have to work overtime next week to make up for it. Then he took me with him out to the parking lot, where there was a squad car with his subaltern Curly sitting in it, listening to the car's radiophone. "Sort of a command post," Dall explained. He then pulled me to one side and said in a hushed tone, "Don't mention it to nobody, cause if word got back to headquarters, they wouldn't be too awfully pleased." Anyhow, he explained, he had had two other squad cars set up out at the southwest edge of town since early afternoon, on the two main routes to Hot Springs, Interstate 30 and at the junctions of Highways 5 and 70, and they had the license number and a good description of Mrs. Austin's old Hudson, and when and if she tried to return to Little Rock, they were going to "detain" her, just in case she might try to get to the Arts Center to stop Margaret from going on stage. "The boys," as Dall referred to his subordinate patrolmen, "is just doin this as a little personal favor for me."

Lights flashing in the lobby signaled the crowd to take their seats, and we went inside. We compared our tickets—which Margaret had given us—and discovered that we were sitting side by side down front among the best seats. Naps and Tatrice were sitting over at the far side, with an empty seat between themselves and the next patron. The theater was small and compact but, like the rest of the Arts Center, the last word in lavish functional modernity.

Waiting for the curtain to go up, I read the playbill for *How Many Times Have You Seen* THE RED SHOES? (subtitled "A Play Around a Movie Around a Ballet Around a Fairytale, or, A Fairytale Within a Ballet Within a Movie Within a Play"), which contained biographical information on the author and cast. James Royal Slater, born November 22, 1915, at McGeehee, Arkansas, the son of James Lewis Slater, a journeyman joiner, and Lillie Royal, a singer; educated at Arkansas A & M, Monticello, later at Memphis State, later at the Sorbonne; since 1939 the husband of Ethel Sharpe Crittenden of Little Rock. Author of seven plays (list followed); Guggenheim Fellow 1948-49, Bollington Prize 1953. Introduced the Morgan horse to Arkansas in 1946, won numerous prizes at horse shows (list followed). Hugh Berrey, cast as "Floyd," is the president of the Little Rock Playmakers, appeared in their memorable *Hamlet* of 1961 and their *The Milkman Doesn't Stop Here or Ring Twice* of 1963. Educated at several universities and drama schools (list followed). Appeared in summer stock six consecutive summers at (list followed). Margaret Austin, cast as "Wanda," was educated at Little Rock Junior College (now Little Rock University), and is making her debut in this production. Previous appearance: "Spirit of Christmas Past" in Dickens' *Christmas Carol*, West Side Junior High School, December, 1949.

There was a tap on my shoulder and I turned to see the patrolman Curly. He handed me a folded note and gestured for me to pass it to Dall. I nudged Dall and gave him the note, and he read it and smiled and passed it back for me to read. "Sarge," it said, "Jack just called in. Caught your party on Asher Avenue. Was exceeding speed limit by 15 mph. And that aint all. Was operating defective equipment, no taillights, bad brakes, etc. Also: Use of abusive and offensive language to an officer. Also: Resisting arrest. Jack says they are remanding to HQ and can probably hold her an hour, maybe more. If not, will nab her myself if she shows up around here, and see if her abusive language is still working. Curly."

"Well now," said Dall, settling back in his seat, "we can watch this here show in peace."

The house lights dimmed out and the curtain slowly rose.

🐢 EIGHT

Mise en scène: a drive-in theater. Upstage there is a curved screen made of large panels of white gypsum board, on which, as the curtain rises, we see projected the lively but fulsome climax of what is known as a grade-C Western. We watch the Bad Men being pursued by the galloping Good Men, one of whom is saying, "Let's head em off at Eagle Pass!" his steadfast voice clearly audible to us. Against its husky sagebrush patois comes the small mid-American but otherwise regionless voice of a girl, whom we descry occupying one end of a carless car seat. "What a pretty pass," she says. Then we notice her companion, a young popcorn-munching man upon whom her punning sarcasm is lost because of his absorption in the thrilling finale of the movie.

Here in the first line of the play there seems to be a collision of interests, a tacit cultural incompatibility which may set the tone for the whole play. The girl, we later learn, is a dental technician whose days are a tedium of bridgework, of uppers and lowers. The young man is an air-conditioner repairman. They are far enough out of their teens to be no longer children; yet close enough to it to still enjoy the drive-in. Apparently they are a typical young middle-class American pair on a semi-romantic date. Beyond this superficial rapport, however, there appears a deep and irremediable rift, a clear suite of cross-purposes. Floyd obviously came here to see the cowpunchers, and now that the bad men have met their just deserts at Eagle Pass and the good men have gone riding off into the sunset, he is bored, his eyes are tired, he would like to get in a little petting. But Wanda patiently endured the Western because she wants to see the second show, which, through one of those common freaks of double-feature programing, is *The Red Shoes*—"co-hit," it is grossly advertised on a large flashing sign at the side of the stage.

By his choice of words and lines we know that Floyd pictures himself as a sharp, oily, swaggering humdinger of a guy, where in fact he is unsure, unsettled, even timid; he masks his nervous insecurity with a façade of boastful garrulity. With Wanda it is almost the reverse: outwardly shy and susceptible, she has iron in her veins, sovereignty in her glands; it might be that she is even vain. He is not going to make out with her very successfully. She knows this. We know it. Floyd doesn't. The only advantage he has over her, if it may be considered an advantage, is that he is a pure realist, a no-nonsense opportunist, a practical and level-headed fellow who is never going to be gyped by the auto mechanics, is never going to be taken for a ride by man or beast, is never going to be caught doing anything except making money and having himself a good time, whereas she, alas, is idealistic, impractical, fanciful, quixotic, an incurable dreamer.

Just as we are about to get wrapped up in the movie, even if we have seen it a dozen times before, we notice a singular fact: although we can hear snatches of the musical sound track, no voices are coming through to us: no word from the lips of Marius Goring or Moira Shearer or Anton Walbrook or Robert Helpmann or Leonid Massine is clear enough to interfere with the duologue of trifling twaddle heaving out of the mouths of Floyd and Wanda—forty-five minutes of compendious, synoptical, leisurely repartee—the essence, obviously, of Absurdity. But it begins to seem that Floyd is bothering her. She wants to watch the show. It is almost as if Floyd were saying (if he knew how): "See here, I want to talk about Man, I want us to make our own small progress in the direction of discussing these little problems of our little people, for only by plodding doggedly through them can we attain ultimate understanding of the big picture of which they are only fragments." And it is as if Wanda replies: "Poo. I want to watch this movie, because only by sharing its enchantment can I lift myself above those petty problems that concern you." Apparently, for a while at least, Floyd has become our champion, the true hero of this drama, while Wanda is relegated to the role of the villain. She lacks common sense. She lacks perspective. What is worse, she has no sympathy, no fellow feeling, she is too wrapped up in herself to perceive the rightness of Floyd's practical point of view. Maybe this guy means to marry her some day, we don't know. She owes it to herself to come down off her cloud. But naturally she won't.

He puts his arm around her shoulders and nuzzles her neck. She shrugs him off. Absorbed in the swelling climax of the movie, she even yet fails to perceive the message that it offers her, the lesson that it holds out to her like a pair of fancy red slippers proffered on a fat silk pillow: *vanitas vanitatum, omnia vanitas*, or, she who desires everything gets nothing.

Moira is yelling at Marius and Marius is yelling at Moira (we see their contorted mouths but do not hear their noise) and then Moira is crying, and then Floyd is yelling at Wanda, "Goddammit, baby, I been trying to get somewhere with you for the last goddamn five months, and it's driving me nuts! What's the matter with you, anyway?" But Wanda does not cry. She looks him coolly in the eye and, obviously thinking of how severely he fails to be as handsome or romantic as Marius Goring, says to him, "Drop dead." Moira leaps from the parapet in time to fall beneath the oncoming steam train. Anton Walbrook quavers his sad, choked speech to the Monte Carlo audience, and Massine begins the ballet without her, and then Wanda begins to cry. Floyd entreats her to dry up. Alternately pitying and disgusted, he is beside himself with confusion. His comforting words make her cry harder. His harsh words make her cry even harder yet. The movie ends. For a while the sound of Wanda's sobbing is drowned by the roaring, gravel-popping noise of several hundred automobiles racing each other to the exit gate. When the last car fades off, we pick up her crying again. Floyd reaches into the back seat (there is none, but we are to imagine that whatever is behind the seat on which they are sitting is the back seat) and finds a tire jack, with which he begins clubbing her. Her red wig is knocked off by one of his blows, but he is too distraught to notice. She expires. He reaches into the back seat again and gets an ax and hacks away at her ankles, severing her red-shoed feet. (A clever bit of stage designing enables this illusion to be created, by having her conceal her real feet in a black shroud beneath the car seat, while a false pair is sent clattering downstage, coming to a stop near the footlights, where an intense pistol spotlight picks them out while all the other lights go off, and the curtain slowly descends.)

A few of us have screamed. The rest of us are speechless. All of us, if we have followed closely throughout and have kept our minds open, clear and active, are asking ourselves: Who is to blame here? Which of them was right, which wrong? Who won, who lost?

There are two polite curtain calls for Hugh and Margaret, but no cries of "Author! Author!" and the New York producer and his entourage have already departed.

Illuminated by the rising house lights, Dall's face was staring blankly at my face as if he were trying to place me. I stared back at him with a similar quizzical expression dulling my own countenance. We just looked at each other like this for a long moment, and I knew that we were probably thinking the same thing: Was *that* what we went to such trouble to get Margaret back from Hot Springs for? Then Dall slowly shook his head. "By doggies," he said finally, "I done seen it all."

It behooved me to attempt an explanation. "You see, Dall," I said, trying not to sound too didactic, "I think what Slater is trying to say in this thing is that the dreamer, the idealist, you know, doesn't have any place in the modern world. The dreamer is too easily conceited, and that kind of conceit may get the dreamer into trouble—in this case, death."

"Yeah," he said. "I read the fairy tale. Slater showed it to me once. It's in this book of stuff by this feller named Hans Christian Somebody or Other, and it tells about this little girl named Karen that gets her feet cut off cause she's so all-fired stuck-up and snotty, but in that there fairy tale she sort of *reforms*, see, she takes it all back and she gets religion and all and her little old heart is so filled with peace and love and all that it breaks on her and her soul flies away to heaven."

But wasn't Margaret beautiful? We agreed she was.

Dall went out to check with Curly, and I joined Naps and Tatrice, who were busily trying to explain their conflicting interpretations of the play to each other. Naps was on Floyd's side, Tatrice was on Wanda's side, and a heated argument was building up between them, so I slipped away. Naps caught up with me and said he had to take Tatrice home and then change into his chauffeur's uniform, and then he would be delighted to drive me out to the Nordens' party. I thought that was superfluous, but he insisted on it. "Us Nobodies," he said, "has got to show them Somebodies that we is Somebody too." Then he winked, clapped me on the back, and rejoined his wife.

I wandered on backstage to the Green Room, hoping to catch a glimpse of the author, but he was nowhere about. A group of people was milling around Hugh Berrey and Margaret, offering reserved congratulations to them, but Margaret slipped away as soon as she saw me. She came over and kissed me on the cheek and thanked me for the beautiful roses. Up close, I noticed the heavy stage make-up on her face, the exaggerated delineation of her eyes and mouth, and more than ever she seemed to be the strange embodiment of that transcendental succubus who haunted so many of my dreams. In that moment, perhaps because it was *I*, Clifford Stone an anonymous member of the audience, talking face to face with *her*, Margaret Austin the star, I felt a sudden profound passion for her.

"You were wonderful," I said.

"Did you like it?" she asked hesitantly.

"Not *it*," I said. "*You*."

She smiled. "But you didn't like the play?"

"Frankly, no."

Then she said, "I told you. I told you it was bad."

I nodded. Then, a great idea suddenly taking hold of me, I took hold of her hand, bowed low, kissed her hand, and said, "Miss Austin, it has been my privilege to have received an invitation to attend a post-theater party at the residence of Mr. and Mrs. Norden, and I will accept that invitation if I might have the honor of your company."

She laughed. "Stage Door Johnny," she said. Then she said, "Jimmy Slater wants me to go out to his ranch and—"

"Oh," I said, crestfallen.

She took my arm. "But I would rather go with you," she said. "Much rather. So I will." My heart did flip-flops, and instantly I visualized the impression that I would make when I arrived at

Norden's in a chauffeured limousine with the star of the play on my arm.

Dall came into the Green Room. "Hiya, Marge," he said and patted her on the back. "Great show. You were just great." She thanked him, but expressed doubts that he really enjoyed it. "Aw, yeah, it was kind of interestin," he said without conviction. She asked him if he felt the time and trouble of his trip to Hot Springs had been justified, "This play wasn't the only reason I wanted you back from Hot Springs."

"Speaking of my mother," Margaret said, "how did you keep her from getting here?"

Dall shrugged. "Aw, I guess she must of run into car trouble or something." Then he asked her, "Where's Slater, by the way?"

"I don't know," she said. "I guess he's back in the wings or somewhere. Why?"

"Just wanted to speak to him a bit," Dall said.

"Why?" Margaret asked again, her face wearing a worried expression.

"Aw, just wanted to tell him what a good show it was and all, you know," Dall said. Then he said, "Excuse me," and went out through the door leading to the stage.

Some old ladies came up to pat Margaret on the arm and tell her how sweet she was and how awful it was that she had been killed. Then a photographer wanted to take some pictures of her holding hands with Hugh Berrey. Then a florist brought her some more roses. Then some more old ladies came up to pat her on the arm and tell her how sweet she was and how awful it was that she had been killed. Then Margaret came to me and told me that she had to go to the dressing room to remove her make-up and costume, and would meet me outside.

I left the Green Room and strolled for a while up and down the sidewalk promenade beside the Arts Center. The last of the audience was leaving; only a few cars remained in the parking lot. An old Hudson drove up, and a fat old woman got out and swiftly approached me. Officer Curly moved to intercept her, but she had a head start on him. "*Clifford!*" she said. "*Where's my daughter?*"

"Ma'am," said Curly, trotting up, "could I see your driver's license, please?"

She turned to him. "I've *shown* my license to *enough* policemen tonight, and I'm *not* going to *show* it *again!*"

"Now, ma'am," said Curly, "don't you go using offensive language to me, or I'll run you in."

She ignored him and turned back to me. "*Where's* my *daughter?*"

"I'm afraid you're much too late," I said. "The show was over half an hour ago, and—" I did some quick thinking— "and Margaret has already gone out to Mr. Slater's place."

"*Oh*, she *has*, has *she!*" She made a movement to return to her car, but then she paused and turned back to me again. "But *what* are *you* doing *here*, then?"

"Waiting for my chauffeur," I said.

She eyed me suspiciously and wagged a finger in my face. "Did *you* steal my daughter *away* from me in Hot *Springs?*"

"Hot Springs?" I said. "My goodness, I haven't been there for years."

"Well, *you* stay away from my daughter *too*, you . . . you *married* man!" she yelled, and then she got back into her car and turned it around and began to roar away toward, most likely, the Slater rancho.

Curly took off his cap and scratched his curly hair. "*Crazy* old *bag*," he said. "Imagine *any*body *having* a *mother* like *that*."

"*Imagine*," I said.

Curly returned to his squad car, and I stood alone, restless, breathing in the spring night fragrances, magnolia and honeysuckle. It was the kind of moment when, had I been a smoker, I would have lit a cigarette. After a while Dall came out. He lit his pipe. I asked him if he would like to go to Norden's party with us.

"That asshole?" Dall said rancorously. "Not me. Wouldn't be caught dead walkin the same ground he walked on. Besides, I don been invited to go out to Slater's. He's feelin pretty low, the way nobody seemed to care for his play. Wants me to go out and play some poker with him or somethin. Just me and him. He don't like people." Dall smirked at me. "And he sure don't like *you*. Cause you done gone and stole his girl away from him."

I told Dall that my heart was touched with pity for Slater, but that all was fair in love and war. Then I told him that if he and Slater were going to play cards, they might have a third for their game, because Mrs. Austin was on her way out there. "*What?*" Dall boomed. I explained. I told him that I had simply been trying to think of some way to keep Mrs. Austin away from Margaret when I told her that Margaret had gone to Slater's place. "Well, say now," Dall said with a speculative smile, "that might not be such a bad thing after all." Then he bade me a good night and a pleasant evening's entertainment. Curly came up with the squad car, and before getting into it Dall said, "When you see Norden, tell him that Doyle C. Hawkins says, and I quote, 'KISS MY RUSTY BUTT,' all capital letters. Wouldja do that for me?"

"Sure." I laughed and waved as he drove away.

Shortly afterward Margaret came out, dressed in a very charming blue cocktail dress which did interesting things for her figure. She glanced nervously from side to side. I asked her if she was afraid that Slater was hunting for us. No, she said, Jimmy had already left. But she was afraid that Agnes Galloway might be hunting for her. Who's Agnes Galloway? I asked. "My understudy," Margaret said. "This dress belongs to her. She left it in the dressing room, and I don't have anything else to wear, so I—"

Naps pulled up in the Lincoln. He jumped out to hold the rear door open for us. Lord, he was lovely, decked out in a full-dress chauffeur's uniform complete with brass-buttoned tunic. He bowed low. *"Monsieur et mademoiselle,"* he voiced in a precise and perfect French appropriate to a Phi Beta Kappa who had had three years of the stuff in college but never a good chance to use it, *"entrez dans ma voiture donc, s'il vous plaît."*

Thus it came to pass that Cinderella and Prince Charming got into the golden coach and, the wicked mother being tied up elsewhere, went off to have themselves a ball.

NINE

Rhododendron Terrace is actually west of Pulaski Heights, and out of it: a winding quarter of a mile of six superaffluent new homes in a special development called Grandwood, carved into the hilly pinewoods between Robinwood and Kingwood, overlooking the river precipitously and toploftily, it is hardly a street at all, but a golden curl, a wisp of honey-blond hair bristling up from a head which otherwise is plain dishwater. Number Five the Rhododendron Terrace is a white-brick peristyled Pompeian villa with Williamsburg touches, a smooth bar of platinum lolling behind two rows of gas lamps in two acres of sea-green fescue on the river side of the street, with marbled patios commanding a grand view of the palisades upstream and the city downstream. No television announcer's salary ever paid for this place, or ever could; its immaculate conception and birth could only have been the fruit of a divine coition between Judge Norden's tainted legacy and the free riches of Marcia Paden's family, fertilizer magnates. The gas lamps, which, like thousands of others all over town, the Arkansas-Louisiana Gas Company burns night and day to supplement their usual income while satisfying a parvenu craving for elegance, were bright enough to gild this homestead with resplendent aureoles of celestial light.

All of the other guests had arrived and were standing around in the patio out back, while white-jacketed Negro waiters plied them with drinks. A small orchestra was providing music for twisters. Naps turned the huge Lincoln into the white gravel driveway and edged it as close to the gathering as he could get. Everybody turned to look at us.

The car motionless, Naps leaped out, raced around the rear of it, and swung our door open with a flourish, standing rigidly at attention while we stood up and debouched. He whispered to me through a closed mouth, "Suck in your gut." I sucked it in. Then he gave me a crisp salute and closed the door behind us.

Hy Norden trotted up as fast as his corpulence would allow, with Marcia hard on his heels. He threw both of his hands at me and clasped my hand between them, pumping. "Great to see you, Cliff!" he oozed. "Glad you could make it, boy!"

"Margaret," I said to her, "I believe you know Hy Norden and his wife Marcia. Hy and Marcia: Margaret Austin."

He squinted his eyes at her. "Your face is familiar. Haven't I seen you somewhere before?" Margaret smiled modestly, her head slightly bowed. Hy went through the finger-snapping routine, trying to place her. "Where was it?" he asked himself aloud.

"Well," Margaret offered, "we were classmates in high school."

"Yeah!" Hy said.

"Hy," Marcia said *sotto voce* to her husband, "she was the girl in that play tonight!"

"No!" Hy said, ogling Margaret up and down. "Well, I'm damned! What a surprise! What an *honor*!" He glanced at me with renewed admiration. "Well, come on, let's say hello to some of the folks."

There followed a round of introductions with old, half-forgotten friends. I remembered only a few of their names, but they all knew mine; Hy must have announced me in advance. A circle opened around us and followed us as Hy took us from one couple to another. My supersensitive ears picked up their hushed asides; wives were telling their husbands that the girl beside me was *the* Wanda of the Slater play; I heard one girl remark to another, "He's *ever* so handsomer than he used to be, don't you think?" and one of the guys said to his companion, "Saw a dinner jacket just like that one in *Gentleman's Quarterly* last month. Costs two hundred and forty-five bucks."

Margaret and I became separated in the crowd. Hy's wife Marcia came up and linked her arm through mine and handed me a drink. She turned her face close to mine and showed me all her teeth; an unmistakable redolence of gin, Schweppes and Rose's lime juice emanated from her. "I've got him," she said. "I'm the hostess and I've got him and I'm going to show him my house." With that she drew me away from the others, led me up more marbled steps and through sliding glass doors into the house. She had to show me every room, all twelve of them. None of it interested me; the furniture was a blend of Empire reproductions and classic moderne pieces of the latest wrinkle, selected for her probably by some popular interior decorator who had been instructed to create ten thousand dollars' worth of opulent but innocuous flash. Bathmats and toilet-seat covers of pinto pony skin. A dead tree growing—or, rather, dying—up through a hole in the bedroom floor. Mirror-lined shower stalls. Book ends of Rodin's "Thinker." Pink satin harem pillows. A round master bed. A Hammond organ. "Nice," I offered noncommittally. "Lovely place."

Her arm still entwined with mine as we drifted along a corridor, she said, "I hope you weren't disturbed at the way we behaved in the Deadline Club the other day. But you see, we had just received word that Hy's aunt, his favorite Aunt Astrid Norden, had . . . had passed away, and we were both terribly upset at the time. I hope you'll forgive our rudeness."

"Don't mention it," I said, giving her wrist a consoling squeeze.

She squeezed me back and said, "I want you to have a good time tonight. A *very* good time."

"I will," I said. "I'm sure I will."

A tall fellow unknown to me—I had missed his name during the introductions—approached, threw an arm around Marcia's shoulders, nuzzled her neck with a quick kiss, and said, "Don't hide from us, honey. Come on out and play." The he said to me, "You'll have to watch out for this gal, Stone. Old Marsh'll snatch you off to bed quicker'n a streak of greased lightning. I'm tellin you."

"For your information, Rex, we've already been there," she said to him and winked at me. "Now let's join the others."

Once outside again, she took up with pesky Rex, relinquishing me to a girl named Teddy Terrell whom I vaguely remembered as one of the high school cheerleaders. Teddy, I soon discovered, was a divorcée and was bored with life, but not sufficiently bored to prevent her from being completely captivated by the slightest bit of chitchat that might fall out of my mouth. I had some fun, during a ten-minute parley with her, observing her breathlessly affected responses to my charmless remarks about the weather and other utterly banal topics. She was an easy mark, every flick of her lashes suggesting an open expectance of a seduction, but before she had time to pursue the matter Cinny Anderson came and took me away from her, and then Marilyn McComb took me away from Cinny, and Chuchu Heffington took me away from Marilyn, and so on—a gallant gallivanting shuttlecock I was, tossed around from one doll to another. Through it all, I kept on the *qui vive*, kept my ears to the ground and my nose to the wind and my eyes peeled, and managed to assemble a good picture of what was what—the naked facts, the inside wire on the private amours, likes, dislikes, infidelities, assignations, peeves and short shrifts of this cabal of restless, dissolute plutocrats. It was not a pretty picture, I must say. They were the cream of Society, perhaps, but apparently it is possible for cream, left idle, to become scum. There was not much post-mortem talk about Slater's play; these people had gone to it to be seen, not to see the play. I cast my eye about for Naps, and finally saw him, over on the other side of the ashlar wall, talking to one of the Negro waiters. I strolled over to ask him if I seemed to be sufficiently Somebody now, and he said I was doing just fine. I told him I was tired and hoped that we might go soon.

I found Margaret, standing alone near the table set up with liquor. She had a highball in her hand. Several males were gathered near her, watching her, but none of them had approached her yet. "Having fun?" I asked her. She nodded and smiled. "Let's dance," I suggested.

She shook her head. "I can't," she said.

"Oh, come on," I said, taking her hand. The orchestra was playing a rather leisurely variation on "Stardust."

"I can't, really," she said. "I never have."

"Well, let's just get into a clinch and sway back and forth and nobody will know the difference," I suggested, and she gave in and let me lead her out among the other dancing couples. I put my arm around her and held up her hand with my other hand. We swayed back and forth. "See?" I said. "Nothing to it." Cheek to cheek, we held each other and rocked gently, our feet stepping slightly without moving. I nuzzled her earlobe with my mouth and whispered, "Going to stay with me tonight?" I felt her cheek nodding up and down against my cheek. I gave her a squeeze, feeling her breasts flatten against me. We swayed and rocked onward, tightly clenched. I whispered, "Tell me more about Slater."

There was a tap on my shoulder. I ignored it, but it tapped again. I let go of Margaret and turned. It was Hy. I glowered at him. "Yes?" I said.

"My turn," he said with a nasty pucker of his peachy mallow mouth.

"She can't dance," I blurted.

His eyebrows went up. "With *me*," he said, "anybody can dance," and he took her and waltzed her away.

I stood aside and watched. Margaret was hanging on for dear life, but not doing such a bad job of it. Teddy Terrell came up and leaned on me and said, "A penny for your thoughts, darling. Why so glum?" I told her I was bored. "Me, too!" she said excitedly, as if it were a great thrill to be bored. The orchestra was changing its tune, and Teddy grabbed my hand and said, "Hey, come on, let's hully-gully!"

"Let's what?" I asked.

She demonstrated. It was some kind of obscenely suggestive variation on the twist, but I joined her in it, having learned the basic fundamentals of the dance the other evening with Tatrice. I had a couple of drinks in me already and my inhibitions were not what they might have been.

"Now," said Teddy, wild-eyed and excited after the orchestra had stopped and then begun a new number, "let's frug!"

"I beg your pardon?" I said to her.

"Frug!" she said. "Haven't you ever frugged before?"

She took my hand and turned around with her back to me. "*Here?*" I said. But it was only another variation, even more obscenely suggestive but pervertedly so this time, on the twist. After that we did the dog, the mashed potatoes, the hitchhiker, and several others which she demonstrated for me. I caught the spirit of the things, and even began to enjoy myself. I turned to see if Margaret was watching me, but I couldn't spot her. I was almost certain she would have to sit out such contortionist antics.

I observed that several couples were, from time to time, sneaking off toward the house or out toward the woods, and they weren't married couples—I mean, the couples weren't married to each other but to somebody else. One of them was Marcia Norden and her friend Rex. Teddy, I noticed, was steering me off into the darkness. When we reached the edge of the marbled patio she took my arm and suggested that we go somewhere and rest for a while. "Rest?" I said. She pointed, over there toward the woods. I was tempted, but I had a date. Where was Margaret? Had Hy taken her off to see the house or something?

Thunder boomed and a sudden heavy shower saved me from Teddy. Some of the guests made it to the house, but most of us took shelter in a small summerhouse behind the patio. The rain came down in torrents. There were fifteen or twenty of us packed into the summerhouse, and it was hot and stuffy. Something bit me. A mosquito. Teddy was in there too, and she came up and bit me on the earlobe and pressed herself against me and wiggled, and kissed me. A mosquito bit her. "Dammit," she said and slapped her arm. Another mosquito bit me. Other people were getting bitten too. "Ouch," several people said. "Open a window, Hy!" somebody said, and I heard Hy's voice explaining that the windows were unopenable. One fellow couldn't stand it, and made a mad dash out and through the rain, and was badly drenched. The rest of us endured. I had been bitten several times now. I wondered if Margaret were inside the summerhouse too. It was dark and I couldn't see any faces. "Margaret," I called softly, but there was no answer. "Who?" Teddy said and pressed herself up against me, and I could feel the shape of her groin against my swollen appendage. "These awful mosquitoes," she moaned. "Got it," came Hy's voice out of the darkness, and he said, "Folks, just keep calm. I found a can of bug spray and I'll kill these little pests in no time." I heard the sound of the button depressed: hisssss, hisssss. I saw the silhouette of Hy's arm passing the aerosol can back and forth through the air. He kept his finger on the button a long time and exhausted the contents of the can. Now the air was not only hot and stuffy but also choked with the pungent fumes of the bug spray. Where was Margaret? Had she made it to the house? Another mosquito bit me, and several other people were bitten too. One of them complained, "Hy, that bug spray of yours is no damn good." "Let's get out of here," somebody said. "I'd rather get wet than eaten up alive," said one girl. "Turn on the lights," said another girl. "No!" said a fellow. "Aren't there any lights in here," the girl said. "I think so," said Hy and groped along a wall, feeling for a light switch. Teddy continued to squash my groin with hers, as if that alone could palliate the pain of the mosquito bites. Where, *where* was Margaret?

Somebody found a light switch and the lights went on at last. Gently I pushed Teddy away from me. Several other couples disengaged themselves quickly, and one guy complained, "Hey! Douse the lights!" But the lights stayed on, and I reeled with dizziness as I discovered that I was in a room full of ghostly apparitions, shimmery phantoms glowing silvery. These ghosts saw each other, and the female ghosts began to scream, and the male ghosts began to rub themselves. "Oh my God!" Hy screamed. "It isn't bug spray! This *isn't* bug spray!" He hurled the can from him, breaking a window. "Oh my God!" he wailed. "What have I done?"

What had he done? He had covered all of his guests with a nice thin but adequate coat of aluminum paint. I looked down at myself. Fortunately Teddy had been pressed against me during the event, and thus the front of my (or Naps's) violet dinner jacket was not coated, although I had a little of the stuff on one of my sleeves. The back of Teddy's pink dress was heavily coated with it and she was craning her neck to inspect the damage. "Norden, you nitwit," said an outraged guest in white (formerly) tuxedo, "I oughta bust you in the nose." And he began to, but Norden ran out through the rain toward his house.

The rain abated, and most of the guests dashed to their cars, and sped homeward in search of cleaning fluid. Teddy crossed the patio huffily and went into the house. I went off to look for Margaret. I looked all around the house, and then I went into the house. Hy approached me with some rags and cleaning fluid. "God, man, I'm sorry," he said. "I ought to be shot. But here, let's see if we can't get some of that off." He dabbed at my sleeve, and fortunately most of the paint came off at once, and then he cleaned some of it off my face and hair. Finished, he said that if that wasn't suitable, just to let him know and he would buy me a new jacket, but please not to instigate a lawsuit or anything. "God, I feel awful about this," he said again, and went off in search of another painted guest.

Margaret was not in the house. I went out to the parking lot to ask Naps if he had seen her, but Naps was not in the parking lot. The Lincoln was gone. My watch said it was after midnight. The Lincoln had changed back into a pumpkin, and Cinderella's beautiful dress had changed back into rags. But she had not even left a glass slipper behind her.

🍂 TEN

Sitting down on the rock retaining wall at the edge of Norden's precipitous property, I gazed down at the river, and out across the dark hills upstream. I did not know what to do. Had Naps stolen Margaret? Had Slater arrived to steal her, and Naps given chase? Had Naps become disgusted at the sight of all those dissolute plutocrats at the party, and gone on home? Had Margaret wandered off into the woods with some seductive male? Had I only dreamed the whole thing from the beginning?

When I got my wits back I would just get up and enter the woods and keep going, walking all night until I found a lost dale up in the mountains and there I would build that log castle and eat those berries and mushrooms and grasshoppers and think those thoughts and live that rustic life. The *voyageur*, a worthless *voyeur*, would become an *ermite*.

The guests were all gone, the last lights of Norden's house were blinking out, the night was utterly soundless, and I began to whistle to myself simply to make a little bit of noise and keep myself company. I didn't know what I was whistling, some old Victor Herbert love song or something. About this time of night, years ago, two crack trains used to pass through Little Rock: one was the Missouri Pacific's Sunshine Special going southwest from New York to Mexico City; the other was the Rock Island's streamlined Rocket, going west out of Memphis. You could hear both of them passing through, the one rattling swiftly under all the viaducts out behind the high school, the other far eastward near the airport then sweeping around the south end of town, with every clack of its wheels clearly audible in the still distance. I always wanted to ride one of them, but I never did, and now they don't run any more, all you ever hear is the switch engines out in the Biddle yards. But what I mean is, you could really hear them, this time of night, after midnight. They blew their whistles several times, and otherwise made a lot of far-off noises. So maybe the reason I had to whistle was to fill in all that long silence. Soon I would think of something to do. *Phee wheu fii bee,* I puckered and blew, *fii bee wheu phee . . .*

How long I sat there whistling and meditating and scratching my mosquito bites I don't know; I know only a few of the questions which bumped around in my mind, questions dancing with each other in a frug or a hully-gully. Was Margaret really Wanda in a way? Is that why Slater had picked her for the role, because he saw that she was the perfect model of the idealistic dreamer who closes herself into a shell and can never turn her thoughts away from herself? But if that were true, why had Slater, who reputedly was both misogynist and misanthropist, sought her out and romanced her? Or had he? And to what extent? My fragile nerves would not bear up under the strain much longer.

"Nyhiss nyhit, aint hit?" said an old country boy's voice behind me, and I turned to see a tall silhouette approaching. He came up and sat down on the wall beside me. "Been lookin high and low for you," he said. "Heard somebody whistlin over here, figgered it couldn't be nobody else but a nut like Nub Stone. What're you doin, anyway, callin your dogs?"

I told him I was waiting to be rescued, and I was glad that he had come to rescue me.

"You ain't the one needs rescuin," he said. "Come on." He led me back across Norden's patio and out to the street. A jeep station wagon was parked there. I asked him if he had got himself a new car. He said no, the jeep belonged to Slater. He was just borrowing it. We got in, and he turned townward. "That nigger sidekick of yours done went and got hisself into trouble," he said. "Peepin Tom. Breakin and enterin. Whole buncha junk." He turned into Cantrell Road and mashed the accelerator to the floor. Over the noise of the speeding engine he said, "Don't know if I can get him out or not, but we'll see."

"Suppose you tell me what this is all about," I said.

"Suppose you tell me how come you let Margaret get out of your sight."

"Well, we were at the party, and it started raining, and I ran into a summerhouse, and—"

"All right," he said. "If I know you, you were probably foolin around with some other girl at the time. Anyway, Margaret's mother come and got her. While you wasn't lookin. Or while you was foolin around with some other girl." I asked him how Margaret's mother had known that she was at the party. He coughed and hemmed and hawed, and then he said, "I told her. Couldn't help it. Me and Slater was playin cards out at his place when she come up and rung the doorbell. Must of taken her an hour to find the place. Boy, I'm tellin you, she was mad. Thing is, she didn't even act mad at Slater, not at first anyway, but boy she really bellered at me, like it was all my fault. Guess it was, come to think of it. '*You!*' she says in that voice of hers like the whole world was deaf and dumb. '*You did it!*' She says, '*You* came and *took* my *daughter* away from *me* in Hot *Springs* and *you* took her *back* to *Little* Rock and *you* let her *be* in that *awful* play, and *now* here you *are* out *here* with this . . . *this* awful *man* who *sins* with her!' Slater turns to me and he says, 'Is *this* her?' And I says, '*That's* her.' And he says to her, 'Madam, I have always wanted to meet you, I've heard so much about you, but I thought I would just have to see you, because otherwise I wouldn't have believed it. Now I know.' And she says, 'Know *what?*' And he says, 'Know how it could have happened that a lovely girl like Margaret was virtually a recluse for twenty-seven years.' Then she got awful mad at him, and she says, 'Mr. *Slater*, you are a *disgrace* to . . . to your *profession*, what*ever* it *is,* and *I'm* going to *tell* your *wife* on *you!*' And he says, real prissy-like, 'Tell what, may I ask?' And she says, 'Tell *her* how *you* have been *living* in *sin* with my *daughter!*' Then Slater sort of looked at me and then he looked back at her and he says, 'Now *where* did you *ever* get *that* idea?' his voice just like hers, mockin her, and that got her madder than ever, and she says, '*Never* mind! Just *tell* me where you're *hiding* her and *then* don't you *ever* even *look* at her *again!*' And Slater says, 'Madam, you have my permission to turn the place upside down, but I don't think you'll find her on the premises.' And she says, '*Well,* what *did* you *do* with her?' And Slater says, 'In all truth, madam, I have not seen her since the curtain went down on the play.' And she studied him and studied him and then she turns back to me and says, '*You,* then! Dall, *you* are a *disgrace* to the *Little* Rock *police* and *I'm* going to *report* you to the *mayor* or the *city manager* or *who*ever and get *him* to *fire* you. Now *you* tell me *where* my *daughter* is, *right* this *minute,* or I'll *do* it!'

"And she just carried on like that somethin awful, so finally

I told her Margaret had gone to a party, and she kept after me about it, so finally I told her whose party it was, but I didn't mention you. Then she left, and I called Norden's place trying to reach you and warn you, but some drunk answered the phone and I had the awfulest time gettin him to understand what I was sayin, and when I did, he went away and come back in a little bit and said that you was nowhere around, so I thought maybe you'd done already taken Margaret off somewheres else.

"So I sat down and played some more cards with Slater for a while, and then the phone rang, and one of the boys at the station house was callin to tell me that they had this nigger that they caught prowlin around inside of Margaret's house after gettin a complaint from her mother, so I borrowed Slater's car to come and try to find you. And so here we are."

There we were, at the police headquarters. Dall told me to wait for him outside while he went in. He was gone for about twenty minutes, and when he returned he had Naps with him. Dall lectured him: "Naps, if you have to go into white folks's houses, don't rattle the damn doors so much."

"Men, we got to get a rope," Naps said to us. "Aint no other way. Miss Margaret's mother put a padlock on the door of that room, on the outside, yeah, and that's how I got caught, rattling that padlock. We got to get a rope and throw it up to her window."

So we got a rope. Dall parked Slater's jeep in the headquarters parking lot, and then he went inside and came back with a fifty-foot coil of rope. Then we got into Naps's Lincoln and drove over to Margaret's house.

There were no lights at all anywhere in the house; Margaret's room was dark too, we noticed as we crept up the back alley. It was two o'clock in the morning now, and we hoped everybody but Margaret would be in deep slumber. We stood beneath her open window—thirty feet beneath it. First Dall picked up some gravel and threw it up against her window screen, but there was no response. "Rapunzel," I called softly upward, "Rapunzel, let down your hair." This aint no time for jokes, Dall said.

Then I saw something, dangling from her window all the way to the ground. "Gone," I said to Dall and Naps, and pointed to the sheets and bedspread that she had knotted together to make a rope to get out of her room and down.

🌑 ELEVEN

In my dream of that night I am again John Linton, the Latin-spouting ex-lawyer in the frontier settlement of Lewisburgh, and I have left my cabin and, fortified with a jug of sour mash, floated my raft twenty miles downstream to La Petite Roche, to hunt for Sam Houston, who had deserted me in the previous episode of this continuing nocturnal serial. Or it is Sam Houston I am seeking? No, old Sam had become old Wes Stone, my father. Daddy is it, then, that I am hunting in the dirt streets of this territorial capital? No, my name is John Linton, and my father's name would be Linton too. In my drunkenness I careen down rows of brick dwellings and the new jerry-built clapboards— *Tristis eris si solus eris!* I yell, and the people stare questioningly at me, and I yell a translation for them: You will be sad if you keep company only with yourself! A constable accosts me and asks, Who are you trying to find? I cannot answer. Your brother? he asks. Your sister? Your mother? Maybe you're lookin for your wife? he says. I cannot answer. Hours and days I spend in that town, and can never learn what I am doing there. I only know that I am not well, and I cry: *Ubi bene, ibi patria:* Where it is well with me, there is my country. And the people stare at me.

I awoke looking into the dark pretty face of Tatrice. She was sitting on the side of the bed, with a tall glass of orange juice in one hand and the Sunday morning papers in the other. I fought down an urge (morning madness?) to grab her and pull her to me. She told me I had been talking in my sleep. What had I been saying? I asked her. She said I had been saying, over and over again, *O rus, quando ego te aspiciam,* and she asked me to tell her what it meant. I told her: O country of my boyhood, when shall I behold thee?

"You just lie here and be comfy," she said, handing me the orange juice and the newspapers. "I'll get you some coffee and doughnuts. Probably Naps won't get up for another hour or two." Then she left me, and I drank the juice and opened the papers. The news was dull and uneventful. I read the comics and then I hunted through all three of the papers for reviews of

Slater's play. The *Democrat* in search of a reviewer had scratched the body politic of Arkansas literati and had come up with another playwright, one Shirley Watford LaPlante, whose *This Is the Way We Wash Our Feet* has been playing to sixth-grade audiences for twenty years. Miss LaPlante gave her solemn attention to the premiere of Slater's play, and grudgingly acknowledged to *Democrat* readers that it was "clever." But her general reaction to it was summed up in the hyperbole of her concluding sentence: "Last night the legitimate theater wantonly ravished the illegitimate theater." The *Gazette*'s critic wrote: "Miss Austin performed admirably in her debut, and in her red wig bore an uncanny resemblance to the heroine of the movie, Miss Shearer, but as a whole the evening's entertainment struck this viewer as simply a case of cinema at its best being defiled by drama at its worst."

Early in the afternoon the delectably crisp smell of fried chicken was filling the house as Tatrice prepared Sunday dinner, when Dall called me. He had found Margaret. Or, rather, one of his patrolmen had found her, eating pancakes in a café at Markham and Main, and the patrolman had contacted Dall and Dall had gone down to get her and now they were at Dall's house. "Bring her on over here and have Sunday dinner with us," I suggested. Well, naw, now, Dall hawed, he reckoned he'd just fix some spaghetti for him and Margaret and come on over afterward. "You've been fixing too much spaghetti lately," I said, "and it's fattening. Come on over." Now look here, Nub, he said, runnin around with niggers is one thing, but *eatin* with em is a horse of a different feather. "We're having fried chicken," I said. "Don't you like fried chicken?" Why hell yes, he said, but— "Suit yourself," I said and hung up.

We delayed dinner pending his arrival, but he wasn't very late. There was a timid sound of a car rolling down the driveway and we went to the window and looked out. His dusty, rust-eaten Pontiac croaked to a halt at the front steps, and Dall got out, dressed again in that suit and porkpie straw hat which made him look so much already like the chief of police. He opened Margaret's door and she got out and the two of them timidly approached the front door of this strange mansion, both of them looking from side to side wonderingly, as if they had the wrong address. Margaret was wearing a full madras skirt and matching blouse, deep blue and green.

Tatrice answered the bell and said, "Won't you come in?"

and I said, "Hiya, Dall and Margaret, come on in. Dinner's getting cold."

But he said in an undertone, "We done ate, Nub. Honest."

Margaret nudged him. "No we haven't," she said, and before he could protest further I grabbed his arm and pulled him into the foyer and slammed the door behind him. I introduced them to Tatrice. "Pleased t'meetcha," Dall mumbled at her, then he added, "Don't want to put you folks to no trouble."

"Not at all, sir," Naps said and beckoned, and we led Dall down into the living room. Naps offered, "How bout a little Jack Daniels, Sergeant?" Dall started to decline, but too late: Naps had already sloshed a couple of jiggers into an ice-filled glass and thrust it into his hand. Dall looked down at the glass, mumbled something about how he didn't guess a little bit would hurt him, grinned blushingly, and took a sip. "Good stuff," he commented.

There followed a brief interlude of silence, during which we all struggled to think of an ice-breaking word. Dall spoke first: "Sure is a swell-lookin place you got here."

"Thank you," Tatrice said nicely.

"You—" Dall bluntly addressed Naps, then he softened his tone. "Naps, what sorta work is it you do?"

"I'm a book salesman," Naps said.

"You mean a bookie?" Dall asked.

"Naw, I don't *make* book. I *sell* books."

Dall did not pursue the matter. We sat in the living room and drank our drinks and exchanged pleasantries. Margaret looked very . . . very, well, tired in a way, and more than that: confused, as if she were not at all certain where she was, who she was with. There were many things I wanted to talk with her about, but I would have to wait until we were alone.

Soon Tatrice led us into the dining room to a groaning board (Duncan Phyfe-type mahogany) laden with three big chickens cut up into golden flaky pieces, mashed potatoes, giblet gravy, stuffed celery, roasted pecans, artichokes, the works. Dall was to be seated on Tatrice's right, Margaret on Naps's right, I beside Margaret, little Lucy and Mart beside Dall. Dall eyed Margaret and me skeptically and waited until he had watched with his own eyes as we sat down at that table before finally sitting down himself. But sit he did, and I was thrilled. A whole era had come to an end. "You the law?" little Lucy asked of him, and Dall gruntingly granted that he was. "You don't *look* like the law," Lucy said doubtfully, and her father explained to her that it was only because Sergeant Hawkins didn't have on his uniform, but that if she would be a very good little girl he might come back sometime with his uniform on. Mart said, "I gonna be the law when I git growed," and Dall said that if he were chief of police by that time he would give Mart a job on the force, and Naps choked on a bite of celery or something. Dall's deportment in general surprised and pleased me, and I was especially gratified to note that his table manners, if not irreproachable, were at least graciously inconspicuous, even genteel.

For table conversation, Naps and Tatrice tried to draw Dall out on the nature of several of his more recent and daring exploits in the performance of his duties as a policeman, those for which he had been cited by the department, but Dall was reluctant to say anything which could be construed as a self-laudatory remark. The talk turned to the reviews of Slater's play, which Dall and Margaret had read in the papers that morning. They agreed that the reviews had been about what they had expected.

Toward the end of dessert and coffee I noticed that Margaret's head was beginning to nod forward at intervals, and I sensed that she was having a struggle to remain awake. Tatrice noticed this too, and offered her the use of one of the upstairs bedrooms for a nap. At first Margaret declined, but eventually she had to do it. She excused herself and went upstairs.

"Poor kid," Dall said after she had gone, "I don't imagine she slept atall last night. Told me she'd just been walkin around town, tryin to make up her mind what to do."

"Make up her mind?" I said. "About what?"

"All kinds of things," Dall said, rather evasively. "Mainly she was wonderin whether it might not be best for her to quit that Slater play right now, cause she don't approve of it."

"I know that," I said, "but I wonder why she had to spend the whole night wandering around town trying to make up her mind."

"Needed to be by herself, I guess," he said. "Caint say I blame her, though I gave her a real talkin-to for it. Them reviews in the papers this mornin kind of upset her, and I think she don't aim to be in any more performances."

Dall could not stay long, he had to go back on duty that afternoon. He got his hat and went up to Tatrice and said to her, "Miz Howard, that sure was a mighty fine dinner, and I'm much obliged to you." She said she hoped he would come again sometime, that it had been good having him.

I walked with him out to his car, and he got into it and I leaned up against the side of it and looked in at him. "Well," he said. "You and Margaret have yourselves a good time now, hear? And thanks for invitin me over for dinner, anyway. I guess if you can pal around with niggers, I can too. You aint a goddamn bit better than me." He let out the clutch and was gone.

When she woke up from her afternoon nap we went out for a walk, through the copse of oaks behind Naps's house and down across the Fourche Creek valley and part way up Granite Mountain on the other side of that plain valley, keeping to no paths or trails but just wandering through woods and bottoms and barrens, a fine afternoon full of wildflowers and clouds. This is the way to take a walk with one's girl, I said to myself, and what we talked about didn't much matter: frivolities, persiflage, waggery, air, nothing. We held hands. She seemed to be feeling much better: rested, less confused, happy even. Starting back, on the way down Granite Mountain, I grew tired of vacant gab and began to ask her little questions. "Who was that Dr. Ashley that your mother took you off to see the other morning?"

He was, she said, the minister of her mother's church, the Reverend Doctor Malone C. Ashley. Her mother had said to her that morning, "I've *told* you time and *time* again you should have *talked* to *him*. That's his *job*, it's what he gets *paid* for. If you won't tell *me* your troubles, at least tell them to *him*, for heaven's *sake*."

But the man's manner, his fat beatific face, his rectory—all had overwhelmed, intimidated her. She had not been able to tell him a thing, although he had persisted: "Unburden yourself, my child. Share your problem with me." And he had told her, "I think I might safely boast that I have never yet encountered a problem of the soul, of the spirit, which I have not been able to deal with. So . . . if you feel that we might be able to bring this thing out into the open, so to speak, if there is any possibility that we might call upon Christ Our Redeemer for some measure of understanding or reassurance in this time of our affliction and our errant but venial iniquity, then by all means let us stand shoulder to shoulder and put our heads together, let us play ball."

She had not been able to think of a blessed thing to say to him.

His Immense, she referred to him—he was not really a fat man, no, not fat like her mother, but he ate well and his ectomorphic build was incongruously draped with flab; his underchin jiggled when he spoke, his lips had drawn a surplus of sebaceous cell tissue and were thickly pursed, distinctly carnal; in Sunday School class years ago when the teacher was out of the room Margaret and the other girls had often speculated about this minister's private pleasures, he being a bachelor and all. "Naturally now I'm aware," he had prattled onward to her, "that you have not been entirely . . . entirely"— he had been rotating his open hand palm upward in front of his belly as if to signal that he was about to heave up his breakfast— "entirely, well, *dutiful,* shall we say? in the manner of your outlook toward the Faith, that is, you seem, to all intents and purposes, to have manifested a rather skeptical approach to matters of theology, all in all, yet at the same time I am given reason to hope that you are not beyond the pale, figuratively speaking, in so far as your basic moral structure is concerned." But she had not been able to talk to him. Alternately jabbing his palm with an anodized letter opener or forming a church roof with his fingertips pressed together, he had leaned forward abruptly across his desk and gripped the front edge of it so hard his pink pudgy knuckles had turned white, and he had tilted his head to one side and his face had become filled with gummy and affected compassion as he whined, "Margaret, why did you not come to me before? Why have you waited so long to seek counsel and comfort? Have you not known, all these years, that Our Lord has a place for you in His heart? Have you been afraid of Him?"

No, she had confessed at last, she was not at all afraid of Him.

Finally he had said to her, "Margaret, in my own way I'm a pretty nice and level-headed sort of fellow, and I think we ought to do business with each other, and if we just work together on this problem, we'll have it licked one of these days." And he had suggested to her mother that she dip into her savings and send Margaret away for a while, out of town, for a rest. He suggested Hot Springs because, by coincidence, he himself was due over there for a few hydrothermal treatments in another week, and they might get together for a little talk or two, no?

No, she had said, but the mother had been persuaded, and had taken—not sent but taken—her to Hot Springs. Before they left she had said to her mother, "You don't have any savings, so tell me, if we're so poor, how can we afford to go to Hot Springs?"

"That's *my* business," the mother had said, "*I'll* worry about *that.* You *run* on *up* and *pack* your *bag,"* and then, as Margaret had started for the stairs, she had stopped her and given her an aerosol can of Glade spring-flower air freshener, and had said, *"Spray* this *around* up *there!"*

"Mother," Margaret had moaned in exasperation, "I told you. It *isn't*—"

"Do *you* think you can fool *me?"* the mother had said. "Do you think *I* believe all your *lies?"*

We were sitting now in the late afternoon sun on the terrace behind Naps's house, returned from our walk and resting now, drinking lemonade with a little gin in it. More than it had yet, the day began to take on that quality of laziness, of idle lethargy, which Sunday afternoons always have, and there was nothing we felt like doing so much as sitting gently in the sun and holding hands and talking. But although I was managing to get a lot of her story out of her, still she was reluctant to talk about Slater, beyond saying that she thought she might at one time have been infatuated with him or she might not have been, but one way or the other, after meeting me again as she had, her feeling toward him, whatever it was, had turned abruptly into revulsion; and now she wished for nothing better than to be permitted to forget him entirely.

"But just tell me one thing," I persisted. "Did you ever sleep with him?"

"No," she said.

"Well, did you ever get into a bed, or a cot, or any kind of horizontal position, with him?"

"No," she said.

"Well, what *did* you do with him, for goodness sakes?"

"Clifford—" she protested.

Naps called to us to come in and eat supper.

Walking into the house, she said, "This is such a beautiful home, isn't it?" I told her I had never seen its equal anywhere. Then she asked, "Is this where we're going to stay tonight?" Sure, if you want to, I said, giving her hand a squeeze.

Supper was interrupted by the ringing of the telephone. Tatrice answered it and said it was for Margaret. I wondered who, besides Dall, knew that Margaret was here at Naps's house.

Margaret went to the phone, which was in the hallway, but not quite out of earshot. "Yes?" I heard her say into it.

Then she lowered her voice and said, "Yes, that's right."

A moment passed, she lowered her voice still more and said, "I'm sorry, but I just can't. It's just the way I feel about it."

Another moment, and she said, "I can't talk to you now."

"I don't know," she said. "Do we have to?"

"No," she said.

"No, of course not!" Her voice rose, and she tried to lower it again: "No, I tell you. What makes you think—?"

"But—" she said.

"Don't you dare—" she said.

"Listen, I can't talk to you now, but just wait, don't even think about it until I talk to you. I'll call you later."

"Please—" she said.

Then, "I'll *call* you. Good-bye, now."

She hung up and returned to the table. She was trembling. "That wasn't your mother, I hope?" I said, but she did not answer. She stared at her plate. In silence she finished her food. We cleared the table. Tatrice motioned to Naps and they went out of the room.

"Margaret," I said, "was that Slater?"

She did not look up at me.

"Margaret, would you like for me to leave, so you could call him back and finish the conversation?"

She shook her head. Then she got up from the table and walked into the living room. I followed her. She poured some bourbon into a glass and sat down. I made myself a drink and sat down beside her. After a while I asked, "What did he want?"

She made up a story. Slater was writing a new play, a kind of folk piece, completely different from his previous work, and he wanted her to have a part in it. It was based on Ozark superstitions and symbolisms, the phases of the moon and katydids and love charms and so forth, and he was going to present it in some small mountain-locked community up in the Ozarks for a tryout, because he felt that the backwoodsmen could appreciate it more than the bourgeoisie of Little Rock. It was a fetching idea, she said, but she did not want a part in it, she did not want to see Slater again, she did not want to be in any more performances of his *Red Shoes* play, she wanted to forget him entirely.

Then she said, "I wish you and Doyle would forget about it, too, and just leave him alone." I told her that it was not Slater, but *her*, that we were interested in. She said that Dall had some kind of obsession with being a custodian of the public welfare, a pillar of strength in a town full of weakness, a vigilant and overzealous guardian spirit, and that it must really tear him up to realize that there wasn't a blessed thing he could do for her any more now. She had told him again and again, lately, that he'd done all he could possibly do, all anyone could possibly do, and that she was very grateful to him for it, but that he was just wasting his time now.

"He wouldn't be wasting his time if he prevented you from killing yourself," I averred.

"Clifford," she said. She just said my name in a tone of tiredness, exasperation.

"It's true, isn't it?" I harped. "Wouldn't you have tried to kill yourself if Dall hadn't come your way?"

"All right!" she said. "But I'm past that now, so forget about it, can't you?"

"No, I can't," I said.

But clearly she would not allow me to pursue the subject. She said we had spent too much time talking about her, and now she wanted us to talk about me. I protested that there was nothing about me worth discussing, but she said I was mistaken. "What do you want out of life?" she asked. "What are your ambitions, your dreams, your plans?" I put her off with a boring synopsis of my project for writing a book someday on the Vanished American Past. She wanted to know more about it, she wanted to know what elements of that vanished past I was most interested in, but I was in no mood for talking shop. She asked me how long I planned to stay in Little Rock. I said I was ready to leave just as soon as she was.

"But why do we have to leave?" she asked. "Where would we go?"

We would see the world, I said. The world!

What about your wife? she asked.

To hell with my wife, I said.

Why don't we just stay here in Little Rock? she asked. Why don't we see Little Rock before seeing the world?

What's there to see in Little Rock? I asked.

Lots of things, she said. All kinds of things. Things you've never seen before. Things *I've* never seen before, in all these years.

Bosh! I said. The world is waiting!

You're an incurable dreamer and wanderer, she said.

"Besides," she said, smiling impishly, "how do you know I would go with you? I don't know anything about you. You won't talk to me about yourself. You're virtually a stranger to me."

"You're *really* a stranger to me," I said defensively. But I told her there would be plenty of time for getting acquainted . . . or re-acquainted.

"Talk to me now!" she said, and in her voice was an echo of the same desperation that had crept into my own voice on that night I met her at the movies. "Talk to me, Clifford!" she said. "Tell me about yourself."

But I couldn't. Had I not written, in my Ring-Master: Familiarity Breeds Contempt? Had I not learned, the hard way, what a dangerous thing it is to reveal too much of oneself to a woman? I was not going to give Margaret the opportunity to acquire the false conception of me that Pamela had used against me. Later, maybe, I could open up a little bit. But not now.

I had it all planned: how we would snuggle up here in a cozy corner of Naps's vast living room with a bottle of Jack Daniels and a bucket of ice and have the most intimate kind of talk all evening until bedtime, and then in the dark I would sneak into her room or (better) she would sneak into mine, or, considering the kind of broad-minded people Naps and Tatrice were, we would be put to bed together anyway. But while I was ruminating on this happy thought, the telephone rang and Naps answered it and said it was for me this time, and I should have known, should have guessed, that the Fates, in the person of people toward whom I had responsibilities, would intervene smack dab in the middle of this opportune time and rob me of all my little pleasures. The caller was my father. He sounded displeased. He said he had been looking all over the place trying to find me. Seeing as how I was in Little Rock, he said, why didn't I visit with my relatives sometimes? How had he located me? He had phoned Dall at the police station, and Dall had told him. Now he didn't want to seem aggervatin, he said, but didn't I think I ought to just drop in and say hello, especially on account of Grammaw Stone coming all the way down from Parthenon just to see me? Grammaw? I said. Yeah, he said. She's here right now, came in on the afternoon bus, and it sure did embarrass me that I didn't know where you was or even if you was still in town or not or what. Well gee, Daddy, I— Hadn't you better get yourself right on over here? he said. And I said yeah, I guessed I had better.

The expression on Margaret's face, when I told her I had to go say hello to my grandmother and would probably be expected to spend the night over there, convinced me that her plans for the disposition of the evening had been similar to mine and that she was equally disappointed. I kissed her and told her I would be back first chance I got tomorrow. Naps drove me home.

My grandmother is a rather large and sturdy old Scotswoman, much bigger than my father, although now, in her late eighties, she is spent: her hair is a plump white leghorn hen roosting upon her head, and her massive Amazonian frame is so stooped that my father and I do not have to look up to her any more.

When I walked in the front door (unlocked and usable now that she was here) her embrace was feeble and limp; all her strength was spared for her voice: "Well, lookie who's here! If it's not little Cliffie!" (Nowhere but in Parthenon was I ever called Cliffie.) I told her I was awfully glad to see her—and I *was*—and she said, "Well, your dad wrote and tole me you was home, so I figured I'd better just hop right on the bus and high-tail it right on down here to see you."

Daddy said, "And she come walkin through that door this afternoon with her suitcase in her hand and without even sayin so much as hello to me her own boy she yells, 'Where's Cliffie?' and be dog if I had the slightest notion where you might be at. Boy, it sure put me down on you. I was mortified."

My sister Cindy (who in honor of the occasion had come with her husband Victor to this house which, I had lately learned, she rarely visited these days) said, "Shamey on you, Clifford Willow Stone. If you're only going to come back to Arkansas ever four years or so, you ought to at least visit with your own folks while you're here, instead of running around all over town or whatever."

Victor said, "Yeah."

Cindy said, "Here you've been home for a week now and haven't been to see me but once, and you sure weren't much company *that* time."

Victor said, "Yeah."

Grammaw Stone said, "Well, I'm tickled to see you anyhow. I tole your dad, I said to him, 'Now I bet you that boy is just out rompin around some'rs and cuttin up with Dall Hawkins like he used to, and I wouldn't be surprised if he don't come home soon's he gets a few burrs stuck on his tail.'"

They had all finished eating except for dessert, so we sat around and divided up an egg custard pie which Grammaw Stone had baked especially for me. Something in the house was missing, and finally I realized what it was. "Where's Sybil?" I asked my father.

He threw me a squint of mingled panic and caution, then he

glanced furtively at his mother and saw that she was waiting for him to answer my question.

"Aw, you mean that cleanin woman that was here the other day?" he said to me in a voice catchy and too loud. "Well, I sorta figgered we wouldn't be needin her long as your grammaw's here." He turned to her. "Aint that right, Momma? No sense in having a cleanin woman come around long as you're here, is they?"

"I can out-sweep and out-dust the best of them" Grammaw Stone proclaimed, brandishing an imaginary broom.

Grammaw Stone did a rare thing that night: she deferred her rigidly habitual bedtime—nine o'clock—in order to sit up with us for a long time, but I was nervous with the vague feeling that I no longer knew how to converse freely with her, so the evening was awkward and long and difficult for me. Long moments passed in which none of us said anything. Eventually she said to me, "Seems like somehow you're not the same folksy little chum as you used to be," then she shuffled off to bed. I looked at my father, and he said, "What's on your mind, boy?" and I said that nothing was. He said, "Sybil told me last time she saw you, you acted like you'd seen a ghost or somethin. What's eatin on you, anyway?" Nothing, I repeated, nothing at all.

I watched the ten o'clock news on television—Hy Norden's program—and listened to him offer his own opinion of the Slater play: "Folks, there's a good movie showing over at the Arts Center theater now, called *The Red Shoes*, with a great British cast, and in color and all. But the trouble is, it doesn't have any sound, and you have to sit and listen to a couple of amateur actors sitting on the stage jabbering some nonsense. Well, I guess there are worse ways to spend one's time . . ."

Before going to bed I phoned Dall at the police station and told him about the call Margaret had received from Slater, and what she had said. I said it was about time that one of us—Dall or I—had a talk with Slater and persuaded him to leave Margaret alone. Dall agreed and said he was going to call Slater and tell him that Margaret was spending the night at his—Dall's—house. "Why?" I asked. Dall said: I'll see you in the mornin and talk it over then.

Sleep for me that night was fitful, almost as bad as it had been the last time I had tried to sleep there. Perhaps I cannot sleep in this house.

Dall came in the morning. His green lynx eyes were puffy and vacant; apparently he too was having trouble with the sandman. But before he could tell me whatever he had come to tell me my grandmother spotted him. "Well, fan my brow!" she exclaimed. "If it's not Sheriff Hawkins Junior hisself, I do declare!"

"Howdy, Miz Stone," he said, smiling and removing his white cop's cap. "Ain't seen you for a right smart spell. How you been gettin along?"

"Tobble," she said, "Just tobble, thank you. Still up and about. How's ever little thing with you?"

"Just fine, ma'am. I'm doin pretty good. How's each and ever one up your way?"

"Okay, I imagine," she said, then she moved closer to him and straightened up enough to look him level in the eye. "Dall, when d'you aim to come home?" she asked. "When air you aimin to come home and run for sheriff up there?"

"Aw, I don't know, Miz Stone," he hemmed. "I sorta like it where I am."

"They's not been a sheriff up there worth two hoots in hades ever since your daddy got . . . ever since he passed on, and we all been kinda hopin you'd come back when you got growed up, and take his place." She put her hand on his arm as she said this.

"Well now, that sure is a nice thought, Miz Stone, it sure is, but like as not I wouldn't have much of a chance of gettin elected since I aint lived there for nigh on to twenty year or so, and don't hardly know any of the folks up there well enough to get em to vote for me even if I was of a mind to try it. But I'm much obliged to you, that sure is a real nice thought."

She squinted her eyes and cocked her head sideways and lowered her voice. "You had any word from Rowena lately?"

"Why no," he said, equally quietly. "It's been some time since I got any mail from her."

"Well," Grammaw Stone said, still squinting, and a trace of a wry smile on her thin mouth, "I'll tell you, you sure wouldn't be proud of the way she's been carryin on and sashayin around up there with that bricklayer Sims and everbody else."

Although Dall protested that it wasn't any of his business any more, my grandmother proceeded to fill him in on all the latest antics of his former wife. He inquired after his children: "Them little boys. Anybody watchin out for em?" and she explained that Rowena's aunt was taking good care of them but that Dall could get them back any time he wanted them, to which Dall said that he was hoping to get them when his promotion came through in September and he could afford a housekeeper or somebody to take care of them.

Then he excused himself, explaining that he had to talk to me about something. He asked her if she was planning to stay awhile, and when she said yes he said he hoped to see her again and would like to talk about "up home" with her.

Dall and I went outside and sat on a front step. He asked, "Did you see this morning's *Gazette*?" I told him I hadn't had a chance to look at it yet. "Go get it," he said, and I went back into the house and borrowed it from my grandmother and took it out to Dall. He opened it and leafed through it until he found the editorial page and then he showed it to me, pointing at something which ran down a narrow column in the lower right corner. "Read this," he said, "and see if you can make any sense out of it."

COMMENTARY VERSES
To Mr. Slater, Occasioned by the Premier of His Travesty Called *How Many Times Have You Seen* THE RED SHOES?

You who art due din and ear pop aye
Yet got not one nod but hue and cry,
And rue the day God had His sly fun,
May Art die ere you let its end run.
Too oft bad men can cut and vil ify
And act the cad and caw the mag pie,
And low the old cow but how odd not
Wit nor fun can rid one cow God wot!
Fie for any mad foe who did not see
The wry way you saw the gal and she
Was shy and wan yet all off her nut;
Her cry was why she got hit and cut.
All she did was wet her eye and mew.
Mim was her air and red was her shu.
May hap her ice got him mad and his
Hot dog got him fey and his ire riz.
Who can say the guy his gut was tin?
But who can say she did owe him sin?
Not let him pet her nor get his way
Nor get far was how she had her say;
And sly art and gyp did she emp loy:
Pry off his lid and rob his one joy.
You let him axe her and you are top.

```
Rot  her   sad  mug  and  rot  her  red  mop.
Our  pal   old  dry  Han  sAn  der  sen  Sir,
Han  sCh   ris  tia  nAn  der  sen  did  err:
His  end   was  raw  fib  all  big  fat  lie.
She  did   not  opt  sky  pie  bye  and  bye.
```

Doyle Curtis Hawkins

It took me a moment to recognize the name at the bottom, and then I said, "*You* didn't write this thing!"

"Haw, naw," he said, abashed. "Slater tole me he was writin some poem for the papers but he couldn't sign his own name to it cause it was dedicated to hisself, so he ast me if I would mind if he signed my name to it, cause he don't have no other friends, and I said, What the hell, don't matter to me one way or the other. So he did."

"Looks like something that came out of an IBM computer," I remarked.

"Yeah, but what does it mean to you?"

"It means," I said, "that Slater obviously is bitter about the reception his play got, and also perhaps he is a little bitter about Margaret."

"That's what I figgered," Dall said. "But you don't think maybe it's a code or somethin? All them three-letter words, looks to me like he might be writing a code or a secret message."

I read the poem again carefully and told Dall that I didn't think it contained any secret messages or veiled allusions. "Well, anyway," he said, and then he told me what was up. He had called Slater last night and Slater was very upset because Margaret would not appear in any further performances of his play. Dall told him that Margaret was going to stay at Dall's house and that Dall would appreciate it if Slater would leave her alone. "You're a married man, after all," Dall said to him. Slater replied that such matters were no concern of Dall's, and that at any rate Slater was no longer very fond of Margaret. Then Slater had said, "You're on night duty at headquarters, and she's over there at your house by herself? Do you think that's wise, leaving her untended like that?" But Dall had said: Aw, I aint worried she'll try to run off or anything. Now why don't you just forget about her, okay?

Then from his shirt pocket Dall took out a ragged-edged patch of cloth, a six-inch-square fragment of some kind of light woolen worsted material in a pale gray-blue herringbone weave; he handed it to me. "When I got home from work last night I found my dog sittin out in the back yard with that piece of somebody's pants in his teeth. You remember that there dog Bowzer of mine, the one me and you had a little trouble with the other evenin, well, he was just settin there, kind of grinnin, with that piece of somebody's pants between his jaws. It sort of looks like fine quality material, don't it? I don't reckon Bowzer ran out and tore it off of some pore nigger walkin down the street."

And what did the patch of pants mean? It meant that Slater was still very much interested in Margaret, *desperately* interested, and that he had gone to Dall's house last night, hoping to find Margaret, and instead had found only Bowzer.

"So it looks like I better go have a little talk with him," Dall said. "Face to face." Now he was on his way out there. He suggested that I keep a good eye on Margaret in the meantime, until he had the whole thing settled. I told him I was going back to Naps's house very shortly. Then Dall got into his squad car and headed off for his showdown.

"Come on back to the kitchen and shell a few peas for me," my grandmother requested.

"Okay." I shrugged and went back to the kitchen and sat down with an aluminum bowl in my lap and shelled a mess of peas while she worked on a pie.

"For a fact," she let fall while rolling out the dough, "Dall has sure got a real head between his shoulders. Just like his daddy was. Slick as a whisker."

"He's all right," I granted, mechanically snapping open the peapods.

"It aint his fault he's not much to look at," she continued reflectively, almost apologetically. "His daddy wasn't no knockout hisself. And his momma . . . Homely! Why, they used to say that when Dall was a baby he had to be blindfolded before he'd nurse!"

I laughed a little.

She eyed me. "Well, you aint lost your funnybone yet, anyway," she said.

While I snapped open the peapods I lapsed into a brown study of reflection. Now that Margaret was successfully removed from her mother and Slater, I could do whatever I wanted with her. I visualized the two of us vagabonding our way around the world, seeing everything, making up for the emptiness of our youths, having a great time. As soon as I saw her again I would persuade her to run away with me.

Oh, of course before we went it might be a good idea for me to learn a little more about this curious creature, to satisfy myself that she really was earnest in her feelings toward me, that she was no longer seriously contemplating her own demise as a solution to her problems, that she was not so dependent on or morbidly attached to her mother that she could not get away from her permanently, that she would not be disposed to embarrass our future guests or friends by decorating the walls with obscenities in mock-feculent colors, that her chronic self-defeating tendencies did not require extensive therapeutic treatment, and that she had not been somehow perpetually corrupted by her deviant contacts—whatever they were—with her former consort.

Golly, son, I said to myself, you've got a long way to go yet.

"You bet you," my grandmother remarked as I was finishing the peas for her, "he aint a real Christian gentleman, I reckon not, but sure as I'm astandin here he's the keenest and two-fistedest jasper that ever come out of Newton County. They broke the mold after he was made, and aint nobody up there got the spleen and spunk of him."

"Who?" I inquired.

She cast me a look of annoyance. Then she said, "Your pal Dall."

"Oh," I said.

The first thing I did after lunch was to call the Missouri Pacific baggage agent once more and ask—rather hesitantly—if they had had any success yet in locating my lost suitcase. There's really no great rush, I assured him, but I *would* just sort of like to get it back, you know? We'll call you, he said.

Then I called Naps's house. Tatrice answered. I asked to speak to Margaret. Who's this? asked Tatrice. I told her. My Lord, she said quietly but intensely. You want to speak to *Margaret*? she asked puzzledly. Yes yes, I said, feeling a stupefying suspicion of something gone wrong. Tatrice said: She's not over there at your house? It took me a moment to realize that this was a question, not a statement, then I answered: No, why should she be? Well, Tatrice said, I thought that must surely be where she went. I said: You mean she's not there? Yes, Tatrice said, she left about an hour ago after talking to—I thought it *must* be you—on the telephone; she didn't say anything at all when she went out, but I simply took it for granted she was going to walk over to your place for a while. On foot? I said. I'm sorry? she said. I said: You mean she just walked out the front door and went walking off up the street? Yes, she said, just went walking up Ringo in the direction of your house; Naps left early in the car to go out to Mr. Slater's place, or else I would have offered to drive her over to your place, but it isn't far, is it, eight or nine blocks? She didn't come over here, I stated flatly. Maybe she went home, I said sadly. Maybe she just went on back home to her mother. Oh, goodness, that *would* be too bad, Tatrice said; I guess I should have stopped her, but I— Hey! I said. What did Naps go out to Slater's place for?

"Well now," she said haltingly, and I sensed that it was going to be hard for her to explain, "you see, what happened was, after you left last night, we sat around talking a long time and . . . well, you know Naps, he likes to see to it that a person gets enough to drink, and Margaret . . . well, I said to Naps, getting him off in a corner, I said to him, 'Hadn't you better let up a little on that girl? She's already had half a pint at least,' but he just laughed and said, 'Honey, don't you want to hear some lively bedtime stories?' and he winked at me and went on back and poured her another one, and after she'd had a couple more and couldn't even turn them up without spilling them I said to her myself, 'Margaret, you are getting kind of pie-eyed and far-gone. Want me to make you some coffee?' but she wouldn't pay me any mind because she was too busy answering the question Naps had just asked her."

"What sort of questions did he ask?"

"Oh, everything," she said. "Just everything, and then after a while he didn't have to ask her very many questions because she was answering them all by herself, I mean, she was just talking a blue streak. At the beginning he would ask her things like what she thought of Little Rock, and what she thought of you, and what she thought of her momma, and all like that, but then before too long he didn't have to ask her much more, because she was doing all the talking, and he just sat back and listened and I . . . well, I did too, because, honestly, some of it was very interesting, even if I'm awfully ashamed of myself this morning for sort of peeking in on her private business like that."

I begged Tatrice to pass along to me anything Margaret had said which might be of interest to me, and Tatrice, after making me promise not to tell anyone that she had told me, told me.

Margaret, in the advanced stages of intoxicated loquacity, had spoken frankly about Slater's wife Ethel, that old, bent, bitter woman confined to a wheelchair and confined to her own room in that large old Spanish hacienda, a woman Margaret referred to more than once as "the last gasp" of the original Little Rock aristocracy—whose people, the Crittendens, had governed and overlorded the town for most of the nineteenth century. Slater implied to Margaret that he was convinced his wife's invalidity was psychosomatic; she wanted to be cared for and babied. He resented his wife because all the money was hers and she knew it and behaved accordingly, was conniving and parsimonious. Horrible woman. He hadn't been between her legs for twenty years. Enough to spoil a man forever. Impulsively Margaret laughed, then realized it wasn't funny. But she felt sorry for Ethel Slater, and liked her; sometimes they talked together over tea in Ethel's room while Slater was busy tending to his horses. "I can't stand men," Mrs. Slater said, "and I see so few ladies worthy of the name, so it is a pleasure to talk with you." At another time (the next day? two weeks afterwards?) the woman said, "My thighs are like iron. Feel them. Ah. There. Now, higher." Now higher Margaret tilts her glass, draining it, gulps, coughs, clearing her throat, says (quotes): Now, higher. Ah. Horrible woman. But she felt sorry for her. No, not because of Slater. They were both victims. We are all victims. All of us are crazy fucked-up victims. (Tatrice leans at Naps and whispers: Can't you see when she starts talking like that she has had enough to drink? Naps answers: Shut up. You say that word yourself sometimes when you're feeling blue. Then Naps says to Margaret: Did he ever do you wrong?) Wrong? You mean, wrong? No. I mean, yes. He was going to help me cover my overdue charge account balances at Blass and Pfeifer's. I had lost my job and couldn't pay them. But then he said, "Ethel has me tied down, it's hard for me to get a cent out of her, but I'll try, only don't you think I ought to get something out of it, I mean, let's be practical and pragmatic about this thing, don't you agree that I'm entitled to get something in return?" (Naps coaches: He was trying to swap for a hump—?) What? (Naps: I mean, he had a flop on his mind—?) I'm sorry, I don't quite— (Naps: That Mr. Slater, what he wanted was to go the route—?) Go the route? (Naps: Yeah, you know, the limit, he wanted to hit it off, take it out on trade, tear off a piece—?) A piece of what? (Naps: Aw, you know what I mean, girl. He wanted to plant his oats.) Oh. No. He doesn't have any oats. (Naps: I see. Well, go on. Don't let me interrupt you.) My glass. Could I— Just a little— (Naps: Sure, Margaret, all you want.)

She passed out. Tatrice said: Now look what you've done. Naps said: All right, make us some coffee.

With the help of the coffee he managed to revive her for a brief time, during which she said, in answer to his persistent insistence: Why do we have to talk any more about this? It's over. Let sleeping dogs lie. He was going to get rid of her so he could marry me and I told him if he did that I wouldn't marry him but he wouldn't let that stop him and he was out of his mind so I told him it was quits leave me alone leave me alone. He left me alone. So let's talk about somebody else let's talk about Clifford or Doyle or you or anybody.

Get rid of his wife? Naps poked.

Yes yes that's what I said yes he was going to push her down the stairs in her wheelchair and make it look like an accident but he's not any more I mean he'll give up the whole idea if everybody will just leave him alone so forget about it leave him alone leave me alone please please don't bother him about it because he is sad and wretched a miserable fool he's under a curse don't make it worse that's a poem of verse good night thanks for all the booze good night.

She went to sleep and they carried her upstairs and put her to bed. Then Naps called his friend Feemy Bastrop at Slater's house and talked to him for a while and then told him that he would be out there first thing in the morning.

"This morning she had an awful hangover, of course, but she didn't seem so very blue or anything," Tatrice said to me. "She was kind of quiet, and seemed to be doing a lot of thinking. But then when she was reading the *Gazette* at the breakfast table she seemed to find something in it that bothered her. Then after breakfast she asked if she could use the phone, and I said sure, and she talked for a little while to somebody—I thought for *sure* it must've been you she was talking to—and then she went out, so I just took it for granted she was going over to your house. Oh, I'll never forgive myself if she's gotten lost again."

I thanked Tatrice and told her to ask Naps to get in touch with me when, and if, he came back from Slater's.

I told her I was going to go out and get Margaret.

🌺 TWELVE

"*There* you are!" the woman said, opening the large Gothic door a brief moment after I had rung the chime. "*Just* the person I've been *looking* for." She narrowed her eyes at me, and what she thought must have been a smirk actually was a sneer. She took my arm and led me into the parlor and parked me among the Victorian gewgaws. She did not herself sit down. "*Now*," she said, fixing me with a schoolteacher's impatiently quizzical stare, "*what* have you *done* with my *daughter*?"

I came back at her unnonplusedly: "I was just about to ask you the same thing."

"Oh, you *were*, were you?" From her standing position above me she was able to look down a very long nose at me, arching her eyebrows and bulging her eyeballs.

"Yes," I said and stood up so that I could be offensive too. I looked her in the eye. "Is she here? I think she is. If she is, I think I have a right to know about it. I want to talk to her."

She laughed. "Oh, you *do*, do you?" She moved closer to me. "All *right* now, you can quit *play*acting. I *want* to *know* where she *is*, and you'd *better* tell me, *quick*."

"Sure," I said and pointed viciously at the ceiling. "She's up in her room. Right this minute. Up there where you're trying to hide her."

"Oh, she *is*, is she?" Again she laughed. "Come *on*, Clifford, you can't *fool* around with *me*. Tell me what you've *done* with my *daughter*."

"*You* tell *me* what *you've* done with your daughter. *I* haven't done *anything* with her." Dammit, the woman's inflections were infectious.

"Oh, you *haven't*, haven't you?" she said.

This sort of insane exchange ricocheted between us for another ten minutes or so, until at last I was convinced that she really did not have her daughter in captivity and really was not hiding anything from me, and until she was at last convinced that I knew nothing about the present presence of her daughter. Then we both sat down. "Tea?" she said. "Thank you," I said.

She poured and we held our cups and sipped gently at them from time to time. I studied the ornately framed chromolithographs on the walls, imaginary Arcadian landscapes.

"That girl," Mrs. Austin meditated aloud.

"Ah yes," was all I could say, and it sounded fruitily phony.

"Such a *trial*," she remarked a short while later. "Such a *burden*."

I slowly shook my head in knowing sympathy.

"I've tried *so hard*," she said.

"Ttch," I clucked, almost inaudibly.

"*Some*where I must've *failed* her," she said.

I slowly nodded my head in knowing agreement. But she was no longer looking at me; her eyes were lost among the dregs in her cup.

A glassy-eyed teacup reader, she read aloud: "I'm *afraid* she's become a *bad* girl. You must *know* it. What*ever* your *intentions* are, I think I *should* tell you that she is *wicked*. And *sin*ful. I tried *so* hard to give her a proper *up*bringing. But it *didn't* work, *some*where I must've *failed* her. I guess you know her *father* ran *off* when she was little . . . well, she wasn't *more* than eleven or twelve years old. He was an *evil* man. *Thought*less and cruel. I didn't want Margaret to *know* that he ran away of his *own* free will, so when she *asked* me, 'Why did Daddy leave home?' I told her that I *made* him leave, I *drove* him away, and she's blamed *me* ever since. *Me!* I told her that her father was *hurting* me. And that was the *truth*. He was a . . . a *cruel* person. He *forced* himself upon me. You *know*?" Her eyes darted away from the cup for a brief glance at me. Then, still looking at me, as if I were to blame, she exclaimed, "*Lust!* Carnal *torture!* God *help* us!"

Then she returned her eyes to her cup and, continuing in a quieter voice, told me how she had tried to prepare Margaret for the eventuality that she might some day encounter such a sex demon herself. Basically, of course, she said, all men are evil and cause pain to women. It was God's way, she supposed. But she wanted to make sure that Margaret knew what the world had in store for her, and she had spared no words in trying to shock Margaret at the prospect of the whole nasty business. "But *look* where it got me," she said. "Just *look* where it *got* me! You'd *think* she *wanted* to be *hurt!* You'd think she was just *dying* to have some *filthy* man take *advantage* of her and in*flict* God knows *what* all kind of *sores and aches* on her!"

"Oh, I don't know," I said.

"*Well*," she said, "I *guess* I had better *tell* you something. It's *embarrassing*, but as *long* as we're discussing this on such a *high* intellectual plane, you know, I suppose I *could* tell you. This may be *hard* to *take*, so *prepare* yourself. It's the *worst* thing Margaret's *ever* done, and it *convinces* me beyond *any* doubt that she is *filled* with *sin and evil*. Oh, it's *awful*, but I'm going to *tell* you, I think you *ought* to know, just so you can *see* what I *mean* when I *say* you ought to *wash* your *hands* of her. All *right*, I'm going to *tell* you, *here* it is: the other day *Margaret* took her own excrement and wrote dirty words on the walls of her room! Understand? Isn't that *horrible?* Now don't you think that—"

"Madam," I politely interrupted. "I'm afraid you're mistaken. It was only paint. Nothing but paint."

"How would *you* know?" she demanded.

"I saw it," I said.

"Then I'm afraid *you* are mistaken. Because *I* saw it *too*. With my *own* eyes. And I *smelled* it with my *own* nose. And I *touched* it with my—"

"Apparently your senses have played tricks on you," I said. "It was really nothing but paint, and as a matter of fact I helped your husband clean it up."

"But don't you *see?*" she ranted onward. "She's past *praying* for! She's *possessed* with the *devil!* She's *ungodly* and *shameful* and *monstrous,* and it was *all* her *father's fault,* there's *nothing* can be *done* about it! Just *wait* till I *find* her," she said. "Just *wait* till I *get* my *hands* on that *girl!*"

"I wonder where she could be," I idly reflected, trying silent telepathy: Margaret, wherever you are, stay there! Keep away from this place and this utterly godawful excuse for a mother.

"You don't have *any* idea?" she asked.

"None whatever, I'm afraid. I'm going to look for her." And then it was time for me to end my politeness. I said, "However, if I do succeed in finding her, I shall do my utmost to prevent her from returning to this house again." Prissy as this sounded, it was nevertheless precisely my sentiment, and I felt an upsurge of pride and, yes, even valor.

"Beg *pardon?*" she double-took.

"I said, if I do find her, I will do everything within my power to keep her from seeing your face ever again."

"*Clifford?*"

"Yes?"

"What are you *saying?*"

"I'm saying that it would be a source of great personal satisfaction to me if I could devise or arrange some means by which she would never again have to have any contacts with you."

"*Why* do you *talk* like *that?*"

"Like what?"

"So . . . so *unfriendly,* all of a *sudden.* Haven't I *just* been *telling* you what a *nice* boy I think you *are,* and what a *high* opinion I've *always* had of you?"

Against my will my face flushed and my eyes moistened in anger. "You never knew me," I protested. "You never knew me any better than you knew your own daughter, and that wasn't much, God knows."

"*Now*, now, Clifford, *don't* be un*pleasant*," she admonished.

"Unpleasant!" I was as close to tears as I ever get. "Good grief, lady, you're telling *me* not to be unpleasant, and *you* are just about the most mean and heartless person I've ever met."

"If you intend to make remarks like that, I'll have to ask you to get out of my house."

"I'm going. I just want you to know that no girl ever deserved the kind of treatment you've been giving Margaret all these years, and you can henceforth consider me your sworn enemy, and I'm going to keep Margaret away from you if I have to take her to the farthest corner of the earth!"

"*You* leave *my* daughter *alone!* You're a *married* man, you . . . *you adulterer!* You just *touch* my daughter and *I'll* have you *arrested!*"

I moved out of the parlor and headed toward the front door. She followed. I turned briefly to say to her, "You would have to lock her up again to keep me from taking her away from you, and even that wouldn't stop me. I opened the front door and stepped out onto the porch.

She stopped me with her hand on my arm and said, "I'm *warning* you, *stay away* from my *daughter*."

I said, "And I'm warning you, prepare yourself never to see her again."

She slapped me.

Considering that she is much bigger than I am, by about fifty pounds, I was tempted to return her blow, but I didn't. I just glared at her. She burst into tears. Such sopping sobbing I have never seen before, such a deluge. It was disgusting, otherwise I might have felt some compassion for her. She buried her face in her hands and thoroughly drenched her fingers. Her hefty shoulders bounced at a rapid clip. I wondered if any across-the-street neighbors were watching. Eventually she peeked out between two of her fingers to see what sort of reaction I was having. My cold hard contemptuous glare set her to sprinkling and spluttering all the harder.

God have mercy on your soul, lady. I can't.

I turned my back on her and walked down the front steps of that house for the last time. That, I think, was the real End of Innocence for me. This thing, this so-called End of Innocence, is supposed to happen in dramatic situations like getting one's virginity lost, or robbing a bank, or performing a Carnegie Hall solo at the age of thirteen. But for me, I think it came when I was able to turn my back on a self-styled poor heartbroken mother who was crying her head loose from its already precarious moorings.

Dall would be proud of me.

🙢 THIRTEEN

If he lived. He had got himself battered badly, the foolhardy paladin, and was hospitalized. When I got home from my unpleasant visit with Margaret's mother, Naps was waiting at the curb and without a word he rushed me out to St. Vincent's, where we were admitted to a small room containing a large swaddled mummy, bedfast, taped and braced and splinted almost beyond recognition. The mouth and eyes alone were untaped and visible, and there was something curiously familiar about them, but I couldn't be altogether positive, until Naps stepped forward and presented the items he was bearing in each of his hands: a bouquet of Arkansas wildflowers and a pound tin of Brush Creek pipe tobacco. "Brought you some flars and terbacker, Sawjunt, suh," he said obsequiously. But even then I would not accept the possibility that this corpse was my old buddy, until at last the old buddy himself spoke: "Goddammit, nigger, when you gonna stop callin me Sawjunt suh?"

"Dall!" I cried out and sprang to his side and placed a solicitous hand on his encased arm. "What in God's name happened to you?"

"I got run over by a horse," he said, vainly trying to manage a feeble grin. "Naps, did you get that horse's number?"

"He didn't have no Arkansas license plate on im, suh," Naps answered, compensating with his own enormous grin for Dall's inability to make one. "But he was headin west so fast, I couldn't tell for sure."

"What horse? Whose horse?" I demanded.

"Sit down, boys," Dall invited us, and we pulled up chairs beside his bed. A nurse came in bearing a vase for the wildflowers, and arranged them neatly and set them on a table. Naps waited until she left, then opened the tin of tobacco, filled one of Dall's pipes, and stuck the stem in the exposed orifice on Dall's face, then lit it for him. Dall could not lift a hand to manipulate the pipe, so Naps periodically performed this office for him. "You know what I think?" Dall said to him, puffing out a contented cloud, "I think you aint really a nigger. You're just one of them mistrel-show boys made up to look like one."

"Have it your way," Naps said.

"I reckon you think you're a hot-shot cause you saved my life, don't you?"

"Nawsuh, that never occurred to me. All I was thinkin of was what my little girl Lucy said to me yesterday. She said, 'He sho a nice man. You gon have him come back again?' And I promised her I'd get you to come back again. So I figured if that horse killed you, I'd have some tough explainin to do to her."

"Will somebody kindly tell me what happened?" I asked.

"Well," Dall said and squirmed a little inside his wrappings, "for one thing, me and Slater didn't get along none too well today. I reckon he got a notion that a wise cop is a dead cop."

"Did you get him?" I asked. "Did you nab him?"

"Naw, Nub, I never nabbed him," Dall said sadly.

Naps said to me, "He let him get away."

"I didn't neither!" Dall objected.

"You did too!" Naps said. "You had your gun pointed right at him, but you wouldn't pull the trigger, so he got away."

"Dammit, I didn't have enough strength left to pull the trigger! Besides, what good would it of done if I'd of shot him?"

The nurse, a kindly-faced nun, came in and said, "Gentlemen, please don't excite the patient. He mustn't be excited. Try to keep him calm." Then she removed the pipe from Dall's mouth and went out again.

"You tell it," Dall said quietly to Naps. "I'll just fill in anything you leave out."

So between the two of them, speaking in perfect accompaniment like Bones and the Interlocutor, or like Huntley and Brinkley, they narrated the story of *Showdown at the JRS Ranch*, or, *How a Brave Cop Confronted a Crazy Playwright and Was Run Over by a Horse*.

Naps, who has been sitting semi-secluded in the Slater kitchen talking to his friend Feemy Bastrop, sees the squad car arrive, watches it coming up the long pine-forested driveway. Feemy excuses himself to go answer the bell. Feemy had not been surprised when Naps told him what he had learned from Margaret of Slater's intentions regarding his wife; with sadness and censure and a sense of helplessness Feemy (as he was known in sobriquetion of his Christian name Blasphemy Bastrop) had admitted to Naps that it was all too obvious that Slater's burning obsession was to do away with his wife, which in a sense, as Feemy saw it, would be a blessing, because Ethel Slater was the most miserable and useless woman on earth. When Feemy returns to the kitchen and tells Naps that Slater and the sergeant are going to have lunch together and he has to get busy and fix them something to eat, Naps sits down at the table and scrawls a note on a piece of paper, and later, when Feemy goes to carry a tray of club sandwiches in to the men, Naps hands him the note and asks him if he can slip it to the sergeant without Slater seeing him, and Feemy nods.

"By the way," Slater says to Dall conversationally, "did I ever tell you about the history of this house? No? Well, it was built quite a long time ago, 1856 in fact, by a Spaniard named Isidore de Carranza who paddled up the Arkansas in a canoe, although steamboats were plentiful at the time and Little Rock was already a flourishing port, because he wanted to retrace the route of Hernando de Soto in his famous but fruitless quest for gold. Somehow he got hopelessly lost and— But wouldn't you like a glass of brandy first? It's a long story."

"Never drink when I'm on duty. Thanks just the same," Dall says.

"I see. Well, this Spaniard, Isidore de Carranza, it seems he was quite a wealthy man, his primitive means of travel notwithstanding. So when night fell, and he realized his position was totally off his intended route, he banked his canoe and walked in from the river a few miles and discovered this property and was so taken with it that he called it Le Agradezco Mucho, which is untranslatable but means, roughly, that he was awfully glad he found it, and he decided to stake out a claim and build this grand *casa*. The fact that a large community of Negroes already held squatter's rights to the place did not deter him. He—"

"Slater, if it's all the same to you, I'd just as soon talk about Margaret."

"Margaret? Heavens, man, what is there to be said about Margaret? Haven't you just said yourself that she absolutely refuses to see me again? Agnes Galloway would be delighted to have her part in the play. So Margaret is a dead issue as far as I'm concerned ... well, perhaps dead issue isn't the right way to put it, but, I mean, she's passé, you know. We've rung down the curtain—*rang*, is it?—for a playwright I sometimes have atrocious grammar. The fault of my education, I suppose. You see, I went to a little hick college down in the southern part of the state, and—"

"Slater, listen—"

"Ah, here's our lunch. Just set it down here on the coffee table, if you will, Feemy, and ask the sergeant what he would like to drink with it. A bottle of Löwenbräu Dark? A glass of Liebfraumilch?"

"Milk," Dall says.

The Negro servant, bringing him his glass of milk, places himself between Slater and Dall in such a way that Slater cannot see that the Negro is passing a folded note into Dall's hands. "Wh—" Dall begins to say, but the expression on the Negro's face silences him, and he takes the note and conceals it beside his hip so that he can open and read it without Slater's knowledge.

"You haven't put any arsenic in the sergeant's milk, have you, Feemy?" Slater says to his servant and titters with laughter. "It isn't time yet. Later. I'll let you know. Ha ha."

Surreptitiously Dall reads the note: MISS MARGARET HAS CONFESSED. UNDER THE INFLUENCE OF INTOXICANTS AND STIMULATING QUESTIONS AT MY DOMICILE LAST NIGHT SHE SAID MR. SLATER PLANNED TO QUOTE GET RID OF HIS WIFE UNQUOTE BY PUSHING HER DOWN THE STAIRS IN HER WHEELCHAIR. FURTHER DETAILS ON REQUEST. THE BEARER OF THIS NOTE IS ANOTHER FRIEND OF MINE. THE JIG IS, AS THEY SAY, UP. NO PUN INTENDED. YOURS COOPERATIVELY, N. LEON HOWARD. P.S. I AM BACK IN THE KITCHEN. SLATER'S KITCHEN, THAT IS. By God, Dall says to himself in unabashed awe. When I get to hell one of these days, that nigger's gonna be down there spying on Old Harry Hisself.

"Well now," Dall says, "if you don't want to talk about Margaret, suppose let's talk about your wife—"

"My wife? Why?"

"Her and you aint gettin along too good, are you? How come?"

"Hawkins, aren't you married?"

"I used to be."

"Ah, that's even better. Then you know what it's like to be a martyr, to be martyred by a woman? You know how a woman can prey on a man with her subtle tortures, her provoking whims, her guileful wiles? You know how utterly gifted all wives are at making their mates miserable?"

Dall, forced to think for a moment of his own former tormentor Rowena, answers, "I sure do." But then he quickly adds, "All the same, that aint no excuse for killin em."

"Beg pardon?"

"You heard me."

"My friend, what wild conjectures have been filling your head lately?"

"I just got a idee maybe you'd like to get rid of her so's you could marry Margaret."

"But I told you I'm no longer interested in Margaret."

Dall reaches into his pocket and takes out the fragment of worsted trouser-bottom and passes it across to Slater, without comment.

Slater casually studies it for a moment and apparently decides not to pretend ignorance. "Thank you," he says. "Although I'm afraid that particular garment is beyond repair, with or without this missing piece." A moment later he adds, as in idle observation, "A competent and vigilant dog you have. My compliments." Then he leans forward and asks, "Where *are* you keeping her?"

"Wouldn't you like to know?" is all Dall can think of in the way of a rejoinder, so, puerile as it is, he doesn't say it; instead he says, "At my place, like I told you. I reckon she must've stepped out for a six-pack of beer or something when you came by."

Slater seems to accept this. "Aren't we friends, you and I?" he asks solicitously. "Didn't you write a beautiful three-letter-word poem to me in the *Gazette* this morning? I wanted to thank you for—"

"Slater, you wrote that yourself. You know it."

"Oh well. No matter, then." He stands up, stretches a little, adjusts his ascot, and says, "I generally take a short stroll after lunch. Care to walk along with me?"

Naps watches them leave the house, the two ugliest white men he has ever seen, walking side by side. They cut across the broad rear lawn of the house and enter the dirt road that winds up the hillside toward the stables. Naps begins to follow them, but the land is so open that he has to remain at a considerable distance from them to keep from being seen. He cuts over toward the pinewoods that encircle Slater's fields, and here he can move from tree to tree, making his hidden progress. Still, the closest he can get to them is behind an outcropping of metamorphic rock some hundred feet away from where they have stopped at the end of the paddock beside the stables. He cannot hear what they are saying to each other.

Dall watches Slater take down a bridle from the nail on which it is hanging, and open a half-door of a stall in which there is one of the roan Morgans. "Would you care to ride a little, Hawkins?" Slater asks. "We could lope down to the lake and back."

"Much obliged, but I aint been on a horse since I was eight years old."

"I give lessons, you know. I could teach you. Usually I charge ten dollars an hour for private lessons, but considering that you're a friend—" Slater has already led the Morgan out of its stall and is placing the bridle on him.

"Slater, look, this aint no time for no horseback ridin. I think we'd best just sit down and talk this thing over. Or else I'd have to let the sheriff in on our little secret."

"You haven't told the sheriff—or your captain—of your suspicions yet, have you? That wasn't wise, Hawkins. Whenever you intend to go somewhere to question a suspect, you should always let your associates or superiors know where you're going."

"Up to now this is just between you and me."

"And Margaret," Slater says and, in one remarkably agile leap, throws himself up upon the bare back of his horse. There he sits stiffly erect, holding the reins loosely in one hand. "Now," he says. "Now I don't have to look up to you. *You* have to look up to *me*. How does that feel? I liked you, Hawkins, but you are too gallant and noble and cocksure. You put me at a disadvantage. I allowed you to become my friend, and that was my only mistake. But I should have known. It has always happened whenever I have taken anyone into my confidence, and perhaps that's why I have no other friends. Hawkins, you've abused our friendship." Then he pats his horse on the neck and says, "This is my favorite gelding, Houyhnhnm. I don't suppose you know Swift, do you, Hawkins?" Then to the horse he says, "Houyhnhnm, say hello to Sergeant Hawkins."

From his hiding place behind the rock Naps sees the man mount the horse and continue talking to—or, rather, now, *down to*—the sergeant, and his first thought is that Slater intends to ride away, to escape, but Naps knows that wouldn't be a smart thing to try, as Dall is armed and could bring him down in an instant. Before Naps has time to do much more speculation about what is happening, he sees that Slater suddenly does something to the horse: spurs it, tugs the reins a certain way, speaks to it. And the horse rears. Its forehoofs dance in a rotating air-fanning movement above Dall's head and then they come down, one hoof striking Dall atop his head, the other atop his shoulder. Dall staggers. The horse comes down, then rears up again, again dancing, again coming down upon Dall, this time clouting him on the side of his face with one hoof, his chest with the other. Dall falls. Lying there, he has only enough strength left to attempt to cover his face with his arms. The horse tramples him, cantering around and around and around upon him. A rear hoof crashes down upon one of the arms, and a bone snaps. Naps hears the snap of the bone and suddenly realizes that the reason he can hear it is that he is standing right beside the horse with a big stick in his hands, a piece of fallen tree limb which he paused to snatch from the ground in his headlong dash toward the horse. Now Slater sees him and wheels the horse toward him. Naps swings back the long stick of wood, and as the horse begins to rear, lashes the stick hard across the horse's face. The stick breaks in two. The horse is stunned, but only for a moment, long enough for Naps to begin a mad dash in search of another stick. He turns to see that Slater is running the horse toward him. Then for what seems a long time Naps runs in circles around the stable, eluding the horse more with fancy footwork than with speed. His footwork is too fancy: he falls. Now I'm dead too, he thinks, waiting for the first shock of the hoofs upon his back, but when none comes he looks up to see that Slater is riding the horse at full gallop off into the woods, and he turns to see that Dall has rolled over and has drawn his revolver and is pointing it at Slater's diminishing back. *Shoot, shoot!* he yells at Dall. But Dall only holds the gun as if aiming a camera at a passing parade, and no shot is fired. Slater entirely disappears into the pinewoods. Naps gets to his feet and rushes over to Dall, who has passed out now, face down. Dall's face is severely cut and bruised, blood is running freely from his nose and from one ear. His uniform is ripped in several places. But his heavy breathing tells Naps he is still alive. Naps slips his hand into Dall's pants pocket and fishes out the keys to the squad car, then begins running toward the house; halfway there he calls loudly to Feemy. Feemy comes out of the house, and they get into the squad car and Naps drives it up the dirt road toward the stable, not pausing to open the paddock gate but knocking it down with the front of the car. He stops the car as close to Dall as he can get, then he and Feemy improvise a stretcher with horse blankets and fence stakes and manage to lift Dall upon the back seat. He tells Feemy to take the Lincoln and meet him at St. Vincent's; Feemy asks him if it wouldn't be a good idea to call the sheriff, but Naps says not until Dall has regained consciousness and can pass approval on it. Then Naps gets into the squad car and barrels it off toward Little

Rock. When he reaches Route 10 he turns on the siren and leaves it on all the way to St. Vincent's Hospital. Always wanted to drive one of these things, he says to himself, watching all the other cars get out of his way.

"Far's I'm concerned," Dall said to Naps from his hospital bed, "I'm just glad you didn't stop to give anybody any tickets. That would of been goin too far."

"Was Slater really trying to *kill* you?" I asked.

"I don't reckon he was just exercisin his horse," Dall replied.

"But why? Why did he want to do something like that, and what made him think he could get away with it?"

"Well, I guess I knew too much and he figgered if he didn't put me out of the way he'd never have a chance to go ahead with what he wanted to do about his wife and about Margaret. A nut like him. Why, sure he could of got away with it. The more I think about it, the more I think I was pretty stupid doin what I done. He could of put my dead body in my car and rolled me into the lake. Or he could of told the sheriff I come out there snoopin around and got trampled accidentally by one of his horses. All kinds of ways he could of got away with it."

Diabolical, I mused in awe, positively diabolical. "What are you going to do now?" I asked him.

"That's a damn-fool question if ever I heard one," Dall said, but only with a tinge of disgust in his voice. He managed to raise one hand just high enough to point his fingers at himself, and said, "Looks like I aint gonna do nuthin for a good little while. Doctor says a week or more before I can even get out of this bed. The Chief, I expect, is not gonna think too highly of me. Might be I'll even get demoted."

"Why?" I asked. "You got injured in the line of duty, even if it was a sort of self-appointed duty."

"Aw, hell," Dall said and he sounded like he was about to cry. "I wasn't on no duty. Hell naw. I'm still supposed to be on the night shift, and I just wore my uniform and took the squad car to kind of *impress* Slater, see? The Chief wouldn't like it none atall if he found out I did that, it bein outside city limits and all, so I'm hopin he won't find out. Still they aint gonna think too highly of a sergeant that somehow gets banged up so bad he has to take a couple weeks off work."

"Do you think Slater is going to hide out, or do you think he'll try to find Margaret?" I asked.

"Well, I caint say for sure, but I guess he's pretty damn sore at her and he might just have a notion to get even with her. Of course, I don't think he could ever find her, long as she stays at Naps's place."

"She isn't at Naps's house any more," I said. "She ran away."

"*What?*" Dall demanded.

"*What?*" Naps echoed him.

So I explained to them what Tatrice had told me over the phone.

"Goddamn that woman all to hell!" Naps moaned.

"Hey, nigger boy, watch who you're cussin about," Dall cautioned him.

"I'm cussin about my wife," Naps said. "Lettin Miss Margaret get away like that. I should of known better than leave it up to her to keep an eye on Miss Margaret."

The nurse came in and said to Dall, "It's time we took a little nap. Your friends will have to leave."

"Nub, we got to find her," Dall said to me. "Maybe she aims to go out to see Slater, and she don't know what's been happenin lately." To Naps he said, "Could you get your pal Feemy to sort of keep a eye out for her if she should turn up out there, and get her away from the place or somethin?" Naps nodded. Then Dall said to me, "Find her, Nub. Get her back to Naps's place and keep her there if you have to tie her down."

"I'll do what I can," I said. "But don't you think you ought to let the sheriff in on this, and have him get a posse out after Slater?"

"I done did," Dall said, and there was a note of regret, of resignation, to the way he said it. "I didn't mean to, or want to, not yet anyway, but it looks like there's not a blessed thing I can do about it any more." He was breathing hard, and the nurse repeated her injunction that we must leave, putting her hands on our shoulders and urging us toward the door. Before I went out through the door, Dall spoke once again: "Nub, feed my dog, will you?"

FOURTEEN

Downstairs in the lobby Naps's friend Feemy was sitting in a chair, waiting. Naps reintroduced me to him, and I said I remembered him well from the old days when he lived on Ringo, and we chatted reminiscently for a while, then the three of us got into the Lincoln and drove out to the Slater ranch. Under any other circumstances I might have delighted in the ride, meandering as it did through the pinewooded hills west of Little Rock, passing around the unique Pinnacle Mountain which I had climbed as a boy, passing through the little hamlets of Natural Steps and Monnie Springs, weary and brown yet still having a quaint rural antiquity in the late but still hot afternoon sun, passing close enough to the lake to see it, the Big Maumelle Lake which had not even been here at all the last time I was out this way. And under any other circumstances I might have been thrilled to see for the first time the Slater property itself, the profuse, almost luxuriant pine forests, the carefully tended fields, and the anachronism of a house, that grand *casa*, an abode of adobe and curved-tile roofs and all the appurtenances of a flamingo-colored Spanish-Gothic style which would have looked out of place even in St. Augustine, Florida, but in Pulaski County, Arkansas, was hopelessly far-fetched, remote, eccentric, and lonely. Even the presence in the front driveway of three automobiles from the sheriff's department could not keep me from feeling an acute nervousness and anxiety, as though I expected Slater's horse Houyhnhnm to materialize out of the sky, Pegasus-like, and trample me; but perhaps my antipathy toward the place came only from my being aware that this was where Margaret had spent many an hour lately of . . . of what, sin?

Naps left us for a while, "just to look around," he said. Feemy made me a couple of roast beef sandwiches and I had a bottle of Löwenbräu Dark to wash them down with, taking some sort of strange pleasure in freeloading on Slater's food. Later Naps came back again, and sat down and ate some sandwiches too. We sat around for a while, then we got up and wandered about through the house. There was nothing particularly noteworthy about any of the furniture; very little in the house was as curious as the house itself. Upstairs Naps pointed at one door and told me not to open that one, because she was in there. Thus I never had the honor of seeing Ethel Slater face to face; and, unless her husband were soon captured, I might never have the honor of seeing him either. We returned to the kitchen and had another bottle of Löwenbräu apiece. A sheriff's deputy questioned us perfunctorily for a few minutes and then went on off. Naps observed that it was not likely that Margaret would show up here, because all the sheriff's cars in the driveway would frighten her away. No use us hangin around any longer, he said. So we left.

It was dark when we got back to town, and I had Naps drive to the Austin house, and I got out and crept around to the side of it so that I could look up and see if there was any light on in her room. There wasn't. Through the living-room window I could see Margaret's mother and stepfather watching television.

Then we drove to Dall's house, stopping first at a grocery store, where I bought four cans of Ken-L Ration, a package of Burger Bits, a ten-pound bag of Gravy Train, and thirty-five cents' worth of beef bones. At Dall's small house I carried these items around to the rear yard, and Bowzer (whom I had somehow expected to find chained) came bounding at me with a terrific yapping and snarling. I dropped his dinners and fled to the safety of the Lincoln, where Naps and I rolled up the windows and talked to Bowzer for five or ten minutes before he was pacified. "Damn mutt is scratchin up the finish of my car," Naps complained. I tried to get it across to Bowzer that the packages I had dropped in the back yard contained tasty tidbits to assuage his hunger, but for all his wisdom he couldn't grasp this essential point. Finally something in the beast's murky memory reminded him that it was I who, less than a week ago, had nuzzled and coddled him in a moment of distress. Licking the hand which I cautiously proffered through the car's window, he identified my scent and concluded that I was no foe. I got out of the car and escorted him back to the rear of the house, keeping up a steady flow of nice doggies and good doggies and head pats. I retrieved my packages and opened the one containing the bones and spread it before him, and he fell to with a vigor and a grateful thrashing of his long tail, slobbering on my shoe from time to time as a token of his thanks. While he was busy chomping the bones I ventured to step up onto the back porch of the house; to my surprise the rear door wasn't locked. I went into the kitchen, turned on a light, and found a bowl in which to mix the Gravy Train with hot water according to directions. I filled another bowl with fresh cold water and, after leaving the remainder of the food in the kitchen, took the two bowls out and put them down where Bowzer could get at them. I gave him a parting pat and told him to keep an eye out for pudgy playwrights.

We got back to St. Vincent's just in time to catch the last fifteen minutes of evening visiting hours, during which we chatted and joked with Dall as best we could, attempting to shore up his obviously flagging spirits. Naps told him that for all we knew Margaret might have already returned to Naps's house and was safe and sound again, to which Dall replied that Naps ought to go out into the hallway where there was a telephone and call his house and find out. Naps did, and returned smiling, saying, "Yeah, what did I tell you?" "You're lying," Dall said to him. "Yeah," I joined in. "Don't lie, Naps." "Aw, man, you got to cheer up," Naps urged, but his heart wasn't in it. We sat in silence for a while, and then it was time to go. Dall said to Naps, "Fore you go, stick my pipe in my mouth and light her up, okay?" Naps said he didn't see how Dall could manage it without the use of his hands. "Aw, I'll just let her burn down on her own, and get a little suption out of her before one of them nurses comes in and yanks her away from me." So Naps did. I wanted to cry, it was so pitiful. Then Dall thanked me for feeding his dog, and we left.

I asked Naps to take me on home. I told him he had done enough for one day, and anyway my father and grandmother would be wondering why I was abandoning them again. So he took me home and we promised to get in touch with each other immediately if either of us found out anything. He had already alerted his Little Rock underground again, the Negro grapevine of porters and red caps and cabbies and bellhops and all, and if this had worked in Hot Springs maybe it would work here. There was nothing more we could do for a while. Naps went on home himself. True to my expectations, my father loudly upbraided me again for missing supper; he said Grammaw Stone had fixed me something special and when I didn't show up to eat it he was so mad he could spit. Grammaw Stone herself began adding to his remonstrations, but I silenced them both by telling them that Dall had had a terrible accident and was listed in critical condition at St. Vincent's. Grammaw Stone got up and put on her hat; my father asked her where she thought she was going; she said she was going to go out and visit with Dall; I told her visiting hours were over. She took off her hat and said she would go out there first thing in the morning. Then she went back to the kitchen to bake him a cake. In answer to my father's searching questions, I told him a little bit of what had been going on, but without mentioning Slater. When I finished he was silent for a while, and then, before going to bed, he asked, "Are you pretty sweet on that girl?" I told him I was very sweet on her. "If you take up with her," he asked hesitantly, "does that mean you'll stay in Little Rock?" I told him I was afraid that it didn't. He shrugged his shoulders, gave me a sorrowful look, and went off to bed. I sat in the kitchen with my grandmother, talking with her while she finished Dall's cake. She put it in the oven and told me that if I was going to stay up for a while I might as well take it out of the oven for her in forty-five minutes, so she could go on to bed. I told her I would; I said I would even put the icing on it for her. Then, as she was leaving the room, she asked, "He's gonna live, aint he?" and I assured her that he would, and she said finally, "Cause if he don't, there's just not ary replacement, just nowhere to be found."

When I finished the cake I pussyfooted into the bathroom and searched the bottom of the dirty-clothes hamper for one of my father's bottles, but there weren't any. I asked myself: If my mother came to visit me and I didn't want her to find my bottles in their usual place in the clothes hamper, to where would I transfer them? After considerable preoccupied cogitation with this knotty problem, I thought to inspect the house-maintenance junk on the back porch, and there, in a bottle labeled SPIRITS OF TURPENTINE, I found some spirits which were distinctly not of turpentine but of corn, and I poured out three fingers into a glass of ice, thinking it would make me sleepy. It didn't. Three additional fingers didn't either; if anything, it only aroused my libido, and I realized it would be futile for me even to take off my clothes, much more futile if I got into bed, ridiculously futile if I tried to sleep. So, sometime after midnight, I left the house and began walking north up Ringo, townward, with no particular destination in mind but simply a desire to walk myself into complete sleepable weariness. But I had not gone a mile through the dark and cool streets of that city before I realized that I was searching for something, or, rather, someone, and that that someone was, of course, Margaret. She might be lurking behind any ashcan or billboard or forsythia bush, and even if she weren't, there was no harm in my looking anyway. Little Rock would be a great place if it were like this all the time, I reflected, relishing the quietness of it at that hour, the calm dark emptiness of it, the spring-night fragrances of people's yards, the distant sounds—traffic downtown, switch engines in the train yards, a correspondence of dogs—which intoned a gentle cadence like the dying of an overture. The sky was starry, the night above the dingle starry, and I looked up and caught sight of Orion and the Dog Star and the Dippers, but instead of feeling small, as I usually do so many light-years beneath these celestial bodies, I felt that I and Margaret were the only two beings in the universe, and were lost from each other, and had to get together again. This illusion, however, was soon shattered when a car pulled up alongside me and began to stop. Remembering all the times that pansies had offered me a ride when I walked alone at night in Little Rock long ago, I was tempted to keep walking, but a second glance told me the car was a familiar one, so I stopped walking. "Give you a lift anywheres?" Naps asked, and I got in. I didn't ask him what he was doing out that time of night, because I didn't have to ask him; I knew he was doing the same thing I was doing. "Seems like we're right back where we started from Friday night and Saturday morning," I observed, thinking of how we had sought her in Hot Springs, and he nodded. I told him I couldn't see how he was ever going to get any of his own work done, the way he was devoting so much of his time to helping me and Dall. He said in reply that he carried his office around with him in his hip pocket; just that day, he proudly reported, he had taken orders for two sets of *The Catholic Encyclopedia* from a couple of staff members at St. Vincent's Hospital, and for a twelve-volume *Home Handyman's Guide* from one of the sheriff's deputies out at Slater's place. That was a good day's work for him, he said.

Then he snapped on the interior lights of the car and handed me a folded note. "Found that on the bed where she slept last night," he said. "I'm surprised Tatrice didn't find it earlier."

The note was short, hastily scribbled in pencil, and it was addressed to me. "Clifford," it said. "Everything is happening so fast. You came at the wrong time, I guess. Three or four years earlier would have been more like it. I still don't know why you came at all, but I am sorry that I have been such a disappointment to you. Now I don't know what to do. Every little thing seems to be terrifying me. If you leave, I will know why. If you don't, you should know why. M."

I offered it to Naps, but he said, "I done took a peek at it."

"Make any sense out of it?" I asked.

"Naw, not much," he said. "But it seems to me she tryin to tell you sump'm."

"Yes," I said, taking the note again and studying it. "It seems she's trying to tell me that she doesn't want to see me again."

"Naw, man, you readin things into it. She just tryin to say that if you *do* hang around, you better make up yo mind *why* you hangin around."

All right: why? Why, indeed.

We drove around aimlessly for an hour, up and down the streets of the old part of town. There was nothing better to do. Naps asked me heuristic questions. Did I really want to take Margaret away, and, if so, what did I plan to do about my wife? Was I contemplating divorce and remarriage? Was I after Margaret only in search of a quick lay? Why, actually, was I in pursuit of her? Just as a favor for Dall? Did I really think I could keep her from killing herself, if that was what she wanted to do? Did I really think there was any chance she would? Did I really know anything about her?

No, I said. I could not answer any of his questions. I could only tell him that I was doing what I felt like doing, that I was looking for answers, that I had never stopped trying to discover why I had come home, and that if there were any answers I felt it had to do with Margaret, who, in my fanciful mind, was so inextricably conjoined with the town.

"Well," Naps sighed, driving me home, "looks like her and the town both are hiding out this time of night." We parted and promised to keep in touch.

Many an old night in my nervous, questing youth, I had let myself into my father's house late on little cat's feet, skillfully, entirely in the dark, lessening the chance that he might awaken and rise to come and smell the exhalation of tobacco (I smoked in those days, for social reasons) or alcohol (usually beer, sometimes stronger) which hung like a stale lotion around the front of my face. Now, for no reason, all the old talent returned to me naturally, the dexterity, the maneuvering, and I jockeyed my way up the back steps, across the junk-littered porch, through the door, into the kitchen (where I paused for a sip of cold water from the bottle in the refrigerator, opening the door of it in such a way that it made no noise and its light did not go on—the little button held down under my deft thumb), on through the hall and into my bedroom, where I closed the door firmly yet soundlessly before turning on the light. The light switch did not even click, the way I adroitly handled it. You know, I told myself with amusement, you might have made a good living as a second-story man; and my weary mind yearning for sleep began already to dream: I would become a highly successful Little Rock burglar, the papers would carry stories of the latest haul by the mysterious Prowessed Prowler, and finally I would have a dramatic showdown with Detective Lieutenant Hawkins, who cracked the case. Ah. Go to bed.

Early the next morning I heard the voice of my grandmother talking to someone on the telephone, and then I heard her yelling into the phone, and the phone slammed down. Then she came into my room, looked at me, and said, "You awake?" Then she said that somebody had called, a man who would not identify himself, and that he had instructed her to tell me I had better get out of town fast and not come back again, if I knew what was good for me. Slater?

After breakfast Grammaw Stone and I rode a bus to St. Vincent's to visit with Dall; he was mighty pleased with her cake; she was mighty pleased that he was going to live; he was mighty upset about the phone call I reported to him; he was mighty disappointed that I hadn't re-secured Margaret yet; I was mighty nervous about everything. Sonofabitch, he said, referring not to me but to Slater. Aw hell, he said later, trying to cheer up me and himself both. They're just bound to catch that bastard soon and—"Don't swear, Dall," my grandmother admonished. "It aint nice."

Later in the morning I went to Dall's house to feed Bowzer again, but Bowzer wasn't there. I called him for a while, and waited half an hour for him to come home, but he didn't. Perhaps he was just out roaming the neighborhood, but I had an awful suspicion that Slater might have done away with him. I left some fresh food in his bowl, and then wandered off through the town, and spent most of the rest of the day in futile walking, soaked with sweat from the hot May sun. A cold shower and a brief nap in the afternoon repaired part of my deteriorating substance, but I felt I would never again be a whole man.

Naps phoned to ask if I had had any luck and to tell me that he had had none. He invited me over for supper, but I felt obliged to eat with my folks. I stayed at home and brooded for as long as I could stand it, and as long as my father and grandmother provided some company and sense of security, but then after they had gone to bed I grew intolerably restless and plunged once more out into the night, and roamed the streets again. It was almost monotonous, all of this roving, but although I damned myself for it I could not help it.

This self-damning frame of mind made me begin to think that my pursuit of Margaret was not out of the purest of motives and that what I really wanted from her was some sex or at least whatever she had given to Slater (and what had *that* been?). I even began to believe that I was a twerp incapable of really loving anyone but myself, incapable of desiring any friends except for their usefulness, incapable of being satisfied with this town, this home—or any place for that matter, incapable of establishing a real trust or faith in anybody, and doomed forever to this senseless rambling.

Was this really me?

FIFTEEN

I remembered that Bowzer was lost. How could I ever face my old buddy again in his disabled and gauze-swaddled confinement and tell him that his good dog, whom he loved so much, was gone? It might complete the defeat of his spirit, and he would lose the will to live. Better that I lie than reveal the truth.

It was too late now, after midnight, to go visit with Dall again, anyway. Perchance before the morrow Bowzer would reappear, if he was in any condition to reappear. Maybe he had already come home. I would just run over and see.

On foot I continued to Dall's house, scanning the dark streets and yards en route, and calling softly to the dog. Various mongrels replied to my call, but none of them was Bowzer. Approaching Dall's house I suddenly realized, for the first time this evening, that Slater might be out after me, vengeance-minded, and my veins froze, but I warmed them with the thought of the worthiness of my mission, to find the lost dog and restore him to his master. If Slater had harmed the poor pooch in any way, and I had the fortune to come across Slater, I would rip him apart from limb to limb with my bare hands . . .

Bowzer was not in Dall's back yard. The food I had left in his bowl was untouched. In turning to survey the surrounding darkness for some sign of him, I noticed that a light was burning in the kitchen of Dall's house. Had I left the light on when I was in there mixing Bowzer's dinner last night?

Or was Slater in there?

Call the police? Run? Die of this apprehension raging in my vitals?

Or confront the scoundrel? I had a fleeting vision of tomorrow's headlines: DOUGHTY EX-ARKANSAN, HOME ON VISIT, NABS ERRANT PLAYWRIGHT. I could hear Hy Norden telling about it on television: "Clifford Willow Stone, twenty-eight, Boston antiques curator and a native of Little Rock best remembered for his victories in the 1953 Golden Gloves tournament, single-handedly found and captured James Royal Slater, whom police and sheriff's department officials had been seeking on a charge of intended murder of his wife, last night at a house on West Fourth Street, after a brief struggle in which Stone disarmed Slater and gave him a sound drubbing. Reports from St. Vincent's Hospital, where Slater was taken after the fray, indicate that Slater is in serious condition but that it is expected he will live to face trial . . ." And an interview with me and all.

But could I do it? I mean, if he really was armed with a gun or something? Could I dodge his fire? Good Lord, it was an awful decision.

Maybe I could sort of sneak in quietly through the back door and club him over the head with something before he had time to turn around.

Stop this damn trembling, Clifford Stone! I rebuked myself. Maybe you just left the light on the other night. Go in and turn it off.

So I went in, very quietly, sneaking with the best of my mouse-soundless skills, and I opened the door a crack and thrust my arm in and flicked off the kitchen light switch. But then I flicked it back on again, because I had caught sight of somebody sitting at the kitchen table. It wasn't Slater. It was some woman. A redhead. When I turned the switch off and then on again, she wheeled around and threw me a really panicked look, and I stared dumfounded at her, wondering if I might possibly have entered the wrong house, these little bungalows in this neighborhood look so much alike, and the next thing I expected her to do was to throw up her hands and scream a banshee's furious wail and go running off into the bedroom, yelling, "Man sakes alive! WES! There's a prowler out there!

Get up, Wes! Quick! A prowler!" But she didn't do this. The panic in her face ebbed and she just stared at me. I had a brief thought that this might be Dall's old wife Rowena returned to badger him, but this woman was much prettier than the Ozark hill gal I had seen in that photograph, and besides she was a redhead and Dall's wife was supposed to be a blonde. Well, maybe she could have dyed her hair and sort of fixed herself up or something . . .

"What are you doing here?" she asked.

"I'm sorry, but I thought—" I began, troubled by something in her voice. "This *is* the Hawkins residence, isn't it?"

"Clifford," she said. "How did you find me?"

"Find? Me? I mean you? I? Who?" I babbled.

And then she took off the wig.

"Good gravy, what were you wearing that thing for?" I demanded.

"Just because," she said.

I sat down at the kitchen table across from her and began to shake helplessly, I know not why. Or maybe I do. "Coffee?" she said, and I nodded and she took a pot off the stove and poured me some. Two cups before I could speak, and then I quavered, "I just came to feed his dog. I didn't expect to find you of all people here. What are *you* doing here?"

"Waiting for Doyle," she said.

"Why?"

"I just wanted to talk to him," she said.

"What about?"

"I just wanted to talk to him," she said again, somewhat adamantly. "He told me once that if I ever needed somebody to talk to, to just come on over any time and talk to him. So I did. It's not the first time I've come over here." She glanced at the clock and said, "But I've been here for almost two days now and he hasn't come home. Would you have any idea where he is?"

"Yes, I would," I said.

"Then tell me. Do the Little Rock police have to go out of town for long spells or something?"

"Some of them do," I said. "If they are investigating somebody who lives outside the city limits, and if they are very brave and rash and determined, like Dall, they will go outside the city limits and let nothing stop them. Even if the person they are investigating happens to be as crazy as Slater, they won't let that stop them."

Her face came to life. "Are you saying—?"

"Yes, I am."

"Well, for goodness sake, what is he doing out at Jimmy's house, if Jimmy is here at *his* house?"

I sprang up from my chair and glanced wildly around me. "Where—?"

"Oh, I don't mean *now*," she said. "He left about an hour ago."

"He was *here*?"

She nodded.

"And you saw him? You talked to him? He didn't *do* anything to you?"

"No, I just told him what I said to him before, and what I've been trying to tell you and Doyle and everybody: I don't want to see him again any more. Ever. So he left."

"He didn't even point his gun at you or anything?"

"Has he got a gun?" she asked. Then her face became very troubled, and she said, "Clifford, you're not saying he . . . he didn't . . . he didn't *shoot* Doyle, did he? Clifford?"

"No, he didn't shoot Dall," I said.

She sighed in relief, and laughed at herself a little. "I've just been so confused," she said. "Sitting here all alone and not knowing who is where or what is what. I still can't figure out how Jimmy knew that I was here, and I can't figure out how you did either."

"I told you. I just came to feed Dall's dog. But it's gone. Did Slater say anything about that dog? Did he say what he had done to it?"

"No. Well, he mentioned something about the first time he came over here, Sunday night, the dog bit him, and he asked me if the dog was still around. Personally, I've never seen the dog, and I don't even understand why Jimmy would have come over here *Sunday* night. I wasn't here then."

"Margaret, pour me another cup of that coffee and I'll try to bring you up to date." She did, and I said, "But first, would you mind too awfully much telling me why you ran away and got yourself lost like this? Everybody's been looking for you— me and Naps and Naps's friends and the police and everybody— we didn't know *what* might have happened to you."

She spent some time thinking about it before she could find an answer, and then she searched my eyes, and put her answer, if that is what it was, in the form of a question: "Did you get my note?"

"Sure," I said, a bit impatiently. "But I still don't understand why you had to run off like that. What good did that do? Did you want to find Slater and console him about the bad reviews of his play?"

"Of course not. I wanted to talk with Doyle."

"Why?"

"I needed his advice."

"What about?"

"You."

"*Me*? Why?"

"I don't know anything about you. I never knew you. I thought Doyle might be able to tell me about you, and he could tell me if I should go with you."

"I see," I said. "You wanted to ask him if—"

"—if I should leave Little Rock to go with you," she said. "Or if I should do whatever you ask me to do when you get around to asking me."

"Why Dall?"

"Who else? I can't depend on myself for answers any more."

"Couldn't you have waited just a little longer, and talked with me about it, instead of running off like that."

"You were asking me to leave, remember? And I don't want to."

"Do you mean you actually want to stay here in Little Rock forever?" I couldn't believe it, and I thought she was out of her mind, and I told her so: "Margaret, you're out of your mind."

"Probably," she said. "But it's what I want."

"So," I said to her accusingly, "your reason for wanting to stay here in Little Rock is that you have such a crazy attachment to your crazy old mother that it would break your heart if you went away and left her. So whoever marries you would have to move into that house with you and help you hold her hand when she feels bad."

"Clifford, I would be just as happy if I never saw her again. And I'm hoping that this town is big enough that I won't have to."

"Fine. So if I will get us a nice ranch-type house out in Broadmoor or Kingwood, and join the Lion's Club and start a subscription to the Arkansas *Democrat* and take you to Razorback football games and to picnics in Boyle Park, you'd marry me? What kind of life is that?"

"It's a better life than being eaten up by wanderlust, and letting one's nights be haunted by constant dreams of faraway places."

"Oh? Haven't you ever had any wanderlust yourself?"

"All my life I've been positively consumed by it. My lust for wandering has tormented me and frustrated me to such a point that I realize that wherever I might wander I would always lust for some place else. I'm just the kind of person who would be unhappy anywhere, and if I'm going to be unhappy I might as well stay in my home town and make the most of it, instead of tormenting and frustrating myself even more by roaming all over the earth in search of some magic enchantment or excitement."

"East, West, home is best," I said sarcastically.

"Yes," she said with conviction. "Yes it is, in a way. Because however you look at it, if a person has any roots at all, those roots are in one's home town and— Now don't you squint those beady eyes of yours at me, Clifford Stone!"

"I'll squint my beady eyes at whom I please, but go on."

"I know you think that this town is bad, that it's corrupt, and that it's decadent and sterile and banal and all that. That's why you got out of it and went away up East in the first place, isn't it? And I couldn't tell you just how often I used to want desperately to get out of it myself. But the basic difference between you and me, I guess, is that you have got to where you are interested or involved in everything that has happened, or is happening, or is going to happen, in this entire country, or the world for that matter, and thus your curiosity and your discontent and your wanderlust are never assuaged, never satisfied, because you couldn't even hope to live long enough to see and do all the things that you want to see and do. But I . . . I suppose that apart from being too much absorbed with myself the only things that could really interest me *now*, the only things about which I could truly care, are those that are happening right here in this small corrupt decadent banal microcosm of a city, in these small dull microcosmic streets and backyards and front porches and vacant lots and parks and all. And I think, oh, I think, if I could just tune myself in to these petty sights and sounds and smells and learn to find some meaning in them and, yes, even to love them, then perhaps I shall never be bored again, I shall never suffer wanderlust and, who knows? I might even become happy or at least content, satisfied, at ease. And that would be the only seventh heaven I could ever want, or find."

"Ah yes," was all I could say, and if I was still squinting my beady eyes it was only to hold back a threatening lacrimal flow.

Then from the depths of my own yearning and chronic perennial homesickness or homeseeking or whatever it is, I called out to her and asked, "Don't you think maybe I could learn to be like that too?"

She lay her hand on my arm and smiled. "I don't know," she said. "It's something you have to decide. That's what I meant in my note when I said that if you stay, you should know why you're staying."

I began to nod my head in a rhythmic, continuing agreement. At length I quit nodding my head and gave it a flippant toss and said, "Well then—"

"I'd like to show you what I mean," she said, "if we could just take a little tour of some of these streets. Maybe it isn't too late for you to change your mind about this town. Tomorrow—" She glanced at the clock and said, "I mean today, because dawn is only a few hours away, isn't it?—we could take a little walk and I'll show you things you've never seen before. After Doyle comes home and I talk to him for a little while, then we could—"

"Dall isn't coming home," I said.

"What?" she said and her face was alarmed. "Why not?"

"He's in the hospital," I said.

"*What?*" she cried.

"I said he's in the hospital."

"What happened to him?"

"He got trampled by a horse named Houyhnhnm," I said.

"Jimmy's gelding! How did it happen? Is he hurt badly? Which hospital? When did it happen? Did Jimmy—?"

So I gave her the whole story, and near the end of my narrative she began to cry, I think it was when I mentioned that business about Dall asking me to feed his dog, and her crying got harder and harder until finally she had to bury her face in her hands. Sitting there like that with her face in her hands, racked with sobs, obstructing the flow of my narrative, she gave me a sudden memory of the way her mother had looked the other afternoon when she had put on that fake weeping show. But Margaret's tears were very real. And they weren't for herself at all.

Even after I had finished the story, down to the last detail, she continued to cry, and I could do nothing to stop it. I told her Dall was getting along just fine and the doctors said they wouldn't have to open his skull after all—and I even tried to make a cheerful joke by saying it was a good thing they wouldn't have to open his skull because they might be shocked to find nothing there, ha! ha!—but I don't think she was even listening to me any longer.

Finally she got up from the kitchen table and went into the living room, where it was dark, and she lay down on the sofa and continued crying. I went in there and sat down beside her and stroked her forehead. Eventually she stopped crying, and her eyes were closed and I thought she might be asleep. Flat on her back like that, in the dusk of the room, her hands crossed upon her waist, she seemed like a Renaissance tomb sculpture, a supine Ilaria del Carretto or some such alabaster maiden lying quietly in a state that is neither death nor sleep but the pure image of both. Her breasts, however, were not alabaster but rising and falling swells palpitant beneath their coverings of cotton and playtex, and I began gently to palpate them, and she did not protest beyond an initial slight squirm. Screwing up courage, I lay down beside her, crowding her over toward the back of the sofa. One nice thing about being short: sofas fit. For a while my fingertips lightly twiddled the lengthening nipples as detected in their embroidered nylon sanctums, and I gnawed on her earlobe. Then my hand went south, but even then she did nothing to stop me. Even when I hooked my finger under the edge of the crotch of her panties and with it found and fondled the growing and moistening clitoral bud in its tender labial cove, the only sound from her was her breathing. *Fortunae cetera mando.* By and by, when it seemed that such titillations would have kindled fires in any woman, I made bold to swing a leg up over onto her, and then another leg, and then slowly and gently to commence a mock, clothes-hindered venery which, make-believe though it was, served to distend me to the point where just the feel of my thick trouser-bound tool riding up and down across her panty-clad canyon would itself have been a fine joy and redemptive and obliterative gratification had I not wanted something better, and it served, too, to give her notice of my intentions so that she could get herself ready emotionally in whatever manner she chose. But if she was doing anything to get ready, emotionally or physically, she wasn't much showing it. Still as still as a stillborn child, she neither stirred nor stiffened nor stopped me. Could she really be sleeping through all this? Now it is my experience to know that Pamela, whenever she gave in, gave in completely to the point of absolute impassive submission and such lifelessness that only a necrophiliac could have enjoyed it. So if

Margaret were going to turn out to be only another Pamela-type dead-end dishrag, I wasn't so sure that I wanted her after all . . . But I thought I might as well try anyway; maybe the act itself would resuscitate her. Wherefore I slipped a free hand down between us and unzipped my fly. The faint whir of the parting zipper, alas, sounded in the dark stillness of the night like some prehistoric pterodactyl grinding his mandibles, and it woke her, it woke her from whatever sleep or reverie or shy withdrawal she was in, and she spoke to me, murmuring some words so timidly stifled that I had to incline my ear against her mouth to catch them, and even then I had to ask her to repeat herself, and she did, just a little less suppressed: "Will you stay?" And I, thinking she meant simply would I stay with her through the night, replied, "Certainly," and then realized my voice was much too loud, and realized too that I might be giving the wrong answer to the wrong question, and lowered my voice, fought it down to this quiet question: "Do you mean will I stay in Little Rock forever?"

She was silent for a moment, a moment during which I felt my manhood flop and shrink and during which I got off of her and lay beside her to ponder this turning of my analogy: that if I wanted the town, I would have to stay in it; if I wanted her, I would have to stay with her. "Yes," she answered. Then I became distressed, beside myself. Clutching her tightly, I awkwardly babbled a nearly incoherent explanation of why I could not stay, and why I thought she should go with me, until she drew away from me and I realized I was not only incoherent but perhaps irrational as well, then I stopped. I just shut up altogether, and pressed my face into that dale between her breasts and became as still and quiet as she. Thus we remained a long while. Sometime later she raised her head slowly and kissed me lightly on the brow. I didn't move. Later still her hand crept across my waist and entered the unzipped fly and parted the curtains of my shorts and took out my dead extension and slowly stroked it back to life. Now, I thought, now the town and its agent, this sorceress and succubus, are trying to seduce me. I didn't move. Awkwardly and unskillfully she did it, hesitantly rubbing the underside of it with her palm, and I wanted to show her how, but I didn't move. For a long time, fifteen minutes or so, she slowly caressed it, beginning to explore it from stem to stern with the pads of her fingertips, until I thought it might explode, but I didn't move. All on her own, she closed her fingers around it and began a rhythm which steadily swiftened to a fierce abandon. Sweat was streaming down the sides of my face, but I didn't move. When the time came that she sensed the involuntary sinews were about to throb and heave, she put her other hand into the pocket of her blouse and took out a small hankie whose lilac scent my nostrils caught in passing, and she wrapped this around the pulsing crown, and then I moved. I clung to her and shook and felt myself thumping inside of her tight fist. When it was over, sudden waves of sleep began to crowd down on me, and I was able to fight them off for only a short while. Then as I let myself be caught up in them and swept off into nothingness, out of detumescent shame and frustration and anger I uttered a final question: "Is that what you did for Slater?"

The drowsiness pressed me down as into a dark well, and as in a dark well her answer had muted echoes, far away and not altogether intelligible, and perhaps only sounds inside my own head already in sleep: "No. It's what I did for myself."

When I awakened, the sun was well up in the sky, and she was gone.

SIXTEEN

I was standing in the morning sunlight at the kitchen window, drinking a cup of tepid leftover coffee and staring vacuously out at the back yard as if I expected to see Bowzer come trotting home at any minute, when she returned. She came trotting into the kitchen with a bag of groceries, threw me a very cheery "Good morning!" and unpacked her groceries and began to fry some bacon and eggs. I didn't say anything in answer to her extravagantly gay greeting. I just watched her. She glanced at me and said, "My, how grumpy you look this morning! Didn't you sleep well?"

"What are you sounding so goddamn merry about?" I asked grumpily.

"I went to see Doyle," she said. "And he's just fine. I told him all my troubles, and he advised me and counseled me, and now I feel much better."

"What did he tell you?"

"He told me I should go with you."

"Bully for him!" I said, delighted, sending the old buddy a telepathic message of thanks.

"But," she continued, "he said that I ought to try to convince you that you should stay in Little Rock. Because he wants you to stay too. Doyle loves you like a brother, did you know that?"

"Yes," I said, "but very rarely do brothers ever spend their lives together in the same town." Then I said, "Well, do you want to go with me?"

"Sit down and eat your breakfast," she said. I sat down, and she put first a bowl of Rice Chex (psychic girl!) and then a plate of scrambled eggs and bacon in front of me, and even buttered my toast, and it was a cozy domestic scene. She sat down across from me and started in on her own plate. The food was very good; I realized how much practice she had had all these years as cook for the Austin-Polk household. I complimented her on the crispness of the bacon, and then I reminded her of my question. She said, "No." Why not? I asked her. "I've already told you," she said. "What's the point? We could spend our whole lives here in this city and never get to know it all. Why should we wander restlessly around the world?"

"All right," I said challengingly. "If I *do* leave, and you stay here, then what are you going to do?"

"I've managed this long," she said, not looking up at me.

"All right," I said. "Those are your terms, then? I stay: I get you. I leave: I lose you."

She nodded.

"Christ!" I moaned in exasperation. "What a decision!"

We ate our eggs and bacon in silence. Then she stood up. "So now if you will finish your coffee," she said, "I would like for you to go with me on that little walking tour of this town."

Never, never before had I ever looked at the old burg with quite the same eyes, as though searching desperately for something I had missed before, as though trying to create quaint and wondrous façades to hide all its lackluster and jejunity, as though the future of my very soul depended upon my success in finding some redeeming quality in this lost city. Far from being any Diogenes-like search for honesty, or Lot-like search for goodness, it was the search of a sophisticated world-traveler trying to find any usefulness in the desolated site of his irretrievable youth. Even though I had convinced myself, at the outset, that regardless of what distaste or boredom or uneasiness I felt toward the town I would still stay here, I would stay here if that is what I had to do in order to have

Margaret, still I was qualmishly skeptical. For her part, she was trying hard to show me the nice things about it: the architectural grace of its old buildings—the classic Albert Pike Memorial Temple and the Old State House and the few fine antebellum houses; and the architectural tastefulness of some of the new modern buildings—the public library (which I had already studied thoroughly), the new office buildings, and even such things as an unusually attractive motel called the Coachman's Inn (where, I recalled, we had planned to stay together, and where we might yet stay together if only I came to my senses). I guess we must have walked a good six or seven miles that day, and even the weather seemed to be co-operating: although the sun was bright a constant breeze came up out of the south and kept us continually cool, and sometimes the soughing sound of that breeze seemed to be carrying the ghost of old Stephen Foster melodies, "Beautiful Dreamer" and "Old Folks at Home" and "Come Where My Love Lies Dreaming" as the straining strings of André Kostelanetz' orchestra might have reinterpreted and haunted them. All in all, I probably never had a finer day in Little Rock in my life. Or a more irresolute one.

Margaret said not a word about herself, or me, but talked only about the town. The Metropolitan Little Rock area, she told me, now had almost 270,000 inhabitants within its 781 square miles, and that was a lot of people, and a lot of room. Little Rock University, which had only been a small junior college when she attended it, was fast on its way to becoming a large, complex institution. The city police force, in case Dall hadn't told me (he hadn't), consisted of a total of 188 ablebodied and benevolent gentlemen. There was a growing industrial complex south of town (I had caught a glimpse of it from Naps's window) which would some day be positively gigantic. The Little Rock Philharmonic was a pretty fair symphony orchestra. In addition to the somewhat lackadaisical Playmakers organization (which was doing Slater's *Red Shoes*), there was also an active Community Theatre of Greater Little Rock, Inc., and between the two of them they put on some fine plays. The Heights movie theater often showed the best of foreign and domestic art-cinema. There were restaurants which, in specializing in Mexican, Italian, and Chinese foods, Margaret (although she had never eaten in one of them) knew had no equals anywhere. The six municipal parks covered a total of 1,600 acres. Little Rock led the entire nation in the progress of its urban renewal. When dredging and lock-building were finished, the Arkansas would be opened up to navigation, and Little Rock once again would be a port city. When Faubus was finally ousted, the state would elect an intelligent and far-sighted man to replace him, and then things would begin to happen all over. Everything pointed to a beautiful future.

After a humdinger sandwich luncheon in the Pebble Room of the Tower Building (I had shaved with Dall's razor and my seersucker suit, although wrinkled, wasn't entirely unpresentable), we spent the afternoon exploring the so-called Quapaw Quarter, which I had never even heard of before. Margaret explained that this was a group of twelve widely scattered historic sites and structures which were in or near a section of the city surveyed back in 1818 and designated as a kind of early reservation for the Quapaw Indians, later usurped by the prosperous white landowners. Here, within a seven-block radius, we could find almost all of the interesting antebellum and postbellum sites and sights of the city, and we did: we spent nearly an hour in the 1843 Trapnall Hall, a low classic mansion patterned after the best Southern style of Gideon Shyrock, elegantly appointed with girandoled chandeliers, gold walls and draperies, and surprisingly good Empire furniture (I deigned to impress Margaret with my connoiseurship by identifying and dating and provenancing each and every piece in the house, from the Chinese Chippendale sofa to the brass padfooted andirons); we spent another hour studying the exteriors of the 1846 Ionic-columned Absolom Fowler House, now a nice day nursery for St. Andrew's, the 1873 "Steamboat Gothic" Augustus Garland House, the 1840 Albert Pike House, and others; we looked at historical documents and artifacts in the Old State House and in the Old Arsenal of City Park, General MacArthur's birthplace; and we spent still another hour on a tour of the extensive Territorial Restoration, its pioneer-rustic Tavern Room with the perforated-tin milk safe that is the twin of Tatrice Howard's milk safe, its old kitchens and parlors, its early print shop, and its beautifully landscaped grounds with massive black walnut and magnolia trees. I had been through the Territorial Restoration at least a dozen times before, once with Pamela after our honeymoon, but this was the first time I could bring to it such a formidable depth of recognition and perception. "If only Little Rock still looked like this," I said to Margaret, gesturing my hand in a wide arc to indicate the rugged primal elegance of the place. "But it doesn't."

Still I had to admit to her that our long walk had made me discover aspects of the town which I had never known before, and I had to agree that this whole area of town, east of Main, had an old and hushed charm—no two houses were identical in the whole section, and this in itself was a great relief from the sameness of the new suburbs. I guess I *could* live here after all, I told myself, spotting a delightful old house or two which, if carefully restored with authentic furnishings, would make an appropriate base of operations for me.

But wait! I cautioned myself. Perhaps you've discovered—or uncovered—more of the town, but you still don't know the girl.

SEVENTEEN

One of the historic sites of the Quapaw Quarter we missed: the Mt. Holly Cemetery, sometimes referred to as the Westminster Abbey of Arkansas. Margaret said it was too far out of the way, but I suspected her real reason was that she thought I had seen enough moribundity already without visiting a cemetery. So our last stop, our last station on the trail of Quapaw Quarter sites, was the Rock itself, *La Petite Roche,* a hefty but comparatively small hunk of greenish-gray schist and sandstone bulging up from the bank of the Arkansas River at the foot of Rock Street beneath the Rock Island Railroad bridge. I had been here before too, but the last time I had seen it this was a weedy junk-strewn shore where the bodies of gar and catfish rotted in the sun and hobos and other vagrants lit their little fires at night and East Side punks and their loose girls came and screwed madly in the scrubby bushes and left behind a litter of toilet paper and used condoms, and a nearby junk dealer's warehouse vomited a hideous black disgorgement of old battery cases down the bank of the river. Now except for broken glass everywhere the place had a certain civic neatness and decency to it, and the Rock itself was capped with a granite monument and a commemorative bronze plaque explaining how Bernard de la Harpe had discovered the Rock in 1722 and how he had called it the Little Rock to distinguish it from the "Big Rock" bluff farther up the river on the other side, and how it was used as the beginning point of the Quapaw Line. We walked down thirty-one steps, holding to a pipe railing, to get to the Rock, and, after reading the plaque, we sat down on the base of the monument with our backs up against it, and stared at the river. It was a secluded place, remote and private.

This river means many things, but the one thing it meant to me at that moment, coming down to it like that, was that it was the ominous instrument with which Margaret might have wanted to destroy herself at one time. I glanced at her suspiciously, and then I said, "Why have we come here to this water?"

She returned my suspicious glance and answered, "I suppose Doyle has told you everything I ever said to him, including that."

"Not everything," I said.

"We have come here to this water because this Rock is the last of the Quapaw Quarter sites," she said. "Or the first, depending on how you look at it. Now our walk, our tour, is ended. And now I can ask you: Would you really like to stay in Little Rock? What do you think?"

She might have picked a pleasanter place for such a discussion. The day's soft and cooling breeze had ebbed in the stillness of the late afternoon, and the hot sun seemed to suck all the foul and rank odors from the river, the smell of mud, of rotting driftwood, of sewage, of dead fish and smelly live fish; and the river itself, dung-brown and ugly and scummed with bubbly swill, rolled indolently and turbidly but with an awful incessant resolve and monstrousness in its unrelenting push to join the Mississippi. I remembered that upstream several hundred yards, behind the old sewage disposal plant, an enormous excretory bubble belched upward from the surface of the river at regular intervals. Beneath us, frothy eddies swirled and lapped against the Rock, filled with little vicious whirlpools; gazing down at them, I felt a slight vertigo and anxiety, and also a curious recognition which soon clarified itself: this pattern of the brown tormented water had been re-created, not abstractly but almost literally, in those murals that Margaret had smeared on the walls of her room. I did not like it here, and I wished we could go some place else to talk, but I didn't want to say this to Margaret. In fact, I couldn't say anything for the moment anyway, because I had suddenly been stricken with an attack of sun sneezes. The heat of the sun on one's face, counteracting the lower temperatures of the nasal chambers, creates a sudden chemical refrigeration in one's head which results in distressing unseasonal sneezes, and I had a whole string of these things, a twenty-one-gun salute. "Heavens!" said Margaret, both amazed and sympathetic. "Excude me," I sniffled. "It habbens eber so offen, whed the sun is sot." Finally I got them under control, and blew my nose into my handkerchief. "I guess I'm just not cut out for this climate," I said.

"Oh, I'll bet you sneeze in the sun in Boston too," she said.

"Well, I guess I do," I admitted. "But the sun doesn't shine so often in Boston. I've been here almost two weeks now and we've had hardly any rain."

"Droughts can be nice too, if you learn to like them," she said.

"Your whole life was a drought," I said. "And so, for that matter, is the life of anybody who lives in this town, or this state, or the whole South. One big drought," I said severely, accusingly. "Why indeed have we come here to this water?"

"Why have *you*?" she said. "You've never really answered that question I first asked you: What are you doing in Little Rock? Why did you come home in the first place? Surely it wasn't just to visit your father again."

I recalled my original notion, that wistfulness which had flitted through my head on that night before I left Boston, of using this vacation as an opportunity for reappraising my old hometown with a view toward resettling here and recapturing whatever stimulus the climate and physical environment had once given me, and I realized that all this time, not just today on this formal tour, but all the time since I got off the train a week ago last Monday morning, I had been searching and reappraising, sweeping the cobwebs out of that homesickness of mine, that nostalgia which corrupts all the wandered sons of this town and makes us keep coming home, again and again, long after we no longer have any use for the town. I told Margaret that even if I left again I would probably come back, perhaps in another year, perhaps not for three or four years, but I would always keep coming back, and, if so, maybe I should just stay here now and never leave, because I think I had found at last that thing which keeps me returning.

And I acknowledged it to her: "Somehow it seems to me that the little lives of all these people, of this town and state, this whole permanently drought-stricken Southland, are intricately woven together, more than are the lives of the people of any other region or country. I don't know why this is. I don't think it has very much to do with the Confederacy or the Civil War in itself. I don't even think it is because our names are Stone and Austin and Hawkins and Howard, or Johnson and Crittenden and

Slater and Ashley. Maybe it's because we have all been victims, in one way or another, of the South's long and continuous tragedy. I don't know. There really wouldn't seem to be much brotherhood or kinship of any kind between a colored man and a white supremacist, would there? But there is. Because they are both Southerners, both permanently doomed by whatever living doom or damnation is the lot of us all. Or whatever honor or pride or shame. Take Naps and Dall, for instance. Both of them, I am willing to admit, are uncommonly intelligent. Naps is a college graduate, did you know that? Did you ever notice the Phi Beta Kappa key which dangles from his watch pocket? But sometimes he sounds like any old illiterate darkie, just as sometimes Dall sounds like the trashiest of hillbilly white trash. But Dall doesn't *have* to talk like that. No, he doesn't *have* to sound that way, neither does Naps. You know what I think? I think those guys, each in his own way, bear some kind of deep implacable pride in their backgrounds, their roots—Nap's descent from poor Delta slaves, Dall's descent from poor Ozark mountain folk—and their speech is a kind of living monument to the past. They *know* it's bad speech, it's improper and imperfect and all, and that's all the more reason why they use it, to flaunt the coarse glory of the Old South in the languid face of the New South, to keep reminding themselves, and us, that the South's past, however bad or improper or imperfect it was, had a rich character which modern civilization is taking away from us. Like a couple of old sailors who won't give up the old ship, even long after that old ship has gone down they still cling to fragments of it because even these fragments, warped and weathered and useless, are somehow more beautiful than a whole new modern ship could ever be."

She smiled. "Let's sit on porches and grow old together and talk about the coarse glory of the Old South," she said, her arm linked cozily through mine. "And Dall will be our best friend, a brother to both of us. He will be the old kindly Chief of Police and he will come and sit on the porch with us, still speaking those same old back-country words, and we will all grow old together and be good friends. And Naps too."

"But I don't know you," I said. "I don't think I ever knew you, and I doubt if I ever could."

"It's because you've never tried," she said.

"I have tried," I said, "but it does me no good."

"You've never tried," she said.

"It does me no good, because you seem to change so much.

You're never the same person twice. It's not just a split personality, it's a fragmented personality."

"You take things at face value," she said, "or you want to, or try to. But my face has no value, and you've never gone behind it."

"All I've ever had to go by is what you say, and you've never said very much to me. You've never told me who you really are. Whom have you every really loved? Are you carrying a torch for somebody?"

"No. I've got a lighted match in my hand, and I'm waiting for somebody to come along with a torch that I can ignite." She paused to light herself a cigarette, then she went on. "Just now you were offering up such a lucid and logical analysis about the South and how we are all bound together and why Naps and Dall talk the way they do, and you sounded so perceptive, so rational, that I was sitting here telling myself: If he can make such brilliant theories about something like that, then maybe he can finally theorize about me. That's why I said let's sit on porches and grow old together. Because maybe we could see each other enough, and talk to each other enough, so that finally you would know who I am. And then you could tell me. And you might even learn who you are."

"I might learn that I am your father," I said.

"Now what do you mean by that?" she asked, but I think she didn't really have to ask, because, uneasily, she knew.

"I mean that whoever will sit on those porches and grow old together with you will have to serve as your father for you. You've heard of 'father figures'? Oedipal or Electral feelings and all that?"

"Yes," she said, smiling wryly. "Somebody to wield a firm hand over me, somebody to keep me out of mischief, somebody to punish me when I'm bad, is that it?"

"You get the idea," I said.

"Probably you're right," she said. "I remember once when I was a girl, oh, eight or nine years old, I was at my great-aunt's funeral, and while all the grownups were inside the house listening to the service, all the kids were out in the yard playing, and I was up in a little tree hanging from a limb by my knees, upside down, you know, with my dress flopping down over my head, and my father came out of the house and reproached me severely, telling me to get down out of that tree and quit showing my panties to all the world. Innocent as I was, I had no idea that there was anything wrong with showing my panties, and if it hadn't been for my father, I probably never would have known any better. So that's what I need, is it? Somebody to tell me when I shouldn't show my panties to the world?"

I laughed. "Sort of," I said.

"Then you wouldn't fill the bill," she said, "because you don't remind me of my father in the slightest, and you aren't firm enough or authoritarian enough, and you are always so preoccupied with whatever is going on in your own mind that you never would notice if my panties were showing or not. I remember once back in high school, when I was a junior and I felt nobody seemed the least bit aware of my existence, nobody ever looked at me or spoke to me, and even you . . . you never complimented me or even commented on my dress or my appearance, so one day I came to school wearing the most outlandish outfit, just to see what would happen, just to see if anybody would notice, I had on one black shoe and one white shoe, one orange sock and one green sock, and a pair of polka-dot pedal-pushers— that was a time when pedal-pushers were banned at high school —and my hair in pigtails and a horrible old plumed hat on my head, but nobody even looked at me! And *you* . . . you never said a word about it!"

"I remember that," I said. "I was so embarrassed I didn't know what to say. I didn't want anybody to see me with you. I thought you'd gone completely off your rocker."

"Oh?" Her surprise lasted for a long moment and then she said, "Well, that's what I mean, then. If my panties were showing, you'd be too embarrassed to mention it to me, wouldn't you?"

"I don't know. Possibly—"

"And another thing. You never once—not once did you ever discuss anything serious with me. You never even brought up the subject of sex. Why not? I remember how you used to paw me, and you always had something wicked on your mind, but you never put it into words. Why not? I didn't know a single thing about the subject, and I needed somebody to tell me what it was all about, and how it was fun, and how it was a normal, decent thing which happens between male and female all the time. I didn't know this, and I worried myself sick about it, and you never said a word. Why not? I ask you."

"Maybe I didn't know very much about it myself at the time. But I distinctly recall that I had the impression you knew all about it, because, after all, I remember you told me what a gigolo was. We heard the word in a movie or read it in a book or some place, and you explained to me what it was. I didn't know. You did."

"I told you it was a man hired by a woman for the purpose of entertaining her. I didn't know what *kind* of entertainment, though."

"Tell me," I said, "how *did* you ever manage to find out about sex, if, as you claim, you're still a virgin?"

"I still don't know much about it," she said. "But in junior college I had three dates—*three* dates in two years—and from those three I picked up the rudiments, at least. Did I ever tell you about them? Well, the first was with a football player named Bink Conley. Bink was a big husky guy but he seemed kindly and decent and honorable, and he was rather shy. He took me roller-skating once, and then afterward we drove out some lonely old dirt road and parked, and drank some whiskey, and when he began petting me I told him I was a virgin and didn't know the first thing about the matter and that he had better explain to me what it was all about. Well, apparently that was one subject he knew something about and wasn't the least bit shy of discussing. So I received my first lecture on the facts of life from Bink Conley. 'See, it's like this,' he explained. 'I got me this big old prick'—that's what he called it—'and you got you that there little old hole, so what I do is, see, I take my prick and stick it up into your hole and sort of work it around in there, in and out'—and he began to demonstrate with the forefinger of one hand clenched in the fist of his other hand—'and it gets faster and faster, feelin real good, see, and before long I shoot my wad, and it's the best feelin there is, I'm tellin yuh, and then I kind of relax and it's all done.' So I said to him, 'Well, that's all very interesting, but what am I supposed to get out of it?' and he gave me this blank look, kind of surprised-looking, and he scratched his head and thought about that for a while, and then he said, 'Well, I guess it must feel sort of good to you too, and that's what you get out of it. Come on, I'll show yuh.' But I asked him, 'What if that big old prick won't fit into this little old hole? What if it pricks me? What if it hurts?' and he said, 'Aw, it won't, I guarantee yuh.' And he kept saying that over and over again, but he had scared the daylights out of me, and even if I had been dying of desire I was probably so tightly constricted he never would have been able to get it in, and I didn't want him to try, so I made him take me home."

She paused to light another cigarette. Why is she so open and frank with me this time? I wondered. A compulsion to confess? Is she desperate again because of the lateness of the hour, because I'm leaving? *Am* I leaving? If she will talk to me like this on porches forever, perhaps not. I smiled at her, and she smiled back, and went on.

"My second date was with a nice, good-looking pre-med student and he was about your size, so I decided that his wouldn't be quite so big as Bink's—I always had the notion, up until last night, in fact, that physical size determines phallic size—and this pre-med student took me to a movie and did a little petting during the movie and he was so nice about it, such a polite and well-spoken gentleman, that I decided I would let him do it, so after the movie we drove toward that same lonely dirt road, but on the way a cat crossed the road and he swerved the car to hit it and made a self-satisfied chuckle and said, 'Got the bastard!' and he had, he had smashed it flat, and I was so upset I slapped him hard and got out of the car and walked home.

"But I was still convinced I might find somebody to do it with, and I was willing to try."

I interrupted: "You mean you were really trying to get yourself laid?"

"Don't look at it that way," she said. "Just say that I was nearly twenty years old and curious to know what sex was all about. My third and last date at JC was with my English teacher. He was a young bachelor and although he wasn't especially good-looking he was very intelligent and an interesting person to talk to. He invited me to come up to his apartment and discuss my grades with him, because I wasn't doing too well in his course. I wrote good themes and always got A's on them, but my test scores were low because I just wouldn't take the trouble to memorize all the facts, William Blake's wife's name and Coleridge's birthplace, and so forth. So I went up to his apartment and he made a cocktail shaker full of martinis and we drank them and talked for a while about the meaning of Wallace Stevens's 'Thirteen Ways of Looking at a Blackbird,' but it was obvious to me what was on his mind, and I think he must have realized it was on my mind too. Well, there was a sort of spontaneous combustion: we both stood up from our chairs at the same time and met in a mad embrace and he kissed me all over my neck and face and began pressing himself up against me and I could feel his thing all stiff and swollen inside his pants against my groin, and he began rubbing it against me, but then all of a sudden he trembled and sprang away from me and turned his back to me and bent over and clutched himself down there, and he was so quiet and reserved for a while I thought to ask him what was the matter, but I didn't know how to put it, I didn't even know the precise meaning of the word *orgasm* and with all those martinis in me I couldn't think of any way of expressing it except the way Bink Conley had put it, and I thought if Bink Conley put it that way it must be current coin, so I put my arm around my English teacher's shoulders sympathetically and asked, 'Did you shoot your wad?' and he turned and game me a look as if I were the most reprehensible sort of uncouth harlot, and he was very cool toward me for the rest of the evening, and my grade in English that semester was an F."

She paused and waited until I had quit laughing, and then she concluded: "Those were my three dates, and I didn't have any others until I got out of college. And still I'm a virgin, and it's all my own fault, I guess, because, like last night, I've had several chances not to be one. I've always been very interested in sex, perhaps obsessed with it, and you'd think I would have learned something about it, but I haven't. I'm still as ignorant as ever. When I was nine or ten years old, in the summertime, I'd take a quilt out to the back yard and lie down on it and open the Montgomery Ward catalog and spend hour after hour looking at all those hygienic devices and contraptions—suspensories and leg-strap urinals and French trusses and scrotal trusses and stem pessories and syringes and douche powders and sanitary belts and all—and I knew they had something to do with sex and the bodily functions but I didn't know what, and I spent so much time trying to figure them out . . ."

"Hell," I said, "I used to study those Ward and Sears catalogues too, and I *still* don't understand them. Suspensories always kept me in suspense."

". . . And those advertisements in magazines," she said, "those elegant, smug, secretive ads, like the ones that said *Modess, because* . . . because of what? I wondered. Because why?"

"Life is riddled with mysteries," I mused aloud. Then I asked, "Why didn't you ever ask your father about the birds and bees?"

"He died before I was ever fully aware that there is a fundamental difference between a he-bird and a she-bird, or a he-bee and a she-bee. But I remember once I found something out in the alley behind our house, and after examining it puzzledly for a while I took it in and showed it to him and asked him what it was. He took it away from me and told me to stay out of the back alley. Years later I saw another one when you and I were walking through War Memorial Park and I asked you what it was and you got all red in the face and pretended you hadn't heard my question. Finally when I was working in the stockroom at Alexander's Shoe Shoppe I found another one in an old box of shoes, so I asked one of the ladies who worked there what it was and she told me. She called it a fuckinrubba. What do you do with fuckinrubbas? I asked her. 'Dearie,' she said, 'I don't do anything with them. My boy friend puts em on his dofunny so I won't get p.g.' 'Oh,' I said. 'So his wad doesn't get loose, huh?' 'You got the idea,' she said. Oh, I was naïve. Really a square. Yet although the mechanics of the business, the implements and the techniques and the chemistry, were largely way over my head, I had some kind of innate, intuitive realization of its relation to Eros; I sensed how my own feelings and drives were bound up into a force which needed only an object, somebody or something to activate them. I told you about how when I was thirteen I discovered the surprising phenomenon of the orgasm. Well, even though I suspected it was some supernatural thing which was unique in me and never happened to anybody else, still I had an overwhelming feeling that it had a potential relation to somebody else, and finally I decided that that somebody else was my father, although he was dead, and it became his hand which stroked me and took me on that ride through heights of weird physical ecstasy. Does that shock you? Clifford? Does it bother you for me to talk like this?"

"Not especially," I said. "Maybe my ears are burning, but my curiosity is too." Large green flies were molesting both of us, but I was in no hurry to go.

"I suppose anything I say would only reaffirm your notion that what I need is a father figure."

"It doesn't need any reaffirming," I said.

"Well," she said. Then she asked me a hestitant question. "Did you ever . . . ever . . . do that? I mean, did you ever—?"

"Play with myself?" I said. "Sure. Who hasn't?"

"Last night—" she said.

"Never mind about last night," I said.

"You were upset," she said.

"It was a lousy substitute," I said.

"But you didn't think it was . . . unnatural? Perverted or anything?"

"No. I thought you learned how to do it by practicing on Slater."

"I didn't. For all I know, Jimmy doesn't even have one. I 'practiced' by—long ago—I used to imagine that I did it to my father. There. Does that shock you?"

"If you want it to."

"I have an evil mind," she said.

"Not evil," I said. "Just wild."

In the wilderness of the river, two men, shirtless, were passing by in a high-speed flatboat outboard. She waited until the roar of the motor had faded off, and then she said, "All right, wild. Would you rather I didn't want to talk about masturbation?"

"That's an ugly word," I said. "One of the harshest words in the language. I remember the first time I heard it. It was at the YMCA. I was twelve or thirteen. After all the other guys had gone into the pool for the daily swim, I had to stay behind to put a fresh Band-Aid on my skinned knee. The lifeguard, a huge fat guy of twenty or so who was supposed to be a benevolent counselor to us boys, came back into the locker room and said, 'Okay, Stone, what's keeping you? Are you masturbating in here?' 'Am I what?' I said. 'Masturbating,' he said. 'Ain't you ever heard of the art of masturbating?' I thought it sounded like it might have something to do with fishing: if one learns how to put the bait on the hook properly, one knows how to master bait. 'How do you spell it?' I asked him. 'Aw, shut up and get your ass on into the pool,' he said. Afterward I went to the library and looked it up, and made some sense out of 'stimulation of the genital organs to orgasm achieved by manual or other bodily contact exclusive of sexual intercourse.' Naturally, because I did it sometimes, I was suspicious that the fat lifeguard was reading my mind or spying on the bathroom of my house. It was another year or so before I learned, from Dall as a matter of fact, that everybody does it, so during that period I had an awful guilt complex and I still get tense every time I hear the word."

"When did you quit?" she asked. "How old were you?"

"I never quit," I sighed. "Not completely."

"Me neither," she said, and we sat side by side on the Rock staring at the surge of the heavy brown river, and we were a pair of confederates, sympathetic chums bound in a synchronous moment of reflection that was lost in time, ageless: we might as well have been eager children, and if this were some barnloft instead of the Rock, and all the grownups were off at some safe distance, then now would be the time to say: I'll take down my pants and show you mine, if you'll take down your pants and show me yours. Why do we have to grow old and acquire hardened candor and nonchalance and blaséness before we can reach this rapport? And now that we've reached it, what do we do with it? Sit on porches with it and grow older together?

"When I was a little girl," she said, still staring reflectively at the river, "I would climb trees. There was not a tree anywhere that I was afraid to climb. But I never knew how to get down. Somebody always had to come up and get me."

"That's you," I said. "That's you all over."

"Because, even then, I was punishing myself? Do you think? Have I always got into these scrapes, these situations, for self-punishment, so that somebody would have to come and get me out of them? When I make love to myself in that way, I feel that I am punishing myself, that I have got myself up into a tree and I don't like it there, but there is nobody to get me down. Can a person punish himself but still not really like it, not want to?" She paused, and because she was asking that question of herself, I made no comment. Then she asked me, "Does this river frighten you?"

"It scares me witless," I said. "I recall once a high school friend of mine was playing around on the bank one evening up above town, and he fell in and drowned. He was an excellent swimmer, the best."

"Jimmy and I went swimming a few times in Lake Maumelle," she said, "back in early April when the water was still pretty cold. We would row out into the lake in his boat, and jump in and splash around until we were nearly frozen. One time, when we were bringing the boat back toward the shore, I had an impulse to dive into the water and see if I could swim all the way to the shore, just to impress him, it wasn't far, four or five hundred feet. So I did. I swam for a while and then turned to see what he was doing, but he wasn't even looking at me. What if I drowned myself? I wondered. Would he care? There I was, paddling madly in that icy water, with him two hundred feet behind me and the shore two hundred feet ahead of me, and I seemed to get the curious notion that if I reached the shore, somehow I would be free of him. I would be saved— because I knew already then that he entertained crazy thoughts of getting rid of his wife and marrying me—but if I didn't reach the shore, I would drown, I would die, and that too might be a salvation, a liberation, a freedom. As I swam I became angrier and angrier at him, because he had pretended to ignore my daring attempt, and because he could've brought the boat up alongside me and hauled me in, but he didn't. I thought I could hear the sound of him laughing at me, but probably it was just my indignant imagination. If I hadn't been so furious, and so obsessed, I probably would have drowned, right then and there, but I fought so hard that I finally reached the shore. And that was when I began to think constantly that the only way I could ever get away from him would be to drown myself or something. So one evening not long ago—just a week ago last Tuesday, in fact—I decided to do it. All day Jimmy had been beleaguering me with a lot of crazy talk about how we were destined for each other and how I could never get away from him because the Fates had intended that I come into his life and restore his lost youth, his lost manhood, and how his wife was a sinister intruder whom he had to dispense with in order to appease the Fates; and to top it all off my mother had been in one of her frequent bitter moods and had been berating me for everything, and Blass and Pfeifer's had sent me letters saying they were going to take action if I didn't pay my bills, and Ethel Slater had just finished telling me that I was the only good friend she'd ever had and she wanted me to come up more often and massage her poor paralyzed pudendum for her, and the trees were blooming and the flowers were blooming, but I wasn't, I wasn't blooming, I wasn't—"

She had begun to tremble and I put my arm around her and she lay her head against the side of my neck, but still she trembled, although her voice became quieter for a while. "And I kept remembering how much I had hated and despised myself, and I remembered that I was still wearing those cotton panties that belonged to some nun named Sister Mary Dolores who had lost them in a laundromat, and I brooded sullenly about how life had mistreated me and I had mistreated life, and how life was supposed to be all a bowl of cherries but I never got anything but the pits . . ."

Margaret wriggled out from under my arm and stood up. She moved to the edge of the Rock and stood there staring down at the water. She continued talking. "So I decided that night to come to this river and plunge into it." Her eyes were glazed; she gazed entranced at the water. "But on the way down here to the river I happened to pass a movie theater and saw that they were showing a movie I wanted to see, *Two for the Seesaw*, so I went in to see it, and in the movie a man held my hand." She turned and smiled at me. "And that man was you."

"My goodness," I responded to the wonder of it. "Do you mean that if you hadn't met me at that movie, you might have come on down here and jumped in?" But she didn't reply. Again she was staring at that water as if it held a particular fascination for her. "Margaret," I implored her, "sit down! Come on back here and sit down! I'm getting dizzy just looking at you." I held out my hand to her, but she ignored it.

"I wonder," she said to the water. "I wonder what would have happened if I *had* jumped in. Would I have drowned?"

"Hell yes you would've, you ninny! Now come away from there!"

"It's such an ugly river in the daytime," she said, spreading her arms wide to indicate the vast ugly length and breadth of it, and, in the act of this sudden sweeping gesture, she lost her balance—or did she?—she lost her balance and fell forward and out, and down, and dove into the river and disappeared from sight beneath its muddily opaque water.

🌺 EIGHTEEN

Now this has all been a hallucination, a bad dream, and she has been only a succubus who now has gone away and left me alone, and now I can wake up. But perhaps not yet. Perhaps I have to be in the water too, drowning too, sinking toward the dark gar-infested slime and ooze at the bottom, and then in that last moment of terrible panicked consciousness I will wake up. I am standing now, and I am kicking off my shoes, and in just another second I am going to dive in after her, but in the last on-shore moment of this fantastic dream I am thinking: Dall, rise up from your bed and come to the river, for there are two people this time who need your help.

Who is going to alert the fire department rescue squad? I am asking, and now I am in the water too. Who is going to bring the boats? The water is very warm, almost hot, and it is full of crud. Where are the boats? Because somebody is always jumping into the river, the fire department has a number of special rowboats, permanently anchored at the base of each of the three bridges, which are used exclusively for fishing the frequent jumpers out of the river. But where are they? I go under water and try to look around, but all I see is crud. Who has seen us, who has noticed? Margaret has already gone to the bottom, probably. The boats, where are the boats? How deep is this river? Sixty-four feet, I read once somewhere. And grappling hooks, too, bring grappling hooks! I surface for air, gulp big draughts of it into my lungs, and once again go under and look around, but it is useless, I can't see six inches through all this crud. I surface again and look around to see if there is anybody anywhere who is watching us, anybody on any of the bridges who has paid any attention to us, but I see no one, except, a long way out in the river already, Margaret, swimming, swimming nicely toward the other shore. I follow her, thinking: What the hell? I am a good swimmer, a regular little frog in fact, but she is just as good, or better, and I cannot catch her. Across the wide stream we go, dodging driftwood and debris, swallowing mud and crud; her arms rise and fall in a slow even breaststroke, while I flail away at the water for all I'm worth, but she keeps ahead of me, and I think: She *would*, being a succubus, a hallucination. But then I decide: This isn't a dream after all, it's just a crazy anticlimax. And you, son, I say to myself, are the fall guy. You've been had. If only she *would* drown.

But she doesn't. Although the river is nearly five hundred feet wide, and although the strong current has shoved us far aslant down the stream, we survive, both of us.

🌺 NINETEEN

Gasping and limp, I staggered up onto the bank of North Little Rock under the span of the new Interstate Highway bridge, took a few steps and collapsed into the sand. I rolled over onto my back and lay there looking up at the underside of the bridge and the sky, now ultramarine in the late afternoon, and I breathed in great heaves. Chasing her up that Hot Springs observation tower had not winded me as much as this did. My seersucker suit was ruined, I mean really ruined; hopelessly besmirched with all the river's foul exudations, and even its inherent drip-dry nature was not meant to withstand such a drenching. I had lost one of my argyle socks in the water. My unwaterproof wristwatch had ceased ticking. But worst of all, my elevator shoes, without which I am reduced to a dwarf of a mere five feet six inches, were left behind on the opposite shore, where any tramp might come along and take them.

I turned and watched Margaret. She had hit the bank thirty feet or so upstream from me, but she had not collapsed from lack of oxygen. She was walking around, sedulously examining a pile of rocks beneath a clump of willow trees, and I thought: Indeed she is loco. But she lifted a large flat rock from near the bottom of the pile, and drew out a cardboard box about thrice the size of a shoebox, and she brought this over and sat down on the bank near where I was lying. I was still too exhausted to speak; I could only watch her. She opened the box and began to remove its contents, which were wrapped in aluminum foil. The first item was a pair of silk panties, and she reached under her wet skirt and removed her wet panties and put on the new dry ones, then flung the old ones over to me so that I could see that name label sewed into them: Sister Mary Dolores. The next item was a brassiere, and she reached inside her blouse and unfastened her wet bra and wriggled loose from it and pulled it out, and put in the new bra and wriggled into it and fastened it. The next item, a larger one which she unfolded, was a gray skirt of pleated gabardine, and, after glancing furtively around to see if anybody was watching (nobody was but me), she took off her wet skirt and put on the new one. She did the same with her blouse, replacing it with a new one made of striped blue-green silk. Then she took out a new pair of shoes, black suède flats, and put them on her bare feet. Then she took out a small make-up bag and checked its contents: lipstick, powder, comb, miniature hair spray, small vial of cologne, and two ten-dollar bills. The only other item in the box was a paperback book, *New York: Places and Pleasures*, by Kate Simon. She riffled through its pages for a moment, then gave it a toss, and it landed out in the water and was carried swiftly downstream, finally sinking. She threw the cardboard box and the wads of aluminum foil in after it, and they too ultimately sank. Then she began to comb her hair.

"Margaret," I said, regaining my voice and my wits and feeling an irresistible urge to give vent to the vexation which festered inside me, "you take the cake. You are a first-class bamboozler, a big fraud. You ought to be put in jail. You— Do you realize you could have got us both killed?"

"I knew you wouldn't drown," she said, "and I knew you wouldn't let me drown even if I hadn't thought I was able to make it on my own."

"But of all the dumb stunts! What was the big idea, anyway? In the name of all that's holy, what—"

"I just wanted to see what you would do," she said. "And you did it."

"Christ sakes Almighty! You capricious female! Why, you couldn't commit suicide if you wanted to! You couldn't do it if you tried!"

"Oh, I could too!" she said, returning part of my vehemence. "And I did try! All day that Tuesday I worked at it! I tried to get some sleeping pills, but the druggist wouldn't give me any without a prescription! I thought of slashing my wrists, but I remembered I can't stand the sight of blood! I put Daddy Polk's old shotgun to my head and pulled the trigger, but it wasn't loaded! And I couldn't find any shells! I tried to jump in front of a bus on Main Street, but I stumbled and fell flat on my prat! I couldn't even write a decent suicide note, because my pen ran out of ink! But one thing I could do, and that was jump in the river, so I—"

"Well, how are you going to explain that box of clothes? Did your goddamn fairy godmother put them there for you?"

"Let me finish. So I decided to jump in the river, but I thought, what if that failed too? what if that failed just as everything else has always failed for me? and I knew I was a good swimmer, and I thought: What if I can't sink? And this is what I decided: I would put that box of clothes and twenty dollars—which I stole from my mother—and that book over here on the bank, and then I would go and jump in the river, off the Broadway bridge, which is pretty high, you know. At night, in the dark. If I sank, then that was the end of me. Fine. But if I didn't sink, I would swim over here and climb out and put on these clothes and take my twenty dollars and see if I could sneak out of town, and out of this state, under cover of darkness, and get to New York. As far as the police would have been concerned, or my mother would have been concerned, or Jimmy would have been concerned, I would have ceased to exist, either way. In one case, it would have been a matter of 'body recovered.' In the other case, it would have been a matter of 'body not recovered.' But either way, I could have escaped the intolerable situation I was in, and Jimmy would have had to give up his plan to murder his wife."

"If you wanted to go to New York," I demanded, "why the hell didn't you just go? Why make it so difficult?"

Because, didn't I see, she said, if she had gone to New York, still "alive," her mother would have written her letters constantly, telling her how lonely and miserable she was without her and begging her to come on back home, and finally Margaret might have given in to her—out of homesickness for the town, not out of any love or pity for the mother? Or, if not the mother, Slater would have written her, or he might even have come up there to find her, after disposing of his wife, so that the two of them, he or her mother, would have hounded her forever.

But how did my arrival on the scene change all of her plans? The very first time I had mentioned the possibility of taking her to New York, she had quickly rejected the idea.

It was the movie, she said. Remember? Remember how Robert Mitchum goes to New York and has to get involved with that Jewish girl in order to discover that he should have stayed back home in Omaha after all? Well, she said, somehow that movie had made her change her mind, it had made her realize that if she went to New York she would want to come home again, and then when she met me and talked with me and discovered how much I wanted to leave Little Rock, she felt she had a mission: to talk me into staying. Curious, because I had felt I had a mission too: to save her, to take her away from her mother. Had both of us succeeded?

"From that first moment we met," she said, "I have wanted to make you stay, but you—"

"If you really wanted me to stay," I broke in with bitterness, "why have you been giving me all this run-around? Do you just like being chased? Are you trying to play hard-to-get?"

"I've had reservations—"

"Reservations! What do you think *I* have been having? I don't know whether you're off your rocker, or not, or what. I don't know if you love me or even if you ever *could* love me! You've got me so bewildered and flustered and exasperated that I don't even know if I have even *reservations* any more! I don't even know if I should keep on seeing you and talking to you!"

"It's your choice," she said, but not coldly. Gently she said it. "It's all your choice. But I just want you to know how hard it has been for me to reach any definite conclusions about you. There are several reasons. One is the fact that you deserted me when you went away to college, and even if it wasn't desertion, I couldn't help feeling resentful about it for a long time. Another reason is that you were always so hard to talk to, even if you are so much easier to talk to now. Another reason is your attitude, some of the things you've said recently. That first night, for instance, when we had that long talk after you found me at the movie. You acted so terribly jaded, you were just a world-weary bird of passage, you said, and you have this raw streak of cynicism in you that sometimes is very galling, because it's obvious to anybody that you aren't really cynical at all, you're just lost and confused. I don't mind your lack of strength or inner conviction, because I'm a pretty weak person myself in that respect, but I wish you wouldn't try so hard to hide it by being so cynical and flippant and all. You make facetious remarks like you wish you were a rat, and you quote Latin like some fusty Oxonian, and you do such a poor job of concealing your sex drives that it's almost embarrassing. And some of my reservations were confirmed this morning when I talked to Doyle. I told him I didn't know who you really are, and I couldn't very well go away with you, or even try to talk you into staying, if I didn't know anything about you, so I asked him please to tell me anything he knew about you which would be . . . well, which might shed any unfavorable light on your character. At first he wouldn't, he said you were the nicest guy he'd ever known, practically faultless he said, but then after I continued to badger him about it, he confessed some things, just a lot of little things, but—"

"Like what, may I ask?"

"Well, for instance you used to pick fights with other boys, just to show off your boxing skills, and because you felt insecure and had to take it out on other people."

"Aw, crap!" I said. "Nobody's perfect. If you'd care to hear about all the bad things Dall used to do, I could entertain you for an hour with them. I could tell you about how he—"

"We're not talking about Doyle," she said. "We're talking about you, and why I had reservations about you. But if you'll just let me finish, I'll say this: Despite all those reservations, and your imperfections and so forth, I've been able to discover recently, very recently"—she smiled impishly—"that you are really a very nice guy, and you have a heart of gold, and you are kindly and courageous and even more intelligent than I thought you were."

"Thanks loads," I said, "but how did you ever arrive at such a conclusion?"

"For one thing, you jumped into the river after me—"

"What was I supposed to do? Throw rocks at you?"

"You could have done one of several things. You could have run up and down the bank in helpless confusion. You could have just stood there hollering for help. You could have gone off looking for a telephone to call the police. You could have hesitated a minute too long before jumping in after me. You could have taken the trouble to remove not only your shoes but also your coat and tie and trousers. But you didn't do any of those things. You just jumped right in after me, and I saw how you kept going under and staying under to look for me. Then when you saw me, and discovered that I was swimming on across, you could have been so disgusted that you might have climbed back out onto the bank and gone away and I would never have seen you again, because I will admit that it was a very silly thing for me to do, a very prankish thing, even a very cruel thing. But you didn't turn back in disgust. You came on after me. You followed me all the way across the river. *Why?*" She stopped and waited for my answer. "Why?" she said again. "Why did you do that?"

I thought about this. Now I was sitting up beside her, no longer reclining, no longer staring up at the sky. My wet clothes were beginning to chill me, although the day was still very warm. I ran my hand across my hair and flung some water from it. I looked at Margaret. The answer to her question disturbed me very much. "My perpetual curiosity, I guess," I said to her, but I knew that was wrong, and I amended it. "No, I guess maybe I really do love you after all. You must have some kind of spell over me. Even if I think you're crazy, even if you exasperate the blue blazes out of me, I think I must somehow be your slave."

She laughed gaily.

"But tell me," I said, "are you sure that was your *only* reason for jumping into the river? Just to test me? You didn't perhaps think there might be a fifty-fifty chance that you would drown after all?"

She said again that she had just been testing me, trying to see what I would do in such a situation, and she was very sorry if her test had offended me. "But if you're going to stay," she said, "I have to know who you really are."

"I didn't say I was going to stay," I corrected her. "I said I *might*. It's a horrible decision to have to make." I wondered if she would continue doing crazy things all her life, and if she knew that she would, and if she had contrived this test just to see if I were prepared to put up with her in the future.

"Will you take me out to dinner," she asked, "and talk to me some more about it?"

"In this?" I said, indicating my drenched and soiled seersucker. "You're all dressed up nice, but unfortunately I didn't think to cache away a box of dry clothes in advance. And they never have found my suitcase yet, even if I had the nerve to go over and get it, looking like this. I'd get arrested for indecent or indecorous exposure or something."

She stood up. "I'll be right back," she said. "What are your sizes?"

"My sizes?"

"Yes, your shoe size and shirt size and trouser size and all?"

"What are you going to do?"

"I'm going to buy you some new clothes. You've worn that seersucker suit too much already anyway."

"What are you going to do for money?" I asked her.

She took out the twenty dollars which had been in her box and said, "I couldn't think of a better use for this money."

"Twenty dollars won't buy much in the way of a complete outfit."

"I'm not going to get you a suit," she said. "Not yet, anyway. Just a shirt and trousers and shoes and socks and"—she giggled—"unmentionables."

"Oh, all right," I said. I took out my billfold. It was soaked, including the bills. I took out three tens. "Here," I said. "Save your own money . . . or your mother's. If you wave these in the air as you walk, maybe they will dry out."

She took the limp bills and said, "Now, your sizes."

I took out my Ring-Master and my ballpoint. The ballpoint worked all right, but the Ring-Master was so wet I was afraid it would disintegrate if I tried to open it, so I put it back into my pocket and wrote my sizes on the underside of Margaret's wrist.

"I will wear your sizes forever," she quipped, holding her inscribed wrist aloft, and then she walked off into the trees and disappeared.

I sat on the bank alone and drew up my knees and hugged myself to fight off the chill. Where was she going to find a men's store this time of day, anyway? My wristwatch wasn't working, but judging from the sky I would say it was close to seven o'clock and the stores would be closed. Maybe I should have asked her to find me a nice commodious barrel somewhere.

Then I thought of my shoes. My shoes! Holy cow, if Margaret bought me some new shoes, they wouldn't be elevator shoes, and if I had to walk beside her, I'd be an inch shorter than she!

I gazed despondently out across the river, tempted for an insane moment to try to swim back over there and get my elevators and bring them back over here. But then I realized I could just as easily walk up to the Rock Island Railroad bridge and cross it. But I might not get back before Margaret did, and what would she do if she found me gone? And furthermore, wouldn't she be curious to know how I had managed to retrieve my shoes, and why I was so determined to get them back?

It was a racking impasse, and I wasted so much time brooding about it that I forgot to brood about why I was in love with Margaret if she was so naughty. When I finally got my mind around to this subject, Margaret was returning.

She had found a small department store still open on Washington Avenue in North Little Rock after only a six-block walk, and she was laden with packages and smiling triumphantly. Her selections surprised me, because they were what I probably would have purchased if I had done the shopping myself. A short-sleeved sport shirt of blue-striped oxford cloth with button-down collar and tapered bottom. Dacron golfer-type slacks of a darker blue, pleatless, and a narrow black belt. A pair of debonair black moccasins which, I noted with some relief, had rather thick heels. Then there were a pair of argyle socks nearly identical to the ones I had, a white cotton T-shirt, and a pair of boxer-type cotton shorts. I remembered why she would have known that I preferred this style to the more common briefs.

I took off my wet clothes and put these new ones on, and she watched me with the pride of a mother seeing her boy dress up in his first Easter clothes. I didn't mind, but impulsively I turned my back while I was donning the shorts.

Dressed neatly and happy again, I wadded up my old clothes and started to toss them into the river, but she stopped me and took them and put them in the hole where her box had been.

Then we walked away from the river. I discovered that I could sort of walk on the balls of my feet, with my heels elevated, and this kept me on a level with her. We reached Washington Avenue and began searching for a taxi.

"Are your legs stiff and sore?" she asked solicitously. "Why do you walk like that?"

But then we found a cab, and got in and sat down.

🌮 TWENTY

One thing I will have to admit: Mexico Chiquita is, for me at least, a finer restaurant than Jake Wirth's, Locke-Ober, Durgin Park, Jimmy's Harbor Side, or any of those other elegant Boston beaneries where I have richly dined with Pamela. I told Margaret, only half jokingly, that if I could cultivate a permanent craving for tortillas, tacos, enchiladas and cherry punch, I would have sufficient reason for staying in Little Rock and taking her to this eating-place once a week forever. Mexico Chiquita, which is in a nondescript building way out in the marshes on the east end of North Little Rock, has no menus; you sit down at one of their rugged oak tables and a Negro girl comes and begins dumping it on you, hot and spicy and filling, until you holler quits, and even after you holler quits they will try to stuff some lime sherbet down you for a chaser. Outside, trucks roar by on their way to St. Louis, and some of the truck drivers stop in and sit at the table next to you, and nobody seems to notice that you are wearing a short-sleeved sport shirt and the fellow on your left is wearing a soiled T-shirt while the gentleman on your right is wearing a dinner jacket. It is a convivial, homogeneous atmosphere, and a nice place to talk. We gorged ourselves, and had refills on cherry punch, and did an impressive lot of talking. But afterward, even though the satiety of Latin dishes imposed a contented truce on our verbal contest, we were no better off than before, no nearer any conclusions.

Unable to make any definite decision, I could only tell her that I would have to think about it some more, and I would have to think about it alone. This was honorable of me, and I am proud that I could be that way about it. I think that it would have been an easy matter for me to have pretended that I was going to stay, just so I could get into bed with her a few times and find out what she was really like, and then to skip on out. As it was, I couldn't get into bed with her until my mind was settled. Even if I could, she wouldn't let me. This is the boat I was in. She was helping me row it, but she couldn't guide it. That was all up to me.

Give me twenty-four hours, I said. To reach such a verdict, to satisfy myself that I could eventually cure my wanderlust and settle down, to make such a decision that would affect the course of the rest of my life, I would need twenty-four hours of solid solitary concentration. I glanced at the clock. It was 9:30 P.M., Thursday. By 9:30 P.M. Friday I would bring her my final word.

Where are you going to stay in the meantime? I asked her. Naps's house? She shook her head. You're not going back home, are you? I asked her uneasily. Again she shook her head, and then she told me that she was going to continue staying at Dall's house. The place was a mess, and the least she could do for him, she said, would be to tidy it up a little, and a day of hard housecleaning would be good for her.

We left Mexico Chiquita and found another taxi, which took us back to Little Rock. She asked me if I knew whether or not Dall had any tools like hacksaws or hacksaw blades. I said I thought he probably did, but why was she asking. Stay with me just a little longer, she said.

The taxi took us to Dall's house, and we searched in his toolshed until we found a hacksaw. Bowzer still had not returned home. I gave him up for permanently lost, strayed, stolen, or put to death. A fine dog, I told Margaret; it is too bad she never met him. A beautiful German shepherd. Now, I said, what are you going to do with this hacksaw? Commit hara-kiri?

She said she had to get her clothes out of her mother's house, and would I please help her. Her mother had padlocked the door of her room, and she wanted to wait until her mother and stepfather had gone to bed and then sneak up and saw off the lock and get her clothes out.

"Now wait just a minute," I protested. "You remember the first time we tried to sneak up there she caught us. And then when Naps tried to sneak up there to rescue you she caught him too. So if you think I'm going to—"

"*Please*," she said, gripping my arm. "We have to try, at least."

Reluctantly I gave in, and we walked to her mother's house. It was near midnight now and the house was dark and, Margaret assured me in a whisper, they would be sound asleep. With extreme caution we tiptoed up the back stairway, making not the slightest sound this time, and I marveled at how skillful Margaret was at this technique—how many times, I wondered, had she sneaked out of the house at night to rendezvous with Slater? We felt our way through the attic without stumbling over all the junk, and found the door of her room and the padlock. I began to pass the hacksaw blade lightly over the lock, but even the slightest of my motions made an awful raspy noise; it reminded me of the startling sound my pants zipper had made the night before. Margaret whispered that the sound would not carry as far down as her mother's bedroom, but I was skeptical. I tried to saw gently, but gentle sawing didn't do much good. Margaret found an old blanket with which we managed to muffle the sound somewhat, and I stood there at that door for half an hour, unbreathing, sweating profusely, sawing away. Margaret listened for any noises from the house. I felt the lock with my fingers; I was making progress. In a rush of excitement to hack the remaining sinew of steel, I sawed too hard, made too much noise. The attic light went on, and Mr. Polk came rapidly up the stairs. We had no time to hide, and could only face him sheepishly. "Why, 'lo, Margaret," he said, confronting us in his nightshirt. "What're you doin?" She said, "We came to get my clothes, but the door is locked." "Oh?" he said, and he was silent for a long moment, then he said "Hold on" and went back downstairs. I urged Margaret, "Come on, let's get out of here." "No, wait," she said and put her hand on my arm. "Look," I said, "I feel the same way about your mother that you do: I don't ever want to see her again. Let's beat it," and I began to head down the stairs. But Mr. Polk came back up the stairs, holding a key in his hand. "Here y'are," he said, and brushed past me and handed the key to Margaret and she unlocked the door to her room. Quickly she stuffed all of her clothes and a few miscellaneous belongings into three cardboard boxes, and Mr. Polk helped us carry these downstairs and out of the house. She gave him a kiss on the jowl. "Thank you," she said with profound sincerity. He said, "Come see us sometime," and waved as we walked away.

I carried two of the boxes, and Margaret carried the other, and we took them to Dall's house. She thanked me and kissed me and then she asked, "How are you going to spend this next day? Are you going to lie on your bed and stare at the ceiling and meditate? Or are you going to go out and walk through these streets in search of some grace?"

"Nothing so idealistic as that," I said. "I have to be practical. I'm going to look for a job."

TWENTY-ONE

Again dusk is falling, the fiery day-star has slumped into those pine forests west of town as though that cacodemon Slater, lurking still at large somewhere out there in those woods, is sucking the sun down out of the sky and casting a pall of twilight over the town and over this cemetery in which I am sitting. What am I doing here in this cemetery? Well, I am not deceased yet, of course, but mainly this seems to be a convenient place to sit and sip from my half-pint bottle in semi-seclusion. I have bought this bottle because I am tired and a little sad, and that seems reason enough. I am not going to get drunk, I am simply trying to relax. Mt. Holly is not any mountain, hardly even a knoll, and it has been swallowed up completely by the city: Broadway traffic raises hell a stone's throw away, houses are aligned along Eleventh and Twelfth streets, the new dormitories of the Negro Philander Smith College are visible across Arch Street, but if anybody is watching me I don't know it. In an open little bell house I am sitting, an old gingerbread Gothic relic of white wood and a cypress-shingled roof; the view of the cemetery is good from here: all around me the swarthy granite pillars, the white marble crosses, the quaint cenotaphs, the proud mausoleums jut up out of the ground in a cluttered, eclectic congregation of memoria. Here reposeth the remains of ten state governors, three United States senators, five Confederate generals, twenty mayors of Little Rock, and one Pulitzer Prize poet, among others, but this impressive assortment of engraved names is not particularly interesting to me at this moment. I did not stop here to be among the famous native dead, but because, as I say, this is a nice cool place to sit down and rest my sore feet and take a nip or two from this half-pint bottle. I didn't find a job.

Naps loaned me a suit, a fine blue tropical worsted which really made me look like some suave executive, and he drove me down to the Rock, where, luckily, I recovered my elevator shoes. And that's not all he did. He offered to give me a job if nobody else would. He said that if I had any talent for selling books, or for keeping an eye on the stock market, he could guarantee me a minimum of seven thousand dollars per annum. That was very nice of him. I am thinking about it. I am sitting here in this cemetery resting and thinking. But I know next to nothing about the stock market, and I'm afraid that my efforts at book selling, especially religious-book selling, would only disappoint his confidence in his friend. Still I am thinking about it. It's good, it's comforting, to have that dernier ressort, that last card up my sleeve.

This morning I went out to Little Rock University and had a talk with a fellow in the History Department. Too late, he said. Should've contacted them earlier, three or four months earlier, when they were looking for a man to handle American History. Still, if I would send them my vitae, my résumé, perhaps next year . . . I hate those words, vitae, résumé, and I hope I never have to have one. Later this morning I went to the School Board office and sat for an hour, to be ultimately told that without Education courses my background was inadequate. Then I went to the Arkansas History Commission and listened to a sad story about how low their budget is. Then I went to the Arkansas Gazette offices and uncomfortably laid bare my plight to a sympathetic editor who told me I was too old to begin at the bottom as a sixty-dollar-a-week office flunky. Finally, after filling out futile application forms at an insurance company, an advertising agency, and the Parks & Recreation Department (which controls the museums), I wound up in a lowly line at the State Employment Office, where they gave me a typing test and a mechanical aptitude test, and then a personnel officer, a kid of twenty or so who was impressed with my background and boasted that an uncle of his had also been to Yale, gave me the final word: "Gee, Mr. Stone, I just don't know what we could do with somebody like you."

Now I am in this cemetery. My feet ache, my head aches, my pride is wounded, I think I have made an ass of myself, and, oddly enough, I even feel a strange resentment toward Margaret, as if she suckered me into this ridiculous quest, as if the last trick she could play on me would be to send me out on such a silly job-hunt and make me the laughingstock of every sadistic personnel director in town. This bourbon helps, but also it reminds me of the last time I was required to resort to it, in shock against that girl, and I decide: Really, I am no less lost than before. No more near discovering myself. This cemetery helps; although it is surrounded by the city, it has a certain placeless tranquillity, a universality that removes me for the moment from any definite *time or space. Here in this grove of stone shafts I will dispassionately evaluate the route of my tomorrows.*

In the taupe light of this gloaming the clustered flowers of tall black locust trees are a vault of pale stars gently swaying. Out of one of these trees come two sparrows, and I am so motionless that they alight on the ground near my feet and begin procreative maneuvers: face to face they smite each other with their wings, they rake their wings together, they thrust their beaks into each other's mouths, they join their bottoms together in a frantic dance. In the dim light they merge into one fluffy feathered mass fluttering constantly in a frank fervent twitter which is a graphic symbolic orgasm, a figurative fuck. They are so near me I can swing out my foot and kick them ... if I wanted to. A long time they keep at it, and then, sated, they return to the black locust tree. I take another pull at my bottle. Sex is everywhere, I muse. They have reminded me of one of the reasons why I came to Arkansas, a reason not any more fulfilled than any of my other reasons: I was going to relieve the hunger in my groin, I was going to have myself a little commerce or two. Maybe I could become a rapist. Do I have what it takes? In dark alleys and back yards and upstairs hallways I will exact final retribution from this city.

Time passes. Another swig at the half-pint: I am not going to get drunk, I am simply trying to relax. Maybe there is some answer. I might, if I could borrow the capital, open a good first-rate antique shop somewhere around town and build it into a thriving business. Or I might persuade a group of affluent Arkansas citizens to establish a Museum for the Preservation of Southern Antiquities and get myself appointed curator. Or I might apply to some national philanthropic foundation for a research grant large enough to support me and Margaret while I finish my VAP book, and once my reputation is established the world will beat a path to my door. Little Rock is as good a place as any, I suppose, for writing a book, or books, on the Vanished American Past. Or maybe I could run up to Petit Jean Mountain and have a chat with Winthrop Rockefeller and convince him that he could find some good use for a man of my ... of my what?

Now in the dull dusk I perceive a dog approaching, trotting with a bouncing wolflike lope, his head low and his tail flailing the air behind him. It occurs to me that he is coming up through the graveyard by the same path I had followed, and that perhaps he is on my scent. Probably he wants to use my knee as a surro-

gate bitch, and I must be prepared to fend him off. Laying my bottle aside, I pick up a rock and cock my arm. Nearer he comes with that jaunty lope, and then he stops and sees me, woofs once, and bounds toward me. I fling the rock; it whizzes cleanly between his tall ears and grazes his tail; a bad aim: I stand and he rises and clutches me, but he does not begin to misuse my knee. He woofs and thrashes his tail and holds me in a tight but civilized embrace. Old Bowzer, I cry aloud. Good old Bowzer. Sit down, fellow, and tell me what you've been up to.

We sit on the grass side by side and I nuzzle and coddle him, as of old. Lost all these days, he rejoices beneath my friendly familiar hand. Obviously Slater didn't harm him after all; probably he just wandered away from home because his master would not return. How far is Dall's house from here? Nine or ten blocks, at least. A long way to wander. He looks up at me with an adoring expression on his face. We sit content. I offer him a slug of my bourbon, but he declines, shaking his head. I drink his drink for him.

I bring him up to date, telling him what has been happening, how his master was hospitalized but is all right now and might come home again in another week or so, and how his master's house is now occupied by Margaret, and so on and so forth. Bowzer is a good listener, better than a lot of bartenders.

"So now," I tell him, "I have paused here at Mt. Holly, as evening cometh, to find myself, for my time runneth out."

"I see," he says understandingly. "You have only another hour or two to make up your mind, but you can't make up your mind until you know who you are, is that it?"

"Precisely," I reply. "And that is a large order, a big question."

"Actually, we are not anything much at all," he observes philosophically, "that is, what we were is more important than what we are, because all of the present is so firmly anchored in the past."

"Indeed," I agree. "So then the question is: Who was I?

"You were an Ozark backwoods boy in the summertime . . ." he coaches.

"Yes. Yes I was, in fact. I'll admit that. Not so Ozarky, nor so backwoodsy as your master, though, even if for a long time I could talk just as hillbilly as Dall or anybody else and I wore a straw hat and fished with a bent pin and all like that. And my girl friend was a feisty barefoot gal in a floursack dress and her name was Bertha Jo and she was as plain as a black-eyed Susan.

Lord, how long ago that was! I can't even think of it as me, I mean I—"

"It was *you*," he avers. "But also you were a town boy who worked on weekends as a caddy at the golf course and you ran around with a little colored boy named Naps and you were a sort of white nigger."

"Right. And I remember once when Bob Hope came to Little Rock, and he played out at the golf course, and although I didn't get to caddy for him, I cornered him before he left and asked for his autograph and he took out his pen and poised it but I didn't have anything for him to write it on, so I offered him the back of my shirt collar—I've still got that shirt collar somewhere, and it says 'To Nub Stone with the warmest best wishes of Bob Hope' —and after he wrote it for me he put his hand on my shoulder and said, 'Son, what do you want to be when you grow up?' and I answered, 'Bob Hope.' But I didn't, did I?"

"No, you didn't," Bowzer says. "You missed it by a mile. One reason was that you became a pugilist and took up running around with my master."

"Yes. Maybe one or the other, the pugilism or Dall, deadened my wit. But by then I didn't want to be Bob Hope anyway. I wanted to be Sandy Saddler, who was the toughest of them all, who won the crown from Willie Pep at Yankee Stadium in a fight so rough that both of them got suspended for violating the rules. That was me. I wanted to violate rules. And another featherweight I admired, more than Saddler eventually, was Davey Moore, and something he said once upon a time still echoes in my sad old head: 'Call me a come-in fighter. Call me a counterpuncher. Call me anything you want. You really want to know what I am? I'm a street fighter, man, the best you ever saw.'"

"And that, too, was you," says Bowzer, "but not any more."

"Not any more," I admit. "Although once there was a time when I could lick any guy on the street. Personally, just between me and you, I can still lick any guy on the street. But I don't. Why?"

"Because you know it doesn't accomplish anything," he rationalizes. "You had to go off to Yale and learn something useful. So you did."

"I did, and then I became a scholar, a Boston pedant, and I didn't like that at all, so now I have come back to Little Rock because maybe I would like to be a street fighter again."

"You can't earn a living that way," he counsels.

"You take me too literally," I protest. "What I mean is that I want to get involved in something, I want to fight again, if only to fight against the evils and corruptions of this world."

"Have you thought of evangelism?" he jests. "There's always room for another Billy Graham."

"The evils and corruptions to which I refer are not so much moral as social. I refer to the sinister forces which have corrupted our society and caused the lovely American Past to Vanish."

"Perhaps," he insinuatingly suggests, "you only want to re-create that lost past so that you can live in it."

"Smart dog."

"Probably what you need to do," he tells me, "is to build that wilderness log castle you keep dreaming about, and live that rustic life. Walden Three."

"You're a very keen-witted animal," I compliment him. "If I build my log castle, will you come and live with me and be my dog?"

"Thanks," he says, "but I'm already committed to Dall. Sorry."

"Well, I wonder if Margaret would come live with me in my log castle."

"If you build it in Little Rock, she might," he says. "But who ever heard of a log castle in Little Rock?"

"Alas. You know, I wonder, if she were a dog, would you consider her a fine bitch? I mean, seriously, would you be attracted to her, caninely speaking?"

"Unquestionably," he says.

"What kind of dog would she be? That is, what breed?"

"An Irish water spaniel, man, the best you ever saw."

"Ah. And I—?"

"A Boston terrier," he says, with a tinge of disparagement in his voice.

"So," I sigh resignedly and dispatch the remainder of the half-pint. "Do you see the quandary I'm in? Do you see what an imbroglio I've got myself into?"

"It shouldn't happen to a dog," he consoles me.

Dark now has set in, the black-locust blossoms are no longer visible, the cars on Broadway are wearing their headlights. I could sit here all night in this cemetery and be no better off. If these souls laid to rest here could rise up by the light of the moon and take a look at this new city and tell me how it seems to them in contrast to the old, that might help. But I don't believe in ghosts, and Bowzer is restless, he is pacing back and forth. I will take him home.

Now through the night streets we go toward Dall's house, where she is waiting for my answer. Bowzer lopes jauntily, eagerly at my side, matching my swift stride; he knows we are going home. Now down little worlds of old sidewalks we go, across a vast and endless firmament of concrete, of cracks and humps familiar as home to any wagoning child, of dips and swells in little worlds a universe in themselves, of, under the street lamps, the circular signs stamped into the cement: GRADY GARMS, *old Mr. Grady Garms the god who has created this cosmos of sidewalks and curbs and steps, this small world changing subtly from block to block, past house and house, past hedges all of a different kind, clipped privet and unclipped privet, barberries and cotoneasters snuggled into by children and cats in search of a small natural house or hiding place, and the profuse honeysuckle and forsythia, and the buckthorn and quince, which now in the evening dapple these cement promenades with wild shadows; and past the walls, low smooth brick walls, ashlar walls and flat stone walls which children walk atop to take the high road above the sidewalk; and all those lawns, and those ladies, and those lavender shadows. I would like to linger longer and look for those redeeming microcosms that Margaret spoke of, but I have promises to keep and miles to go before I sleep. Besides, I have walked down these streets a thousand times before. I don't think I will again.*

3

BRIDGE BURNING

Julia and I did lately sit
Playing for sport, at Cherry-Pit:
She threw; I cast; and having thrown,
She got the Pit, and I the Stone.

—ROBERT HERRICK

ONE

"**Y**our grandmother called," Margaret said. "She thought you might be here. She said she wanted to tell you that the Missouri Pacific people called and said they've found your suitcase."

Ah. "Timely," I mumbled, "timely."

"What? Oh. Then you mean you are—?"

"Yes." I said. "Yes I am."

"Then I shouldn't have mentioned it," she said ruefully. "I shouldn't have told you they found it."

"Doesn't matter," I said. "That's the *causa finalis*, but I'd already made up my mind."

She took both my hands in both of hers and said, "I'm sorry."

"That's the way the cookie crumbles," I stoicized with a stiff upper lip, "that's the way the ball bounces, or the Stone rolls."

"I'm sorry for you," she said.

"No," I responded. "I am sorry for *you*."

"Don't be," she said. "It's you, in the long run, who will be unhappy."

"You think so?" I said.

"Yes," she said. "You'll have to keep going out into the world,

)299(

moving from place to place, trying to find yourself, until finally you'll come back here again and again. As the saying goes, 'a man travels the world over in search of what he needs, and returns home to find it.'"

"Well, that's a matter of opinion," I allowed, "and if I really believed it, if I really *could* believe it, I'd stay, but I'm passionately convinced, you see, that this town, for all its niceties, is, by and large, a goddamn—"

"Don't say it," she said. "Let me believe what I want to believe, and let's not spoil it with more bickering."

"All right. But are you absolutely certain you won't reconsider? Because if there is any chance—"

"I'm absolutely certain, Clifford," she said. "There's not even any doubt any more, not even any misgivings. But why don't you go and talk with Doyle about it? Perhaps he could persuade you to stay."

"No, my mind is made up. There just isn't any place for me here."

"Well, go talk to him anyway. He's beginning to wonder what happened to you."

"How do *you* feel about Dall?" I asked her.

"What do you mean?"

"I mean how do you feel toward him? What do your emotions register when you think of him?"

She smiled. "He's my favorite brother."

I smiled. "So if I am a father figure to you, that would make Dall my stepson?"

"No, because he's your brother too."

"Then he would be your uncle, not your brother."

"But actually you are my brother too."

"So that would make me my own son, and Dall's nephew and—"

"Oh," she protested, "you're confusing me. Let's just all be friends, and let it go at that."

"When I leave," I asked her, "what are you going to do?"

"Don't worry about me," she said.

"Where are you going to stay? Where are you going to sleep at night?"

"Oh, just anywhere I can find an empty bed. Here. Naps's house. Any place where they will have me."

"You're going to stay here when Dall gets out of the hospital?"

"Yes. Somebody has to take care of him until he's recovered, and then somebody has to be his housekeeper, because he wants to get his two sons back home again. I've been a housekeeper for my mother ever since my father died. I'd much rather keep house for Dall—or anybody—than for my mother."

"Why don't you just marry him?"

She laughed nervously. "Well," she said, "the first time I ever came over here, and saw what a mess the house was in, I said to him, 'Dall, you ought to get married again,' but he got all red in the face and said, 'Aw hellfire naw!' and he said he'd had enough experience with women, after that Rowena girl, that he was just going to be a bachelor for the rest of his life. But I don't suppose he'd mind if I became his housekeeper, in return for room and board."

"Dreary prospect," I mumbled.

"Not at all," she said. "He's a very interesting person to be with."

"Which reminds me. I guess I'd better go visit with him for a while."

I opened the back door and whistled, and Bowzer trotted up onto the back porch and came into the house. I made the introductions, and Margaret, having never had a dog of her own before, was timid and unconfident: she patted him lightly on the head. For his part, he leaned his massive flank against her legs and almost bowled her over. I bade him sit, and then I explained to Margaret that it would be wise to keep him in the house for a while, until Dall came home again or until Bowzer had become more accustomed to the place. Then I went to the icebox to get the poor dog a bone, but the icebox was bare of the bones I had left there; I asked Margaret about them, and she said she had mistaken them for soup bones and had made a soup out of them. We gave him a can of Ken-L Ration and closed up the house. I took note, in leaving, of how nicely she had swept and dusted and mopped and waxed the place; she had rearranged the furniture and put up some new curtains in the living room, and the house, homely and squalid as it was, was beginning to bear her own stamp.

I started walking in the direction of the bus stop, but she stopped me and said that we could go in Dall's old car. He had given her the keys. I offered to drive, but she said she had to get as much practice as she could. Obviously, I reflected, as we got into the car, she was bent on devoting herself for a while to Dall, that coarse but kindly police sergeant who had helped her out of her doldrums and changed the course of her life. I suggested to her, half jokingly and teasingly, that since the doctors said some plastic surgery would be required for Dall's battered face, she ought to give them an old photograph of her father and ask them to "copy" it, and then Dall could become a perfect father figure for her. I said I suspected that Dall, wrapped in all those bandages, might seem to her to be, not simply the reincarnation of her lost father, but her father himself rising, Lazarus-like, from the dead. She laughed, but again nervously, because she knew that what is spoken in jest is often close to the truth. I told her that she couldn't see Dall's face because of all the bandages, and she didn't remember how ugly he was, and as far as she was concerned it could be anybody beneath those layers of gauze and adhesive tape, anybody, particularly her lost father. "Oh, stop it!" she protested.

I lay my head back against the car seat and folded my hands over my chest. It had begun to rain. Margaret fumbled for the windshield-wiper switch, and turned it on, and that rain, like any Southern rain when it finally comes, came in great sheets of noisy splatters. There now, she said; there goes your drought. The headlights could scarcely penetrate it, it was so heavy; we had to slow down.

"Why else," I asked her, "would you be the least bit interested in Dall, unless he is a father figure for you?"

"Would I need anything else?" she replied candidly. "Wouldn't that be reason enough?"

"Yes, I guess it would," I had to admit. "Probably that was what attracted you to Slater as well, because Slater was even old enough to be your father. But you couldn't get him, at least not unless his wife died or was disposed of, so you had to give him up. So then you considered me, but I was too small to be your father; you couldn't have a father who is shorter than you."

"Are you shorter than I?" she asked innocently. "I wasn't aware of that."

"Sure," I said. "A good inch shorter. I might as well tell you, since it doesn't matter any more, that I wear elevator shoes."

"I don't care. I still love you."

That pierced me down deep, and I could say nothing, there was nothing else for me to say. Margaret was a good driver—better, probably, than I would have been. I watched the rain splash against the windshield, I looked at the trees along the street swaying, pitching in the watery wind, and I listened to the sound of the cascade of raindrops on the metal roof of the car, and the sound of the busy windshield wipers speaking to me: you *big* chump you *big* chump you *big* chump . . .

"Margaret," I said finally, "it's silly of us to disagree over something so irrelevant as whether we go or stay—"

"Is it?" she said. "Then why don't you stay?"

"I can't. Why don't you go?"

"I can't."

"Why not?"

"Why can't you stay?"

"We already discussed it," I said. And we had. Could anything else be said?

It could, and she said it: "The difference is that you will keep coming back—I'm sure of it—but I won't ever have to go."

TWO

"Why, hi there, Nub old buddy!" he said, raising his head a little off the pillow.

"Hello, Lazarus," I said.

"How you been doin?" he said. "Aint seen you for a little spell."

"Just fine, just fine. How're you getting along? They feeding you well enough to suit you?"

"Aw, I caint complain. Them nurses is kind of uppity, but they aint put nuthin over on me yet."

"Nice flowers you got," I observed, scanning the arboretum that surrounded his bed.

"Aint they, now?" he said. "Them gladiolies yonder there was sent to me by the boys down at the station house . . . and these here chrysanthemumses come from your Grammaw Stone . . . and I got that there potted lily from Naps—you should a seen the way them nurses was carryin on and carryin on when he brung it in, cause lilies is supposed to be only for when you're dead . . . and them poinsettias come from the florist with a little card said 'Remorsefully, J.R. Slater,' wasn't that nice of him? . . . and them hyacinths is from the Ladies' Auxiliary of the police officers . . . and them red roses is from Margaret . . . and that there bunch of yellow roses of course come from my old buddy Nub Stone and I thank you very much."

I smiled to say that he was very welcome.

He turned his head to the window. "Hey, look at that toadstranglin rain pour down, will you! I'm sure glad I aint out on a night like this. You get very wet comin in?"

"Not very. It's really a hard rain, though."

"It really is," he agreed. A moment of silence ensued, and then he said idly, weakly, "Yes sir, it is. It's sure a real pour-down."

Another silence came and hung over the room like a pall of formaldehyde, and I struggled mightily to think of something to say. Now that our adventures were at an end, had we lost the need for talk?

After a while he asked, "How's my dog?"

"Just fine. Eats like a horse. Misses you something awful, though. Moans and whines for his master to come home."

"Aw . . . that old dog . . . that old fleabag . . ." he said, but then he ran out of words, and it was up to me, after another long silence, to say something.

"How're your injuries and all? Coming along nicely?"

"Pretty good. They're going to take some of the catgut out of the stitches tomorrow, so I reckon they'll leave off some of these overgrown Band-Aids and I might get a look to see if I can still recognize myself."

I made a friendly little laugh, but I couldn't think of anything more to say.

Eventually he said, "What all you been doin lately?"

"Thinking," I said.

"Yeah? What about?"

"Oh, I've just been trying to make up my mind whether to go back to Boston or not."

"That right? Well, have you decided on anything?"

"Yes."

He waited, then he said, "Well, do you aim to tell me, or do I have to get out of this bed and wring it out of you?"

I laughed. "Dall, I'm going back, I guess."

"Naw!" he said. "You caint, you just *caint!*"

"I'm sorry, Dall, but I have to. Vacation's over."

"When you goin?"

"Soon. Tomorrow or the next day."

"Listen, Nub," he said, "I got a idee. If you could just wait till I get out of this hospital, I'll help you, and me and you will rig up one of them big packin crates like they ship tigers in, and then we'll sneak up behind old Marge and grab her and put her in it and ship her off up to Boston on the same train with you. Okay?"

Again I laughed, but I shook my head. "No, we'd better not do that. I wouldn't have any use for an angry tiger."

"Aw, I bet she'd be just tickled pink."

"No, Dall. For better or for worse she is absolutely determined to remain in Little Rock."

He tried to scowl but the bandages dampened the job and the best he could manage was a fierce, penetrating glare of his green lynx eyes. "Don't you want her?" he demanded in such an incredulous voice that my negative answer would seem not just unbelievable but entirely stupid. "Here you've been goin to all this trouble to smooth the way for you and her, and now that you've got her free and clear, you skip on out."

"Speaking of all this trouble," I inquired, "what's the latest word on Slater? Have they found him yet?"

"Naw, but you aint got nuthin to worry about, far as he's concerned, if that's what's botherin you."

"That isn't what's bothering me," I said.

"Well, what *is*, then, for godsakes?"

At a loss for a more suitable explanation, I could only offer a cliché: "Little Rock is a nice place to visit, but I wouldn't want to live here."

"But what about Margaret?" he asked.

"She wants to be your housekeeper. Didn't she tell you?"

"Aw, hell yes, but she don't know what she wants. If she came to stay at my place, she wouldn't last two weeks. I'd be droppin my pipe ashes and stuff slab dab in the middle of the rug, and she wouldn't like that none atall. And she'd have to take care of them little boys of mine whenever I get em back, and, by God, I'm tellin you, them is the nastiest little fellers this side of Polecat Creek, if I do have to say so myself. Caint you just see us settin down with her at the supper table, and me and them boys both a-burpin and a-belchin fit to kill ever other bite or two and sloppin gravy on the tablecloth and eatin peas with a knife and God knows what? And me—I never shave on my day off or any time I'm on any kind of vacation, and I look bad enough even when I do shave. Ye gods! First time she catches me settin in the kitchen cleanin my toenails with a dinner fork she's gonna turn on her heel and light out for home. And snore! Why, I've had neighbors call me up in the middle of the night of a time and ast me to please feed my dog or sump'm to get im to quit growlin, and that wouldn't a been so bad only I never had no dog up until I got Bowzer. But worst of all sometimes I feel like scratchin, and by dang when I feel like scratchin I'm sure enough gonna *scratch*, and they aint nobody gonna tell me—"

"But your heart is pure," I interrupted his outrageous parody of himself. "Your heart is good and benign, and you will be like a father to her."

"I don't want to be her goddamn father!" he raged.

"Look at the economic side of it," I said. "Obviously, when you get out of the hospital, you aren't going to be able to do anything for a week or two, and you'd have to hire a nurse to keep you in bed and bring you your pills and all, and you could have Margaret as a nurse and housekeeper both and it wouldn't cost you a cent except for groceries and what you'd have to pay to buy her some fine new clothes ever now and then."

"It wouldn't look right to the neighbors," he protested. "I mean, her being so young and pretty, she just don't look like no goddamn nurse nor housekeeper."

"Did you think of the neighbors when she lived with you for a week that other time?"

"Well, no, but that was different. It was *me* helpin *her*, not her helpin me."

"But now she wants to repay you for all you've done for her."

"I was just doin my duty. She don't owe me a damn thing."

"But she still needs you. What she really needs, of course, is a father, but if you can't be a father to her, then you can be a brother. She never had a brother, but she always wanted one, and she told me tonight that you were her favorite brother."

"Aw, gee," he said, touched in spite of himself.

"Just be nice to her, and provide a willing ear for her to talk to, and sometimes a shoulder for her to cry on, and you'll get along just fine. If you can afford it, take her to dinner sometimes at the Embers or Bruno's Little Italy or Shakey's or the Lamplighter. She's never been to any of those places. And take her out to ride the Ferris wheel at War Memorial Park, and take her for long walks at night down all the streets." In a counseling mood, I continued, "And it might help if you could be a gentleman, and maybe watch your language, and also attempt to use honest grammar and diction more often."

He scowled. "You don't like the way I talk?"

"I love the way you talk," I said. "It's like a creek rippling across rocks, like crawdads scurrying for shelter, like whippoorwills and crickets out in the dark night, like coon hounds baying on a distant mountainside, like chiggers chomping into flesh . . . But it's not true, not really natural, and you may think you have fooled me into thinking it is, but I know that you really know that you're not fooling me."

"Aw, get out," he said, but it was an objection, not a command.

"Come on," I urged him. "Let's hear you say something properly."

"I'll make you a deal," he said. "You stay in Little Rock, and I'll come over every day and say all the proper sentences you'd ever want to hear."

"Thou almost persuadeth me," I said. "But even that would not be sufficient reason to get me to remain in this godawful town."

"Nub," he said, "me and you used to have such good times together. Why don't you stay here, and it'll be like old times again."

"Old times never come back," I said mournfully. "That's one lesson I've learned recently, and the sooner I get out of this town the better off I'm going to be."

"Then this is good-bye?"

"Oh, I'll come back and see you again before I go. But Margaret's waiting downstairs to see you, and I guess we've been keeping her waiting long enough."

"Nub, even if I don't see you again—"

"You'll see me again. I'll come back tomorrow."

"—even if you don't, I just wanted to say thanks for everything."

"Thanks? Why?"

"Helpin us out and all, I mean. If you hadn't come along when you did, and done what you did, no tellin what might've happened."

"Dall," I said sadly, "everything I've ever done in my whole life has been done out of a selfish motive, and nobody owes me any thanks for anything. I was just a friendly, willing pawn."

"Well, then, thanks for being a friendly, willing pawn."

"You've done a lot for me too," I said. So now, having said it, I could go. I took a step away from his bed, but then I stopped, turned back, stared at him a long moment and said, "There's just one more thing. I suppose it really doesn't matter any more, but just out of curiosity—you know what an incorrigible busybody I've always been. Well, I was just wondering if you might know what sort of relationship there really was between Slater and Margaret. I mean, what was *really* going on? Did she ever tell you? She claims that she's a virgin, but I got the idea from you that he must have done *something* to her, and I was just wondering if you knew what it was."

He was silent a moment, and then he spoke very quietly. "I thought you'd done guessed it on your own," he said. "You remember one of the things she wrote on that wall: 'Slater, put your money where your mouth is.' He wasn't no more potent than that there gelding horse of his. Ever now and then he'd just lick her off, that's all. Poor bastard, I reckon it was the only way a screwed-up sonofabitch like him could get any kicks, any fun."

"But she didn't . . . she didn't—" I couldn't say it.

"No," he said. "She never did."

🐟 THREE

Across the municipal golf course fairways and through the woods of War Memorial Park in the darkness and the staggering rain I ambled, all the way to Twelfth Street before I decided that I couldn't go on getting myself and Naps's suit so wet, so at Twelfth Street I stopped and stood under a large hickory tree whose heavy branches partially sheltered me. A few taxis eventually passed, and I hailed them, but they wouldn't stop, probably because I was a sorry spectacle, standing rain-drenched under a tree on a barren stretch of West Twelfth. I took a five-dollar bill out of my wallet and waved it in the air as the next cab came along, and this fellow spotted the lure and screeched to a stop. I got in and rested. "Where to?" he asked.

Margaret had stopped me as I was passing out through the lobby of St. Vincent's and had asked me to wait for her while she talked with Dall. Why? I had asked her, and she had said that she would give me a ride home or anywhere but she would like it if she and I could go somewhere and talk some more; there were still many things to talk about, she had said, before I could consider my Little Rock visit completed. But I had declined—out of weariness, of lingering shock, of vicarious disgust, I don't know, I only know that I had had at that moment an irresistible urge to get out of that hospital, so I had told her I would see her again tomorrow but for the time being I wanted to go my own way. She had released my arm, looked at me for a long moment with a searing gaze both quizzical and wistful of those gray-green eyes of hers, and then she had let me go. Out into the rain I had plunged, asking myself: What kind of squeamish puritan are you, anyway?

"Where to, buddy, huh?" the cab driver said again, glancing at me over his shoulder with a suspicious and contemptuous stare. I gave him Naps's address: 3700 Ringo. Why am I going there? I wondered. Just to return his suit? For solace, sympathy? Do I always—have I always wanted to seek out Naps in moments of distress or anguish? Or is it just his bottle of Jack Daniels that I am seeking? The old white landowner of the South, the master, ole massa, did he, beset with inextricable problems economic or domestic—a failing crop, a nagging wife—seek out a favorite, trusted slave and confide in him and share a bottle of Southern Comfort with him and receive reassurance from him? Nub and Naps, a perfect pair.

When we turned finally into the last dirt-road stretch of the southern part of Ringo Street, the cab driver, seeing the dilapidated slums, called annoyedly over his shoulder, "Hey, you sure you know where you're goin?"

"Quite sure," I said. "Just shut up and drive." I hate cab drivers, as a rule.

"Listen," he said, suddenly slowing the car and turning to glower at me, "you caint talk to *me* like that, I don't care who you are."

"You're the driver, I'm the fare," I said menacingly. "I tell you to go somewhere, you go there, hear?"

He stopped the car completely. "Hey, how would you like to just get out and walk?" he challenged me.

"How would you like a poke in the mush?" I retorted.

"You and who else, Shorty?" he platituded.

"Me, myself, and I," I trited.

"Ganging up on me, eh? Hawr! hawr!" he said mock-jovially, and then he opened his door and stepped out, and he opened my door and said to me in a very cold voice, "Get out."

I got out. He wasn't much taller than I, albeit a good bit stockier. About thirty I would say, and a veteran of numerous altercations. We were near a lone street lamp, whose light gave an ominous, sinister quality to his scowling face. I wondered if I had arrived at my Waterloo, and, thinking of Waterloo, I remembered that the suit I was wearing belonged to Napoleon Howard. I removed the coat, folded it neatly and placed it on the rear seat of the cab, out of the rain. Then I said to my adversary, mock-prissily, "My dear fellow, I suppose you know that if we engage in fisticuffs, you will lose not only the fare but the tip as well."

"You can take the goddamn fare and tip and—" and he suggested a coarse way of disposing of them. Then he swung at me. He swung again. And again, harder. It must be awfully frustrating to swing constantly at a target which is never motionless long enough to be hit.

Then I swung. *Oof!* he uttered spontaneously as his gut caved in. All my grudges against the nasty playwright I would vent on this stupid cabbie. "Take that, Slater, you bastard!" I spat at him and threw another one at him, on the jaw. "That's for Dall!" I let him know. Then I slugged him in the stomach again. "And that's for me!" I said. He was beginning to crumple, but I had time for one more shot, a real beauty right between the eyes. "And *that*," I said as he fell face forward unconscious into the mud, "was for Margaret."

I picked him up out of the mud and placed him on the front seat of his cab, but he rolled off onto the floor. I left him there, and, after replacing my coat, I continued down Ringo Street on foot. Maybe some local colored citizens would find him and rob him and roll him into the gutter.

Tatrice answered the door. "Heavens, Nub, get yourself in out of that rain!" She led me into the living room and told me to make myself a big drink while she ran upstairs to fetch me some dry clothes to put on.

"Where's Naps?" I asked.

"He's out at Slater's place with his friend Feemy," she said.

I helped myself to the Jack Daniels, pouring several fingers into an oversize tumbler filled with ice. She returned with some fresh sport togs and a bathrobe. She asked me if I had eaten any supper. "Of course," I said. It was almost ten o'clock. But then I realized I hadn't had any supper, and I said, "No, not really, but that's all right, I'm not very hungry."

But she insisted on giving me something to eat. While she was occupied in the kitchen, I removed my wet clothes and put on the dry ones. Then I searched through Naps's collection of stereo tapes, selected Dvorak's New World Symphony, and put it on the hi-fi. Then I sat down on the deep-pile rug to drink and relax. Tatrice returned with a tray of club sandwiches, olives, pickles, potato chips and all, and put it down on the rug where I could get at it. Then she made herself a small drink and sat down in a nearby chair.

"Awful rain," she said. "What were you—?" She stopped, then spoke again, in alarm, "Nub, your hand! What happened? Your knuckles are bleeding."

I looked down. Sure enough. "I—" I said.

She dashed off down the hall, and returned in a twinkling with a medicine kit. She took my hand in hers and mercurochromed the knuckles, then spread two Band-Aids across them. "What happened?" she wanted to know. "What have you been up to?"

So I told her. I don't suppose it was a very good conversation topic, but it seemed to amuse her. Just the sound of my own voice speaking conversationally, pleasantly, quite convivially, seemed to restore some of my equilibrium and replenish my dwindling humors. Tatrice is an excellent listener, that much must be said for her. The Dvorak stereo tape had reached that excruciatingly poignant portion known as "Going Home." Loosened up, I decided to tell Tatrice other things too, about Margaret, and about Dall, and about myself: the things that had been happening lately. She listened a long time, nodding her head at this point, shaking it at that point, contributing an occasional word, a "Lands!" or a "Heavens!" or a "Sure enough?" which opened floodgates of fresh confessions and grievances. Between her and Jack Daniels my soul was laid bare.

When I came finally to a long pause during which I was momentarily taxed for words, she spoke up. "Nub, what can we do for you?" she asked, her head tilted sideways in an expression of warm compassion.

"How do you mean?" I said, taken slightly aback. It had not occurred to me that there was anything anybody could do for me.

"To cheer you up," she said. "To make you believe that you haven't come home in vain."

I was about to answer when there came a great knocking at the front door. Tatrice and I exchanged puzzled glances, both wondering who it could be that was not bothering to use the doorbell. Then she got up and went to the front door. I remained seated on the rug and watched.

She opened the door, and three white men came quickly into the house. One of them I recognized to my horror: the vanquished cab driver. He spotted me and pointed a long shaking finger at me and said, "That's him!" and then the three of them advanced. One was carrying a two-foot length of lead pipe, another brandished a tire jack, my cab driver raised a stiletto. Tatrice screamed. One of the men grabbed her and clamped his hand over her mouth.

"This nigger gal your wife?" he said to me. "Tell her to keep her mouth shut if she knows what's good for her."

The cab driver appraised her. "Got him a piece of dark meat for a wife," he said. "He's the type."

They roamed leisurely around the room, enjoying their moment, relishing their grand entrance. "Fancy place you got here, buddy boy, even if it is in Niggerville," one of them said. "Too bad we got to mess it up for you."

I was standing up now. Come home, Naps, we need you, quick. They began to circle around me. Little Lucy came into the room, rubbing her eyes. "Tell the pickaninny to git back to bed if she don't want to watch her poppa git his ass dragged," said the fellow who was holding Tatrice, and he released her mouth.

"Ask her to leave the room," I said to Tatrice, and she, calmer now, instructed Lucy to return to bed. The girl did.

"Well now," said the cab driver, "think you're the champ, don't you?" He slapped me viciously with the back of his hand. "Think you're a hot-shit, huh? When we get through with you, Shorty, you aint gonna be a cold turd."

The one holding Tatrice said to her, "Honey, I got to let go of you now, cause I got to help my buddies beat the crap out of your white lover-boy, but if you open your mouth again or try to do anything, see, I'm gonna take this here pipe and ram it all the way up your sweet black cunt." Then he let go of her and she stood rigidly as if paralyzed.

They came at me. Tatrice reached out a hand and flicked a switch which turned off all the lights.

When she turned them back on again, less than a minute later, she was holding a .45 pistol in her trembling hand. She surveyed the room, then looked at her pistol and said, "Well, looks like I don't need this after all, do I?" and she put it aside and fetched her medicine kit again. "You all right?" she asked, looking me over. "No cuts? No bruises? No concussions?" I assured her I was just fine. "Naps told me you were a holy terror," she said. "But I still don't see how you did it." An old trick, I explained: you take your knee, see, and you drive it up against their privates, which is just about the awfulest pain there is, and then, as they double in awful torment, you take the side of your hand and slash it down across the back of their neck. Puts them out cold. She giggled. "Busts their balls too, I bet!" she said, and then she flushed in embarrassment. "But *three* of them . . .?" she said, puzzled. Well, I said, I only got one of them. I guess the other two must have taken care of each other . . .

I called Curly at the station house and asked him to send somebody out to remove the bodies. He came himself, accompanied by Jack. He looked the place over, studied Tatrice and me carefully, and then asked me, "What am I supposed to charge them with?"

"Assault and battery. Breaking and entering. Indecent language. Possession of illegal weapons. And if you need anything else, call Dall at the hospital and he'll tell you a bunch of other things. He's not going to like this. Not at all."

They revived the ruffians and herded them into a squad car. I asked Curly before he left, "Any luck finding Slater yet?" He said the sheriff had spotted him on his horse out in his woods during the afternoon and they were closing in on him, but hadn't caught him yet.

We made more drinks, stronger this time because of nervous prostration; Tatrice had to break out a new bottle. But within half an hour we had managed to forget entirely the upsetting visitation. We told each other cheerful jokes. I told her anecdotes I had picked up at Yale; she told me old Negro tales. We had a good time.

I asked her when she thought Naps might come home. She said she didn't know. "That man comes and goes, just comes and goes. I never know when to expect him. Sometimes I don't even know where he is. Most likely he's going to stay the whole night out there."

We talked about names. *Naps,* she said, was not simply an abbreviation of Napoleon. "Naps" is also a venerable old word used by Negroes to refer to themselves in the plural, meaning the "nappy-haired" Negroes, those with thick woolly hair. Well then, I suggested, his name is symbolic of the whole ulotrichous race? "He likes to think of it that way," she said, and then she examined my nickname and analyzed it for me. "Nub" can mean, in addition to a small person, many things in various argots: the point or gist of a story, a small or imperfect ear of Indian corn, anything small or imperfect or—she hesitated—worthless. Some darkies use it to mean an unborn child. That's me, I said, an unborn child. Nub the Unborn Child, I repeated, turning it over and over on my thickened tongue. Then I asked her what her name meant. She said her maiden name was Thelma Be*a*trice Plunkett, and the "Tatrice," which rhymes with mattress, came from that particular pronunciation of Beatrice. She was from Hamburg, Arkansas, and she had met Naps at Arkansas A. M. & N. College in Pine Bluff, where she had been a Home Economics major. "Be*a*trice," I said, rather tipsily, "you're the cutest colored chick I ever did see." You're not such a bad ofay mortal yourself, she said.

Hastily and with no little abashment we changed the subject, and began to talk about that one interest which we most had in common: antiques. I swear, that girl knew more about the subject than my boss Clara Ovett did, and we thoroughly explored it as a topic of conversation, treating particularly the early primitive furniture of the Southland. The hour was late, but she showed no inclination to retire, and for my part I welcomed with open arms the opportunity to get my mind off Margaret by talking at length with somebody else.

I don't know how it happened. Somewhere long after midnight I was all wound up in a dissertation on American folk art and why there is no folk art being created in America today because of the dissolution of our society, and probably I was rather incoherent and drunkenly plaintive: I remember citing the old wooden folk sculpture as an example, the beautiful ship's figureheads, the cigar-store Indians, the carved weathervanes, the quaint old merry-go-round horses, the shop signs and other examples of wonderful American wood carving which were not being made any more, would never be made any more, because the America of today had completely lost touch with its roots and . . . And she said something to me and then she had to say it again before I stopped talking and I realized how tight and wandering I must have been. "I've got a lovely wooden statue of an old dancing Negro down in the workshop," she was saying.

"Dancing Negro? Dancing Negro? Dancing? Negro?"

"Yes. I just found it yesterday in a junk shop over on East Ninth."

"Junk shop? East Ninth?"

"That's right. Would you care to go down and take a look at it?"

"Down?"

🙵 FOUR

In the cold light of dawn, waking up in the same bed I had slept in the last time I stayed there, I gazed up at the ceiling and asked myself what kind of dirty bastard was I, anyway. Outside it was still raining; in the grove of post oaks the rain was a loud jeweled curtain. Margaret was right, I reflected, she was absolutely right in the reservations she had had about me: I am dishonest, I am a dishonest cheat. What have I done? *What have I done?* Of all things, my good friend's own wife. An overpowering and disconcerting sense of *déjà vu:* the cluttered repository of old furniture, the single shielded bulb burning from somewhere up in the dark vault of the ceiling, yea, even the words: pick it up, see how solid it is, and: virgin oak, beautiful finish, so nicely put together, and: so rare, I wish I had it for my own, and: I'm tempted to steal it. I had been irresponsibly drunk and my eyes had been purblind; all I could remember distinctly was the table, a long drop-leaf harvest table with peg legs, circa 1815, from which all the paint and varnish had been removed. Hard birch. And I remembered my debased mind asking: the white landowner of the old South, ole massa the profligate and dissolute wretch, did he, beset with unresolved lust because of a cold wife, seek out a favorite slave girl and receive relief from her? We are all victims of the South's final damnation. But then what? What had I done? It was all empty. *Tabula rasa.* Somehow I must have got up here to this guest room, and to bed . . .

Now, by thunderation, what pangs the morning brought! My anxious heart, thumping, said: repent repent repent. Kill yourself, a panicked conscience urged me; if you don't, Naps will come home and do it for you. Or run away: sneak out the window and off through the oak grove; get back to Boston; you got what you came for. Base scoundrel!

The sound of an automobile coming down the driveway lifted me out of bed. I went to the window and looked out. It was the Lincoln. It stopped at the front entrance, and Naps got out. Then Margaret got out. Margaret?! Pity sakes, everybody is coming, coming to accuse me! Next will arrive an ambulance, with Dall on a stretcher. Then will come a Chevrolet with my father and grandmother. Bringing up the rear will be a television truck with Hy Norden and a station wagon with the entire press corps. All of them coming to point their fingers at me and prosecute me and condemn me. I crawled under the bed and lay there trembling, waiting.

Presently I heard soft footsteps in the hallway and then my door opened, and in walked a pair of dark feet in lady's houseslippers. The slippers paced the floor of my room for a while and then the owner of the slippers got down on her knees and looked under the bed, her face a few inches from mine. She smiled.

"I see you," she said.

"Good morning," I said.

"Looking for something?" she asked.

"Dropped a cuff link," I explained.

"How you feel this morning?" she asked.

"Awful. I wish I were dead. My God, what have I done?"

"Hush," she said. "Let's just play like we never even met before. Just forget it."

"But what did I do? Did I—?"

"You were bad drunk, that's all. Don't even think about it any more."

"What's Margaret doing down there with Naps?"

"Well, Naps just brought her over here because she doesn't feel too good."

"What's wrong with her?"

"A good friend of hers just died."

"Who?"

"Fellow name of James Slater."

I crawled out from under the bed, and stood up to face her. "They shot him?" I asked.

"No, he drowned himself. In Lake Maumelle."

"Does Naps know I'm up here?"

"Not yet."

"What if I sneaked out the back way, and then came around to the front and rang the doorbell and pretended I was just arriving?"

"Just fine, just fine." She turned to go, but I stopped her. She stared at me.

"About last night . . ." I said. "You have to tell me—"

"No," she said. "You were lonely and blue. And very drunk. Just put it out of your mind. I won't say anything."

"But—"

She smiled and touched my mouth with her fingertips and then she left the room. I hurriedly dressed and tiptoed down the hall to the back stairway, and down it and out of the house. It had stopped raining. I walked around to the front and pushed the doorbell button. Tatrice answered. "Why, hello, Nub!" she greeted me cordially, then she called over her shoulder, "It's Nub!"

Naps came up out of the living room as I entered the foyer. His face was grave. Was he suspicious? Or was it just the news he would have to give me? I shook hands with him, and then I nodded at Margaret, who was sitting in the living room. "What's up?" I said to Naps.

He took me into the living room and we sat down. Margaret's face was pale and vacant. She had a glass of straight un-iced whiskey in her hand. We all sat in silence for a moment, not looking at each other.

Then Naps cleared his throat and said, "Mr. Slater tried to ride his horse across Lake Maumelle. They didn't make it."

"No!" I said.

Margaret looked at me and said, "But he wasn't trying to get to the other side. He didn't want to."

Naps said to her, "You want to let Nub read it?"

"Why not?" she said, and she reached into her purse and took out some sheets of paper and unfolded them and handed them to me.

Naps said, "Slater gave that to my friend Feemy and told him to see to it that Sergeant Hawkins got it. So I told Feemy I'd take it to him. I took it to him, and after he'd read it, he told me to go and find Miss Margaret and let her read it too."

FIVE

For whatever salivary sensation it may give to the people of this town, to Margaret and to that half-pint Boston Casanova who took her away from me, for whatever fiendish satisfaction my death may provide for them or for any other vindictive person or persons concerned, I hereby oblige them, willingly but joylessly. I hope that my act is sufficiently histrionic and spectacular to indulge their most urgent need for requited pleasure: I hope they will consider it an acceptable substitute for doing the job themselves: I hope they are gratified abundantly. To you I shall address these parting remarks, these last words, this valedictory: not that you should bear any guilt yourself, nor that one drop of my blood fall upon your hands, but only that one sympathetic human creature might be exposed to the final outcry of my oppressed brain. (Of course I am making two carbons: one for Ethel, the other for the sheriff, but I do not presume to expect a careful reading from either of them; it is only a formality.) Into my watery grave I carry your clever poetic tribute: "You who art due din and ear pop *aye*, yet got not one nod but hue and cry . . ." the most elating words I have ever received, and I am very grateful to you for them. You are a gifted and sensitive poet, Hawkins, and you must take care not to let your art stagnate. I am very sorry if differences grew up between us, I am very regretful that we parted company at such a violent and painful moment, and I would like to set my house in order and make good my unwavering respect for you and wipe off old scores . . . and sores. Therefore, Hawkins, I am proud to have this opportunity to appoint you executor and sole beneficiary of my estate, such as it is. No posthumous thanks, please. Who else is so worthy? Dispose of my humble effects however you like, they are all yours. More of this later. First, hearken to my farewell. I am not altogether certain I can finish this. I am up again in my study, for the last time, sitting at my desk. The hour is late. The cloudburst drones on and on outside my window. I see a crack of light under Ethel's door; perhaps she is reading, perhaps she has parked her wheelchair at the window and is watching the rain . . . or watching for me. Coming upstairs a moment ago, I ran into one of the sheriff's deputies. Fortunately he seemed unvigilant from lack of sleep. "Have they found the guy yet?" I asked him. "No, sir," he replied, hardly troubling to give me more than a glance. I came on up into my study, closed the door, and laughed for a while. But perhaps my time is short. This old Hermes portable is quiet, almost noiseless, but somebody might come to check on this room and when they find the door barred from the inside they will knock it down. I must hurry. Forgive me my rambling. The heavy raindrops plunge into the lake relentlessly, and with desperation; soon Houyhnhnm and I must join them. What peace then! The whole world obliterated! I hate to do this to you, and if there were any possible way I might spare your life and let all others perish, I would not hesitate, but this is the only way: I must wipe out the whole universe, wreak death on all! All! Every living thing, every beast of the field, and flower, and all that God has created, I must destroy, with a great flood more terrible than that last flood which Noah survived. No one will survive this one. I am sorry, for you, but not for the rest of mankind, which deserves this destruction, which has brought it on itself. All human life and conduct are a disguise, a permanent play-like, a constant procrastination from reality, a shameless sham, an everlasting pretense in which we are all fools fooling each other and ourselves. We call ourselves "civilized"! We have "lifted ourselves up out of our animal origins." Thrice-damned poppycock! In my book, *civilized* means *artificialized*. Man is a pose. During the "Dark" Ages, after the destruction of the pretentious and mannered Roman Empire, there was some hope that man could save himself from further affectation. But, as ill luck would have it, things got worse instead of better. Today, particularly in this country, life has been romanticized and fabricated and camouflaged out of all reasonable proportion. Everything contributes: our way of speech, our institutions, our government, books, movies, advertisements, television, all! We are living a dream wherein the awful chasm between our true inward natures and our outward behavior is so wide and irreconcilable that life is a perpetual hell of frustration and disillusionment and heartache. Out with it! This show cannot go on! Ring down the last curtain! Destroy this fake world and build a new one! As the Great Playwright, I will wipe out this farce and write a fresh drama in which man is genuine and true. I will banish: television and radio. All advertisements, particularly cigarette advertisements. Suburbs. Trading stamps. Motels. Politics. Clothes. Plastic Christmas trees. Bread without holes. Wood-grained plastic. All plastic, period. TV dinners. John Birchers. Pop art. Pop-top beer cans. Psychosomatic illnesses. Bridge. All other card games, including solitaire (except perhaps poker). Lawrence Welk. Confession magazines. Highway junk yards. Superman comic books. Calvert "Soft" Whiskey. Jerry Lewis. Tourist traps. Houses made of artificially aged brick. Edward Teller. Polyunsaturates. Built-in obsolescence. "LBJ" stamped on everything. All Texans, period. Elizabeth Taylor. Folksongs which are not real folksongs. Dick Tracy, Nancy, and Donald Duck. Innocuous Broadway comedies. Adam Clayton Powell. The togetherness and the mindless conformity of organized religion. Barry Goldwater and all other rabid extremists. Metrecal. Insurance. Messrs. Presley, Nelson, Clark, the Beatles, et al. The Christian Anti-Communist Crusade and Billy James Hargis. Presidential primaries and conventions. Telephones. California. Jack Paar. Baptists, Episcopalians, Methodists, Presbyterians, the whole stinking lot of them. Catholics and Jews too. Orville Freeman. Orval Faubus. Orville Prescott. Billboards, or, for that matter, all outdoor signs. Taylor Caldwell. Garage mechanics. ZIP Code. Richard Nixon. Daytime soap operas, particularly "Love of Life" in which everybody hates life. Leander H. Perez. News leaks. Kahlil Gibran. Credit cards. Anti-intellectualism. George Wallace and his nasty sneer. All nasty sneerers. Sex manuals. The nine-to-five working day. Bosley Crowther. Paper plates. Mobile homes, and trailer camps. Low minds in high places. Mouths and teeth of models, beauty queens, stars, and starlets. Other-directed people. All! Everything! Out! *Out!* I am constipated, literally and figuratively. Old age encroaches, and my worn body will not function any more. I worry ceaselessly about it. Does my constipation affect my emotions? Does my gout determine the particular state of my mind at any given moment? Will my migraine warp my perspectives? Can I do creative work on those days when my liver is out of kilter? Should I propitiate the gods of nature with burnt offerings on the mornings when my postnasal drip clogs my throat? What exercise can help my lumbago? What miracle of geriatrics could ease my palsied bulk down into slumber each night? Must I give up food to avoid halitosis? My one cure, my one good remedy, has been withheld from me now for nearly two weeks: Ethel has inexplicably cut off my whiskey ration, without which I am not strong enough to face the sheriff and these other pests hanging around here. With only two or three strong jiggers in me I could go down there and run them all off. They want to kill me. I do not want to die: I tremble at the merest thought of it. But something will get me, the sheriff or old age. Here is what I would really like to do: I'd really like to get out of this place and go to some lost and peaceful hollow up in the hills, free from all distractions and interruptions and annoyances, and have some place with a good bed in it, and somebody like Feemy to wait on me and me alone, to bring me all my meals and make me just as comfortable as I could possibly want to be, and I'd just loaf around and read and listen to music and recoup my energies and my brains, and be born again. Born again! If I could just sleep for a week. But without money what can I do? The really horrible thing about our civilization is that it costs money just to sleep. Even the sleep of death is frightfully expensive: somebody (not you, I hope) is going to have to shell out a tidy sum just to give my remains a decent disposal. But I want that sleep. I must have it. You are a poet, Hawkins, do you know what is the favorite subject of all poets of all time? Not love, alas. Love is not quite popular enough, although it runs a close second. Not war, not nature, not death, not even life itself. But sleep. Sleep is. Search your anthologies, your collections, your miscellanies, and see for yourself how often all poets have eulogized sleep, almost to the point of being obsessed with it, that thing which knits the raveled sleeve of care, that great gift, that sleep which gives what life denies, nature's soft nurse, perchance to dream, the universal vanquisher. Good night. The babe is at peace within the womb, the corpse is at rest within the tomb, we begin in what we end. I am going soon. Forbear a few more words. You must accept my apologies regarding Margaret. And I am indeed sorry that my careless equestrianship caused you personal bodily injury. I hope you are much better now. I was, as you said, obsessed: Margaret was the only answer. Without her I could have had no future. She alone might have restored to me the precious power of potency, had time and fate and her own inclination allowed. As it turns out, I had already lost her to another man. Do you know this Stone fellow? Margaret said he was a friend of yours. I hope not. But if so, make him miserable for me, will you? If you cannot kill him, do something to him, castrate him, bludgeon him senseless, make him prematurely old: what a fine favor it would be for me if somehow my afflictions could be transferred to him. Do what you can. I am leaving you everything. Such as it is. This Hermes portable typewriter, eight dollars and thirty-six cents in cash, my books, all of them, including the Complete Variorum Shakespeare, the Complete Wilde, the Complete Shaw, the Compleat Angler, everything; also my tape recorder, two good metal filing cabinets along with contents: memorabilia, letters, souvenirs, the original manuscripts of my plays, my collection of phonograph records, which includes, as you know, the entire recorded *oeuvres* of Tschaikovsky, Sibelius and Ravel; also assorted miscellaneous objects: personal jewelry, fountain pen, pencils, erasers, paper clips, etc., etc. I have three cartons of Pall Malls which I will not have time to finish; they are yours, too. In the third drawer from the top on the right side of my desk you will find an envelope which contains three pawn tickets, and should you wish to redeem them, you may take them to Moorhead's Pawn Shop and receive a fine wristwatch, a Leica camera, and an Argus slide projector. That's all I can think of at the moment; undoubtedly you will discover other things which may be of some interest or value to you. I wish I could give you the house, but it isn't mine. Even my horses are owned outright by Ethel. The stable, however, I built with my own hands, so if you want it, take it. I guess Ethel will stay here in this house forever, she will stay in that room forever, in that wheelchair forever. Why don't they hurry up and legalize euthanasia? Put the poor bitch out of her misery. Well, good night, I guess that's about it. No, wait, there's one other little item. I have just one request to make of you. As my executor you are empowered to determine method of burial. I would like to ask that if my body be found, it is to be taken to some convenient hilltop and there placed upon a pyre of pine boughs and branches, and burned, and the ashes afterward not collected in an urn or anything but scattered to the winds, freely broadcast on the breeze out across the fields and valleys.

This is the way everybody should be interred, that they might find final union with nature. I heartily recommend it to you. As for me, please ask them to do it, or do it yourself as soon as you get out of the hospital if there are objections from others. Now I must go. *Fiat justitia, ruat caelum.* I hate to leave my desk. I have said so little, I have left so much unsaid. Ah, there is one more thing I meant to mention. You know my work-in-progress, my Ozarks morality play? Well, it is yours too now, and I dearly wish you could find somebody to finish it for me. I think it has some merit. The folklore of your country people, the old superstitions: amulets, talismans, the phases of the moon, philters and charms . . . That might be some solution, you know? As for now, is this the end? Yes, I'm afraid it is. Do not shed tears for me. If you must weep, weep for this world I have destroyed.

> In death as in life, with admiration, your
> friend   *James Royal Slater*

SIX

"I never met him," I reflected aloud. "I never saw him, I never even saw a picture of him or anything." The four of us were sitting now at the kitchen table, having breakfast. The children had finished theirs and had been sent out to play; the sun was out of the clouds again. Tatrice was serving French toast and Canadian bacon.

"It's like Feemy said," Naps offered. "Mr. Slater was a fine man once, but he's been goin downhill a long time. A long time."

"He was still a fine man," I said, touched by his death and his final words.

"Naw, now, man," Naps objected. "Anybody writes sump'm like that, you just know they not entirely *rational.*"

"Ethel's fault," I suggested.

"That's right," Naps said.

"I hope she's satisfied," Margaret said.

"But why did he have to go and kill himself?" Tatrice asked. "Surely, if they'd caught him, the most he would have got would have been a few years in jail . . . or the state asylum."

"He couldn't afford those few years," Margaret said.
"He was unhappy," Naps said.
"He hated everybody," I said.
"I wish they could have left him alone," Margaret said.
"He might've gone on and killed himself anyway, even if they had," Naps said.
"A world like this," I said. Then I said, "I guess I would have done the same thing if I'd been in his place."
"You're like him in several ways," Margaret said. "You really are. I never thought of it before, but you and he had the same opinions about a lot of things. Of course," she added hastily, "I don't mean you're the same kind of eccentric he was, no."
I nodded. "I might almost have written that document myself."
She and Naps nodded, and Tatrice said, "Well," and then we lapsed into silence as we finished our breakfast.
Over the second cup of coffee Naps remarked, "Well, it's something not to have to worry about any more. It's all over."
"It's all over," I said.
"Now you and Margaret can have a good time, without worryin about—"
"Naps," I said, "my train leaves tomorrow night."
Naps laughed uproariously, but then he hushed and glanced at Margaret for confirmation, and she nodded her head. "Aw naw, now, man!" he protested. "You doan wanta do *that*. Y'all stay here awhile and us'll all have a lot of fun."
"Margaret will," I said. "But I have to get on back to Boston."
Naps was incredulous. "You mean you're gonna go by your*self*?" He look back and forth between the two of us.
Margaret explained to him why we had been unable to agree about the city of Little Rock.
As if to lend substance to her explanation, I burst out, "Little Rock killed Slater!" Then to Margaret I said, "The same apathy of this town that made your life lonely and colorless for years also drove him to death!"
"No," she said, "I can't go along with that. You didn't know Jimmy. This town—us—" she gestured at herself and me and Naps—"we can't be blamed for what he did. Like everything else he's ever done, he did this all on his own. All on his own."
"Do you think," I asked her challengingly, "that you could allow yourself to stay in this town, after what happened to him? Do you think you'll ever again be content here, knowing what he did to himself?"
She did not answer. She hung her head reflectively. When, a

moment later, I said "Do you?" once more, she replied, "I don't know. But I'm going to stay here, and I wish we could consider the argument settled. You'll come back again, wait and see if you don't. You'll come back again and again, and finally you'll settle down here to stay."

"And I'll wind up, at the age of fifty, drowning myself in Lake Maumelle." Then I said, "No. No, I don't think I'll ever come back."

"Yes, you will," she said.

"Aw, yeah," Naps joined her, "I bet he will."

"He will," Tatrice said. "He can't help himself."

SEVEN

That afternoon, at my request, Naps took me home. I had had a surfeit of these friends, and I wanted to go on home and spend my few remaining Little Rock hours with my father and grandmother. The common herd values friendships only for their usefulness, and I reflected how I had used Naps: first as a chauffeur, then as a private detective, a valet, and finally I had used his wife. Or hadn't I? But even to think of it, even to want to ... I was a bastard. And was I any less evil and sinful than Slater? The man had been a crackpot, obviously, and wicked and murderous as well. Good riddance, in a sense. But still, some of the things he said in that farewell letter to Dall led me to believe that he and I were, as Margaret had implied, like-minded in a number of ways, both oppressed by the same oppressions, and that therefore I should not send to know for whom the bell tolls, because it tolls for me: in his death I too was diminished. I began to see why Margaret had pitied him, and why she had tried so hard to keep Dall from finding out about Slater's criminal intentions in the hope that the whole thing would blow over and Slater could find some peace. Was there really a villain in this whole business, and, if so, who? Me, I decided: yes, I am the real villain. The sooner I returned to Boston the sooner I would have a chance to forget it all.

My father was watching a baseball game on television. My grandmother was writing postcards to friends and relatives. I sat for an hour or so reading my father's current issues of *True*

Adventures before they took any apparent notice of me, then my father turned in his chair, gave me a cantankerous look, and said, "Enjoying yourself?" Yes, I said; as a matter of fact, yes, I am. "Gonna eat with us tonight?" he said. Yes, I said, I had planned to. "Gonna sleep here tonight?" he said. If I could, I said. Then I told him I was going back to Boston tomorrow and wanted to spend these last few hours with my family. "Well, that's nice of you," he said with unconcealed sarcasm. "It's a wonder to me how you managed to stay as long as you did. I don't guess you would of, if you hadn't found some doings to get mixed up in." I told him that if I hadn't got mixed up in those particular doings I probably would have stayed longer. He said, "Sorry I wasn't able to entertain you more." I told him that for my part I was sorry that the nature of my activities had kept me away from home so often, and I hoped to make up for it, in part, by spending this last day at home. "You don't have to do that," he said. "Go on out and play with your friends if you want to. I aint worth talkin to." *Daddy*, I protested, feeling awful. Let's talk, I urged him. Let's you and I talk. "What's there to talk about?" he said. "Aint nuthin I could say would interest you any." Tell me about your job, I suggested. "It's just the same old job," he said. "It never changes. Same old wires. Same old tools. Day in and day out." Do you enjoy life? I asked him bluntly. "Same as everybody, I reckon," he said. What do you like to do? I asked. He answered, "Eat. Sleep. Read. Watch TV. Shoot pool some." Are you a good pool shot? I led him on. "Better'n some," he said. Do you prefer snooker or eight-ball? I asked. How do you like caroms? Do you use a light stick or a heavy one? Do you top the cue ball to loosen a frozen ball, or how? And thus I managed to build up about twenty minutes' worth of conversation between us, but ultimately the talk fizzled out like an eight-ball falling off into the corner pocket. I tried. No one can say I didn't try. But he was peevish and obstinate; in two weeks I had let him get too far away from me. Bless me, Father, for I have sinned.

I approached my grandmother and talked with her for a while, but without any more luck than I had had with my father. She shared his resentment. I was too good for my own folks, she said. But she suggested a way I could save face: go back up to the hills of Parthenon with her and visit for a spell. It was a fetching idea, and I gave it serious consideration. I had never disliked the Ozarks as I disliked Little Rock. But I understood at last that I was really impatient to get back to

Boston as soon as possible. Was I actually lonesome for Pamela? No, that couldn't be; I simply wanted to plunge back into my work again and lose myself in the tedium of curatorship. After my unsuccessful job search around Little Rock I was beginning to consider myself quite fortunate in having the job I already had.

I loafed around the house, trying unsuccessfully to think of other things to talk about with my father or grandmother. As on dull Saturday afternoons of my youth, I wished somebody would call me on the phone. Finally somebody did.

"Cliff, *pal*, Hy."

"Hi. Who's this?"

"Hy."

"Hi yourself. Who's calling?"

"Hy Norden."

"Oh, 'lo, Hy. How's tricks?"

"Great. Listen. Wanted to ask you. We're having the Tenth Reunion Banquet of our Little Rock High School graduating class at the Marion Hotel the twenty-ninth of this month. I'm M.C. And I want you up there on the dais with me, boy. Make a speech or two. Crack a few jokes. Give the home folks a look at a real walking success story."

"Thanks, but I won't be here then. Leaving tomorrow."

"Aw, come on, Cliff fellow boy. You can't let us down. We're counting on you. Where's the old school spirit?"

"Up your ass," I said.

"How's that? Hey, come on, be a pal. I got to get the program printed next week and I want to put your name on it in big letters. We all want you there. Honest to God."

"Sorry," I said. "Pressing business in Boston."

"Well look, tell me now, level with me: Is there *anything* I can do for you? Any little favor before you go? Any big favor? Just tell me. Give me a chance to be a pal."

I thought about it. But I decided Hy wasn't the type to offer gratis favors unless he wanted something in return. "What's the catch?" I said. "What do you want?"

"Hell, I'm telling you, I want to be a pal, do something for you, any little token—"

"You could drop dead for me."

"Aw, *Cliff*. Think of old times. Think of the good old days when we used to—"

"I've thought of them," I said. "Too much. Now suppose you either tell me the purpose of this call or get your sweet mouth off the line. I'm busy."

"All right, Cliff, I'll make it short. I've got a deadline to meet myself. I need some information. You could be a big help to me, and I'll repay you the favor any time, believe me. Now here's the deal. I've been told you had an inside wire with James Slater and some girl he was involved with. I was wondering if you could give me some dope on the situation. If you have any idea why he killed himself . . ."

"Oh, sure. Got your pencil ready? Good. Quote me if you wish." I began to dictate: "James Royal Slater, forty-eight, Little Rock's own Bollington Prize-winning playwright, took his life in Lake Maumelle near his home early Saturday morning. Friends revealed that a typewritten note left by the former playwright indicated that he was despondent over the moral and ethical contamination of American life, particularly as evident in and around the city of Little Rock, which he had come to consider a cultural and societal wasteland . . ."

"Yeah, but that's not exactly what I meant. There was some girl he was involved with. Do you know her name?"

"Christine Keeler."

"How do you spell that last name?"

I spelled it for him.

"You know her age?"

"Thirteen."

"Address?"

"RFD, Bald Knob, Arkansas."

"Thanks. Now, could you tell me what sort of relationship he had with this Keeler gal. I mean, you know, was he getting any?"

"Oh, heavens no! Much worse than that."

"Well, what? I won't quote you."

"It's entirely unspeakable."

"Well, tell me anyway. I won't speak it."

I lowered my voice to a whisper. "She was collecting his belly-button lint to stuff pillows with."

"Good Lord, how awful!" he exclaimed, but then he changed his tone. "Wait a minute. Are you sure this is on the level?"

"Well, of course I never *saw* her doing it, but that's what I heard."

"Clifford—"

"Yes?"

"Are you playing around with me?"

"Look, Hy, I don't know anything. You're wasting your time."

"Sergeant Hawkins told me to talk to you, he said *he* didn't know anything. If you don't know anything, I'm sunk. I've got to get this story on the air. Please, Cliff. Old times' sake. Can't you give me any information on this Keeler gal?"

"I'm afraid not. Why don't you speak to John Profumo?"

"Where do I reach him?"

"I don't know his phone number."

"Where's he live?"

"Sixty-nine Codborough Way, London, W.C. 1."

"London? . . . Profumo? . . . Keeler? Oh— Cliff, you old clown! Come on now, quit your fooling. Help me. This is a big thing. Slater was an important person."

"Says who? He produced only one play in this town, and you, among others, panned it terribly. Personally, I never even met Slater, so I can't help you. Sorry. Just say he was a lonely horse rancher who got more than he could take from all the shitty Nordens who rule the earth."

Then I hung up.

🐢 EIGHT

Supper was an unsociable ordeal endured in silence. I hazarded a few occasional remarks or conversational questions which were met with either a Stoney silence or the minimum acceptable response. They dropped a few baited or catty observations, to which I could make no reply. So goes the eventual disintegration of the American family. Fed up, I retreated to my room for a while and there I tried to recapture some enthusiasm for the past by collating my mementos again, but this had the opposite of the effect I had anticipated: it offended and nauseated me. Sitting there in that pile of yearbooks, scrapbooks, clippings, souvenirs, letters, and other dross of my teen years, I became actually sick, physically sick, and before I could move or make it to the bathroom I had begun to retch: my entire supper was regurgitated in a helplessly cataclysmic heave which fell upon those tokens and keepsakes and irreparably blotched them. I gathered them up in my arms, the whole heavy pile of them, and took them out into the back yard and stuffed them into the trash burner, and set them afire. I stood back and watched the blaze, and scorching tears burst out of my eyes and streamed down my face. *Burn*, my bridges. At the perimeter of the flames I descried a large photograph, a portrait of Margaret, and as her young face curled and frizzled in the heat she asked: What are you doing? Burning my bridges, I said. All of them? she asked, and her voice was so plaintively clear that I understood no photograph could be capable of such speech. I turned and she was standing beside me.

"All of them," I said. "Just like you burned yours. When you did what you did to the walls of your room and then when you took all of your clothes out of there, you were burning your bridges too."

She nodded, and her fingertips came up and lightly touched the water on my face. "I've never seen you cry before," she said.

"I never have," I said, and I ran the back of my hand briskly across my face and wiped it almost dry. Then I asked, "What are you doing here?"

"Doyle," she said. "He's worried that you'll leave town without seeing him again. He wants to talk to you. I told him I would come and get you."

"Wants to recant, does he?" I asked, thinking of how he must partly blame himself for Slater's death.

"Recant? No, he just wants to see you again before you go."

"I'll come out there tomorrow. Tonight I'm going to stay with my folks."

"No you aint neither," said my grandmother, and I looked up, and she and my father were standing together on the back stoop, looking down at me with compassionate expressions. "You go on out there and talk to that pore boy," she said. "And I'll go along with you and see to it that you do."

My father's face was soft in sympathy. "Goddamn idiot," he said tenderly, "don't you know there's a law against burnin trash after dark in this town?"

"Don't swear, Wesley," my grandmother said to him. "I'll wash your mouth out with soap like I used to."

"Burnin trash after dark," he grumbled.

I cried harder.

Margaret took my arm and led me around the house and out to Dall's car, which she had left at the curb. We got in and waited for my grandmother to go through the house and get her hat and handbag. Margaret asked me why I was crying. I told her I was a broken man. She asked me why I was a broken man. I said because no man is an island, and every man's death diminisheth me. She was silent and then she said that was not really the reason I was crying. Then Grammaw Stone came out and got into the car with us and we went out to the hospital.

In the lobby of the hospital I told my grandmother I would wait while she went up to visit with him, but she told me I should go first. After a few moments of quibbling over the matter I agreed to go first while she and Margaret waited in the lobby.

He greeted me pleasantly as before. His bandages had been removed and new ones put on, but not enough new ones to hide, to conceal his face. I gasped aloud. He was grotesque. Every bone and cartilage in his nose had been shattered, and it didn't look like a nose at all. Several sutured and unsutured cuts scarred his brow and jowls with various tints of red or pink. Grayish slough in places. Welts, pocks, pustules, and scabs. He was horrid, and he knew it. "Aint I the sorriest mess you ever saw?" he asked me, and I granted that he was. I sat down beside his bed, and tried to avoid looking at him any more than was necessary.

"You got a picture of yourself I could have sometime?" he asked.

"What for?"

"I'm gonna give it to the plastic surgeons and tell em to make me look like you." But he was grinning and I knew he didn't mean it.

"Why me? My face is bland."

"Aw, just foolin," he said. "No, if they give me any say about it, I'm gonna tell em to fix me up to look just exactly like I was before. Take it or leave it."

"That's a highly commendable expression of principle. However, if I were you, I wouldn't object if they wanted to make a few improvements upon nature."

"Like what?"

"Like giving you a kindly mug to match your kindly heart."

"A cop has to look mean. I been practicin all my life. I caint be Chief of Police if I look like some Sunday School teacher or anybody."

"All right. Tell them to restore your fierce glower and your sullen brow, and to leave a couple of wicked scars still visible."

"I might just do that," he said.

After the first caesura of this meeting, during which I got up to stand at the window and look ponderingly out into the darkness, I said to him without turning that Margaret had told me he wanted to talk to me and I wondered if there was anything particular he wanted to say or ask.

He said he wanted to know if this was the last time he would see me.

I told him that it might as well be, because it was painful for me to keep saying good-bye to him.

He said he still didn't understand why I had to leave. What did I have against this town? he wanted to know.

I said the environment of Little Rock had ruined us. All of us, I said, had, in some way or another, been stifled or stunted or stigmatized by the baleful influences of this arid, errant atmosphere.

"So our environment ruined us, did it?" he said contentiously. "So what kind of environment do you think we should of had?"

That was a big question. I was exceedingly pained to realize that I could not successfully answer it. I could postulate the ideal qualities of some Utopia, but I could not cite any specific real place which might have made us better than we were.

Because I was unable to answer his question, he answered it for me: Given the kind of woebegone bastards we was, maybe we'd of been ruined wherever we'd been brought up. As for him, he just wanted to make the best of what he was and where he was.

The grass always looks greener on th'other side of the fence, he said. But it aint. Stay here.

No! I squawked. Don't make me argue about it any more. Let me go! If you say one more word I'll break down and stay here, but I'll hate myself for it. There's no place for me here! I can't find a job! I just don't *belong!*

"Nub, don't cry," he said. "You're too old to start that."

I turned and glared at him. His mangled face was all wet: beads of tears trickled over the scars and scabs. I went to him and hugged him as fiercely as I could without hurting his sores or aches.

You old half-assed bastard, I said.

You stupid prick, he said.

You big stinking turd, I said.

You worthless old egg-sucking polecat, he said.

You old shit-eating dog, I said.

"We never even went fishin," he said, his one partly usable arm around my shoulders. "We never did nuthin. We just sat around and talked a little. Seems like just this afternoon that I first saw you, and now you're leavin already."

"I'll be back," I said, admitting it to myself now. "I'll always keep coming home."

"You do that, Nub. We'll always keep lookin for you."

"And you'll be the Chief of Police and you'll fix tickets for me."

"Damn right. And you'll be a big-shot world traveler, and you'll bring us all kinds of presents from the four corners of the globe."

"And we'll go fishin," I said.

"Man, *yes,* we'll really go us afishin. There won't be no end to the fish we'll get us."

"And sometimes you'll do me the favor of talking good English."

"I'll talk good Russian and Hindoo too if you want me to."

"Just English."

"Whatever you say, Nub."

I released him and stood up. Thirty more seconds with the guy and I'd be lost; a team of horses wouldn't be able to drag me away. I shook his hand. "Well," I said, "take care of yourself, old buddy. And take care of Margaret. I know you will. But if you don't, my genies and sprites will find out about it and they'll descend on you and thrash you soundly."

He wished me good luck and he told me to set the world on fire.

"So long," we said in unison, and I waved and departed.

Later I congratulated myself that I had successfully withstood the temptation to mention Slater.

NINE

But Margaret said he didn't feel very guilty about Slater anyway, and she said she couldn't blame him. While my grandmother was visiting with him, Margaret and I strolled down a long corridor and went through a door and found a balcony in the open air overlooking the broad city. From this vantage point the whole town was laid out in a grid of little white lights and the red neon glow that pulsed above the business district far away, and, farther away, the beacons of the airport. It was a mild spring night, and the scintillating lights of the town were reflected in the stars of the sky. We stood at the edge of the balcony and took in the breeze. Margaret lit a cigarette. Just to be sociable I took one too.

"His only feeling about it," she said, "is a sense of relief that there won't be any trial, and thus he and I both are spared the embarrassment of having to testify. He's glad of that."

"Aren't either of you the least bit sorry about Slater's death?" I asked.

"Of course," she said. "But, you know, the only thing that passed through my mind when I first heard about it was that I had been cheated. I envied him that final spectacle. Every suicide gets some kind of pleasure out of showing off, or of showing people. Jimmy really *showed* us, didn't he? That's partly the way I felt when I went to jump into the river, I was going to put on a show by killing myself. But he was successful. He went through with it. I couldn't. So I can't help feeling a little envious in a perverse sort of way."

"Suicide expiates self-guilt, is that it? It allows the person to inflict his guilts on others. So now we are all carrying Slater's guilts around with us. But you have to carry your own too. Unless you can inflict some of them on Dall."

"I am guiltless," she said. "Of course I feel very sorry for Jimmy, and I think it's just horrible that he couldn't have found some other solution, but I really believe that I don't have to answer to anybody, not even to my own conscience."

"That remains to be seen. You'll be haunted, I bet."

She shrugged. "I'll be too busy trying to be happy to be haunted."

I stared at the side of her face. She was leaning with her arms on the balcony rail, her hands clasped together. She gazed out at the distant pinpoints of light in the townscape. The night breeze ruffled her long black locks. I swear, her face was almost beatific. "You know," I said to her, "I don't think I really like you. In fact, I don't think I like you at all."

If she heard me, she didn't respond. After a while she said, "Beautiful night, isn't it?"

"I don't like you, Margaret," I said.

She turned and gave me a quizzical look with a touch of superciliousness to it. "Is that why you were burning your bridges?"

"Possibly. I'm glad I'm leaving. I don't think I could ever have got to know you well enough to really like you."

"As it is," she said, "you'll be carrying a false conception of me around with you for the rest of your life. You know something? It's silly to cry over spilled milk of course, but have you ever stopped to think that if you had really known me back when we were dating each other in high school, none of this would have happened? None of it. I would have gone away to college with you—at your invitation, which never came—and we would have had a very close and intimate relationship during our college years, and then probably we would have married, and you would have taken me with you to Yale or beyond, and both of us would have forgotten about Little Rock, and we never would have known that Jimmy Slater even existed. But now look where we are. Now see what things have come to."

Indeed. In the mnemonic speculativeness of it I lapsed into silence and languished languor. I was not going to admit, even to myself, that the reason I didn't like her was that my failure to understand her lowered my estimate of my own intelligence. I decided not to spoil our last rendezvous with further hostilities or ill humors anyway. Say a few nice parting remarks and be gone, that's what I would do.

But what could I say? What deserved a nice remark from me? The town, perhaps. I gazed out at all the lights, sucked in the spring-laden air, and delivered myself of an equivocal accolade: "From here the old town almost seems to have a dreamlike enchantment."

"It's the *new* town that does that," she said. "In the old Little Rock, that you mourn the loss of, they had candles and coal-oil lamps and that didn't give enough light to make much of a display from afar." She turned and looked into my eyes as she continued. "I've been thinking about us—you and me—and how we're different, and one thing I've decided is that you like old things but I like new things. Why? Because every new thing, whether it's a building or a house or a car or a work of art or anything, is still loose and free, I mean it's still open to change and fluctuation, it hasn't settled down into a mold. We can't put it into a pigeonhole yet. We can't freeze it into history. You want to make history out of everything. If there were any word to describe the opposite of history, to mean for the future what history means for the past, then that would be my favorite word, my favorite subject, just as history is your favorite subject. Futurity? Would that do? Then you are lost in history, and I . . . I want to be lost in futurity."

"That should make it easy for you to forget about me . . . and Slater and everybody."

"I don't want to forget about you." Very intently she said this, gripping my arm. "I'm not going to. Whenever you come back, I guess I'll still be around."

"Well, thanks," I managed to say, choking up. "I guess I won't forget you either. I hope not. I—"

We stood as though transfixed upon some ultimate pinnacle of time and kinship, both of us (same size, same height) caught together in final speechlessness and the realization that we had either said all that could be said or else we would never have time to say what had to be said, we had lost the chance forever. What happened next was so natural that it didn't surprise me at all, it simply tickled me down to the soles of my feet: we sprang at each other in a wild, uninhibited enfoldment that was all a tangle of impetuous arms and legs, mashing our mouths together eagerly and entwining our tongues; her sharp breasts pierced and deflated my lungs and my hips squashed her hips against the balcony rail. On and on we squeezed and squirmed in a long mad kiss that seemed it could never stop. I have never been kissed like that before, and I doubt very much if I ever will be again. It defied description, really, and I can only say that one vertical kiss like that was better than all the horizontal sport I had ever had with Pamela. Gasping for breath at last, I pried my lips away from hers and breathed, but I didn't let go of her; as soon as I had my wind back I began to kiss her hair and her face and her neck, and it was while I was nuzzling her neck that she whispered something very strange into my ear: "I don't suppose that my persistent virginity is so precious that I couldn't give it to you, as a farewell present." Then she suggested that after my folks had gone to bed I should sneak out of the house and come over to Dall's house and spend the night with her.

Ah God, that was a beguiling temptation if ever I had one, and it literally *faire venir l'eau à la bouche*, and I was on the verge of expressing my slobbering thanks and taking her up on it, but something held me back, probably the realization that I had no real rights on her, but also the realization that this was the first time I had ever kissed anybody without having Stone-ache afterward. Why not? Had Tatrice already released me? I had to confess to somebody eventually, so I decided it might as well be Margaret.

Stepping back, disengaging myself from her, I told her I could not make love to her with a clear conscience. I told her that it was she herself who had told me that I had a streak of dishonesty in me and that because of my dishonesty I did not deserve to have her. Then I told her I had laid Tatrice.

"You did *what?*" she said.

"I laid Tatrice. I think. Last night. Naps was gone, he was out at Slater's place with his friend Feemy. I went over to his house and got drunk. Then I went downstairs to Tatrice's workshop with her and I picked her up and put her on one of her antique harvest tables. I was so drunk I can't remember what happened, but she was sort of drunk too, so—"

Margaret stared at me in awe, her mouth open and her head tilted to one side.

"You don't believe me?" I asked. "You don't think I have what it takes to do a thing like that?"

"No, I believe you," she said quietly. "But why did you want to do it?"

"It's like you said, frankly, that other afternoon on the riverbank: I do a poor job of concealing my sex drives."

"But you don't know for sure whether or not you—"

"No, and that's the hell of it. She wouldn't tell me. Maybe she doesn't know, herself."

"But why Tatrice? Did you just want to see what it would be like to have sex with a colored person?"

"No, as a matter of fact, I don't think that idea hardly entered my head. She was just convenient, that's all."

She studied my eyes. Old barriers had risen up between us again, for good this time. "But that couldn't be *all*," she objected. "Surely your only motive wasn't—"

"All right, if you need a high ulterior motive, some lofty reason for such a thing, then let's just say that I was a man in search of salvation, and she . . . well . . . something Tatrice said to me . . . She told me that my nickname, Nub, has a special meaning in the vernacular of the old darkies. It means an unborn child."

"So did she give birth to you? How does it feel?"

"I don't know," I said. "I can't remember a damn thing—"

She smiled forbearingly, and turned and placed her arms again on the balcony rail, and leaned there, looking out at the town lights. We stayed there a while longer, not talking, and then it was time to go. We re-entered the hospital and walked down the corridor. We saw my grandmother sitting in the lobby waiting for us.

We would all get into Dall's old Pontiac and Margaret would take us home. But first, before we rejoined my grandmother, Margaret said to me, "You spent so much time accusing me of needing a father figure. Did it ever occur to you that what you've always been looking for is a mother figure, somebody to replace the one that died when you were a boy? That's something I probably never could have been for you. And as it turns out, perhaps it's just as well."

And that was about the last thing she said to me.

TEN

Sometimes . . . I feel . . . like a motherless chile: some . . . times! I feel . . . like a motherless chile: sometimes I feel like a motherless chile! So far, far away from my home . . .

"Now what are you singing *that* for?" I asked Naps, eying him suspiciously. We were loitering on the upper deck of the Missouri Pacific station, above the tracks and platforms. The train would be late, after midnight. My father and grandmother were sitting in the waiting room. Naps and I had wandered out to the upper deck to look at the trains and to talk, but we hadn't been able to say much to each other yet, and he had begun to croon old spirituals to himself, dolorously. It was a sad occasion, my leaving. He had a rich, moving voice, and I liked to hear him sing, but it disturbed me that he had chosen that particular refrain.

"Jes my favorite song, is all," he said, quitting.

"Do you really feel like a motherless child?" I asked him.

"My old mom been dead a long time too," he said, and his "too" told me that he was aware my mother had been dead as long as his. This, too, we had in common, and I wondered if Tatrice was a suitable mother substitute for him. Then my self-reproach caught up with me again, and I wanted more than anything to confess to him my sinful error and ask him to forgive me. But I lacked the nerve. "Besides," he said, "don't you know what day this is? Sunday, May the tenth. It's Mother's Day, man." Yes, I know, I said and then I said to him, Go ahead and sing that song. But he shook his head. Then he turned abruptly and put his hands on my shoulders and spoke with profound sincerity: "Sure wush they was some way I could talk you out of leavin." I told him it was too late, nothing would do any good, I had already bought my ticket. He began to shake his head sadly, and then he turned again and looked out across the dark railroad yards and improvised a last song:

"Went to the station, to tell my friend good-bye,
He doan like this place, but he never did try.
He got dose runnin-off blues, oh yeah he got dose runnin-off blues.
Train gonna come, whistle gonna moan,
Got de runnin-off blues dat makes him groan.
Yeah, he may go wherever he choose,
Caint help but get dose runnin-off blues."

Yeah, I agreed when he finished and turned grinning to me: wherever I go I'll always get the running-off blues. Then I asked if he didn't think he would ever want to leave this town himself. He said, Oh yeah, I got de runnin-off blues too. Everybody got em, he said. Not Margaret, I said. Aw yeah, she got em too, he said. Cept she wanter keep em. Keep em till dey go runnin-off demselfs. Then he quoted another old blues song, to the effect that: *Now, when a woman gets the blues, Lord, she hangs her head and cries. But when a man gets the blues, Lord, he grabs a train and rides.*

"But we not gonna be no different, wherever we go," he said. "We just gonna *feel* a little different maybe."

We are just going to make it a little harder for the world to stomp all over us, I said, alluding to the sermon he had given me.

Dat a fack, he said. You just gon get a better chance to be Somebody, stead of Nobody.

Ah, I said. Amen. Naps and I began to pace up and down the deck, restlessly. Would that train ever arrive? I was reminded of the previous time I had thought of leaving town, when Naps had first given me that fine parting aphorism: if you obliged to eat dirt, eat clean dirt; and the time, before that, when I had actually come on into the station (wondering: Do I, leaving, leave, or come, or, rather, by coming, go?) but had discovered that the train wouldn't leave for hours, so that I had wandered off through the town and wound up in the movie theater where I had met Margaret; and I reflected that if I had stayed in this station and read a book or found some way to amuse myself I would never have met her again and I would never have become involved in these entanglements of the past week—but I knew that if I had stayed in this station and not met her again she might not still be alive at this moment. The dirt I had eaten had been clean dirt; I could bear no grudges, except a single large unfocused grudge against the town itself.

We tried to talk, Naps and I, but there really wasn't much that we could say on this occasion. Why is it that the more desperate the need for talk the less likely the talk will come? We had agreed to write each other occasionally. I knew I *would* write to him sometimes, and to Dall and Margaret too, for a long time, and then, as the letters became less frequent—then it would be time for me to come home again. Naps had given me, as a going-away gift, a really sumptuous two-volume gilt-edged morocco-bound set of the 1834 edition of William Dunlap's *A History of the Rise and Development of the Arts of Design in the United States*. Where he acquired this rare treasure I have no idea, but I was no longer surprised at the things he could accomplish: I was both humbled by his generosity and distressed by his extravagance, and I wanted to tell him I was no longer worthy of his friendship, but I couldn't.

Making conversation now, I inquired after his friend Feemy. I said I wondered what Feemy was going to do now that Slater was dead.

"Aw, he done already quit and we got im over to my place," he said, and he paused, then resumed speaking, but he spoke this time without a tinge of any dialect, as if he were desperate that I should share the significance of this last bit of news with him, that I should know exactly what it meant: "Feemy called me this afternoon and asked me to come out there and get him. I went out and got him and took him to my house, and he's going to stay there for a while until he can get him another job. I'll be glad to help him out. Tonight at supper he told me what had happened out there this afternoon. All of Mr. and Mrs. Slater's old friends, people they hadn't seen or heard of for years, most of them, came out to pay their respects to Mrs. Slater and help her mourn or hold a wake or whatever she wanted to do. Feemy let them into the house and served them coffee. Thirty or forty people, he said it was. Then he started to go upstairs to get Mrs. Slater and wheel her down to meet her friends. But just as he started up the staircase, there she came down it, walking, walking on her own two feet to meet all those people."

❧ ELEVEN

Out of the darkness of the southwest the train came thundering into the station. My father and grandmother came out of the waiting room and, with Naps, they walked me down the steps to the platform. I had given the whole Sunday to my folks, and thereby reclaimed some of their lost love. After sleeping Saturday night in the same house with them I had risen and eaten breakfast with them and talked with them and read the Sunday papers with them, and then my father and I had taken my grandmother to church and we had sat and listened to the Baptist preacher talk about the coming doom of mankind and both my father and I had taken communion with my grandmother, and she had been well pleased. He had bought her a new hat for a Mother's Day present, and I had given her a corsage of white carnations. After church we had gone home to a big Sunday dinner of fried chicken and it was like a thousand Sunday dinners I had had before in Little Rock, and like a thousand Sundays, with Sunday's long listless lethargy, that encompassing feeling of having eaten more than enough and having read too much of the newspaper and having nothing whatever to do. We had been genial to each other. A kind of old Southern gentility had suffused the whole day with comfort and warmth and peace. Although it had been a very dull day, even a very boring day, I had reflected that it was much more like a typical Little Rock day of my youth than had been any of the other days in these two weeks; I had remembered all my other visits, all my other homecomings, and had recalled how monotonously uneventful all of them had been: and there in a long moment of that Sunday ennui I had permitted myself a last consoling but hopeless fantasy: none of this had really happened, all of my days during these past two weeks were just like this day, dull and uneventful, just like all the other times I came home, I had gone fishing with Dall a few times and that was about the extent of the excitement, I had never even met Margaret, I had forgotten she existed, and the same for Naps too, and as for Slater he was but a figment of my lazy thrill-seeking mind. There I had lounged indolently in the living room with my father and grandmother, and there I had tried to believe that